LESSONS IN LOVING

"Ty," Serra murmured ⸺ away from his.

He allowed her ⸺ body close to his. "This ⸺ ra?"

Heat sparked w ⸺ and a burning need rippl ⸺ her mind protested against what ⸺ oing. "Ty, I'm not sure," she stammered.

He sighed with frustration, then his fingers gently stroked her hair. "No, I suppose you're not. To be honest, I'm not sure myself."

Serra wrapped her arms about his waist, realizing that Ty was no longer the boy she'd once known. Things were much more complicated between them now. Whatever this strange desire was that gripped her, it consumed him as well. Perhaps they could regain the lost years, heal the rift that divided them, and come together . . . make things the way they were before.

Tilting up her face, she stared into his cobalt-blue eyes. "Teach me, Ty."

"You don't know what you're asking."

"Yes, I do," she replied.

SURRENDER TO THE PASSION

LOVE'S SWEET BOUNTY   (3313, $4.50)
by Colleen Faulkner

Jessica Landon swore revenge of the masked bandits who robbed the train and stole all the money she had in the world. She set out after the thieves without consulting the handsome railroad detective, Adam Stern. When he finally caught up with her, she admitted she needed his assistance. She never imagined that she would also begin to need his scorching kisses and tender caresses.

WILD WESTERN BRIDE   (3140, $4.50)
by Rosalyn Alsobrook

Anna Thomas loved riding the Orphan Train and finding loving homes for her young charges. But when a judge tried to separate two brothers, the dedicated beauty went beyond the call of duty. She proposed to the handsome, blue-eyed Mark Gates, planning to adopt the boys herself! Of course the marriage would be in name only, but yet as time went on, Anna found herself dreaming of being a loving wife in every sense of the word . . .

QUICKSILVER PASSION   (3117, $4.50)
by Georgina Gentry

Beautiful Silver Jones had been called every name in the book, and now that she owned her own tavern in Buckskin Joe, Colorado, the independent didn't care what the townsfolk thought of her. She never let a man touch her and she earned her money fair and square. Then one night handsome Cherokee Evans swaggered up to her bar and destroyed the peace she'd made with herself. For the irresistible miner made her yearn for the melting kisses and satin caresses she had sworn she could live without!

MISSISSIPPI MISTRESS   (3118, $4.50)
by Gina Robins

Cori Pierce was outraged at her father's murder and the loss of her inheritance. She swore revenge and vowed to get her independence back, even if it meant singing as an entertainer on a Mississippi steamboat. But she hadn't reckoned on the swarthy giant in tight buckskins who turned out to be her boss. Jacob Wolf was, after all, the giant of the man Cori vowed to destroy. Though she swore not to forget her mission for even a moment, she was powerfully tempted to submit to Jake's fiery caresses and have one night of passion in his irresistible embrace.

Available wherever paperbacks are sold, or order direct from the Publisher. Send cover price plus 50¢ per copy for mailing and handling to Zebra Books, Dept. 3367, 475 Park Avenue South, New York, N.Y. 10016. Residents of New York, New Jersey and Pennsylvania must include sales tax. DO NOT SEND CASH.

Terri Valentine
Outlaw's Kiss

ZEBRA BOOKS
KENSINGTON PUBLISHING CORP.

Between 1854 and 1929, more than 150,000 homeless children were "sent West" on orphan trains through the Children's Aid Society of New York. This book is dedicated to those brave souls and their descendants.

ZEBRA BOOKS

are published by

Kensington Publishing Corp.
475 Park Avenue South
New York, NY 10016

First printing: April, 1991

Printed in the United States of America

Chapter One

There's nothing worse than being alone, unless it's being lost and facing the terrifying possibility of never being found.

Her heart pounding in her throat, Serra Paletot stared out the window of the New Hope Opera House from her assigned seat on the stage. Her fingers clutched a square of paperboard number twenty nine-printed in big red numerals.

Number twenty-nine. She swallowed so hard it hurt. Soon it would all begin, and she wasn't sure she could do it.

She tried to ignore the rows of empty chairs below fanning out from the stage in brown austerity. In just a little while, those seats would be filled with curious faces. Thick lashes flicked down over her amber eyes as the lines of the poem she'd been trained to recite ran through her mind. What would happen if she forgot the words? Would people laugh? Or worse, would they turn away from her?

Fear snapped her eyes open, and her gaze returned

5

to the window. Framed in the dirt-streaked panes was the train yard, a locomotive sending out puffs of smoke as it rolled into the station. She had to remember. To make a mistake might mean she would be one of those not selected.

Her focus adjusted closer. An unadorned moth fluttered against the inside of the windowpane, beating its brown wings in frantic uselessness, trapped and fighting for mere existence.

Serra understood exactly how that poor moth must feel, as she, too, was struggling for mere existence. They all were. Her gaze scanned her surroundings once more, taking in the other children seated in an arc on the stage with her, their distinctively different faces revealing their kindred anxieties. Thirty of them in all, orphans from the streets of New York sent west to be "placed out," the unwanted offered the singular opportunity of starting over.

At least, that's what the Reverend Millboone had told them from the moment they had stepped aboard the train in New York. They were the lucky ones. They would have the chance to select a new family, not just take the dregs that nature had given them.

Serra's bow-shaped mouth arched downward. No matter what the reverend said, her parents were *not* like the others. They had simply lost her and didn't know where to find her.

Her pink tongue darted out, licking her dry lips in anticipation. A family. That was all she yearned for . . . to know that after years of abandonment, she'd been found. Real parents to claim as her own, a surname she could be proud of. Her nose, lightly dusted with adolescent freckles, wrinkled. Not Paletot. The orphanage director had simply given her that last name when he had discovered her, cold and hungry, huddled on the steps of the home nearly eight years ago, wearing little more than a woman's expensive but tattered paletot, with a note pinned to the collar that read: "Please take care of Serra."

No one knew for sure why she had been abandoned. Alone in her bed at night, she tried to call forth forgotten memories. Instead, she drew a blank when it came to the first four years of her life, a frustration that drove her forward with determination to face each new day. No matter what happened to her or where she ended up, she *would* find her rightful place — or at least discover what had happened to her parents. She wouldn't give up until she did.

"Are ya scared?" rumbled a voice beside her.

Serra looked up into the steady cobalt-blue gaze of the boy seated next to her. Tyler Ramsey, his youthful face framed with ink-black hair topped with a tweed cap, as most younger boys were wont to wear, grinned down at her. Trying to judge what answer would please the sixteen-year-old boy the most, she shrugged. "I don't know. Are you?" She whispered.

She wasn't sure what reply she wanted from him. If he said yes, she wouldn't feel as foolish about her own fears, yet the thought of Ty being afraid left a cold rush of uncertainty coursing through her veins. But should he answer no, how could she justify her own childishness? Holding her breath, she waited, willing to mold her opinions around his more mature words of wisdom.

But, then, her loyalty to Ty was unshakable. From those first frightening days in the orphanage, he had been there for her, giving her the attention and companionship she'd craved. Why he took time with her she didn't know, but gratitude rushed through her. Someday she'd find a way to pay him back.

"Naw," he boasted, in that cocksure way of his that made the older girls in the home giggle and say he was cute.

Serra frowned. He was cute, she supposed, but she didn't really think of Tyler that way. Strong and brave, he always knew the right thing to do.

"Besides," he continued, his eyes darting to Reverend Millboone and his wife, the agents sent by the Children's Aid Society with the orphan train on its long journey, "if I tell ya somethin', will ya keep it secret?"

Her amber eyes widened. A secret? Whenever Ty revealed one of his well-guarded secrets, it was always something worth hearing. Nodding vigorously, she mouthed, "I swear."

He leaned closer to her ear, which peeked out of the copper-colored mop of hair that crowned her head like a halo of shiny new pennies. "I ain't gonna stand up and recite some dumb ol' poem. I don't want to be adopted. I'm gonna run away first."

"Ty, no!" Serra gasped. "Reverend Millboone will catch you and box your ears for sure." Somehow, she'd always imagined they would stay together, perhaps even be adopted by the same family.

"Naw, he won't," the boy declared.

Serra studied her friend . . . her protector. Tyler Ramsey had been one of those boys on the streets of New York who could pick a pocket in the blink of an eye. She'd seen him do it on a dozen occasions, and no one had ever been any the wiser. But that was New York, a big city. Her gaze drifted to the window and the waiting crowd beyond. It would be so much different out here in the West. "How you gonna live?" she asked. *How am I gonna make it without you?* she wondered.

"Ain't ya ever heard of Jesse James or Billy the Kid? They were younger than me when they shot their first man," he boasted, as if such a feat deserved his praise.

"Ty, ya plannin' on shootin' somebody?" Serra asked, horrified.

"Uh-uh," he assured her after a moment's hesitation. "I'll just rob 'm."

"But what will the reverend say?" Serra edged forward with concern. If Ty did manage to run away, it might mean she'd never see him again.

The boy placed his larger hand on her arm, as if he feared she was going to jump up right then and there and tattle on him. "Ya swore, li'l Serra," he murmured.

Serra stared at his restraining grip. A man's hand in every way, it even carried the scars of maturity.

"I know, Ty. I won't tell," she promised, slumping forward, a little part of her wrung dry with the feeling he was going to desert her no matter what she said or did. "But how are ya gonna git away?"

He gave her a long look, as if trying to decide if he could trust her with details. "I'll find a chance; don't ya worry none about me."

And Serra knew he would. Just like some penny dreadful hero, he would make his own chance, and then he would be gone. The fear of desertion welled up within her, and she couldn't hold it back.

"Ty, what about me? Take me with ya," she pleaded. As much as she wanted a family of her own, she didn't want to lose Ty in the process.

The cold blueness of his eyes melted with concern. "Naw, li'l Serra." Reaching out, he fingered those coppery curls he'd always said would be her pride and glory someday. "Outlawin' ain't for little girls." He clucked her under the chin, giving her a rakish grin—

9

a look she would never forget. "But don't concern yourself. I'll come back for ya."

She reached up and grasped his hand in hers. "Promise me, Ty. Promise me you'll come back when I ain't little no more."

Staring at their clasped hands, he lifted a finger and placed an *X* on his chest. "I cross my heart 'n hope to die." His face, which was so dear to her, grew solemn. "I'll be back for ya as quick as I can." Leaning over her upturned face, he dropped an unexpected kiss on her lips. A promise made and sealed.

With a rush of strange, new emotions, Serra's innocent heart quickened. Maybe the other girls had been right after all. Tyler Ramsey was sort of cute. She smiled, knowing she could trust him, as he was the one constant she could count on no matter what.

"I'll look for ya, Ty. I'll expect ya."

"Tyler Ramsey, sit up straight," boomed a voice from across the auditorium.

Ty shot the Reverend Millboone a sullen look but did as he was told, turning away from Serra to stare straight ahead, his strong fingers kneading the nappy tweed of his knickers.

"Now, children," the reverend began, moving to stand at the foot of the stage, his hands clapping like thunder to get their attention. "In a few moments the doors will open, and I want each of you to remember everything we've taught you. Be polite, be retiring, and above all else, smile. All those people out there are looking for a child to take home." He swept his arm in a wide arc, indicating the crowd outside the building. "If you want to be one of the lucky ones . . ." His words trailed off on a warning note.

Mrs. Millboone began moving amongst the children, straightening a collar, brushing back an unruly lock of hair, wiping off a smudge from a cheek with a tongue-wetted thumb. When she at last reached Serra and Ty, she ran her fingers through the girl's coppery mop and shook her head in defeat, then turned to Ty, attempting to fasten the top button of his shirt.

With a growl, Ty knocked away her hand. "Goddamn it, I'll do it myself."

The woman gasped indignantly but snatched back her hand nonetheless.

"And you, Mr. Ramsey," the reverend threatened in a loud voice fit for a hell and damnation sermon. "I'll have none of your infernal cussing, young man."

"Go t' hell," the boy mumbled, but he grew silent when Serra turned pleading eyes on him.

Minutes later the doors swung open, and a file of chattering people began pushing their way down the aisle. As soon as the auditorium was filled, the Reverend Millboone moved center stage, his hand outstretched in welcome. "Thank you. Thank you all for coming. I assure you, you won't be disappointed."

At his signal, the group of children stood. Beginning with a boy of six, each gave a little performance: a song, a recital, a shuffling dance, a magic trick.

When her turn came, Serra stepped to the forestage in eager anticipation. She recited her poem with ease, then returned to her seat with a bow, beaming with her success, fully expecting Ty to take her place. Center stage remained embarrassingly empty.

The Reverend Millboone cleared his throat and glared at the rebellious boy.

"Ty," Serra hissed, but he shook his head, refusing to put himself on display. She glanced at the reverend, noting his angry frown as he moved toward them. If someone didn't do something quick, Ty was in a peck of trouble.

Without thinking about what she was doing, Serra claimed center stage again. Taking up her skirt, she dipped a little curtsy as if to apologize. "Tyler's shy," she improvised. "But he's a real nice boy."

The crowd laughed and Serra reddened, realizing she was the source of their amusement. She glanced at the Millboones. The reverend didn't look as mad anymore. As long as she'd helped Ty, she didn't mind it that much if people made fun of her.

Stealing a glimpse at Tyler, she saw him frown at her. But before she could justify her impulsiveness, the performance was over, and the crowd surged toward the stage.

A plump, pasty-faced farmer's wife knelt in front of her and smiled. "Do you like dolls, honey?" the woman asked, pinching Serra's still-rosy cheeks with icy fingers.

Serra nodded and smiled back, but kept glancing behind her to catch glimpses of Ty, not wanting him to stay angry with her. A large-boned man felt Ty's muscles and quite rudely poked him in the chest, trying to assess the boy's stamina and strength.

He refused to look at her, and Serra knew he was doing it on purpose. Then the crowd blocked her view for a few moments.

When they parted, Ty was gone.

Had the man taken him? Or had he simply disappeared as he had promised her he would do? Surely, he wouldn't go without saying good-bye. Frantically, Serra raised on tiptoes, looking for him. Tyler Ramsey was nowhere to be seen.

Turning back to the woman who had been speaking to her, Serra found herself deserted. The farmer's wife had moved on, apparently disappointed with Serra's lack of enthusiasm, and was now bending over little

12

Ellen, a fair-haired child of ten who had danced a jig while humming "Yankee Doodle."

Disappointment raked through Serra, and she eyed Ellen with envy. How could she have been so foolish as to squander her first and quite possibly only opportunity to find a family of her own? She scanned the opera house once more. *Oh, 'Iy, where are you?*

Her roving eyes slowed and came to a halt. From below, the charismatic scrutiny of a tall, nicely dressed man captured her attention. He studied her intently, then tilted his head to say something to a pleasant-enough-looking woman beside him, his gaze never leaving Serra's face.

He smiled; Serra reciprocated shyly. Realizing he intended to approach her, her heart accelerated. The world narrowed to a corridor of vision that ran from her eyes to his dark ones. She tried to glance away but found she couldn't. His look was almost frightening, yet at the same time it was reassuring, calling to her, demanding that she accept the mesmerizing spell he wove between them.

Is this what the future held for her? Serra swallowed a strange lump of apprehension. This was what she wanted, wasn't it? A family.

The couple mounted the stage stairs, moving closer. In order to maintain the powerful eye contact, Serra lifted her face. When the man's hand reached out to stroke her coppery hair, an uncontrollable shudder coursed through her.

"Amazing," he observed in a gentle, refined voice.

"Uncanny, Doctor," the woman beside him agreed, her eyes lifting to the man, then settling back on Serra.

His hand flattened on Serra's head, patting her as if she were a puppy, his other hand falling to his waist to finger the watch chain strung across his middle. Serra's eyes widened. Gold. Link upon link of the precious metal. This doctor must be very rich. He knelt down in front of her, their gazes leveling. "What's your name, child?"

"S — S — Se — rra," she replied, her eyes darting down once again to the watch chain, which he eased from his pocket and began to swing in front of her face.

"It's pretty, isn't it?"

Serra nodded, her eyes following the path of the pendulum. Oh, how she wished he would hold the fob still so she could study it.

"How old are you, dumpling?"

"Twelve," she replied. Back and forth. Completely entranced, she couldn't tear her eyes away.

The watch stopped abruptly, and to Serra's disappointment, the man stuffed it back into his waistcoat. For the first time his gaze left Serra's, making contact with the woman who stood over and behind her. "How perfectly lovely. A most apt subject."

Blinking away the strange feeling that had seeped into her bones, Serra tilted her head and found the woman staring down at her. The lady smiled, and she followed the movements of her palely painted lips.

"Tell me, dear, do you have a birth certificate?" the woman asked.

The question sent fear coursing through Serra's childish heart. Some of the lucky orphans carried copies of official papers that named their real parents. She was so afraid that her lack of such a document might make her undesirable. "No, ma'am," she answered in an unsteady squeak, "but my momma weren't crazy and weren't no whore."

The woman's eyes narrowed, and Serra just knew for sure she'd said the wrong thing. Fear of rejection

14

set her mouth to trembling.

"We'll have to work on her speech, Lionel. Much too quaint for our needs."

"I agree, but that won't be so difficult. Her age is right. With her looks and her intelligence . . ." His hand came to rest on her coppery curls as he stood. "And the name, the hair color . . . By God, she's perfect."

"Dare we, Lionel, do something so bold?"

"Dare we not, my dear? Our entire future rides on our success. Think about it. An orphan. Who would ever know or suspect?"

Looking from one adult face to the other, Serra read their hesitation and indecision. "I can do it — whatever you tell me," she promised. She needed them to want her, to agree to take her home. Without Ty . . .

Ty. Chagrin bubbled up from her lapse of memory. How could she have forgotten him so easily? Her head snapped about to scan the crowded opera house.

"Serra, is something wrong?"

Glancing up at the tall man, she noted his frown. She couldn't afford to bungle another opportunity to be adopted. Torn in her need to be found and to find, she shook her head. "Oh, no, sir," she lied, swallowing the lump of indecision clogging her throat. If only Ty could see whom she was going with, then he could find her later. He would come for her still, wouldn't he? She hadn't made him that angry. She blinked back tears. Or had she?

"Excellent." The doctor's frown metamorphosed into a smile. His fingers curled about her chin, his mesmerizing gaze capturing hers once more with that inescapable way he had of looking at her. "Would you like to come home with Mrs. Chelsey and myself?"

15

Without hesitation, her head nodded, though her heart clattered a protest.

"Good, dumpling. Good. You're a wise little mite."

Reaching down, he took the paperboard square from her fingers and tucked it under his arm. As they moved around the crowd, Serra's feet stepped on something on the floor. She looked down. The piece of paperboard boasted the number thirty.

That had been Ty's number. The fact that the square lay deserted on the floor confirmed her worst fears. Tyler Ramsey had indeed disappeared without saying good-bye.

Ty, her heart cried out at the sudden severing of everything she'd held near and dear for as long as she could remember. He would be back, she assured herself, even if he was angry with her. He had promised, and Ty Ramsey always kept his word. When he returned for her, she vowed, shyly squeezing the adult hands that held hers, she would gladly share her good fortune with him in order to make amends for upsetting him earlier.

With that first sweet kiss still lingering on her lips, Serra knew that when he did come back for her, nobody or nothing would ever separate them again.

Hours later the morning sun streaked across the horizon, accenting the echoing wail of the departing train. Tyler Ramsey stood on a busy street, squinting up at a sign that boldly stated "Shalladay's — The Finest Dry Goods In Joplin." That's exactly what he would have — the finest — now that he had managed to escape and was fairly confident no one would bother to follow him. But he hadn't really expected them to. After all, who gave a damn if another street arab from

New York disappeared?

Uttering a deep sigh of relief mixed with exhaustion, he snatched his cap from his head and tossed it beneath the step tiers. God, how he'd despised that thing from the moment old Millboone had forced him to wear it. Glancing down at his knickers and stockings, he grimaced. He was too old to be dressed like some mealymouthed schoolboy. Who had they thought to fool? Short pants or not, he was almost seventeen. Nobody wanted to adopt him; they only considered the prospects of getting free labor.

If Ty did nothing else with his life, he swore he'd never be a slave to anyone or anything—especially not to poverty. Not ever again. He was his own man now and could take damn good care of himself. Just like Jesse James and Billy the Kid. He glanced about the streets already crowded with freight wagons and pedestrians, worry puckering his dark brows. But could he be as ruthless as those two? He wasn't so sure.

But, hell, there wasn't anybody who could relieve a man of his wallet as smoothly as he could. He studied a couple who crossed in front of him, forcing him to take a step back. His mouth flattened into a determined line. Everybody—even people out west—carried their money in their pockets, he assured himself, and they deserved a little relieving.

Without warning, he yawned, for one moment nothing more than a sleepy-eyed youth. All through the long night he had crouched in a boxcar until the freight train he had snuck aboard in New Hope had reached the end of the line. Though freedom had hummed a gentle lullaby through the wheels of the rolling train, sleep had refused to come.

All he could think of as he watched a golden moon between the crack of the two doors of the train car was

17

Serra Paletot . . . of the sweetness of her unsuspecting lips when he had kissed them . . . of the innocent way she had stepped forward in his place to cover up his defiance . . . of his promise to return—and he meant what he'd said, he really did. But what haunted him most was the look on her oval face as she stood between the couple who had chosen her—so proud and happy. He had intended to say good-bye, to assure her he wasn't angry with her, but the opportunity hadn't presented itself.

He was glad for her. Perhaps only a little jealous that it had come so easy for her, when he had to fight for every inch of progress he made in his life, but he would never do anything to destroy what she had found for herself. Not to Serra. She was the one person he truly cared about.

But now he had to think about his own future. For the time being, he would settle on finding an easy mark and filling his empty pockets with pilfered cash. Then he would buy himself some decent clothes and a meal worth sitting down to—and he wouldn't get up until he was so stuffed that he couldn't move.

Ty rubbed his growling stomach. Never, as long as he could remember, had he ever had all he'd wanted to eat.

With a practiced eye, he canvassed his surroundings. Joplin, Missouri was a bustling town. Businesses lined the streets, every other one seeming to be a saloon, and even at this early hour he could hear the discordant clash of music and laughter pouring out of the divided half doors. What he needed was a crowd; a distracted one would be best.

Several doors down from the dry goods store he found what he was looking for. A group of men fanned out around a pair of those swinging saloon doors, laughing, pointing, totally engrossed in what took place inside. Ty moved forward, slowly flexing the fingers of his right hand, a ritual of long experience. Hunching his shoulders, he looked about one last time to make sure no one noticed him in particular. A successful pickpocket was one who blended in.

Meshing with the crowd, he fished his way into the open jacket of the man beside him. His fingers curled around what they found and eased out. A wallet, and judging from its thickness, he had chosen his victim well. Without once glancing at his prize, he slipped it inside his shirt and moved on.

Why not? he laughed inwardly. Why stop at one when it was so damn easy? These pigeons apparently had never had their pockets picked before, at least not by the likes of an expert. They deserved what they got, and it was only fair that he be the one to give it to them.

He edged about the crowd, his hand darting into exposed pockets, pulling forth his booty. Soon his shirt was so full that anyone who might notice him couldn't miss the bulge of his incredibly easy morning's work. With the consummated control of the best professional gambler, he stepped back, satisfied with his winnings, willing to walk away.

And just in time. The crowd parted as a thin, balding man came flying through the doors, which flapped and squeaked an unoiled protest. The smell of stale beer and perfume trailed the unfortunate man like a kite tail. The woman who followed him was twice his size and wielding her broom as if it were a sword, swinging and jabbing as she screeched at the top of her lungs, "James Ludlow, you're a swine."

Clutching his shirt closed, Ty moved off and rounded a corner into an alley, just as the man began to whine, "Ah, sugar, I was comin' home. I was." A harmony of laughter followed the sound of the broom whacking the woman's lack of belief.

In the shadowed confines of the alley, Ty sat down to count his takings. Removing the cash, he tossed everything else into a nearby garbage can. Ignoring the angry yowl of the alley cat he'd disturbed, his eyes widened as he shuffled the bills from one hand to the other. He'd never seen so much money. Missourians apparently didn't believe in banks, and he couldn't be happier at their lack of trust.

Stacking his money, he shoved it back into the safety of his shirt. Then, with a satisfied sigh, he lowered his lashes over his cobalt-blue eyes, his thoughts returning to Serra. Sweet Serra. At this rate, he'd be able to go back for her in no time at all.

Not so fast, he chided himself. It would be best to give her time to grow up. Just like he'd told her. Outlawing wasn't for little girls.

Pushing up from his squat, he brushed the sleep from his eyes and set about to implement his plans. New clothing. And if he wanted to be a real desperado, maybe he should get himself a gun as well.

He ambled into Shalladay's dry goods store and looked around. There were stacks of ready-made pants and shirts, rows of boots in different sizes . . . and hats. God, there were piles of them. Ty patted the wad that pressed against the bare skin of his middle. Whatever he wanted he could have just by asking.

He made his selections quickly, then turned to the counter and the man standing behind it.

"Nice duds you picked there, sonny boy. You got money to pay for 'em?" old man Shalladay asked.

Ty knew what the storekeeper was most likely thinking. Kid of the street . . . Suspect him. Well, he'd show the old gaffer a thing or two. Reaching into his shirt, he stared back. "How much?"

The old man stiffened, his gaze shifting to Ty's shirtfront. "Twenty-five dollars," he stated, never taking his eyes off the boy's hidden hand.

Grinning, Ty pulled out his wad and, licking his fingers, counted out the required amount with exaggerated slowness, then slapped it on the counter. Shalladay scooped it up and deposited it in a money box, his relief evident that he'd been presented with payment instead of the wrong end of a revolver. Ty couldn't help but notice that the money box was brimful.

"Anything else?" the clerk asked.

Behind the man's head was a display case of guns — large ones, small ones, plain ones, ones decorated with beaten silver — mostly six-shooters.

"Yeah," Ty grunted, pointing at one with a pearl handle that caught his fancy. "How 'bout one of them?"

The storekeeper turned, noting the side arm Ty indicated. "Ain't cheap, sonny boy. You sure you got enough?"

Irritated by the condescending way Shalladay spoke to him, Ty narrowed his eyes. "Bullets to go with it." In his mind's eye, he kept seeing the overflowing box of money stashed under the counter. The old codger had more than his fair share.

Confident the boy was harmless, the storekeeper turned and took down the gun Ty wanted. Then he reached behind him on a low shelf and collected a box of ammunition.

"Forty-five with the bullets," he announced, slapping them down in front of Ty with the same deliberate challenge the boy had given him earlier.

Forty-five dollars! That was highway robbery. Did the old swindler really think he'd just fallen off the banana cart? Ty swallowed his anger; he wanted that gun, wanted it in a bad way, but, hell, he wanted to eat, too.

He shot a look at his opponent and knew the storekeeper was laughing at him from behind his benign expression. *Son of a bitch*, Ty simmered. *You don't deserve my money. What you do deserve is . . .*

Slowly, Ty picked up the weapon and spun the empty cylinder. Opening the shell box, he filled the chambers one by one and snapped it back into place. Then he pointed the gun at the old man.

"I don't like your price."

The man looked down at the pointed weapon and swallowed so hard Ty could hear the spittle sliding down his dry, wrinkled throat. A rush of pure excitement coursed through him. This was a hell of a lot more fun that just picking pockets.

"In fact," he drawled, taking to outlawing like a pigeon did to bread crumbs, "I think you overcharged me for the clothes, too. So I think *you* oughta pay *me* for pickin' your store over all the others in town." He grinned and waved the gun barrel in the direction of the money box. "I think you've got enough in there to satisfy me. What do you think?"

"I think, boy, you should either use that gun or put it down." The flatly stated suggestion accompanied by the click of a hammer being drawn back came from behind him.

Ty stiffened with surprise, his hand tightening about the pearl handle of his weapon. His options flashed before him. If he used it, wouldn't that make him like Jesse James and Billy the Kid—someone to be reckoned with, somebody important? Then he remembered the promise he'd made Serra not to shoot anyone. But if he gave up, what would happen to him then?

Most likely he'd be thrown in some stinking prison, his newly acquired freedom snatched from him. He was tired of having to answer to others, tired of being treated like the dregs of society, but did he really want to die?

A hand clamped him on the shoulder. "Give it here, son," urged the faceless voice, rich with authority.

Looking up into the frightened eyes of the storekeeper, Ty's determination wavered momentarily. Then his hand gripped the gun anew, his finger seeking out the trigger.

"Are you sure that's what you want to do? Only a fool or a desperate man refuses to back down to such odds."

He wasn't a fool, but desperate? Damn right, one might say that. Desperation born from years of neglect. The only one to never try to take advantage of him, to never deceive him, was Serra Paletot. That's why he was determined to go back for her someday. . . . He could trust her. But he couldn't keep that promise if he was dead.

The gun slipped from his fingers, and he found himself jerked around so roughly his feet flew out from underneath him. Scrambling to right himself, he stared up into the meanest-looking eyes he'd ever seen. He swallowed down the fear churning in his belly.

"Jasper, take your goods back," his captor said, never once lifting his intelligent brown eyes from Tyler as he sized him up.

"Boy paid me for the clothes," Shalladay mumbled, grabbing the gun off the counter. Ty could hear it being unloaded with nervous fingers. One of the bullets

23

hit the floor and rolled, probably underneath the counter, never to be retrieved.

"I bet he did," the mean-looking man said with a derisive laugh. "I saw him pick the pockets of half the miners in town less than an hour ago."

"Stolen money?"

Ty heard the scrape of the money box. The bills he'd just given the storekeeper passed beside his head and into the other man's outstretched hand.

"Where are you from, son?" The man pocketed the money in his shirtfront.

"I ain't from nowhere," Ty answered sullenly, angry that what he considered his was being taken away.

The man's dark gaze slid over his knickers and stockings. "The way you're dressed, it looks to be the truth." He snagged Ty under one arm and began pulling him along.

"Mr. Langston," the clerk called. "If you plan on takin' the little thief to the sheriff, I'm willin' to file charges."

"I don't plan on turnin' him in—at least not right away." Langston's mouth skewed and he shrugged. "I think I'll take him home with me, feed him, clean him up a bit first . . . see if there's anything worth redeemin' underneath all that dirt and toughness."

"Mr. Langston. With all the goin's on at your house, you think you oughta do that?"

"Probably not, Jasper." Langston took a deep breath and let it whistle out between his even white teeth. "Probably a big mistake." He looked down at Ty and pressed his lips together. Then he smiled, and Ty decided he wasn't so mean-looking after all. "But, then, desperate men have been known to do desperate things, haven't we, son?" He looked up at the storekeeper. "Put the boy's purchases on my bill, Jasper."

Ty forced his face to remain impassive and refused to answer Mr. Langston. He'd take this man's offer of a meal and some new clothes. Hell, why shouldn't he? But more than that? He'd just have to wait and see.

Tyler Ramsey was not about to make the basic mistake of trusting a stranger—at least not without a damn good reason. That was the one thing he'd learned on the streets of New York . . . the one thing he wasn't about to forget.

But he did allow Mr. Langston to lead him out of the dry goods store without protesting. If he didn't like what he saw, he'd simply run away again and take up where he'd left off—if the need arose.

Serra followed the movement of the swinging watch with concentrated fascination. It was so pretty, the loveliest bauble she'd ever seen. How she wished Dr. Chelsey would hold it still so she could get a better look at it.

But more importantly she wanted to please, so she said nothing, her amber eyes swiveling from side to side like the pendulum of the tall case clock in the foyer.

Ticktock. Back and forth. Back and forth.

From the other side of the room, she could hear the rustle of Mrs. Chelsey's silk gown, along with the purring of the cat that curled in her lap. From down the hall, the musical chiming of a mantel clock drifted into the parlor. All sounds of contentment, sounds to trust.

"You're getting sleepy, Serra. It's all right to close your eyes," the doctor assured her, his voice and the rhythmic tapping of his fingers superseding all of the other homey noises about her.

Suddenly her eyes were so heavy; it was impossible to keep them open. Her eyelids lowered once, then she snapped them back up, struggling to fight the blanket of oblivion. But it was so warm, so comforting, so . . .

"Sleep, Serra. I only want to help you . . . make you feel better."

And she did feel better. . . . So relaxed . . . Soon she heard nothing but the sound of the doctor's voice crooning reassurance to her. Even the ticking of the foyer clock ceased to exist.

"Serra . . ." The doctor's voice sounded far away, as if he were speaking from deep down in a well. "I want you to envision yourself as a little girl."

The image of the orphanage, of Tyler Ramsey holding her hand, blanketed the backs of her eyelids. She smiled in remembrance.

"What do you see, dumpling?"

"The orphanage . . . my friend Ty."

"Go back further in time, before you lived in the orphanage."

As if someone had placed a series of photographs in a kinematoscope and spun them backward, Serra felt herself growing younger. The memories grew sporadic; then there was nothing. Though she tried with all her might, she just couldn't remember. "I don't know," she squeaked in a frightened little voice, fearing that her failure would somehow displease the doctor.

"Then let me help you. Open your eyes."

Her lashes parted, and her vision filled with an image — a big house with gables, fretwork, and a turret. Before it stood a carriage that looked as if it belonged in a fairy tale, a rotund fairy godmotherlike woman sitting on the plush upholstery. Standing between the big spoked wheels was a man and a woman as beautiful as the castlelike house in the background. Between them was a little girl. And though the picture was in brown and ivory, Serra could tell from the way the child's hair sprung about her head that it was very much like her own.

She stared hard, sensing that what she looked at was merely a photograph, yet her heart began to race out of control. A family—a mother, a father, and the plump woman in the carriage who must be the nanny. Oh, the household was so much like the one she dreamed of for herself.

"Do you know what that little girl's name is in the picture?"

Serra shook her head, her eyes refusing to tear themselves away from the frozen imagery.

"Serenity. Serenity Langston. That's a pretty name, isn't it?"

Serra couldn't think of a more perfect one.

"Don't you wish that were your name, dumpling? Serenity." The *S* sound seemed to echo in Serra's mind.

She wet her lips with mental hunger. "Oh, yes," she murmured, her head bobbing with enthusiasm. Her gaze skimmed over the two adults in the picture, her heart crying out, wanting more than anything to grasp, if only for a moment, the unattainable.

"Then you can have it, Serra. Ser—ra. Ser—enity. All you have to do, dumpling, is reach out and take your mother and father's hands."

For a brief moment she hesitated, almost feeling foolish, knowing she shouldn't even consider doing what the doctor suggested. It was wrong, wasn't it? That wasn't her in the photograph. . . .

Or was it? Serra's head tilted sideways. As if by magic, the couple from the photograph were standing on either side of her, reaching out and smiling.

27

Their flesh was so warm and real when she touched it. She clung, tears of happiness bursting forth.

From somewhere deep inside of her a voice cried, "No, Serra, don't do it." Cobalt-blue eyes challenged her. Frowned at her. Rejected her the way they had on the opera house stage.

But now she had a family. Was that so wrong?

The condemning gaze faded away.

She turned to the couple — real parents — who called out to her, wanting *her*. "Serenity, Serenity, where are you?"

"I'm here, Momma," she whimpered, gripping the hand tighter.

"Sleep, dumpling, sleep," commanded that faraway voice that had the magic to make dreams come to life.

Serra Paletot, neglected child from the streets of New York, willingly obeyed. In her place emerged the seedling of a new personality, someone who demanded to be nurtured and developed. Serenity Langston, adored daughter. A little girl found and determined never to be lost again.

Chapter Two

"Serenity, dear, contain yourself."

Serra's white gloved hands stilled in the lap of her rosewood and ivory plaid dress only with a conscious effort. How could Doc expect her to show patience at a moment like this?

She was going home.

After six long years of guidance and therapy, as the good doctor called it, she was ready to face her future — and her past.

Oh, God, what would her father think of her after all of those lost years?

She glanced at Dr. Chelsey. As if he understood the turn her thoughts had taken, he reached out and patted the back of her hand that was beginning to fidget once more. "You'll do fine, dumpling. Not to worry."

"What if Father asks me something to which I don't know the answer?" Her voice sounded calm, cultured, mature.

He looked at her in that way he had. As always, it soothed her troubled mind. "Then be truthful. Tell him you don't remember."

29

With an accepting bow to her lips, she turned to stare out of the window. The world beyond the train rolled by with regularity. Stretches of spring-lush pasture, rocks painstakingly cleared stacked along the fence line, a farmhouse, a stone barn with a matching silo, green pasture again. The rhythmic clack of the wheels went unchanged except for when they crossed an occasional trestle bridge that spanned a river, going on and on endlessly.

She hoped her father was as kind as he appeared in his picture — and in her memory. Her hands began twisting in her skirt again.

The locomotive blasted an unexpected warning that echoed away like dying thunder, shattering her worrisome thoughts. Serra stiffened and stretched to see beyond the panorama framed in the window. "Are we there?" she asked breathlessly.

"No, we couldn't possibly be in Joplin already," the doctor replied, straining beside her to also see what was ahead.

In contrast to his statement, the wheels beneath their feet rumbled a protest as brakes were applied, the alternating squeal, release, then squeal again suggesting an unscheduled stop.

With a resigned hiss of steam from its underbelly, the train came to a shuddering standstill. Serra's murmur of protest mingled with those coming from her fellow passengers, but oddly enough no one bothered to rise. They all just remained in their seats as if glued there, waiting to see what would happen next.

Pop. Pop. Pop . . .

Under different circumstances, the faraway noise could have easily passed as pine knots crackling on an open fire grate.

From three seats up, a woman screamed. The

30

sound worked like a catalyst.

"Gunfire," someone gasped.

The announcement ricocheted several times about the car.

Serra looked to Dr. Chelsey, her amber eyes wide with apprehension. Doc would tell her if she should be afraid or not.

"They're mistaken, Serenity," he assured her. "What earthly reason would there be for someone to be shooting? Train robberies became obsolete years ago with the death of Jesse James." His logic was so sound that she relaxed and gave him a smile.

The passengers remained in their seats. No one moved or spoke after the last declaration of "gunfire."

The door to the train car swung open and slammed against the wall like a loose shutter in a storm. Someone shrieked.

Serra found her hand plastered against her mouth and realized the sound had slipped from her own lips.

A figure filled the doorway, so tall that the top of his Stetson brushed the upper frame.

Black. That was all she could see. Black hat, black drover's coat, black boots, even the glimpse of pants and shirt revealed more black. A black bandanna covered most of the intruder's face, a face that was framed with raven-black hair that billowed over the upturned collar and blended with the coat's shoulder cape. The only relief was the silver conchae banding the crown of his hat and . . .

In the black gloved hand was a pistol, shiny steel cradled with such casual expertise that she was more frightened than if he had held it in a firm grip.

Above the concealing neckerchief the intruder's eyes roamed about the passenger car. They lit on Serra, traveling from the flower-topped straw hat perched atop her red curls to her kid-covered hands, then down to the tips of her dainty white high-top packers. The gaze moved back up to study her face.

Blue, she thought in amazement. *Among all that black, his eyes are so very blue.*

The black figure moved forward. Down the aisle, and for some crazy reason she knew he would stop before her.

He didn't disappoint her.

Serra's chin tilted upwards. Her heart grown as still as the moments just before a tornado, she watched his progress. Spurs jingled when he walked. She glanced down at them. Another touch of silver to contrast with the ominous black.

The melodic clinking stopped when he halted in front of her.

"I'm lookin' for someone claimin' to be Serenity Langston." He directed his slightly muffled inquiry toward Serra.

"Don't know her," Dr. Chelsey piped out.

But her head was already nodding, denouncing Doc's protective lie.

The black-clad man ignored the doctor's denial. "Who is *he?*" he demanded, notching his weapon toward Chelsey. A lock of crisp ebony hair fell over his forehead. A crazy urge to reach up and brush it away overwhelmed her.

She restrained her impulse. "Dr. Chelsey's my guardian."

Blue eyes narrowed, studying the doctor, who conjured up his most powerful stare, one that never failed to affect Serra. The man in black was unimpressed, and he flipped his ice-cold gaze back to her. "You sick or somethin'?"

"No," she answered at the same moment the doctor

32

said "yes." It never occurred to her to lie.

"Good."

Somehow, she sensed the man in black's relief was not on her account.

"Then if you don't mind, ma'am," he drawled in a deceptively lazy voice, "you're to come with me."

Though he mouthed his demand ever so politely, she doubted he would accept a refusal from her, courteous or not, for when she hesitated, his grip tightened on the trigger guard of his pistol—a warning.

Serra rose; Doc stood with her.

"You can't do this," Chelsey protested. "Miss Langston's father is a high-positioned businessman in Joplin, and—"

"Sit down, you ol' charlatan. I *know* who John Langston is."

To Serra's complete surprise, Doc dropped into his seat without another comment.

"Now, ma'am"—the stranger touched his gloved fingers to the brim of his black felt hat in an almost respectful gesture—"nobody will get hurt if you come along peacefully."

There was no question of obedience. What else could she do? Stomp her daintily shod foot and say no? She had a hunch such a spectacle would only make this dark-clad desperado laugh. She further suspected his laughter would not be a pleasant sound.

With all of the grace she possessed, Serra gathered up her Spanish lace shawl and her reticule, and she stepped into the aisle.

One dark brow above the bandanna arched in surprise, but her show of courage was not enough to make the man in black reconsider his actions. He took her by the arm, and then, as if escorting her to a Sunday social, he led her forward, out of the train car, and

33

onto the tiny platform beyond the rear door.

A circle of riders waited below, each one as unsavory-looking and nervous as the next. Their faces were covered, their weapons drawn, all seeking instructions from the man in black. His iron-strong arm swept about her waist. With a squeak of protest, Serra squirmed, to no avail, so she ceased her fruitless struggle. Pure fear gripped at her insides, twisting, grinding. She swayed on the platform.

"Why are you doing this?" she asked in breathless fright when he dragged her against his hard-planed chest.

He laughed, and just as she'd surmised, it was a chilling, demonic sound. His bandanna sucked against his face, and for a moment she could make out the faint outline of his features. They were as strong and chiseled as the rest of him.

"If I find out you're lyin' about who you are, your life won't be worth the price of a shot of rotgut," he answered in that uncompromising manner of his.

Before she could voice her objections, he tossed her over the rail onto the back of his waiting horse, which was surrounded by his men. A black horse. Of course, the man in black would have such a beast.

Then he dropped down behind her and gathered up the reins, the circle of his arms squeezing about her ribs.

Turning his horse in the opposite direction that the train headed, he jabbed his spurs into his mount's sides. They leaped forward, the instant pounding of the horse's hooves taken up in multitude as his band of outlaws followed his lead.

Serra looked back over her shoulder and his much broader one. All she saw was her flower-topped straw hat fly through the air and roll in the dust near the tracks. Doc stooped and picked it up, standing and lifting his fist in belated defiance. Red curls and the hem of her captor's duster whipped by the breeze prohibited her from seeing more.

They rode. Over the course of time the other riders, one by one, split off from the main group, suggesting such tactics had been worked out ahead of time. As if the hounds of hell snapped at their heels, the man in black never seemed to notice. He just kept up the grueling pace, until the great black gelding beneath them began to stumble in exhaustion. With a barely perceptible tightening of his arm that brushed against her waist, he slowed the grateful beast.

His head sagging, his glistening sides heaving, the horse came to a ready halt. But her kidnapper apparently harbored no sympathy for his mount's plight. She felt his legs tighten as he made the poor loyal animal move forward again, but at a much slower pace.

Serra glanced about. To her left the sun rode the western horizon, seeming to dip and rise behind the rocky jut of a mountain. She was alone with the dark-clad stranger, and it was nearly dusk, yet she could make out the flecks of frothy sweat dotting her gown. More freckled her abductor's long coat, and against the black the lather stood out like snowflakes on coal. She shivered in the cooling spring air and felt a kinship with the poor abused horse.

In sympathy, Serra reached out to pat his neck. The animal was coated with perspiration, which stood out like soap foam across its ebony shoulders.

Such a harsh taskmaster, this man of gloom. Neither the animal nor she deserved to take the brunt of his cruel disregard.

35

"Can't you see fit to allow your horse a moment to rest? Surely you don't mean to kill *him*." She wondered if the stranger had caught her show of uncertainty regarding her own fate.

"Just what do you think I oughta do—ma'am?" The *ma'am* came a bit belatedly, as if he mocked her.

The answer seemed only too obvious to Serra. "What anyone decent would do. Let him stop long enough to catch his wind and cool down."

He laughed cruelly, throwing back his head. Beneath his mask Serra caught a glimpse of his unshaven chin, the strong, protruding cords of his neck, the up-and-down action of his Adam's apple as he spoke. "You hear that, Cochise? The li'l lady thinks I oughta let you stop. What do you think?"

The tired horse snorted but continued his slow, even pace.

"Goes to show how much you know about horses," he snapped. "If I did what you suggested, miss, he'd colic and be dead by mornin'. The kindest thing I can do is make him keep walkin'."

Cochise tried to stop. True to his words, her captor gave the horse a nudge with his spurs to keep him going.

"I hope you're better informed when it comes to John Langston. He won't be as amused by a wrong answer as I am."

Serra stiffened upon hearing her own inner concerns voiced aloud. "You make it sound as if I've been groomed to play a part."

"Haven't you? Serenity Langston disappeared over fourteen years ago. Doesn't it seem a little odd, even to you, that you show up now? Where have you been keepin' yourself all of these years?"

"I don't have to answer to you." And she didn't. She

36

sat up as straight as she could, trying to avoid his touch. The injustices life had dealt her were none of this stranger's business.

"Well, Miss Whoever-you-are, that's where you're wrong. You'll answer to me in one way or another."

His arm gripped her about the middle, and he leaned into her. His actions made her tense and tremble at the same time. They also caused Cochise to step up his pace, just enough to take the next rise in a matter of moments.

At the bottom of the hill a stone fence ran from left to right, as far as the eye could see. A wooden gate hung neglected on a post, partially blocking the trail, clumps of grass growing up between the slats. Apparently no one had ever bothered to take the time to shut it—or fix it.

Through the gate and up another rise. From the crest she saw where they were headed. A small, natural stone cabin. Uncurtained windows stared out like soulless eyes. The wooden steps were in need of repair, the railing between the porch pillars warped and bowed from the lack of a coat of paint. A pair of old rocking chairs, weatherworn and unpadded, swayed in the light breeze. It all offered an unfriendly greeting.

What kind of grudge did this man hold against her father? That was the only logical reason she could come up with for his strange actions. Just what did he plan to do with her?

He seemed familiar with his surroundings as he led the horse into a small shed in the back of the house and dismounted. Reaching up, he dislodged her from the saddle and stashed her in a corner, the horse and his own wide body between her and the door making escape impossible—not that she'd know where to go even if she could get away.

Once he lit the oil lantern hanging on a nail on the wall, Serra was able to watch as he uncinched the saddle and tossed it over a low divider in the lean-to. The horse gave up the bit in his mouth with relish, standing quietly as his master scooped out a tin canful of grain and tossed it in the feeder.

Picking up the tack, the man in black slung it over his shoulder with a grunt and turned to her.

The lantern hissed softly. She looked at his face, still concealed by the dark bandanna, and tried to imagine what he looked like beneath it. How sinister he appeared hidden behind his black mask. Why didn't he just take it off? The palms of her hands began to sweat as she conjured up all kinds of crazy reasons for him not wanting her to see his face.

"What's wrong?" he demanded, coming to a halt in front of her.

She dare not confess she was afraid; it might serve to further incite his contempt for her. Yet the shadows cast by the light, which threw strange configurations against the wall, intensified her fear. Her eyes darted about and settled on the horse, who was contentedly munching on his meal. The lather had dried on his body, leaving the imprint of the saddle blanket across his back. For some strange reason she couldn't fathom, Serra could still feel the imprint of this man's arms about her waist. "I thought you said he would die if he stopped."

"Jesus, woman. Don't you know nothin' about nothin'?" he asked in exasperation. With his free hand, he shoved the lantern into her gloved fingers and grabbed her arm, leading her out of the building.

She stumbled on the rocky footpath leading from the shed to the back door of the cabin. She glanced down at her white-kid boots, highlighted by the lantern suspended beside her feet. They were ruined, the expensive leather that had been a gift sent from her father scuffed and torn. The discovery made her so angry with this man, who had had the audacity to interfere with the culmination of her dreams from at last coming true, that she drew herself up, refusing to be polite — or cowed — for another moment.

What right did he have to do what he was doing with her?

The second his fingers relaxed on her arm, Serra jerked away. Racing up the overgrown drive, she headed back the way they'd come earlier in the evening, the lantern still clutched in her fingers. The blessed illumination allowed her to see her way yet at the same time pinpointed her exact location for him. But she refused to give it up.

On she went, like a will-o'-the-wisp, over the rise, her shoes shuffling along on the gravel path that her beacon revealed step by grueling step. At the gate, which partially blocked the road, the hem of her skirt snagged on something. To the tune of a loud renting sound, she fell to her knees, bits of slate rock scraping the unprotected skin of her legs. The lantern somersaulted through the air, landing with the tinkle of shattered glass several feet away.

Trapped by the blackness of the moonless night, Serra cried out her pain and distress. Biting down on her tongue to squelch the wayward sound, she tasted blood. Her hand flew backward, seeking to untangle her skirt. The sharp barbs of a piece of loose fencing speared their way into the soft leather of her glove.

It was ludicrous the way her thoughts turned to something so irrelevant as the condition of her gloves when so much more was at stake, but nonetheless her eyes welled with frustration that they were now as ruined as her shoes. It was all his fault.

"Oh, damn you," she railed, her curse directed at the man in black, who had forced her into this most unacceptable situation. With her good glove, she swiped at her nose and sniffed. With the other, she groped in the darkness behind her, carefully relocated the wire, and tried to disentangle it from the hem of her dress. But it clung like cocklebur, refusing to let go.

"Oh, it's ruined, too," she grumbled, meaning her dress. "It's all ruined." Meaning her life. Gathering the pretty plaid wool in her fist, she ripped it away from the fencing, freeing herself.

But freeing herself to do what?

She glanced about and could see absolutely nothing, not even when she held her splayed fingers up inches from her face. She couldn't even be sure which way she should go. Which way led to freedom, which back to the man in black?

She thought of the times Dr. Chelsey had shown her inkblots on paper and asked her what she saw. The one that came to mind now had almost completely filled the page, except for two light spots in the middle. A black cat on a black night, hiding beneath a black rock. Doc hadn't thought her humor so funny then. Well, she didn't find it funny, either, at least not anymore.

To her left something crunched—and jingled. A puppylike squeak erupted from her throat. She leaned in the direction from which the sound had come, but no matter how she strained, Serra couldn't see a thing. A black cat on a black night—and it was stalking her. Only this predator wore boots and a black felt hat with silver conchae banding it. Her heart registered her absolute terror, flaying its prison like a trapped beast.

She couldn't just sit here and let him stumble upon her. It seemed the coward's way out.

Carefully, she tucked her feet beneath her. Like a fingerling fish she darted forward, skipping over the surface in an attempt to avoid the waiting jaws of death — so close she could hear his intake of breath. She took the path she thought led away from the danger, praying that for once her sense of direction was accurate.

She crashed into something as solid as a tree trunk. As her mind went spiraling, Serra couldn't remember seeing one single tree when they had ridden onto the property earlier.

Great limbs curled about her. She screamed, certain that the devil's henchmen had hold of her and would drag her down into the pits of hell. They heaved her forward all right, and she sensed that hell awaited her in a tiny, lifeless cabin made of stone.

"Let go of me," she demanded.

"Not likely, not unless you're willin' to give up your false claim to what belongs to me," her tormentor responded. As if he had the night vision of an owl, he pulled her along, hoisting her up about the waist and dropping her every few feet, his strides long and confident.

Up the rise through the darkness they moved. The steel band of his arm dug into her rib cage as he hauled her back toward the stone cabin. Her own hands plucked at his sleeve, but the leather gloves kept her from wreaking much damage to the flesh beneath the material.

"Oh-h-h," she grunted, snagging the finger of one glove in her teeth and tugging her hand free as he again lifted her up and carried her a yard or two, only to dump her on her feet with a bone-jarring thud. She would claw his eyes out—those wretched blue eyes—the moment her nails were unsheathed. Fervently, she hoped she'd be the first to draw blood.

The glove dropped to the ground, the same one she had grieved and sniveled over moments before, and she didn't care if she ever found it again. Reaching upwards, she scraped her fingernails across his face.

One finger hooked in the bandanna he had so painstakingly kept over his features, and it slid down around his neck. She heard his hiss of protest at the same moment they crested the hill. A beacon of light shone from the cabin's uncurtained windows and gaping door, a giant jack-o'-lantern squatting at the bottom of the hill.

The thought that he had not bothered to chase after her right away but instead had taken his sweet time to open up the cabin stung her already-injured pride. Had she been such easy prey that he'd known for sure he could catch her?

The not-knowing-why blended with the humiliation and worked like a catalyst, churning her anger into courage. She'd come too far and suffered too damn much to lose it all now. Balling her fist, she swung with all of her might and plowed into his belly.

He grunted, doubled up, and teetered at the top of the hill. Then they were falling, rolling, but he refused to let go of her. Down the hill they tumbled, over and over, rocks cramming against her spine and skull, then his. At the bottom of the incline they landed in a heap, arms and legs tangled, his duster wrapped beneath her in such a way that they were soldered together like Siamese twins, neither able to move without the other's consent.

A single streak of light poured out of the open door

of the cabin and fell across them like a ribbon. The man in black rolled to his side, and the illumination touched his face for a split second.

Serra caught her breath. She had seen his features for only a moment, but she knew she wasn't mistaken. It was older, it was bearded, but it was a face she would never forget.

"Tyler Ramsey," she whispered so softly she wasn't sure she'd said it aloud.

His familiar blue eyes narrowed at her, their burning intensity hard and uncompromising. There was not a smidgen of the compassion she had squirreled away in her subconscious and treasured for six long years.

Her need to find her family faded away like the sweetest of forget-me-nots left too long in the hot sun. All that seemed to matter at the moment was to put the remembered kindness back into his cobalt-blue eyes.

Chapter Three

Apparently, the little trollop wasn't as dumb as he'd figured. Tyler Ramsey's blue eyes hardened like steel tempered by the fires of righteousness as he appraised the willowy, yet curvaceous body he held pinned to the ground. The pink and white plaid of her dress front rose and fell each time she inhaled, reminding him of just what she was—all woman. A conniving one without a doubt, but one with rich red hair a man could easily get lost in.

His body reacted with a familiar tightening, his mind with anger. The fact that she knew who he was and now stared at him with such confidence could only mean one thing: This bit of brazen baggage had done her homework. She probably knew as much about John Langston as the damn sentimental fool knew about himself.

Forcing his arm beneath her back, he encircled her slender waist. He rose to his feet, dragging her up with him, her long coppery tresses trailing behind her like a signal flag. Red-haired witch. He'd known plenty of women like this one in his twenty-two years. Out for a free ride, or whatever their femininity could buy.

Easily a foot taller in height, he stared down into her amber eyes, noting that her arms hung lifelessly at her sides, showing not a sign of resistance. Her face tilted upwards, indicating no fear. In fact, those damned golden eyes seemed to search his face for . . . something. . . . For kindness, perhaps?

Not in a pig's eye. His jaws snapped together, and his mouth flattened. Consummated actress that she was, he had almost been sucked in by her pretty little performance. Reaching up with his free hand, he unknotted the bandanna slung about his throat. All the while, she watched his movements with trusting eyes. Speared by uncalled-for guilt, he wrenched his gaze away, twirled her unresisting body about, and grabbed up her wrists, securing them behind her back with the black neckerchief.

"Just where did you think you were goin'?" he growled, the unwarranted war going on inside his head making him jerk the final knot a little tighter than he'd intended. When she flinched in martyrlike silence, he wanted to shake her, make her show her real nature by saying something nasty back to him.

"I'll tell you now, Miss Whoever-you-are," he warned. "There's nothin' out there for miles but rocks, and there's nobody but me." He gave her a shove toward the cabin, and she stumbled forward in resilient fortitude.

She braced her shoulder against one of the porch rail posts and hung there, speaking at last. But what she said was not what he expected. "I *am* Serenity Langston," she assured him in a low, even voice, her gaze as steady as a Sunday morning sermon.

He met her look with a challenge. "Yeah? And I'm Jesse James," he mocked with a curl to his upper lip.

Her eyes widened, as if she considered the feasibil-

45

ity of his declaration. Then her chin lifted ever so slightly. "Impossible. Jesse James is dead. Besides . . ." Her thoughts trailed off incomplete.

Besides what? he thought, but let the matter drop as well. "That's right, ma'am," he confirmed. "And chances are Serenity Langston has fared no better."

At last she gave him what he'd been looking for: A flicker of uncertainty tempered with ire flashed in her amber eyes. Her mouth curved down, and he could almost see the angry retort forming in her mind.

Then she disappointed him. She soldered those pretty lips of hers together and straightened, staring out long and hard at the rolling hills that stretched out before the cabin. With a lingering examination of him, she turned and moved with the dignity of the persecuted into the cabin and waited, without glancing back, for him to follow.

Ty eyed her rigid spine and straight shoulders. Damn her. Damn the scheming little bitch to hell. Even if she was Serenity Langston — which he was fairly confident she was not — what right did she have to appear at this time and stir up old hurts and losses for John Langston? What justified her looking so vulnerable?

Above all else, he was honor-bound to protect his mentor. It was the least he could do after all John Langston had done for him over the years. Langston deserved better than to be duped by a money-grubbing female.

Reaffirming his dedication to the one person who had shown concern for him — even if it had been harsh at times — Ty strode into the cabin and slammed the door behind his back, determination manifesting itself in the frown that creased the bridge of his nose. He would break her, somehow, someway — any way he had to. But he would have to do it soon.

John Langston was a man who carried a vengeance into hell if need be. As soon as he discovered his supposed daughter missing, he would come after her again, no bars held. Ty shot his captive a stoic look. Unless Miss Innocence was ready to confess her dupery, there would be no way to stop the man's fury, and there was no doubt in Ty's mind which one of them would suffer the consequences. It wouldn't be her, he assured himself.

How could Ty have changed so completely over the years? How could he have forgotten her so easily? *Oh, Ty, Ty,* her heart cried, wanting more than anything to reveal herself. *Don't you recognize me?*

Serra dropped her head and felt the tears of disappointment well, filling her eyes, threatening to spill down her cheeks. He had always been there in her mind, something to keep faith in, to dream about, to await. Never once had she suspected that her memory would be wiped clean from his mental slate. But apparently that was the case. There had not been even a flicker of recollection in his cold blue eyes.

Serra lifted her face to the ceiling and swallowed down the urge to cry out. Rejection hurt. Oh, God, how it hurt to know he had probably never intended to keep his promise to come back for her. Fool that she was, she had truly waited, even up until this very moment. The thought of sharing her new found fortune with him had been her secret desire. Someday. Always in the back of her mind, the possibility had seemed so real.

Now, suddenly, Tyler Ramsey threatened to take away all she had worked so hard for over the last six

47

years.

She wouldn't let that happen. Whatever his reasons were for doing what he did, she wouldn't allow him to destroy the culmination of her dreams. But just as important, she couldn't let him see that his threats and bullying affected her.

Taking a deep breath, she turned to confront this man who represented so much to her, but who was now nothing more than a stranger. The fact that she knew his name had thrown him off guard. She felt no qualms about taking further advantage of the situation.

"Mr. Ramsey, if there is nothing out there" — she tipped her head toward the door — "but rocks, like you say, why do you feel it necessary to tie my hands? If you truly fear I'll try to run away again, don't you think binding my legs would be a much smarter move?"

At the word *smarter* the muscle under his left eye twitched and his large, gloved hands fisted. Was that his Achilles' heel? she speculated. An intellectual deficiency? At one time in her life, she would have felt an affinity to his sensitivity, but Dr. Chelsey had seen to it that she received every advantage he could give her, including an education. Yes, she supposed Ty had always been overly self-conscious about his lack of formal learning. She waited, wondering what further reaction he would give.

"No woman," he said with vehemence, " 'pecially a brazen little hussy like you, will ever outsmart me. Run, Miss Know-it-all." He indicated the door by sweeping off his hat in a mocking show of chivalry. "See how far you'll get."

But Serra wasn't thinking about escaping. His raven-black hair that showed the imprint of his hat reminded her of how he used to be—young and wild and, oh, so full of wisdom. "Please, Ty," she whispered, the throes of remembering roughening her voice, "won't you release my hands?"

Instead of softening with her plea and familiarity, he seemed to grow even harder. "Shut up and sit down," he ordered, refusing to even look at her.

Serra glanced around the one-room cabin. Sparsely furnished with a cookstove and a rickety old table with two chairs, one broken and haphazardly propped against the wall, the other already occupied with the gear Ty had hastily flung in the seat earlier—saddle, blanket, bags, and bedroll—the inside wasn't much to look at. In the far corner stood a bedstead that sagged so deep in the middle it looked more like a sinkhole than a place to sleep or even to sit down.

"Where?" she asked, cocking her head.

Ty glared at her, but she didn't flinch. She'd seen him in a surly mood before, plenty of times. An oath hissed between his teeth, but he gathered up the tack, slinging the saddle over a bracket near the front door that had apparently been put there for that purpose. The rest of his gear he dropped on the table.

Serra smiled to herself, feeling somewhat mollified. So he *had* been in a bit of a hurry to come after her earlier when she'd attempted to run away.

Once the chair was cleared, he turned to her expectantly.

Wiping the smugness from her face, she sat down, her back arrow straight, her head at a proud angle. The demanded silent vigilance maintained, she watched him shrug out of his drover's coat and hang it on a peg beside the door, along with his hat. The silver conchae caught the light from the lantern on the table and they twinkled. The reflection glanced off the pistol slung about his slim hips in a leather holster, as if it were a permanent fixture. She remembered how easily he had handled that weapon aboard the train.

Her earlier smile transformed into a small frown of concern. Just what had Ty been doing over the last six years? Had he indeed kept his boyhood vow to take up outlawing?

Perhaps she should feel a little more fear. Six years had made Ty a man. Her gaze swept over his broad shoulders and powerful chest. Definitely a man. Time had also hardened him; it could have altered his basically good soul as well.

She glanced up at his face. Why did he find it so important to keep her from her father? He had called her a liar, challenging her claim to the Langston name. But perhaps he was only testing her, for if she did prove to be Serenity Langston, he might have ulterior motives for kidnapping her.

Her heart cried out a denial. Ty—at least not her Ty—would never do something so sinister. But what if he had changed, truly turning into the desperado he'd bragged about becoming all those years before? Then chances were he would be after one thing—money.

The Langston money, and he planned on getting his hands on it by intimidating her.

Her amber eyes narrowed as she took in his countenance, the close-cropped beard, the critical blue eyes, the perpetual lines between his brows that made him look so cynical, the downward curve of his lips. The urge to reveal herself as the little street waif who had trailed after him in their youth vanished, at least for the time being. If he was testing her, then she would simply best him at his own game.

* * *

50

The fact that she plotted something was only too evident in the way her feline eyes flicked over him. Like the predator he knew her to be, she sat there, practically preening her self-assuredness. Didn't think he was too smart, huh? Well, he could outthink her and snooze at the same time, if he had a mind to.

Ty smoothed back his dark hair with one hand, soothing his crimped ego with thoughts of just what he had in store for the little snip. He'd turn that overconfidence into fear, make her only too happy to admit the truth of her identity. If she'd figured John Langston for an easy target, she had another think coming.

"Well, what are *you* starin' at?" He didn't like the way she had of almost seeing into the private recesses of his soul, as if she fathomed things about him he didn't even know about himself. But, oddly enough, a stab of guilt pierced his conscience as he watched her sit there, her slim shoulders straight, her hands still tied behind her back.

She was right; there really was no point in binding her other than to boost his own flagging ego. He reached down into the top of his boot and pulled out a knife.

"Turn around," he ordered, his thumb resting against the razor-sharp edge.

She stared at him, openmouthed, as if she were deaf and dumb. Then she angled her body, offering up her unprotected back. The moment he stepped toward her, she squeezed her shoulder blades together, as if she truly thought he might plunge the weapon between them. The little snip was worried, was she? As well she should be. He touched her spine with the pointed tip, and she jumped. Savoring her reaction, he chuckled as he sliced through the knotted bandanna, releasing her hands.

51

Her arms dropping to her sides, she twisted around. Relief edged the fear on her face and she huddled there, staring at him, rubbing the circulation back into her wrists. "Thank you," she murmured.

He shrugged, then bent at the waist to return the knife to its sheath in his boot. "I figured you won't try anything 'til mornin'."

Giving him a defiant look, she stilled. "And if you are wrong?"

From his crooked position, he stared up at her and arched one brow. "I'm not," he assured her, straightening. And he knew he wasn't.

"Until morning, then," she conceded to the temporary cease fire. Lowering her hands, she placed them sedately in her lap. Her gaze flicked down from his face to examine the revolver slung low on his right hip. "Tell me, Mr. Ramsey. What would you have done if I had refused to come peacefully with you on the train?" She glanced back up into his blue eyes to judge his response.

Surprised by the turn of the conversation, Ty cocked his head and hooked his thumbs about the holster strapped across his flat belly. Amusement spurted from deep within his chest, and he noted the way the corners of her mouth quivered as if he derided her. And he supposed that he *was* laughing at her, but mostly at her ridiculous question. "Done? Whatever I would have had to do, miss," he answered, simply implying he would have taken her by force.

Again her eyes slid to the side arm, as if she interpreted his words to mean he would have shot her. For a second he thought her gaze touched elsewhere, someplace more intimate, but he must have been mistaken, for then she was staring back up at him in what he figured was intended to pass for a sanctimonious look.

"I see," she replied, as if *he* had committed some unspoken sin.

Piqued, he lowered his hands and leaned toward her. "So tell me, ma'am, if you will, what would *you* have done if I had left you on the train?"

She shrank back, her pious look turning guarded. "I would have continued on my way, of course, home to my father, and picked up the pieces of my splintered life." She smoothed the wrinkles from her skirt and gave Ty an expression that dared him to deny her the right.

He'd had just about enough of this damned charade. Grabbing her by the arms, he shook her. "No, ma'am, that's where you're wrong. While you whine about splinters, you should be worried about the real consequences of your actions. You can't go after big game with a popgun and expect to come out unscathed."

Reaching up, she dug her nails into the flesh of his fingers in a futile attempt to escape his punishing grip. "Yes, I suppose I am naive by your standards, Tyler Ramsey," she blurted out. Her lips were pressed so tightly together they were white with indignation.

God, she could play her role to the hilt, couldn't she? Standing there so pitifully yet so bravely, looking so righteous. The strangest urge knotted in his stomach, leaving his mouth dry. How would she react if he called her bluff and ravaged that pouty little mouth of hers? He nearly laughed aloud at the crazy notion, for at the moment, he doubted he could pry her lips apart even with a crowbar.

To his surprise, her moist mouth parted of its own volition, revealing even white teeth and the tip of a pink tongue. The overpowering need to take what they offered intensified. What would she taste like? No doubt sweet and tantalizing, the epitome of the forbidden fruit.

"But the standards of someone like you can't be very high, now, can they?" she continued in a voice laced with emotion. "Stealing from those who are meeker than you apparently doesn't bother you too much."

Her accusation served only to stoke his raging desire. "Stealin' is stealin', darlin', whether at the mercy of a loaded six-shooter or the lies of a sweet-faced angel who would rob you blind without a second thought. At least my victims know what they're up against."

"A thief claiming honor. I doubt that seriously." Her hands lifted and clenched in emphasis.

Locked together, they swayed, and Ty prepared himself for the blow that was sure to come. But to his utter amazement, she controlled her temper. Most of the women he knew would have struck out. So why did she bother to restrain herself? The image, that's why, he assured himself. Always the calm and collected Miss Langston. Her ability to maintain that ruse made him grind his teeth in frustration.

"Honor doesn't have a damned thing to do with it." He captured her balled fingers in his much larger fists and glanced down at them. How small her hands were; how easily he could snap the delicate bones if he so desired.

But that wasn't what he wanted to do. What he wanted was to crush her full, tempting lips beneath his, to feel her willpower shatter beneath his stronger one. That's what she deserved for indulging in the cruel, self-seeking games she played.

Without further justification, he dragged her against his chest, twisting her arms behind her back, and felt the gentle rise and fall of her breasts beneath her bodice.

Soft on the outside, ruthless on the inside. The world had plenty of women like that.

His mouth ground down on hers and encountered the hard barrier of her teeth beneath the silky pillow of her lips. If he could just break through that defense, he knew what lay beyond — the velvety contours of her mouth. But what resided behind the cool facade of a hard-hearted woman who could deceive a grieving man like John Langston, Ty wasn't so sure. There could be bedrock, or there could be nothing . . . a void. He found it hard to believe there might be tenderness.

Not that he needed tenderness, mind you. He'd been shown very little of that in his life, and he'd gotten on just fine without it.

He thrust his tongue against the enamel barricade, limning the ridges and contours as if seeking the secret release lever. To his smug satisfaction, he found what he sought in the vulnerable corner of her mouth, and he took advantage, prizing his way into the revealed crevice.

She struggled once at his plunder, a little whimper of protest welling from deep in her throat. A fine performance of innocence, and when he was done with her, he must remember to tip his hat at her cleverness.

Slaking his thirst, he at last pulled back, the pleasure he found eroding the sharp edges of his anger. Looking down upon her upturned face, he noted her lashes lay like sooty feathers against her high cheekbones. Her lips, slack and trembling from his kiss, were tinged a bright pink.

And that is what it had been — a kiss so full of fire and passion he had nearly lost his head, not the unwilling ravishment he'd intended. He could still feel the warmth of her tongue entwined in his, the softening of her mouth as it had molded to his, the featherlike touch of her fingers on the nape of his neck.

They were still there now, those conniving tentacles, stroking, coaxing. He reached up and jerked her hand away, his grip so tight about her wrist she gasped in pain.

With a knowing curl to his lips that still tingled with the unbidden tenderness the kiss had evoked, he jerked her hand, palm up, to his mouth. "I'm not some callow youth or old man to be toyed with, lady. Strike flint to steel and you make fire. You'd be wise to watch out. You might stoke a flame that could rage out of control."

He took his tongue and traced the thundering pulse in her wrist, then he tossed her hand away from him as if he had no further use for it. "You've been forewarned, darlin', which is more than I can say you've done for dear ol' dad."

Completely mortified, Serra retrieved her branded flesh that burned to exact its own vengeance upon the arrogant blackguard who dared stand before her as if he were the victim, not her. Her lips, still flush and moist with his savage kiss, ached to tell him just what she thought of the man he'd become, but something squelched the venom. Perhaps it was the overwhelming passion he had stirred in her, or perhaps it was the rekindled memories of a wild, unbridled boy who had promised to come back for her someday and had sealed that vow with a gentle kiss. Her first kiss, nothing at all like the second she had just now received.

The Tyler Ramsey she knew and cared for was trapped in there somewhere. Her gaze swept over his lean, powerful figure, seeking a point of vulnerability. She would find him, she would, and then she would release him from the black-clad demon that held him in its clutches. *Oh, Ty, how could this have happened to you?*

She clamped her lips together with resolve. There was only one way to accomplish the task at hand. Her plans to beat him at his own game were impossible, she knew that now, as she had no defenses against his brutal, sensual assault, but her goal to reach him was easily obtained. And she knew just how she had to go about it.

"Ty," she whispered, her voice wrought with kindness and concern. "I'll tell you what you want to know."

His blue eyes scowled, giving her a dubious look, as if he found it hard to believe how easily she'd given in to his demand.

"All right." One dark brow jutted upward in skepticism. "You can start by tellin' me who you really are," he challenged.

"Don't you know?" She stared deeply into his eyes, looking for even the tiniest spark of recognition, but she didn't find what she sought.

"Should I?"

Oh, how his failure to remember pierced through her heart, wounding her pride.

"I'm Serra, Ty," she choked. "Serra Paletot. How could you have forgotten me so easily?"

Chapter Four

Serra?

Ty dug down deep into his cache of memories and pulled out the image of a young girl . . . a coppery mop of curls, freckles that spanned the space from cheek to cheek, and amber eyes that had followed him just as they did now, waiting, anticipating the approval of her every thought and deed.

The color of her hair had matured to a burnished bronze, the wildness now disciplined but still as shiny as he recalled. The freckles were practically nonexistent, her skin as unblemished as a pure mountain stream.

Serra.

Never in his wildest dream had he suspected. Joy rose like bubbling lava in his heart, but the smile never reached his lips.

Oh, Serra.

How had she come to stoop so low as to masquerade as the long lost daughter of John Langston? A clever ruse it might be, but a lie just the same. One he could be sure of now, one unworthy of the sweet child he remembered from his youth. She had always wanted a family, needing to believe, more than anything, that frantic parents were out there looking for her, refusing to give up the search. But John Langston? How had she managed to find him?

Long ago he hadn't thought he'd had the heart to destroy her dreams. Now he didn't bother to deceive himself. Crushing her wouldn't take heart; it would take the lack of one, something Tyler Ramsey prided himself in. He knew loyalty, he knew what it meant to owe, but to truly care about another human being? It had just been too long.

"Serra."

He was frowning, he knew that he was. He could see the proof reflected in her eyes . . . pools of liquid hurt.

"Ty?" she asked in that breathless way she had. "Aren't you glad to see me?"

"Of course I am." And he was. Glad to see she'd done all right for herself.

Like a tender young willow, she swayed toward him as if she needed him to put his arm about her, to physically reassure her. But he couldn't give her that; he wouldn't. There was still this . . . dispute between them. He owed John Langston his loyalty, owed the man his very life. Besides, at this point, he owed *himself* to think *only* of himself. He couldn't be made to feel responsible for Serra, not again.

But she looked so forlorn, like a lost little girl, with nowhere to turn, nowhere to run . . . just as before.

"Aw, Serra," he said in a voice so strained from having to choose that it broke. "Li'l Serra."

She fell against him, her face upturned in trust and relief. Though he tried desperately to restrain the impulse, his arm snaked about her shoulders in almost brotherly affection. God, how he'd missed her, but until this moment he'd never realized how much.

"I waited, Ty. I waited," she informed him with unguarded openness. "Why didn't you come?" She looked up at him, contemplating what his explanation would be, apparently assuming he had a good one.

"I don't know, Serra." He found it impossible to return her honest, open look, so he stared out over her head at his drover's coat, which hung on the peg near the cabin door. "I always meant to come for you, but . . . but . . ." His excuses were so damn feeble.

How could he tell her he'd figured she had found what she'd been looking for, a family that cared? Now he knew why the man accompanying her on the train had looked so familiar. He was the same one who had been standing beside her that day at the New Hope Opera House. How could he explain that he'd felt he had nothing to offer her that was better than what she already had? He couldn't let her know he had been unable to take care of himself, much less her. Having failed miserably, he'd been forced to accept the conditional help of another man. He had had to compromise his own dreams and desires in order to just survive.

Not really much of a hero for her to look up to, was he? It had been better to allow last impressions to prevail. For her sake—and probably for his own, as well. He wasn't sure he cared to know this new Serra, just as he wasn't too sure he wanted her to get to know the real Ty.

"The time just never seemed right," he offered

60

lamely.

She dropped her head against his chest. Her hair smelled of lilacs . . . intoxicating. He had to consciously force his hand to remain at his side to keep from running his fingers through its fiery silkiness.

"I understand," she said, her hand moving up to splay across the broad expanse of his chest. At her touch, his heart nearly burst from his chest like a wild beast trapped and unwillingly confined in a cage.

Oh, God, he just wished she wouldn't be so understanding. If she yelled at him, cursed him, attempted to scratch his eyes out, he could deal with those responses with equal fervor, but not with her simply lying her head against his heart in acceptance. Damn it, how unfair.

"Serra, no, you couldn't possibly understand." Pushing her away, he held her at arm's length.

She placed a long, delicate finger against his sullen lips and issued a patient "shhh." Then she raised up on her toes, took his cheeks between her palms, and brought his face down to hers. The image of her lashes lowering over those big, trusting amber eyes chipped away at his obduracy. But the feel of her soft, comforting mouth seeking his own was his final undoing.

He wanted her, heart, body and soul, and he sensed they were his for the taking. Brushing aside the suspicions that had brought him here in the first place, he gathered her into his arms, claiming his right to her lips, open and beckoning beneath his.

This time the kiss was just as fevered, but it was also gentle, sensual, meant to arouse and pleasure. His tongue dipped into her mouth and encountered

61

hers, a bold and seeking spear of fire that sent rushes of excitement coursing through him.

His arms tightened, his hand finding the soft roundness of her breast.

She gasped, as if shocked by his movement, as if she had no idea that he would want to touch her so. Ignoring the warning bells in his mind and the rabbitlike pounding of her heart against his palm, he gently rubbed his thumb across the nipple over and over, until it hardened and strained against the fabric of her bodice, a response he'd expected to elicit.

What he didn't anticipate was the way her face reddened with embarrassment and confusion, even though she didn't pull away. Serra just stood there, breath held, waiting, trusting.

Damn her, why did she always have to trust him? He still wasn't sure if he should believe in her. Perhaps this was just another game she was playing to gain his favor. If she lied about her identity, how hard would it be to pretend to be innocent? Six years was a long time and could make for many miles. He'd known plenty of well-used whores who were younger than Serra and just as good at appearing to be unsoiled.

God, it was hard to think with her warm womanliness filling his hand.

How could he be sure what to think?

He couldn't.

Pulling away, he filled his lungs and wiped his aching, empty palm against his pant leg, trying to eradicate the feeling of her aroused nipple pressing against it. The sensation refused to go away.

Her sooty lashes fluttered, and she stared up into his face, trying to read the emotions he strove so hard to conceal. "What is it, Ty? What's wrong?"

The innocence of her questions produced a tight knot in his throat. Clearing it away, he shook his head. "Nothin', Serra. Absolutely nothin'. But your little ploy won't work."

As he turned away, he read the hurt she projected, not only with her eyes but also with the way her trembling hand clutched at her heart, the way her mouth quivered in the corners.

Damn her desirable mouth. Damn the way he was losing sight of his goals.

He didn't want her. Her attempt to reach him had been in vain. Serra watched him shrug his wide, manly shoulders into his caped duster and cram his black hat on his head.

A hiccup of self-pity rose in her throat, but she quickly swallowed it down. The last thing she'd expected was for Ty to reject her, to shove her away as if she were an old, used-up rag.

What made it worse was that she had wanted him, had truly wanted him to touch her. Her mind sought the words to express the unfamiliar, raging desire. Like . . . a man . . . touched a . . . woman. She could only assume that was what he had done when he had covered her bosom with his hand.

Her breast had responded as if a sweeping cold had encompassed her, tightening into a hard, aching bud. But she had felt anything but cold. Instead, a flash fire of liquid heat had engulfed her and was still there now, tingling and tugging, demanding her attention, demanding . . .

God, she didn't know what it meant, but there

63

was no ignoring the sensations radiating from deep down inside her.

Tyler Ramsey had been the first and only man to stir such a whirlwind of emotion within her.

And now . . .

He wanted no part of her.

"I'm goin' for a walk," he grumbled.

"Ty . . ." She whispered his name on a soft sob as the door of the cabin banged shut, the wind it created stirring the loose tendrils of her hair against her flushed cheek.

How could she get through to him? she agonized, chewing on her bottom lip. She must find a way.

Seeking whatever might aid her, she glanced about the sparse cabin. The only items that even remotely offered promise were his saddlebags, still on the table where he had dropped them. She hesitated, feeling somewhat guilty for considering going through them. But what choice did she have? Her gaze darted to the door he'd exited. Better yet, what choice did he give her?

The blame rightly placed on his broad, capable shoulders, Serra stepped forward and unbuckled the clasp on one of the pouches. What she found there wasn't encouraging. A clean snow-white shirt, which was surprisingly neatly pressed, fresh socks and underwear.

She moved to the other side and peered into its depths. A can of beans and a package covered with butcher paper. At least he had planned to feed her. With a sigh, she pulled out the supplies and set them on the table, contemplating her next move.

Opening the door of the cookstove, she found what she sought—a cast-iron kettle for cooking the food. She turned to unwrap the meat but abruptly stopped when the cabin door was flung open.

"What are you doin'?" The anger, the suspicion, the distrust rang in Ty's voice like a bell cutting through the thickest of fogs.

"I'm cooking us some dinner," she answered matter-of-factly, turning to wipe from her hands the residue of the slab of salt pork on a bit of rag hanging beside the stove for just that purpose. "I know you must be as hungry as I am."

She slid him a look from the corners of her eyes, hoping to find approval on his face but prepared for the opposite. What she found was curiosity, a reservedness that suggested he was again testing her.

Well, that was better than outright anger, she assured herself. Opening the tiny cupboard above the stove, she frowned her frustration when she didn't find what she was looking for. Then she turned to Ty and stuck out her right hand, palm up. "Your knife, please."

He glanced down at her outstretched fingers. "What?" He eyed her suspiciously.

"Your knife," she replied patiently. "How else do you think I am going to slice up the meat?"

He crossed his arms over his chest. "Are you sure you wouldn't rather slit my throat?"

She stared back at the man in black, deciding he didn't look so sinister any longer. Fisting her left hand, she plopped it on her hip in response to his defiant gesture. "I've considered it, but remember, we've called a truce until tomorrow morning." Crooking the index finger of her right hand, she smiled. When he didn't respond immediately, her smile turned saucy. "Surely you can't fear a mere woman like me might overpower a strong man like you, now, can you?"

Challenge issued and accepted. He whipped out the blade and placed it in her hand, handle first. Their fingers touched for a mere second, but Serra experienced the explosion of sparks. Shaken by the exchange, she turned her attention to the meal she was preparing, suddenly finding she wasn't so hungry anymore.

He moved in closer, the heat of his larger frame radiating like a raging fire. When she shivered, not from a chill but from a fever of excitement burning deep inside her, he reached out and rubbed her arms, as if trying to warm her. The flames flared that much brighter.

"You're cold. I'd better start a fire in the stove." His words were so ordinary, so civil, but they set her heart to racing as if he spoke impassioned words of love.

"Yes, please," she replied, relieved yet disappointed when he released her to carry out the chore.

She watched him select kindling from the woodpile beside the stove and place the pieces in the firebox. The flexing and relaxing of the muscles of his back beneath his shirt as he knelt and arranged the small logs mesmerized her. Until now, she had never been aware of how beautiful the human body could be. And in her eyes, Tyler Ramsey was more than beautiful.

"There," he said, dusting his hands together and rising, looking back at her over his shoulder.

Aware she stood holding the piece of salt pork suspended in the air above the table, the knife poised over it, she pulled her eyes away from him, dropped

66

the meat back on its wrapping paper, and began sawing away at it, cutting off chunks to add to the beans.

"Careful with that," he warned, encompassing her hand with his. "The blade's so sharp, you could lop off a finger before you knew it."

The way her heart pounded and the pulse in her temples and wrists jumped, she doubted if she would realize it even if she did manage to mangle herself. With his hand covering hers, the prospects of pain seemed so remote. Instead, the churning in the very center of her being began to hum, the sound waves radiating to the farthermost reaches of her body, even to her toes, which curled in her shoes in response.

Slipping from his grasp, she grabbed the kettle and carried it to the stove, placing it to one side as she lifted out the grid to check the fire beneath. Satisfied, she replaced it and set the kettle over the heat.

"I daresay, it shouldn't take too long," she assured. Wanting more than anything to avoid touching Tyler again, she concentrated on taking down a couple of tin plates, cups, and forks, wiping them clean of the dust of disuse with a towel. "We could use some water," she informed him.

Ty took up a wooden bucket from near the door and stepped outside in silence. A few moments later he returned, the pail full. Then he moved to the broken chair propped against the wall and squatted down, inspecting the damage.

"With a few strips of leather, I can fix it." He glanced up at her for approval. "At least temporarily."

"That *would* be nice," she replied.

Their eyes met and held. Both obviously aware of the strangeness yet pleasure the moment inspired, they nonetheless returned to their respective duties.

With the thongs from his bedroll, Ty managed to strap together the broken spindles and legs just as the food was ready. Ladling up the steaming beans and dipping the drinking cups into the bucket of spring water, Serra served the meal.

Sitting across the table from each other, they maintained the strained silence, the only sounds the occasional clang of a fork on the bottom of a plate, the clearing of a throat, the scrape of a chair leg against the rough planks of the floor, and the hiss of the lantern sitting on the table between them.

Once they were finished, Serra took up the dishes and quickly washed them in the water remaining in the bucket. Ty stoked the fire in the stove, the only source of heat in the cabin.

"You take the bed," he ordered.

Serra had to admit, if only to herself, that she was tired and grateful and more than willing to obey. With a nod, she moved across the cabin to inspect the handmade bedstead.

"Tomorrow," Ty continued, then his voice trailed off. "Well, we'll worry about tomorrow tomorrow," he summed up, grabbing his bedroll and moving to the opposite corner of the room. Then, as if sensing her uneasiness, he lifted the glass from the lantern, cupped his hand about the wick, and blew out the flame.

Serra stood in the darkness, broken only by the flicker of light emanating from the cracks and crevices of the stove. She could hear him moving about, probably undressing—the thump of his boots hitting the floor, the creak of his body as he bent and strained, the clank of a belt buckle as his pants joined his other clothing.

She found herself unable to move, unable to breathe. The thought that Ty was so close in the darkness, his torso bared most likely, left her mouth dry. Was he thinking of her? Nothing in his manner indicated that he was. The rustle of a blanket as he settled in his bedroll suggested just the opposite, just like the groan he issued as he tried to get comfortable.

Her trembling fingers touched her forehead. This was crazy, the way she was acting. Propelling herself into motion, she sat down, unlaced her packers, and slipped them from her feet. Of course she cared for Tyler Ramsey—she always had, she rationalized—but this ridiculous way her heart pounded in response to the mere touch of his hand had to cease.

What must he think of her, mimicking one of those doe-eyed girls at the orphanage all those years ago? *Tyler Ramsey sure is cute. Giggle. Giggle.* God, how disgusting she had thought them then. And Tyler. She rolled her eyes toward the ceiling. He had ignored their feminine titter, having practically ridiculed the girls for their silly behavior.

Pulling back the covers, she crawled into the bed and yanked the blanket up to her chin. Did he mentally ridicule *her* now in the same way?

Serra was so pretty, so damn sophisticated. What must she think of his rough edges, his lack of polish and education—all the things she had obviously received? Hell, he'd not even known what to say to her when she'd looked up at him so damn innocently time and again, those wide amber eyes of hers round with confusion and wonder. He should have been able to comfort her, to reassure her, but no. He'd just stood there like a big, ignorant oaf, staring back.

Frustrated, Tyler twisted, pounding the saddle blanket he used for a pillow, trying to get comfortable on the cold, uncompromising floor. He'd had more luck on wet, uneven ground. But in those days, he'd not felt like a moony-eyed, tongue-tied schoolboy. Life had been simple then: Right was right, wrong was wrong, his loyalties a single-minded goal. With Serra's reappearance, he couldn't be so sure of that anymore.

From across the room he could hear her settling in, the rustle of the quilt as she turned in the bed, her sigh of exhaustion. Had she undressed? Try as he might, he couldn't prevent the images that invaded his mind. Serra naked beneath the quilt, the nappy, worn fabric caressing the silkiness of her breasts, her belly, her thighs. He could almost feel her rounded contours against his palm as his hand slid down his own body to cradle the aching hardness his visions evoked.

Serra would be soft and pliable, sweet and unspoiled, his to do with as he pleased. Nothing like the women of his experience, who knew what they were about. Nothing like . . .

Ty pulled away his rough, calloused hand, finding it an inadequate substitute for his fantasies, and stuffed it beneath his head. There would be no relief for him—not tonight, not ever—not until he reestablished his claim to the little girl of his past who had grown up into the vivacious woman lying a mere hairbreadth away from him, so near all he had to do was get up and go to her, touch her, feel her heart racing once more beneath his palm.

Groaning, he turned on his side, seeking escape from the throbbing need between his thighs. Making love to Serra—even the fact that he *considered* it—was about the stupidest thing he could ever do.

Serra was taboo. Until he unraveled the deception of her claim to be Serenity Langston, she was a poison to be avoided at all costs. Be that as it may, rationalization did nothing to alleviate the desire raging in his veins like hot, flowing lava.

How had his life managed to become so goddamn complicated in just a few short hours?

Chapter Five

"Tyler?"

Ty opened his sleep-ladened eyes to the dingy light and stared up into the angelic face bending over him. It was early; it had to be. No daylight penetrated the cracks in the alcove wall beneath the staircase where he lay.

The acrid smell of the entryway hall, which often enough was used as much as a urinal as a means in and out of the building, rose up to greet him. He sat upright, bringing the bit of sackcloth he used as a cover with him, and yawned.

"Serra," he mumbled.

It was cold as usual, even though spring was right around the corner. Not that there were signs of warming to be observed. On the Lower East Side, there were no trees or flowers to mark the change of season. On the Lower East Side, there wasn't much but decay, poverty, and filth. And rats.

Ty wiped his nose on his sleeve and sniffed. Yes, in his opinion, the worst part of the city was the wharf rats the size of the fat, overfed squirrels that the wealthy in the fashionable Upper End pampered and oohed and aahed over in Central Park.

In the darkness, he could hear them scratching inside the walls. The rats. The mascot of the homeless and abused children of the slums of New York City.

The dirty-faced moppet of no more than three who had awoken him moved closer, squatting down and huddling against his shoulder, her lanky copper-colored hair that drooped into his face smelling of fried onions and garlic.

"Ty—ler," she whispered in that baby voice of hers that had only recently learned to talk. "Papa hurt." She hiccupped her distress.

Without a word, he lifted his arm like a wing to allow her to crawl in next to him, only too glad for the added warmth her small body offered, though he wished to God the circumstances of her arrival had been different. "It's all right, li'l Serra. It's all right," he murmured sleepily.

But it wasn't. One day he would see to it that everything was all right—for both of them.

"Tyler."

A gentle hand shook him, something unheard of in the squalor of existence he called life.

His eyes popped open, and he saw her bending over him. Serra. No longer the filthy little urchin who needed and sought his protection, but a woman, one so damn beautiful it made his heart ache and his mouth dry with want.

A sweet scent wafted toward him—her hair, riotous coppery curls, wreathing her face. He took a deep breath. Lilacs . . . and lavender soap. Oh, God, she smelled so good. He wanted to reach out and run his fingers through the soft, fragrant mass, pull her face near and kiss her. Lift up the covers and invite her to join him now in the present as he had in the long forgotten past.

But he didn't dare.

Instead, he reached for his pants she held gingerly in her fingertips and slipped them beneath the blanket to pull them on. Once that task was accomplished, he scrambled to his feet, gathered up his shirt, and slid his arms into the sleeves.

As he buttoned up the front, he turned to face her. There were decisions that had to be made regarding not only his future, but hers as well.

The best thing he could do was to take her back where she'd come from and rightly belonged.

As he opened his mouth to tell her his plans, lightning streaked across the sky, filling up the window behind her. The earth-shattering crash and rumble that followed seconds later shook the cabin, choking off his intended words.

He would take her home, but not today.

Staring at her long and hard, Ty found it impossible to say anything. Dear God, what was he going to do with her until he could return her to New Hope? How would he manage to keep his hands off of her another day . . . another night?

Spinning around, he hurried to the door, gathering up his coat and hat on the way.

"Tyler, where are you going?"

How many times had she asked him that in the past? He wondered if she even remembered those long nights they had spent in the dirty tenement hallway. He doubted that she did. He prayed that she didn't. The inability to recall hell was truly a blessing she deserved.

"Out," he mumbled. "Cochise needs lookin' after."

"Without your shoes and stockings?"

74

"What?" Ty glanced down to discover his bare feet sticking out of his crumpled pant legs.

Damn, what a fool she must think him. Angry more with himself than with her, he issued a vile curse, dropped down in one of the chairs, and pulled on his boots. Ignoring the hurt look on her face, he rose and headed outside. But before he could close the door, she thrust the empty bucket at him.

"We could use more water," she said in a voice much calmer than he knew she felt.

"Water," he echoed in response, accepting the pail without looking at her and slamming the door.

Then he was free to breathe, to gather his thoughts and his willpower. Stepping off the front porch, he turned up the collar of his coat against the cold drizzle and hunched his shoulders forward to face nature's protest of his actions. All of them. From the moment he had decided that John Langston needed and deserved his intervention, he had made one heck of a mess of things.

Oh, hell. When would he learn to stop sticking his nose where it didn't belong? One would think that by now he'd have figured out it was wisest to be concerned only for himself.

From the window, Serra watched his dark figure sprint across the open ground between the cabin and the shed, avoiding the puddles and rivulets. She frowned to herself. No doubt Ty was in one of his surly moods. She was familiar with his ways, understood them, knew eventually he would come around if she remained patient. He always did. But, oh, it was so hard to show restraint when he acted that way for no apparent reason.

Then she remembered him during their years together at the Children's Aid Society orphanage. From that very first day she had arrived at the doorstep, frightened and confused, he had been there, his protection something she had come to depend on immediately, almost as if he felt a kinship to her . . . as if he'd known her long before.

But that would be impossible. Tyler had told her he had been little more than a street arab before finding the home, and she . . . well, there was no doubt in her mind that she wasn't a product of the slums of New York City. For some reason she'd been snatched from her parents, and they had never been able to find her. Somehow, but that was a mystery she had never solved, not even with Dr. Chelsey's logical explanations. Everyone told her it didn't matter—the orphanage director, Doc, even Ty.

But to her it did matter; it mattered a lot.

Serra chewed her bottom lip, and once Ty slipped from view, she turned away from the window to concentrate on the task at hand—reheating the beans from last night's dinner. Perhaps once she reached home, her father would explain it all to her, fill in the lapses of memory.

The vision of a sullen-faced boy faded, to be replaced by the present-day image. Ty was all man now. There was very little left of the boy he had once been—so impetuous, full of wild and wonderful dreams and ambitions. He had always been a bit remote, at least to others, but now, after so many years, he was shutting her out as well.

But then, what could she expect? She hardly knew

him any longer. Yet, she was more aware of him than she could ever remember being as a young girl.

His cobalt-blue eyes had deepened, hardened, become much more intense. His body had matured, gone beyond the gangly youth she had worshipped. But it was his mouth that held her transfixed in thought . . . its fullness, its sensuousness. She could still feel it, even now, pressed against her own lips, the soft pinpricks of his beard heightening the pleasure his kisses had stirred in her; still churned within her like a pot of boiling, bubbling . . .

"Ouch!"

Serra jerked back her hand, releasing the hot metal handle of the kettle of beans she'd been clutching during her daydreaming. Sticking her burned fingers in her mouth, she sucked on them, trying to soothe away the pain her absentmindedness had caused.

Then with a crash, the cast-iron pot hit the floor, beans splattering everywhere — the wall, the floor, the sides of the stove.

"Oh, no, what have I done?" she cried, brushing at the brown splotches dotting the front of her plaid dress. Snatching up the hand towel hanging beside the stove, she scrubbed at the stains, but her efforts only made matters worse. With a senseless sob trapped in the back of her throat, she fell to her knees, striking out at the spilt beans like a bear swiping at a swarm of angry bees, doing little more than spreading the mess farther.

And that's how Ty found her, kneeling in the middle of the cabin floor, burying her face into the sleeve of her gown to keep back the flood of tears, the towel cupped about a mound of escaping pork and beans.

"Serra," he exclaimed, spying her hunched over the floor, not pausing to set down the sloshing bucket of water that tipped over as he dropped it at the threshold. "Are you all right?" he demanded with earnest concern as he squatted before her, his hands gripping her under the arms and pulling her forward.

Through her tear-blurred vision, she saw the tidal wave of water wash over the mess she was trying to corral with the towel. Recognizing the uselessness of her actions, Serra finally accepted the fact that her cataclysmic emotions had nothing at all to do with spilt beans but ran much, much deeper.

Ty was there. It didn't matter that he had changed most likely for the worse . . . that he might not understand how she felt . . . that he might possibly be using her to get to her father's fortune. Her protector was there, holding her.

Throwing her arms about his neck, she buried her face into the damp collar of his coat. "Oh, Ty," she choked, refusing to allow the tears to surface.

Gathering her face between his large, work-roughened hands, he tilted her head back, staring down into her eyes with a look she welcomed. "Serra, I need to know. Are you hurt?" he demanded.

God knew she was hurting, but not in the way he meant. She shook her head, wanting more than anything to tell him how deeply his calloused treatment, his unwillingness to believe in her, had wounded her. Instead, she lowered her lashes, parted her lips, and prayed.

Let him kiss me.

His fingers brushed back her unbound tresses, be-

78

coming entrapped in the fine, coppery filigree and curling to cradle the back of her head.

Serra waited, her heart clattering in its prison. Unconsciously, her tongue darted out, moistening her anticipation-dry lips. Was he gratified by what he saw? *Oh, please, please, let him want me.*

Like a slow-moving steamroller, his mouth came down over hers, covering, crushing, molding her pliant lips to fit perfectly to his. Spears of pure joy tinged with relief shot through her and she shut her eyes, surrendering completely to the wondrous feelings she'd only recently discovered whenever he caressed her so.

Her hands moved up and splayed across his shirtfront. Beneath her right palm she could feel the strong thumpity-thump of his heartbeat, steady, reassuring. Pressing closer, she grew bold, her tongue slipping forward to touch the moist rim of his lips, his teeth, to dip into the cavity of his open mouth.

As if a dam burst forth, Ty groaned, his arms about her tightening with a fierceness that almost crushed the air from her lungs. She welcomed the breathlessness, the mindless, uncontrolled giddiness that encompassed her, meeting his probing tongue with her own explorations.

She arched her back, straining forward, knowing her actions were wanton but not caring. He had touched her . . . there . . . once. Would he do so again?

She wanted him to. Oh, God, how she needed him to.

The fires burned hot and low, waiting to be stoked by his knowing hand. And this time she would not let him see her ignorance, she vowed, no matter what he did. Ty knew about these things; she would trust him.

Trust him no matter what.

Directed by pure instinct, she moved her hips against him, her palms fanning out to encompass his wide shoulders, then back to the broad expanse of his chest. The once unerring beat of his heart sped up, thundering beneath her fingertips, an irreversible tidal wave. And she had done this to him.

His hands moved down her spine, cupping her posterior, pressing her pelvis against his own.

A gasp of surprise rose in her throat, but she quickly swallowed it down. She'd not anticipated the thickness of his groin, but to be honest, she'd had no idea what to expect. There was more to this than mere touching. She wasn't so sure anymore that she should go further.

Panicked, she balled her fists and pushed against his chest, her hips twisting to escape the intimacy of his touch. "Ty," she murmured against his mouth, tearing away from his kiss.

He allowed her lips their freedom, but he wasn't so generous with the rest of her. He undulated his hips against her imprisoned ones, the flame in his blue eyes burning deep into her brain. "This is what you wanted, wasn't it, Serra?"

Heat sparked where they touched, and a burning need rippled through her. Her knees buckled, but her mind protested against what he was doing, what she was feeling. It was all happening too quickly. There wasn't time to think, to make a decision.

"I'm not sure," she stammered as she turned trusting amber eyes up to him.

"Damn it, Serra, don't look at me like that," he

80

groaned. Releasing his grip on her hips, his fingers moved up to curl about her shoulders. Then he sighed with frustration. "No, I suppose you're not. To be honest, I'm not sure myself." He pressed her face against his chest, his fingers stroking her hair with gentle understanding.

Feeling safe once more, she wrapped her arms about his waist, allowing a smile of satisfaction to flutter across her lips. But his heart still thundered in her ear, reminding her of what had just passed between them. Reminding her that Ty was no longer the boy she had turned to to soothe away her childish tears. Things were much more complicated between them now.

Her heart skipped a beat. Whatever this strange desire was that gripped her, it consumed him as well. Perhaps this was the way to reach the Ty she knew and cared for. They could regain the lost years, heal the rift that divided them, and come together . . . make things the way they were before.

Tilting up her face, she lay her chin upon his chest and stared into his cobalt-blue eyes. "Teach me, Ty," she requested.

He frowned, his hands reaching behind his back to unlace her clutch. "You don't know what you ask."

"Yes, I do," she replied with whirlwind insistence, refusing to release him even when the strength of his fingers dug into the tender flesh of her inner wrists. "I want to know, Ty. I want *you* to teach me. I want—" She groped for the right words to express her feelings. "I want us to be as close as we can possibly be."

"Are you sure, Serra?" His softly spoken question was strained as he cupped her face. "There's no goin' back, you know, once we — "

Rising on tiptoes, she pressed her mouth to his, cutting off his warning. At first he stood there stiffly, allowing her access but refusing to respond. Then he conceded, taking control of the kiss, his hands moving up her slim waistline to mold about the rounded globes of her breasts. In unison, his thumbs brushed over the aching nibs, stirring the banked desire within her to a flaming passion. She arched, allowing the moan trapped in her throat to erupt and melt into a sigh of pure delight.

Yes, she was sure of what she wanted. So sure of her rationalization.

Ty scooped her up and stepped over the congealing beans on the floor, carrying her to the bed on the far side of the room. Through the window above the stove, streaks of lightning filled the opening, splashing across the old, worn quilt like an on-again-off-again limelight in the otherwise darkened corner.

Gently, he placed her on the mattress. The flickering illumination haloed her face and fiery crown of hair, spilt down over her shoulders and chest, catching the row of mother-of-pearl buttons on her bodice to highlight the rainbow colors.

His hand touched the first one, high against her throat, his gaze never leaving hers as his fingers manipulated the small, ornate frog that held it fastened. The two halves of the lace collar fell apart, and Serra sighed softly as he merely brushed her windpipe.

The second button met with the same fate as the first, exposing the hollow just above her collarbone, then on down the line, his movements smooth yet unhurried until he reached the knotted sash about her waist.

The corners of his mouth lifted, his finger lingering on the swell of her breast just above the lace of her chemise. His smile was all that she'd waited for. Flashing, heart-stopping, accenting the dimple in his right cheek. This was her Ty, the one she remembered from her youth, the one she was more than willing to yield to if it would only mean that he would stay.

She filled her lungs, and not until it was too late did she realize the chain of events that simple action initiated. Her breasts swelled and rose a little higher against the gathered ribbon of her undergarment. Ty's gaze flicked downward to watch, his finger that lay ever so gently in the start of her bosom's valley drifting lower, covering one partially exposed mount. As if concerned about her previous response, he glanced back up into her eyes to judge her reaction. When she lowered her lashes and arched her back in acceptance, he quickly tugged at the ribbon bow, releasing the knot, the gathered material of her chemise, and the aching tips of her breasts.

"I'm not sure I deserve what you offer," he said, slowly stroking one of the budding peaks until she gasped from the pure pleasure of his caress, "but I would be a fool to turn it down."

Placing one knee on the mattress beside her hip, he bent over her, gathering her beckoning flesh in the circle of his hands and lifting it upwards. Her head thrown back, her spine bowed like a willow twig to assist him, Serra could only imagine what he would do next.

Yet when his tongue flirted across the sensitive nipple, wet and exciting, she was ill-prepared. Poised in space, she told herself she had only imagined that he had caressed her so. A woman's breast was meant for the suckling of an innocent babe, not the passions of a man, yet the sensations his touch had created were anything but maternal.

If only he would do it again.

This time his fondling was much bolder. His lips encompassed the entire areola, tugging gently, his tongue wrapping about the nipple with an undeniable possessiveness, as if he, and only he, had the right to taste of her flesh in this manner. The haunting ache that had encircled her heart burst into flame to the accompaniment of thunder, like Greek fire ignited by the moistness of his caress. It became all-consuming, racing through her veins, boiling her blood, finally settling deep inside her, an epicenter of sensation and pressure that demanded release.

But how could her wanton body demand more than her imaginings could begin to conceive of?

As if in answer, Ty slid an arm along her back and lifted her body higher, his other hand tugging at the confining material of her bodice and underclothing.

"Wait, Ty, wait," she cried, her hands moving up between them. If he should tear her gown—and she suspected that was what he was about—she would have nothing to wear.

He raised his head with obvious reluctance, his eyes greedily devouring her naked flesh, but he nonetheless honored her plead, holding himself in check.

"My dress," she responded to his questioning look. "It's—it's all I have with me," she stuttered her explanation.

"Of course," he said, releasing his tight grip about her waist, allowing her to drift back down onto the mattress. The movement returned her clothes to their proper position. Disappointment cast clouds in his blue eyes.

Shifting, he made as if to move away. Serra reached out and clutched his sleeve. "Where are you going?"

He smiled as if caught in a memory, one side of his mouth slightly higher than the other. "I figured you'd had enough of my teachin'."

"Then you figured wrong," she informed him, rising up on her knees beside him. Reaching for the sash at her waist, she untied the intricate bow in the back and began unwinding the length of rose-colored material, allowing it to slip to the floor.

His gaze fastened on the gap of her unbuttoned bodice. Serra watched him, undetected. Did he think her too bold? With fingers numbed by self-doubt, she fumbled for the hem of her dress to pull it off. If he should reject her as he had done earlier . . .

The gown slid up and over her head with ease. Ty was there to take the garment from her shaking fingers, and mindful of her earlier concern, he carried it across the room to drape it over the back of a chair.

Lightning flashed once more, outlining the wideness of his shoulders, the bunched muscles of his arms, the ruggedness of his beloved profile. In the seconds between the sight and the sound the storm outside made, Serra discovered what it meant to be truly vulnerable. Tyler Ramsey had not only the strength to dominate her physically, but also the power to control every nuance of her emotions. Closing her eyes, she swayed on her knees in the middle of the bed and prayed he would be gentle.

The mattress sagged beside her, and Ty's powerful arms curled about her bare shoulders. With the tip of his thumb, he snagged one lacy strap of her camisole, lowering it down her arm. Then he bent and kissed her bared shoulder so gently, she wasn't sure if he had touched her or if she'd merely imagined it.

His mouth brushed against the base of her throat, alternately nibbling, licking, lipping as he slowly moved up her neck to her ear. His beard was rough, yet at the same time downy-soft against her skin, heightening the pleasure he evoked. The moment his tongue touched the shell-like curve of her ear, she felt herself melting.

"You're so beautiful, Serra," he whispered, the rush of his words, his beard, his mouth, setting her aflame.

Before she could respond his warmth vanished, leaving her feeling like an untried sapling abandoned to the mandates of the wind that raged outside the cabin. But then he returned, capturing the knob of her shoulder between his lips. As he inched his way down her arm, he dislodged the strap of the camisole that barred his path. At some point he laced his other hand into the remaining strap, and slowly peeled the undergarment from her body, leaving it draped about the upper edge of the lightweight corset riding just beneath her bosom.

Freedom. Serra took a deep, cleansing breath. She could never remember feeling so unrestrained. The baring of her body to Ty's perusal, the way he touched her, almost seemed to worship her offering, set her heart to soaring.

His hands formed a temple about her breasts, lifting them. His mouth paid homage, as if she were a fragile goddess to be adored. Lacing her fingers in his dark hair, she surrendered to the flames, but mostly to the man who stoked them.

Soon he had the corset strings free of their eyelets. Continuing his slow exploration, he kissed each of her ribs as if he counted them. Then the tie on the waist of her drawers drifted apart and he slipped his hands inside them, pulling them down over her hips, knees, and feet. Completely nude, she willed herself not to shudder, not to act uncertain or afraid. This was Ty. She could trust him.

Lying beside and just a little over her, he reached out like a blind man. First he cupped her breast, then his hand slid down her flat belly, brushing over her navel and down. At the crux between her legs, he paused, combing through the dark thatch. When his finger slipped between her legs Serra experienced thunder. And though reason told her it was the violent storm outside the cabin that she heard, she could have sworn it was her heart that beat so frantically against its prison.

She'd had no idea. No idea at all that he would want to touch her there. No inkling that she would find such excitement in him doing so.

"Ty," she murmured as his hand moved lower, deeper, strumming untried strings of passion she'd never known existed.

"Let me, Serra. Please," he implored, his tongue grazing her ear persuasively.

Could she ever deny him anything? Even this? She said nothing as he pushed her legs apart, unveiling the secret part of herself she had never thought to share with anyone.

It was as if he'd discovered the growing ache balled deep inside of her, his caresses slowly unfurling the pent-up energy. And then she knew that this was the secret to assuaging her need . . . to calm the raging storm within her. Pressing her feet against the mattress, she lifted her hips to receive his gift.

"That's it, Serra. Let me pleasure you."

Pleasure couldn't begin to describe the tide and ebb of sensations that engulfed her. The waves crashed forward as if striving for something, but just before they got there they went tumbling backward, only to move forward again before she could voice her disappointment. Forward, forward. She gripped the hand-sewn loops of the quilt and pushed toward the elusive pinnacle. So close. So very close. Then the rising tide took over and she was atop the crest, riding it to the heretofore unknown destination.

She gasped, aware that she gave an almost guttural groan but unable to stop the sound even when she trapped her tongue between her teeth and bit down.

It was a few moments later when she realized she was lying sprawled in the bed, Ty bending over her, his mouth capturing hers in a passionate kiss that barely gave her time to catch her breath before the liquid fire of desire washed through her again.

Lifting his face, he smiled down at her. "So tell me, sweet Serra, what did you think of it?"

How could she begin to describe what she had felt. "I . . . I," she began, stumbled, and stopped. "It . . . it . . . was . . ." she trailed off.

"Ah, I know. Beyond words."

"And for you?" she asked in innocence, believing they had shared the wonderful experience.

"Well, no, to be honest," he began to explain.

Serra sat up and grasped his hand. "But that's not fair. I want you to have—" She gave him a worried look. "A man can, can't he?"

"Oh, yes," he assured her, chuckling at her naivete. Squeezing her fingers, he brought them up to his lips. "But I didn't want to—"

"Why wouldn't you want to feel what I felt?" she demanded rashly.

He turned her hand over and traced the lines of her palm with his tongue. "Believe me, darlin', I want to. I've wanted to from the moment I laid eyes on you aboard the train." His intense blue gaze burned into her brain. There was no doubting his desire. "But, Serra, I don't think you understand."

"Make me understand." She angled herself so that her swaying breasts pressed against his shirtfront. There was more, and she wasn't about to be left in the dark, not now. "Please, Ty, please," she pleaded in the same fashion that he had earlier.

Ty rolled, pinning her beneath his weight. She could feel that strange bulge in his pants again. "Damn it, Serra. This is not one of your little games we're playin'. Don't you know better than to go around askin' men to . . . make love to you?"

"I'm not asking just any man. I'm asking *you*." When they were children, he had never chastised her for her honesty. Why was it any different now? Besides, if this was called "making love," there was no one she could think of she would rather "make love" with than Tyler Ramsey. She curled her arms about his neck and trailed her fingers through the dark

89

hair spilling over the collar of his shirt. Then she lifted her chin, proud of her deduction, finding no reason why he should disagree, confident he would come to see it her way—with the right encouragement.

"Serra," he chided, shaking his head as if to dislodge her distracting fingers from his hair.

Undaunted, she took his hand and lay it over her beating heart, against her bare bosom.

"Serra," he groaned.

She slid her hand inside his shirt, her fingers threading through the dark chest hairs, so soft, so exciting. His heartbeat accelerated, hammering in rhythm to the rain that pounded against the tin roof over their heads. His nipple grew hard against the sensitive center of her palm.

"Damn it, Serra. You always were a willful brat." His hand cupped about her breast possessively, kneading, massaging, striking fire.

"I know," she replied. "And you were always there to temper me." She arched against his weight. His belt buckle ground into her lower belly, but no pain registered, only frustration that the bit of metal separated his body from hers. Then his hand was between them, releasing the silver clasp. With eager fingers, she helped him shed his clothing. The ominous man in black was no more. Just Ty, naked, as vulnerable as she, lying over her, his manhood pressing hard against her inner thigh.

Instinct guiding her, she opened to him, no longer surprised with the newness of it all. Whatever Ty did would be right, would bind them irrevocably. Even when he slipped inside her and there was a stab of momentary pain she had not prepared for, her determination never wavered.

His hands clutching her hips, he paused when she flinched. She could feel him trembling with a need she was now most familiar with. Remembering the all-consuming thirst, she truly marveled at the way he considered her. While striving for her own release earlier, she had never even once thought about what he might be feeling. But not Ty. Always there for her. Always in control.

Wanting more than anything to give back three-fold, she tilted her hips forward, a sacrifice to his desire.

"God Almighty," he murmured on a great rush of air as he buried his face into the contour of her neck. He pulled his hips away, and Serra thought for sure he was leaving her . . . had changed his mind.

"No," she cried out her disappointment, grabbing at his taut buttock to keep him from escaping.

His response was to plunge within her so deep that it took her breath away. The pain was now no more than a distant memory as a new sensation took over. There was that building pressure again. But this time his body was in the middle of it, the cause as well as the effect. With each rise and fall of his hips the need grew stronger, until she thought she would surely burst apart.

The crescendo came with an explosion. Colors in her mind, electric shocks through every nerve of her body.

"Oh, Ty," she cried, clutching him to her heart. Forever. Always forever. "Tell me that you feel it, too."

"I feel it, Serra," he cried. "God help me, I feel it like never before."

Chapter Six

Hours later, the rain pattered gently against the tin roof over their heads, the storm outside having expended its passion as surely as they had spent theirs. Lying under the worn quilt with his arm about Serra, Ty savored the smell of her fragrant curls cascading over his arm, his shoulder, and across his chest. She slept so peacefully when molded against him, but then she always had, his warmth being hers. But now they didn't crouch beneath some cold, stinking stairwell, but instead reclined in a soft bed in a warm, cozy cabin.

Just he and Serra. The rest of the world be damned.

At least for a little while. Expelling stale air and impossible dreams, he reached out and brushed a shiny tendril from her cheek. A terrible yearning, one he feared could never be assuaged, stirred in his heart, that part of him that until now had been a carefully protected void, the one place he felt no pain. Just he and Serra. If only it *could* be that way forever, but oh, God, how he knew better. They would be found . . . eventually.

But before that happened, he knew what he must

do. Take Serra home. And if he cared for her at all, he would do it now. Glancing out the window over the stove, he saw a ray of late morning sun finger its way past the dripping eaves and into the cabin. There was still enough time to travel a good distance before dark. They would easily reach New Hope on the morrow, and she could return to the security of her adopted family.

Even though he knew what he should do, he couldn't bring himself to wake her. Oh, hell, he had to admit the truth. He couldn't bring himself to let her go.

So, what other solution was there? Now that this . . . thing had begun between them, there was no way he could resist the temptation she presented. In her innocence, she had given all. In Ty's experience, there weren't many women like her—even the so-called good ones. They gave of themselves all right, but expected retribution—a wedding ring. A couple of times he'd come close to giving in to such a woman's demands, but somehow the thought of spending the rest of his life with a conniving female hadn't seemed palatable.

But the thought of always being with Serra just seemed so right.

Ty nearly laughed aloud at how simple the answer to his dilemma was. He could marry Serra. His heart began to race, his mind churning out valid reasons why his solution was the perfect one. As his wife, the things she wanted most would be hers: security, love . . . the Langston fortune.

He frowned at the turn his thoughts had taken. No, no, he chided himself, staring down at her innocent, unlined features, refusing to accept that sweet

93

Serra might have ulterior motives for what she did. It wasn't the money she was after, but the fulfillment of her dreams—a family. For as long as he could remember, she talked of parents. By marrying him, she would finally have what she deserved. John Langston would welcome her with open arms as the nearest thing to a daughter-in-law he would ever have. There would be no need for her to continue to claim to be his missing daughter.

Eager to share his conclusions with her, Ty bent over and kissed her gently on the mouth. Smiling with contentment—perhaps the first he'd ever known—he pulled back to watch her awaken. Serra's mouth worked, almost turning pouty, her tongue swiping at her lips, moistening them into tempting ripe cherries. Then she settled back into sleep.

Situating himself so he rested on one hip, he pushed her hair away from her face and placed his mouth against her ear. "Serra," he whispered, nudging the pearly shell with his tongue.

This time she groaned so softly it was a sigh. Nestling deeper into the curvature of his shoulder, she twisted, flinging one silky leg over his naked hips, her arm across his chest in what appeared to be, at least to Ty, a possessive move.

Ty's heart began to pound, and he wanted to laugh out loud from the sheer pleasure of finally knowing what love must surely be. Being possessed by Serra was freedom of the purest kind.

"Serra," he urged again, chuckling softly, unable to restrain himself one more moment from telling her all the wonderful things he had discovered in the last few minutes—about himself, about her . . . about them.

Her lashes parted, and he saw the momentary confusion register in her amber gaze when she realized where she was — sprawled wantonly across his equally naked body. She blushed . . . so prettily, and Tyler knew he wasn't making a mistake, both in loving her and deciding to make her his wife.

"Wake up, darlin'," he insisted, kissing her once more. He couldn't help it if his body stirred when she returned the ardor with open honesty, her arms curling about his neck.

He wanted her, oh, God, how he desired her, but first he must share his newly awakened feelings with her. Pulling back his head, he placed a restraining peck on her forehead.

"First we need to talk," he informed her.

"Are you sure, Ty, that's what you really want to do." A mischievous glint sparkled in her amber eyes, her fingers feathering a fiery path down his spine. He reached behind his back, grabbed her wrist, and brought her hand back around in front, caging it in his larger one.

"It is." He rose from the bed, dragging her with him. Moving to the table, he gathered up her clothes and turned, handing them to her at arm's length. "Now get dressed, so you won't make me forget my good intentions," he muttered, indeed most distracted by her lithe figure, the way her perfect breasts rippled with each breath she took, the flair of her feminine hips that offered so much. He swallowed down the passion that was beginning to clog his brain. With undeniable regret he spun about, locating his own pants.

"I've figured it all out, Serra," he said, refusing to look at her until he was sure she was properly cov-

95

ered. He glanced at his gun holster casually tossed on the table and rejected the idea of strapping it on. Until now he would have felt naked without it. But Serra had changed all of that.

"You've figured out what?" she asked, a touch of caution coloring her voice.

"Our future." He turned and found her lacing up the ties of her corset, her fingers knotting a pretty bow in the satin ribbon. Most intrigued by her actions, he moved forward and reached out to trace the intricate tatting on the edge of the undergarment. "This—this misconception you have about John Langston. It's so simple. We'll get mar—"

The front door of the cabin crashed against the wall, cutting off his revelation. Serra screamed, and instinctively, Ty pushed her back down on the bed to protect her from whatever danger confronted them. Spinning on his heels, he lunged for the table, his one thought to reach the gun he had carelessly left there.

But before he could grab up the weapon, the blow came swift and hard. Through the pain, all he could think of was Serra. What would happen to Serra if he was not there? . . .

To explain.

Serra huddled in the far corner of the bed, the quilt drawn up about her shoulders to conceal the fact that she was dressed only in undergarments. It was all happening so fast that she couldn't think, but in her confusion, she did know that Ty, dear, wonderful Ty, had thrown himself into the path of the invasion and now suffered for his brave actions.

The intruder's back was to her, so she had no idea what the man looked like, as she had been concentrating on what Ty was saying when the door had crashed open. His body that had given her so much pleasure now writhed in agony on the floor as a well-aimed kick caught him in the side.

She screamed and wasn't even aware of it until the rawness of her throat left her mute.

"Damn it, boy," the stranger yelled, lifting his foot to strike again. "I've tried to understand you, but this—" his voice cracked with emotion, "this time you've gone too damned far."

The man turned about, and Serra gasped aloud. There was no mistaking the face from the old photograph Dr. Chelsey had shown her time and again.

"F—f—father?" she stuttered, searching his rugged countenance for kindness and recognition, a sob clogging her throat, keeping her from uttering more. This was happening all wrong. Their reunion was supposed to be a time of joy, the fulfillment of a lifelong dream.

"Serenity." John Langston said the name not as a question, yet she could feel his gaze travel over her huddled form bundled in the quilt, his expression demanding an explanation. "Are—are you all right?"

Serra pushed back the disheveled hair from her face and glanced down at Ty. From his position on the floor he simply eyed her back, no longer the man who had loved her earlier that morning, no longer the man who claimed to have the solution to all of their problems, but rather a stranger—the man in black who had ruthlessly forced her from the train. Unable to stand the pain of his withdrawal, she returned her gaze to Langston.

"Yes, of course, I'm fine." She glanced back at Ty, seeking—praying—for approval, direction. He stared at her stonily, unblinking, giving nothing.

Langston knelt beside the bed and clutched her shoulders in his hands, drawing her attention back to him—this man she honestly believed to be her father. His scrutiny slid over the thin straps of her chemise, across her bare shoulders, and then returned to her face. "Did he . . . take advantage of you?"

Her eyes darted between Ty and her father. She understood what he was asking her, yet it wasn't at all the way he figured. "Father, I—" she began and faltered, unable to find the proper words to explain and not make herself look bad in his eyes.

"Did I take what the she offered? Is that what you're wantin' to know, John?" Ty barked a derisive laugh that could have been a denial or an affirmation, depending on how one took it.

Apparently, Langston took it to mean he had. Like a wounded bull, her father released her and spun about. Ty was on his knees by then and could have easily stood to defend himself. Instead he remained stationary, his hands relaxed at his sides, and didn't attempt to fend off the fist that caught him under the chin. Crashing backward, he struck the chair he had so carefully bound together the evening before. His large body and the broken spindles crumpled to the floor. Except for the splintering of wood, Ty's grunt of pain, and her father's labored breathing, there were no other sounds.

"Father, no," she cried when Langston made another move toward Ty, rising from her crouch, dragging the quilt with her when she stood.

Langston glanced over his shoulder, his clenched fist suspended in the air, his anger softening when his gaze skimmed over her. "Get dressed, Serenity," he ordered. Relaxing his hand, he bent and roughly jabbed a finger in Ty's exposed rib cage. "You, boy, get up. I'm not done with you, not by a long shot."

Without protest, Ty rose to his knees and silently rubbed his bruised jaw with his knuckles to staunch the trickle of blood oozing from the cut in the corner of his mouth, tingeing his beard a light crimson. Then Langston grabbed his arm and pushed him toward the still-open front door.

Fear for Ty brought Serra stumbling after them. "What are you going to do?"

Langston shot her a look—a most paternal glare—that she knew was not one to be defied. "Just get dressed, girl, like I told you." Then he shoved Ty over the threshold onto the porch and slammed the door in her face.

She seriously considered following, still wrapped in the quilt, but again she stumbled over the trailing ends and knew she would be ineffectual so incapacitated.

Twirling about, she gathered up her dress and tossed it over her head, the yards of material that made up the skirt bellowing around her like a wind-filled sail. From outside, she heard the bone-crushing blow, then another one. Squeaking a protest, she rushed forward, still buttoning up the front of her garment, and threw open the barrier.

What she saw was worse than she'd anticipated. Bleeding from the mouth and nose, Ty dangled like a broken shutter from one of the porch railing posts. It was obvious he planned to do nothing to stop the beating. But why?

She knew only too well how stubborn he could be in his misplaced pride, but she refused to just stand there and watch her father beat him senseless. Rushing forward, she latched onto Langston's upraised arm. "Please, Father, you must stop, or you will kill him."

Like an angry bear hounded by bees, the older man merely shook her off. "Stay out of this, Serenity. The boy has it comin', and he knows it." His open hand caught Ty across the mouth with a sound akin to the crack of thunder. Ty swayed and fell against the railing, falling forward from the porch into the rain-splattered yard, taking one end of the splintered board with him.

How many times in the past had she interceded for Ty when he refused to do something for himself? Like the time at the New Hope Opera House. Or when the orphanage director had accused him of stealing from the money box. She had been the one to prove his innocence. The instances were too many to count, too numerous to change her ways now.

Her mouth flattened into a slash of determination. Knowing what she must do, she ran back into the cabin and grabbed up Ty's revolver from the table where he'd left it. She was not that familiar with weaponry, never having had a need or a desire to be until now, but at least she did know how to cock the hammer and pull the trigger. Her only fear was that the gun might not be loaded.

Framed in the doorway, she took a steady aim at the unlatched gate at the far end of the drive. Then at the last moment, she lowered her lashes and turned her head away before squeezing the cold metal with her index finger.

Like cannonfire, the shot reverberated in her ears. Until now, she had never realized how loud the roar of a discharging pistol could be. Her ears ringing, her palm curled about the gun handle cold and numb, she opened her eyes to find both men staring at her. To her horror, Langston's hat had been neatly lifted from his head by the bullet she had fired.

The older man assessed her with surprise, Ty with cold contempt, both seeming to find it hard to believe she was such a crack shot. If only they knew how poor her aim really was. Dear God, she had drawn a bead—or so she'd thought—on a target a safe distance away. In the process, she had nearly killed her father without meaning to.

Her hands began to tremble with the magnitude of what she had almost done, the quake rolling through her body until she thought her legs would no longer support her weight. She focused on Ty, searching for understanding amidst the anger on his face, for some reason his opinion most important to her. Her intervention always did make him look at her in just that way, as if to say he didn't need her help. With time, he'd come around and accept—if not be grateful—that what she had done had been for him, she tried to reassure herself.

With time. She relaxed her death grip on the pistol butt, allowing the gun to swing down and point at the porch steps. It seemed she was always biding her time when it came to Tyler Ramsey.

Riveting her attention on her father, she announced in a quiet, steady voice, "I think you've done quite enough."

As much as she wanted to tell him Ty had never

101

hurt her, had never done anything she hadn't asked him to, she kept the truth to herself, knowing it would only anger Ty more if she defended him verbally.

Langston frowned but nonetheless lowered his fist, and for one fleeting moment, Serra was sure she had pushed him too far. Fear clutched at her heart. What if he decided he didn't like her . . . found her too forward . . . didn't want her as his daughter? All the years of preparation would be for naught, her dreams scattered like dust before the wind.

She lifted her chin. Then so be it. Ty's life was much more important.

To her surprise, Langston laughed aloud as he snatched up his mangled hat from the ground to examine the bullet hole in the crown. "By gum, girl, right now you remind me of your mother . . . so full of starch and vinegar."

Such a statement should have made her heart soar with joy; it would have had the circumstances been different. Langston's declaration now would only serve to push Ty farther away, to make him more of a stranger than ever before. For as long as she could remember, Tyler Ramsey never had liked to be contradicted by anyone.

"No," she cried, "I'm nothing like her. Nothing. I don't want to be. . . ."

"Serenity."

The voice that spoke her name surged over her like a bucket of cold water, instantly cooling her passionate outburst. She turned to confront the one person who understood her deepest needs . . . who had guided her through the difficult years . . . who had shown her the path she must take . . . who had

102

given her the opportunity to fulfill her dreams, relieved yet distressed by his unexpected presence.

Standing beside the hooded buggy, Dr. Chelsey's dark, magnetic gaze stared down at her, drawing her into the realm of his powers, his fingers drumming against the footboard of the vehicle. His look, the rat-a-tat-tat of his strumming, mesmerized her as surely as a moth is trapped by the flicker of a candle, reminding her in no uncertain terms of the grueling hours they had spent together dredging up the memories she had been unable to find for herself. Their shared experience, her unquestionable loyalty to him and his to her, restored Serra's wavering sanity.

She blinked and inhaled, feeling as if her lungs couldn't get enough oxygen. The need to be needed that had driven her thus far welled within her breast, consuming her mind, putting everything back into its proper perspective.

But there was still that tug at her heart. Ty.

Oh, Ty, she cried inwardly. She glanced down at him, and had he given her even the slightest indication, she might have struggled against the debilitating spell Chelsey wove about her, with the promise of security that her dreams of family offered.

Instead, his glare never altered; in fact, he stared through her, refusing to acknowledge that what they had shared earlier that day had meant a damn thing to him. She thought back to what he had been saying to her before her father had burst through the cabin door. "This misconception you have about John Langston."

Misconception? Her eyes narrowed with the belated sting of his statement. Just what *had* his solution been? Perhaps he had thought now that she had so easily . . . relinquished her virginity to him, she would renounce her rightful claim as well. He had to have known her father would come looking for her, had to have realized he would find them in a compromising situation. It had all been part of Ty's well-conceived plot to make her look bad in her parent's eyes. Now she understood just what Ty had meant by his response when her father had demanded to know if she had been taken advantage of. His derisive words suggested she had thrown herself at him.

And in truth, hadn't she? Yet in her innocence she had been the victim, no match for his ability to seduce her so easily. How stupid could she have been?

And now she had nearly sacrificed it all to foolishly try to protect him. He had been confident she would intercede, had known it, and most likely had figured just such a reaction into his plans.

Looking up into Dr. Chelsey's eyes, she read affirmation in his gaze. Tyler Ramsey had used her and had almost pulled off his elaborate scheme to unjustly expose her as a fraud.

How could he have done this to her, to the Serra who had trusted him for as long as she could remember? She forced herself to look at him, now standing on the ground below her. The answer was in his hard, uncompromising gaze. She wasn't Serra; he wasn't Ty. They were adversaries squabbling over the same bone.

And Serra feared in her heart that her savage enemy—the man in black, watching her with the haunted, hungry eyes of a betrayed wolf—could easily best her in such a beastly contest.

"Easy, girl. I see no call for that."

Serra tore her gaze away from Ty and glanced at John Langston, who covered her still-trembling hand with his. He gave her a kindly, worried look and squeezed her fingers, subduing them against the cold metal of the pistol she'd forgotten she still held.

Glancing down, she discovered she had raised the gun, and it pointed directly at Ty's bare chest. His lungs expanded, deflated, swelled again, but other than his breathing, Ty didn't move a muscle, daring her to follow through with her threat. Yes, *betrayed* rightly described the message his icy gaze sent her.

Appalled that she would do something so barbaric, she dropped the weapon as if it burned her, gladly allowing it to slip into her father's hand. Langston touched her arm, guiding her back into the cabin, and she didn't resist him, still in shock that she had aimed a loaded weapon at anyone, much less at Ty. It wasn't until the older man pointed down at the floor, indicating she needed to don her stockings and shoes, that the full impact of her actions for the last few moments rammed home.

Staring down stupidly at her bare feet, she realized how she must look, so slatternly, her gown wrinkled, torn, splattered, and still not buttoned properly. And her hair. Her hand flew up and probed. She had spent so much time prior to leaving New Hope the day before, making it look just right. Now it hung about her shoulders in wild, coppery disarray.

Was that how they saw her? How Ty viewed her as well? Afraid to look at him, to confirm her worst suspicions, she turned instead to Dr. Chelsey, seeking solace in his calming gaze. She absorbed the worry and concern reflected there, but his look was different than the one her father gave her. But she couldn't quite pinpoint what the distinction was. Perhaps his gaze reflected disappointment in her. Ah, yes, the doctor had every reason to be disheartened with what he had witnessed.

How could she have failed him so? He had spent time and energy unselfishly helping her, molding her into the woman she must be to at last take her rightful place with her real family. And she had paid him back by carelessly tossing it all to the wind on the flight of a silly young girl's fancy. How could she have thought Tyler Ramsey would still be the same as she remembered him?

She hung her head in shame, bending to gather up her high-top packers and noting their ruined condition.

Ruined. Just as she had been, by a man who had thought of nothing and no one but himself.

She pulled on her boots and laced them with quick, determined movements. Ruined or not, she must wear them.

Ruined or not, she must go on with her life.

Serra stood, turning to gather up her Spanish lace shawl that was draped over one of the crude foot posts of the bed. Though she tried not to, she couldn't help noticing the crumpled sheets, remembering the feel of Ty's hands and body touching hers, the passion they had shared . . . the love.

Spinning about, she pushed away such numbing thoughts. Regardless of what he might think, the betrayal was not of her doing, but of his. Yet such reasoning did nothing to lessen the pain ripping through her heart.

Holding the tears at bay, Serra raised her head high as she stepped over the pile of spilt beans and waltzed out of the cabin, gracefully taking the rickety steps down to the rain-soaked front yard. Ty stood in her path, damn him, refusing to move. Notching her chin, she pushed by him, his arm brushing against her shoulder.

Accepting Dr. Chelsey's hand up into the buggy he and John Langston had arrived in, she held her spine ramrod straight while the two older men took their time joining her. She would not give Ty the satisfaction of seeing her break under his scrutiny. And he *was* staring at her; she could feel it as if it were a living thing clawing at her back.

He had been such an important part of her life for as long as she could remember, even in his absence. But now chances were she would never see him again, and it was probably best that way. In the footsteps of Jesse James and Billy the Kid he'd vowed so long ago to make his way, and just like them his punishment had been justified by his crime. But, oh, how she wished it could have been different.

It's over, Serra, it's over, she told herself time and again. Yet when Langston snapped the reins across the horse's back, she couldn't resist the urge to glance over her shoulder as the vehicle turned into the rutted road heading away from the stone cabin.

The image of Ty still standing in the muddy yard, shoeless, shirtless, glaring back at her, tore an irreparable gash through the center of her aching heart.

Chapter Seven

The rain began once more. At first it was merely a light sprinkle, no more than an annoyance. Watching the Langston high-wheeled buggy crest the first hill, Ty swiped at the moisture gathering on his lashes. And it was the rain he brushed away, nothing more. Not the humiliation nor the disappointment he suffered. Rain. The damn stuff just wouldn't stop blurring his vision.

Then with a crack of spring thunder the sky burst open, pelting the already-saturated ground around him. The drops clustered in his hair, plastering it to his head and running in rivulets down the valleys of his face and chest. Still he refused to move, not until the carriage, with the calash thrown up to protect the passengers from getting soaked, climbed to the top of the last ridge, its red wheels spewing out the water of the muddy puddles it skimmed through.

Then the buggy disappeared. And Serra was gone with it.

Ty reached up and pressed a knuckle against the corner of his mouth that still stung from the savagery of the beating he had taken. Now that it was over and he was alone, he succumbed to the pain.

Inspecting the blood smeared on the back of his hand, he watched until the torrents of rain washed it away, leaving behind his naked fist. Turning, he slammed it into the railing post, savoring the pain of his own making, pain that assuaged the need to strike back. Had it been anyone but John Langston . . .

But it had been his mentor, his friend, and there had been no question of doing other than what he had done. To have struck the old man back would have been the same as . . . committing murder.

Turning his back to the storm and to the woman, who for one brief moment of time had captured his heart and dared him to dream of having what others took for granted, Ty dragged himself up the steps and into the cabin.

Serra had made her choice. Oh, she had staged quite a show of defending him, making him look the fool for his own refusal to protect himself. But he knew her better than that. Had her intentions been sincere, she would have spoken up. The fact that she had kept her silence meant only one thing: She chose to continue the charade. Chose the security she thought her claim to the Langston name would give her over what he offered her.

Well, Serra, darlin', you made a poor judgment call. But then, watching Doc Chelsey with her, it was as if they shared some deeper bond, as if . . .

Hell, if he didn't know better personally, he would have thought them more than guardian and ward. He knew the physician played an important part in the scheme, quite possibly was the driving force. But why and how? What did the old charlatan think to gain?

Ty gathered up his gear, including his empty holster, and made ready to ride.

The deception had been bad enough before, but now . . . it was personal. If Serra thought that what they had shared would make him pull back, she was wrong. Dead wrong. More than ever, he was determined to get to the bottom of this entire affair and expose those involved.

Several hours later, the Langston buggy entered Joplin from the southeast, following the creek that wound through the town. Once the country lane turned into city streets, Serra was surprised at the broad thoroughfares that were macadamized . . . as hard and solid as rock. Amazing. Even the streets of metropolitan New York had been mud or at the most bricked.

Healthy businesses lined the ways, with webs of electrical wires crisscrossing the street, the first Serra had ever seen. Sidewalks, each section of different heights and widths, were traversed by men and women dressed in the latest styles. And ahead, a mule-drawn streetcar lumbered toward them, clanking its warning bell, forcing vehicles and pedestrians alike to move aside.

Joplin was nothing like she imagined. Nothing like she remembered. She frowned, momentarily doubting herself.

"Progress. It's said all roads eventually lead to Joplin," John Langston offered with pride, taking her cold, ungloved hand in his and squeezing it, conveying warmth and assurance. "It's been a long time, girl. Things have a way of changin'."

110

Serra turned a dazzling, grateful smile on him. "Yes, of course they do, Father." Only too well she knew how people and places could alter. Look at Ty. Angrily, she pushed away the haunting images that tried to scale the wall of tranquility she'd thrown up in self-preservation.

Jarred back to the present when Langston brought the carriage to an abrupt halt at a cross street, Serra watched with mild curiosity the convoy of rock-filled wagons that passed in front of them.

"That's jack from the lead mines. It's worthless chat for our purposes," he explained. "But we dump it outside the city, and then much of it is used by the road crews to pave the streets. A fair exchange as far as the Langston Mining Company is concerned."

With a snap of his wrists, he started the horse forward, turning the buggy into a tree-lined lane. Recognizing the name on the street sign, Serra's heart quickened. A house came into view, large and opulent. She leaned forward, looking for familiar landmarks, but nothing was as she . . . imagined.

"Our neighbors," Langston supplied.

She frowned. Serra didn't recall having neighbors nearby.

"The Stokes built here only last year. You'll like them. They have a daughter about your age and a son who's gone into business with his father."

But Serra wasn't listening. Instead, she focused on the house just coming into view, the one from the picture, just as she remembered it. The twin garrets with the round oculus windows, the sloping dormers of the second story, the big bay window of the spacious dining room on the first floor. Yes, yes, it

111

was all there.

Yet, it was different. There were trees, large ones, all around, and a shrub-lined fence with a wrought iron gate at the bottom of the driveway. The image in her mind was open—all around. How could she have forgotten so much? Confused, she turned to Dr. Chelsey.

He smiled and patted her hand in reassurance. "Like your father said, dumpling, things change and grow over the years."

Yes, she supposed that was true, but would nothing be as she thought it should be? Disappointment riddled her heart.

By the time they turned into the drive, Serra made up her mind to persevere. She was home. At long last, she was finally where she belonged.

Yet even with her resolve intact, a strange feeling assaulted her when she swept through the entryway of the Langston mansion, the front door held open by an immaculately dressed butler, who issued a stately "Welcome home, sir," without a blink. She had thought she would experience relief, feel a certain something akin to belonging. Instead, a sense of isolation washed over her, especially when the servant looked through her as if she didn't exist.

No rush of arrival. No giddiness of at last realizing her heartfelt dreams. It was almost as if she were an outsider entering where she didn't belong. She glanced about the high-vaulted foyer and had to keep her feet firmly planted to keep from turning back toward the front door—to escape.

"Well, girl," Langston boomed, stripping her wrap from her stiffly held shoulders and handing it to the servant, "what are you waitin' for. Go on up to your rooms."

Serra pivoted, stood blinking at the man she considered her father, and found she couldn't move.

He frowned, and over his shoulder she could see that Doc mimicked his expression. "Don't tell me you've . . . forgotten the way."

"No, of course not," she replied rather quickly. How could she forget? She had been rehearsing this particular moment for years. Glancing up the massive staircase, she noted the mahogany banisters, knew the polished wood would be smooth and cool to her touch, even knew how many steps there were. Twenty to the first landing, then fifteen more. Down the hallway, third door on the left.

This was hers and yet . . .

Damn it. She was letting things Tyler Ramsey had said to her interfere with the happiness she should be experiencing. Terrible things. Lies.

She moved forward and grasped the banister, feeling relief that at least it was familiar, then started up the stairs.

"Serenity."

Three steps up she turned to glance down at John Langston's face, which was awry with emotion.

"I hope you don't mind, girl. I had your rooms redecorated. I think you'll find everything you could possibly need where it belongs. Freshen up and then come back downstairs." He smiled, almost shyly. "W—we can talk. Catch up . . . on things."

At last the delayed joy washed over her. "Oh, yes, Father," she gushed. "I would like that. I would like that very much." Spinning on her toes, she raced up the stairs and right to the room that she knew belonged to her.

113

Without hesitation, she entered her domain, stopping in the doorway to bend and begin unlacing her shoes. Then like a giddy, young schoolgirl, she kicked them off, ignoring the fact that one flew underneath the high poster canopy bed that dominated the space.

Yes, this was how she was supposed to feel. Welcomed. At home.

" 'Cuse me, miss."

The unexpected voice startled her, and she squeaked her alarm, spinning to face the intruder.

The girl in the doorway, not much older than herself, was obviously a servant. She even held a pitcher of water and several hand towels to confirm the fact. The maid dipped a curtsy and waited to be invited in. "I'm Tess. If there's anything you be needin', I'm to be gittin' it for ya."

Suddenly self-conscious, Serra reached out, accepting the proffered water and towels, wanting first to familiarize herself with her surroundings before allowing anyone else to enter.

"Th—thank you, Tess," she stuttered, her own humble childhood crowding her mind . . . the years spent in the orphanage with Ty . . . the vision of someday finding a better place a driving force in her life. Did the servant have similar ambitions?

"Tell me something," she impulsively asked as the other girl turned to leave. "Are you happy here?"

Tess stared at her as if somewhat surprised by the question. Then remembering her manners, she glanced down and flexed at the knees once more to show respect. "Very happy, miss," she replied, stepping back.

Serra frowned, quickly depositing the items in her

hand on the dresser, then she reached for Tess's arm, stopping the girl's retreat. "Don't you have dreams of things getting better?" she asked, needing to assure herself she wasn't all that different from others. Didn't everyone have those ongoing hopes?

"Better, miss?" the girl asked. " 'Tis a roof over my head and warm food to eat." She look up shyly. "And the master—and hopefully the new miss—is kind. What more could I be wantin', except one day, perhaps, the love of a good man?"

What more? Astounded with the girl's simple wisdom, Serra pulled back, retreating into a shell of self-examination. "Perhaps you are right. Nothing more, indeed."

The servant scurried away, and Serra closed the door, turning to press her back to the barrier as it clicked softly shut. She ruminated over what Tess had said to her, then shook her head. Well, there was more *she* wanted, at least at the moment.

She glanced about the room, absorbing her surroundings. And what she needed most was to feel a part of everything around her. Once she and her father had a chance to talk together, the feeling would be there, the security she'd craved for a lifetime.

Clamping her lips together in determination, she crossed to the wardrobe, an ornate piece of furniture that covered the majority of one wall. She whipped open the doors to discover an array of gowns and costumes in every color of the rainbow, more than she could imagine any one person possibly ever wearing or needing.

"Oh, my," she whispered in awe, finding it hard to believe they were all at her disposal. Tess had been definitely wrong. There was more to life than the basic requirements. So much more to strive for.

Making her selection, she took one of the gowns, a pale green one, from the closet and tossed it on the bed. Then she chose a pair of dainty-heeled shoes from the floor of the wardrobe, which were a darker shade of green. Stripping the plaid dress she wore from her body, she tossed it aside with the intention of giving it to the servant. It could perhaps be tailored to fit the other girl, most of the rips and stains worked around. Her first act of charity to someone who had less than she had, and it felt good. Yes, giving felt so much better than receiving, especially when she had so much to share.

A half hour later, she'd washed away the dirt of travel and dressed herself in the new gown. Plucking at the crisp leg-of-mutton sleeves, she descended the stairs to the foyer. Off to her right, she caught the sound of voices, recognized her father's boisterous timbre and Dr. Chelsey's quieter one, and directed her steps toward the . . .

She paused, conjuring up the mental map of the house she carried in her head. The library. Yes, that would be right. The library.

When she swept into the room, the conversation paused, and the two men gave her their attention. The doctor's smile encouraged her. Langston's welcomed her, and he waved her toward the chair next to the one he occupied.

"Serenity, join us." His paternal gaze devoured her, from the coppery chignon on her head to the dainty green heels on her feet. "You're just as lovely as I knew you would be. Come. Sit, girl. There's so much for us to—" He paused and swallowed.

Serra's heart welled with compassion, her eyes

116

with tears. Reaching out, she gathered up his big, work-gnarled hand in hers. All those years she had endured and clung to her beliefs, she had never once thought about what he must be suffering. Not knowing where she was nor how to find her. And her mother who had died just a few years after their separation. Had she succumbed to a broken heart from the loss of her child? Such pain they had all encountered.

Her bottom lip trembling, she wanted to speak but found it impossible.

Finally Langston began in a broken voice. "If only your mother could see you." He touched her hair as if it were made of the finest spun gold. "After—after your disappearance, she was so strong, so sure we would find you, but the years began to take their toll, and the trail and her hope grew cold. By that last spring, Laura Lee lost her will to go on. I watched her fade away one day at a time. Right after she died, I brought the boy home. Thought maybe he would fill the void. But, damn his soul"—he slammed his fist against the arm of his chair—"he wasn't lookin' to find a place in anyone's heart. I've loved that boy, tried to raise him like he was my own, and this," he declared, waving his hand in the air, "is how he pays me back."

Serra froze with shock. Could her father be referring to Tyler Ramsey? Her thoughts scrambled to find firm footing, to make sense out of what the man was saying. Remembering how Ty had accused her of being a fraud, she had automatically assumed his motives for kidnapping her from the train were purely self-serving. But what if he had been trying to protect the one person who had befriended him—

117

John Langston?

She glanced up and stared hard at the man whom she wanted more than anyone to be her father, wondering for one fleeting moment how truthful she should be with him. She needed him to accept her, to never doubt for a minute that she was his daughter, but if he misinterpreted Ty's actions just as she had, she felt it her duty to point out his error.

"I think, Father, you do Ty an injustice."

Silence prevailed. Then in the distance, she heard the sound of Dr. Chelsey tapping his fingertips against the smooth surface of the end table next to his chair.

The familiar, overwhelming feeling of lethargy rushed over her. Glancing up, she caught the disapproval in her guardian's dark eyes.

"Serenity, do not question your father's judgment," Chelsey instructed in a quiet, yet demanding tone, the one that always made her shrivel inwardly.

"No," Langston interceded. "Let her speak. What do you mean, girl?"

But Serra found her tongue stuck to the roof of her mouth, her breath jammed in the deepest recesses of her lungs, her brain refusing to organize her thoughts. She wanted to respond, to express her heartfelt convictions, but whenever she felt like this, there was no way she could disregard the doctor's wishes. All she could hear was that inner chorus insisting over and over, "Family and dreams. Nothing else matters."

"I didn't mean anything," she murmured in a small voice, unable to tear her eyes away from Chelsey's magnetic gaze, unable to ignore the rhythm of his tapping fingers.

The drumming stopped, and Chelsey's confident smile expressed his approval.

Feeling as if she struggled to escape from a trap that pulverized her normal pluck and verve into spineless dust, she sat there in silence, trying to conjure up enough nerve to tear her eyes away from Chelsey's spell. It was with relief that she glanced down at her own hands and watched them twist about each other. Why, oh, why, couldn't she make herself do what she wanted to do?

"Tell us, Serenity."

From some remote corner of her mind, she heard the doctor's request.

"Tell your father what has happened to you over the years."

Ah, now, here was safe ground. She had told this story so many times, preparing for this day, that she knew each precisely chosen word by heart. She began her recital and found herself listening to what she was saying as if someone else were speaking.

Yes, that part was true. She could visualize the Langston house as it had been all those years ago—her mother, her father, the nanny, herself. But she didn't really remember the terrifying trip to New York with strangers, even though Dr. Chelsey had told her that's probably how it had happened. Then wandering the streets of New York alone . . . that part was definitely real. And she had been looking for someone very important, just as her recital indicated, but the thought of her parents had frightened her, not spurred her on to continue looking as the doctor had insisted she say.

Doc had explained away her doubts about that as well. Confusion. The people who had kidnapped her

119

and had abandoned her to the streets of the big city had taken the place of parents in her mind. Yes, she supposed that could be, but why couldn't she recall that for herself?

Serra paused in her oration, stumbling over the memorized words. "I . . . I remember . . . standing on the steps of the orphanage, the note pinned to my collar, 'Please take care of Serra,' scrawled in a cramped, uneducated handwriting."

"That's right," the doctor said, reaching into the inner pocket of his vest and taking out some folded papers. "Here," he said, offering the packet to Langston. "These are the only documents that came with the child when I took her in out of the kindness of my heart. The note is there among them."

Sitting on the edge of her chair, Serra watched anxiously as Langston unfolded the papers to study them. Then he looked up at her. "They called you Serra over the years, then." His eyes were misted.

Serra nodded.

"That's very close to the nickname your mother used, you know. Seri. I imagine it got muddled a bit along the way."

The audible sound of the doctor's relief reached her and she should have experienced it as well, but instead the knowledge took her by complete surprise. Her memories, even though they were sketchy, merely broken bits of images, were crystal clear. She remembered her parents calling her Serenity . . . always Serenity when she thought of them. To forget something as intimate as a nickname seemed inconceivable to her.

She pressed the heels of her hands against her temples, trying to stop the jumble whirling in her head, flipping forward, then backward, until her thoughts became a blur. So confusing. For the first time, she found herself doubting her claim. Was any of it real, or was it all just figments of her imagination . . . her desire to find her family? The only part of it she found she didn't question . . .

Tyler Ramsey.

And not once in her discourse had she mentioned him. She straightened, then stood to emphasize her determination to say what was on her mind. Such an omission must be corrected.

The iterative tapping of Chelsey's fingers reverberated more like thunder in her ears, and she clapped her hands over them to escape the deafening sound, the power it had over her. Her father was there beside her, grasping at her shoulders. Couldn't he hear the noise?

"Serenity, what's wrong?" Langston scrambled to his feet to kneel in front of her.

She didn't have the ability to answer except with a plaintive moan.

"What's wrong with her?" Her father directed his demand for an explanation toward the doctor.

Then Chelsey's hands were on her, the silent action of his drumming fingers playing along the flesh of her upper arms, and he turned her toward the door.

"She has these spells now and then. Nothing to worry about, as they always seem to pass. Usually they're brought on by overexertion, exhaustion," he explained in that authoritative physician's voice that everyone accepted as indisputable.

"Then she should rest. We can finish our conversation later." Langston moved as if to take control.

121

"Perhaps you should allow me, Mr. Langston. I'm familiar with what she might do. I have powders in my bags which will calm her."

"I'll be here if you need anything," her father offered in a voice full of sincere concern yet uncertainty.

"We'll be fine, sir."

Serra heard the conversation through a thick fog, an inescapable heaviness she couldn't shrug off even though she tried. Rebuttal burned on her tongue, yet she couldn't speak. She just followed Chelsey up the stairs to her room.

Then she was lying on the bed, the cool pink spread as soft as satin beneath her. A damp cloth was pressed to her forehead, and she heard Chelsey muttering to himself.

"I can't imagine what could have gone wrong. What influence could be superseding mine."

The stroking of the cloth against her hot skin paused.

"That man. It has to be that damned, interfering—"

Chelsey snapped his fingers, the sound as loud as cymbals in her ears.

"Look at me, Serra."

Obeying the command, her eyes popped open. Before her swung the gold pocket watch, in then out of her view. At first she refused to focus on it, instead, struggling to direct her gaze straight ahead, to keep her thoughts clear.

"Follow it, Serra. You know you cannot resist the urge to watch it."

Back and forth. Back and forth. Soon the shiny fob filled her vision, her mind washed clean of all

122

other images.

"That's my dumpling. So sleepy. Rest, Serra, rest. And you will remember only what I tell you to remember."

The spell gripped her, cold hands of destruction dragging her down, down, drowning her, wiping clean the slate in her mind. The feel of Ty's hands, his mouth, on her . . . his warmth . . . his caring, evaporated like cooling waters before a hot desert wind, leaving nothing but the memory of his rejection.

Leaving nothing but the ravagement of the lingering sweetness, nothing but the bitterness of the way he'd used her for his own gain and tossed her aside.

In the background the clock in the hallway gonged the hour, imprinting itself in her mind.

"Now, Serra," Chelsey instructed, "here is what you will do."

Chapter Eight

Darkness lingered, dawn still an hour away, when Ty led Cochise into the stableyard.

He was home. He should be glad, he supposed. Normally, it was with relief that he rode onto the Langston estate. But this time was different.

Not that he expected to be turned away. Quite to the contrary, nothing more would be said of the incident at the cabin. That was John Langston's way . . . justice rendered swiftly then forgotten. The only reminders that lingered were the bruises and cuts Ty carried, both physical and mental. With time they would fade; they always did. But now there was one memento that would not disappear: Serra.

He didn't doubt for a moment that he would find her there, occupying the rooms no one had been allowed to desecrate, not until John Langston had been informed of his daughter's miraculous resurgence. He further suspected her boon companion, Dr. Chelsey, would have managed to install himself into the household, too. Where one found the dog, usually the tail wasn't far behind.

Loosening the saddle cinch with an unnecessary roughness, Ty muttered a curse. As if Cochise knew his master well, the horse snorted his discomfort, twisting his neck to look at Ty in disapproval.

"Sorry, boy," Ty murmured contritely, forcing his hands to be gentler. "There's just something about that man . . . the way he looks at people . . . the way he absorbs *her* attention. I don't like him. Just don't trust him."

The horse nickered what Ty interpreted to be agreement, and he took the time to brush out the gelding before turning him into an empty box stall. Picking up his saddlebags, he tossed them over his shoulder. Then he left the stables, following the brick-lined walk to the house, noting that the first faint rays of the morning sun fingered the horizon. The servants would be up and about by now. Damn, he had hoped his arrival would go unobserved.

He entered by the back stoop, a door used only by the staff. There on the service porch he removed his muddy boots and left them, knowing that when he returned for them later they would be shiny and clean.

Adjusting the weight of his saddlebags, he moved on stockinged feet up the back stairwell to the second floor. There, to his relief, he found the hallway empty, the wall sconces still burning low for the night. At the first door he paused and made to enter. Then several rooms down he saw a servant exit, her head bent with exhaustion.

Mild alarm sounded in his mind. That had been Serenity's room the maid had just left.

"Tess?" he called softly.

The servant spun about at the sound of her name, and even in the dimness of the hallway, Ty could see her eyes light up when they settled on him.

"Ty!" she cried in an excited susurration, moving forward to throw her arms about his middle with familiarity. "You're back." Turning up her face, he knew she expected a kiss.

But the taste of Serra still lingered on his lips, and he couldn't bring himself to give the girl what she wanted. Casually, he placed an arm about her shoulder and pushed his hat away from his face. "What's goin' on?" he asked.

" 'Tis Miss Serenity. She arrived yesterday," Tess whispered.

"What's wrong with her?" The question laced with concern tumbled from his lips before he could stop it.

Tess shrugged, then pressed her face against his chest. "Seems she had some kind of fit last night. That Dr. Chelsey had to calm her down."

"You mean he gave her some kind of medicine?" An uneasy suspicion wedged its way into his brain.

"I'm not sure, but whatever he did, it put her into a deep sleep." Tess yawned and arched her back, stretching, her body sidling against his, a signal he rightly interpreted. "I was ordered to stay with her in case she should wake up, but she slept through the night without movin' once. It was creepy, Ty," she said with a shiver as she wiggled against him, "watchin' her, almost like sittin' vigilance with the dead."

"The dead?" Ty frowned, pushing the girl away, and started toward the bedroom where Serra slept.

"You can't be goin' in there," Tess warned, grabbing his arm to stop his progress.

He brushed her hand away, a bit roughly. When it came to Serra, he could do any damn thing he pleased. Pushing open the door, he saw her lying in the middle of the canopied bed, her hands clasped

126

across her stomach, her eyes closed, her coppery curls spilling across the pillow. And indeed, she did seem unnaturally still.

Stepping forward, he moved deeper into the room, near enough to the bed to reach out and touch her. Her flesh was warm and alive, thank God, but still there was a translucency to her skin he'd never noticed before, making her appear so fragile, so vulnerable, so . . .

"What are *you* doing in here?"

Ty released her hand and spun about to face Chelsey, noting that Tess stood behind him. The way the man looked at him was most unnerving, but Ty held his position beside Serra's bed.

"I might ask you the same thing."

Chelsey's gaze narrowed, his mouth turning ugly. "Miss Langston is my ward. I have every right to be in her room."

"I suppose. But Miss *Paletot* is my friend of long-standin'."

Alarm flickered in the doctor's dark eyes, then they narrowed with calculation. "Just how long?"

"Long enough to know who she is and where she came from."

Chelsey straightened and slipped into a deceptively relaxed stance. "I can't imagine what you mean. Miss Langston has no intentions of deceiving anyone. And even if she did, there's nothing you could do about it. After yesterday, I doubt John Langston would listen to anything you had to say." He smiled with confidence. "In fact, I think you'll find Miss Langston will also refuse to have anything further to do with you."

"Perhaps." Ty shrugged, disguising the pain of possible rejection that shot through him like a bullet. "As

127

long as she," he said, indicating Serra with a nod of his head, "and Langston don't get hurt, I won't interfere. But let me warn you, Chelsey." He took a step toward the other man and grabbed him by the front of his long nightshirt, giving him an ugly glare. "I will get to the bottom of this. You can bet on that."

He released the doctor, shoving his way past his opponent and out of the room.

What difference did the damn lie make if Serra could give Langston a little happiness now? What did it matter if she was his daughter or not? If he were the kind of man he should be, Ty chided himself, he would care less, but the thought of that old charlatan possibly taking advantage of them all left a foul taste in his mouth.

And if anything should ever happen to Serra . . .

Ty paused and shook his head with bewilderment. Why was it that he always felt this inescapable need to protect her—in the past, in the present, and now in the future as well?

Serra woke. For a few moments she lay there, eyes shut, listening to the noises about her. From beyond the window the plaintive song of a bird burst forth. Though the sound was a mournful one, it nonetheless was beautiful, and when it came to an end, she strained, waiting for it to erupt once more.

A few moments later her vigilance was rewarded.

Chick-a-dee-dee-dee.

Sweeping open her lashes, she tilted her head to look out the window. There on ledge sat the tiniest little bird.

Chick-a-dee-dee-dee, it sang once more in a voice much too loud for its petite size.

"Chick-a-dee to you, too," she murmured, scooting to a sitting position in the bed and stretching. At the sudden movement, her serenader flew away. Then the hall clock outside her door began striking the hour. One gong. Two. As if her mind rode a carousel, it started to spin. She felt so stiff and sore. . . .

And so very strange.

Gong. Gong.

Touching the tips of her fingers to her temples, she sat that way, trying to gather her jumbled thoughts, to just remember what it was that had upset her last night and what had happened afterwards. But even when she furrowed her brows in concentration, she just couldn't quite put her finger on it.

Gong. Gong.

Ty. Somehow it all had to do with Tyler Ramsey. An unaccounted-for anger welled up in her chest, blighting out all other emotions.

Gon—n—n—g! The final peal of the hall clock echoed in her head.

Without really understanding what compelled her, Serra scrambled from the bed, administered her morning ablution, and quickly dressed in a light morning gown of green silk that was already laid out on the foot of her bed. She must get downstairs and . . . and . . .

She wasn't sure what it was she had to do, but she lifted her skirts and hurried down the hallway to the main staircase. Hurry. Hurry. But, oh God, why this need to rush she didn't understand, but she didn't stop to analyze it. She only knew that she was late.

The sound of conversation came from the dining room.

Serra ran in that direction, pausing just before she reached the door to gather her decorum.

The picture within was a typical breakfast scene. Her father sat at the head of the table, a servant pouring coffee in his cup from his left shoulder. Across from him sat Dr. Chelsey, lavishly buttering a muffin.

The physician looked up at her entry, then slipped out his pocket watch to note the time. His unspoken thoughts registered in his dark eyes. *You're late.*

I know, her darting gaze replied. But for what, she couldn't begin to guess.

Then movement to her left caught her attention from the corner of her eye. She turned to discover Tyler Ramsey preparing himself a plate from the buffet on the sideboard.

Disbelief rushed through her like a rain-swollen creek. She frowned, her mouth flattening with anger. What was *he* doing here? After that final terrible scene at the cabin, he was the last person she expected to see having breakfast in the Langston house.

"Serenity!" A chair scraped against the oak parquet floor.

Serra pivoted and smiled at her father, who stood to welcome her. "Good morning, Father."

"I'm so glad you've joined us."

"Yes, Miss Langston, we're so very glad."

Serra swiveled to face the sarcasm in Tyler's voice, so obvious from the way he called her "Miss Langston." Dressed in a white shirt, rolled up at the sleeves as if he'd been working, and a pair of fawn colored pants, Tyler looked completely at ease in the dining room — as if he thought he owned it. But his blank face gave no indication of his feelings. If it weren't for the dark shadow of a bruise under his right eye and the cut in the corner of his mouth, she might have doubted that the last few days had ever happened, being merely a nightmare she was relieved to awake from. Perhaps she imagined his flippancy?

"Mr. Ramsey," she murmured. "To what do we owe the honor of your visit?" She'd couched her inquiry in perfect politeness, so why was he looking at her that way, as if she had no business being there? Pressing the heels of her hands to her forehead, she sensed she should know the answer to that question, but the information eluded her.

Ty dropped the serving spoon back into the platter of eggs and laughed. "Amazin', Miss Langston. You're so well-informed about this household, and yet you don't know that I live here?" This time when he turned to look at her, his gaze mocked her openly.

Serra swallowed down the panic clawing at her throat. There were things she couldn't remember no matter how hard she tried, but she couldn't forget the way he had abducted her at gunpoint and . . . used her so vilely. Never would she forget that.

"Enough, boy," John Langston interceded. "Eat your meal and get back to the minin' office."

Ty's gaze lingered on her—on her lips, on the swell of her breasts—then his mouth curled derisively before he turned and took his seat at the table.

She spun around to face Langston. After the terrible things Tyler had done, after the horrible beating her father had given him, how could he allow Ty to stay here? This was her home, her family. . . . It wasn't right, an inner voice that seemed in charge insisted, overriding her usual kindheartedness. She glanced at the doctor, seeking support, and he sent her encouragement.

Go on, Serra, his look seemed to say. *Do it.* She knew then what her mission was—to tell her father just how horribly Ty had treated her—and yet . . .

Chelsey flashed a confident smirk at Tyler before

focusing his attention back on Serra. "You should eat something, dumpling," he suggested soothingly. "I think part of your problem yesterday was dietary infrequency, in addition to the stressful events of the last few days." He patted the chair next to his.

"Are you tryin' to say because she didn't eat regularly, that caused her to have some kind of fit last night?" Skepticism tainted Ty's voice.

"That's enough, Tyler." John Langston stood in place, tossing his napkin beside his still half-filled plate, and glared at the younger man.

Ty, in turn, stared back his defiance, but said nothing as he threw down his own fork into his untouched food, as if disgusted with them all, and pushed back his chair.

Standing in front of the buffet, Serra reddened, her empty plate suspended in midair. How could Ty possibly know what had happened to her last night when she couldn't even be sure herself? Uncapped anger welled within her. Leveling her amber eyes on Ty, she listened to that inner voice insisting she open her mouth and utter the condemning accusations demanding to be spoken.

But then a cold shudder raced through her as his gaze slowly, methodically stripped her of what little self-confidence she still possessed, taking with it the blessed shell of bias that her mind had wrapped about itself.

The accusation surfaced in his cold blue eyes, and memories came flooding back, stripping her of her indignation. Ty's denial of her right to the Langston name. Her father telling her how he had taken a young boy into his home and apparently felt a kinship with him. Having given up hope of finding her, had he planned to give Ty not only his affection, but his

132

fortune as well?

Serra straightened. So that was it. The money. Ty was afraid she would try to usurp his claim to her father's assets — the house, the mines, and whatever else he owned. Prompted by the revelation, memories of what had taken place in the cabin came flooding back, things she had somehow forgotten in the confusion of last night.

True, at first he had been cold and cruel to her, but there could be no denying the wonderful moments they had shared wrapped in each other's arms. She refused to believe that he had simply resorted to seduction as a means to an end. And that final attempt to talk to her just before her father had burst in on them . . . Just what had his intentions been? Did he really think her motive for being here was the Langston money?

Her brows furrowed in denial and pain. "Ty," she implored, her hand reaching out, wanting more than anything for him to refute her assumption. *Please, Ty, tell me it isn't so.*

But Tyler would have none of her — nor of any of them. With a disinterested sweep of her trim figure, he spun about and left the dining room without looking back, his shoulders stiff with pride.

"Father, I . . ." She stammered her distress, turning toward the table.

"Don't let that boy upset you, Serenity, girl," Langston consoled, settling back down in his chair with a resigned sigh. "He's a stubborn cuss, but he'll come around after a bit." But the way his gaze lingered on the empty doorway through which Ty had just departed revealed Langston's inner feelings. He cared about Ty . . . truly cared about him.

Such a revelation shouldn't have surprised her, for

133

she cared deeply for Ty herself. But seeing the emotion reflected in her father's eyes left her bewildered. Indeed, for one fleeting moment, Serra felt like an intruder. Perhaps Ty was right. She had no right to be here. Her hands shaking, she deposited the unused plate she held back on the stack on the sideboard. Then she bunched her skirts in her fists and aimed for the door.

"No, Serra."

At the call of her commonly used name, a name she would always feel rightfully belong to her even if nothing else did, she swung about to find Langston coming toward her. Draping his arm about her shoulder in order to stop her escape, to ease the way her breath rasped in and out of her lungs, he held her firmly, yet so gently that she found it hard to believe this was the same man who had ruthlessly beaten Ty just the day before. She struggled for only a moment with her emotions and his kindness, then succumbed to the feel of his parental warmth. Burying her face against his shirtfront, she gave in to the inner needs that had driven her for so long—the need to belong permanently, to know just who she was.

"There's no sense in rushing off, girl. With time, you'll get used to Tyler's straightforwardness. And once he realizes you aren't a threat to what's his, he'll accept you, too. If nothin' else," he said with a soft chuckle, "you got to give him his due for his honesty."

Tilting her face, Serra offered her father a thin smile. He was right. With time, Ty would come around. How often had she said the same thing to herself. Things might never be the same between them, but with time, they would learn to make the best of the situation. Learn to share. There was plenty for both of them—love for her, money for him.

Oh, Tyler, she thought, dropping her head in resignation. From the corner of her eye she caught sight of Dr. Chelsey sitting at the table watching them, the corner of his mouth lifted in what she interpreted as a sneer. His unguarded expression alarmed her.

It appeared as if he wasn't so pleased with her father's solution. In fact, he seemed downright upset. Serra studied him, unobserved, for a few moments. Why wouldn't Dr. Chelsey be happy for her? This was the goal they had worked toward for so long, her triumphant return to the bosom of her family. She had to be wrong about her longtime guardian. Surely she must be.

Her father gave her a final squeeze and turned her toward the sideboard, placing her plate back into her hands. "Now, I think Doc there made a good point. You got to eat right, girl, if you want to feel better."

Serra followed his urgings and spooned some of the fluffy scrambled eggs onto her plate. But to her surprise when she sat down, Dr. Chelsey jumped up like a jack-in-the-box whose handle had been cranked. "Tell me, sir, how can you treat your daughter this way?" he demanded.

Langston's countenance turned quizzical. "I'm not sure what you mean, Dr. Chelsey."

"That . . . man." The physician lifted his hand and pointed to the dining room door through which Ty had disappeared earlier. "Don't you understand how much his presence upsets Serenity?"

Serra understood her guardian's concern, truly she did, but it wasn't necessary. She placed a restraining hand on his arm to stop him, but he merely shook it off, giving her a squelching look.

Langston blinked matter-of-factly. "You mean Ty?" He shuffled his feet as if he were the one who stood

135

accused. "Aw, hell, I know what the boy did was wrong, a mite heavy-handed, but he's been punished for that."

"But don't you see that Serenity still suffers greatly from his "heavy-handedness," as you call it, whether you think he's been properly punished or not," the physician criticized in that authoritative voice of his. "Good Lord, man, he abducted her at gunpoint, and God knows what vileness he forced upon her." He threw up his hands as if he found the situation unbelievable, totally unacceptable.

"Doc, please," she cried, trying to stop his tirade.

"Be quiet, damn you," Chelsey snapped.

Serra sat back, shakened that he would curse at her. He had never done that before.

"No," Langston countered. "Let the girl speak." He moved to stand behind her, placing his hands on her shoulders. "Tell me. Is what the doctor says true?"

Serra's heart skipped several beats. Staring up into her father's eyes, she realized he would accept whatever she told him. If she confirmed Doc's statement, Ty would suffer. If she even admitted to the reality that she had stupidly fallen for a man's honeyed words, Ty most likely would still suffer. A simple indication from her, and Ty would bother her no more. Her father might even be inclined to send him away. Then it would all be hers. All of it. If that was what she wanted.

She swallowed hard, torn between her own conscience and that nagging inner voice insisting that she must bring Ty down before he had the chance to do it to her first. That voice belonged to Dr. Chelsey, as if he had somehow crawled inside of her head, controlling her.

Like a drowning person, she fought. Standing, she

pivoted to face Langston. Hurting Ty was something she just couldn't be made to do, no matter what he did to her.

"No, Father, Dr. Chelsey is wrong," she answered in a strong, sure voice, her undeniable loyalty to Ty overriding all else, including the anger she felt toward him. "Ty has done nothing to upset me. He never forced himself on me. Never. In fact," she further confessed, wondering if her openness might make her father doubt the validity of her claim to the Langston name, "Ty and I have known each other for a long time." She glanced at Chelsey and saw the shock register in his dark eyes, as if he couldn't believe she possessed the fortitude to stand up to him. Then she heard the sound of his fingers impatiently tapping a familiar rhythm against the table.

No. No. She barred her mind to the power that sound had over her. She had something to say, and she would say it.

"We—we grew up together in the . . . orphanage." It was so hard to force the words through her lips, but closing her eyes, she continued. "I know Tyler Ramsey well . . . probably better than I know myself. Just like you said, he'll eventually come to accept my presence."

Trapping her tongue between her teeth, she prepared for the inevitable. The world would come tumbling down now, wouldn't it? Now she had committed the worst of sins, broken the unwritten commandment by speaking out against the man whose will had claimed absolute authority over her for the last six years of her life. But instead of the total ruination she'd expected, there was only the sound of her fearful breathing rasping in and out of her lungs. Even the drumming of Chelsey's fingers had ceased. Lifting her lashes, she tilted her chin. The approval and adoration

137

in her father's gaze shone down on her.

She dared to glance at Chelsey. There was no denying that the physician was furious, so much so that his mouth slanted at an ugly angle. But to her amazement, he said nothing . . . did nothing.

But, then, what could he do? She almost laughed aloud at how silly she had been to think he had the power to punish her for her show of resistance. He couldn't call down the lightning to raze the ground and strike her and her father dead. The earth wouldn't open up and swallow them at his command. She stood there unharmed, her beloved father's arms about her, and there was nothing Dr. Chelsey—or anyone else, for that matter—could do to alter the situation.

"I already knew that Ty wouldn't hurt ya." Langston crooked a finger beneath her chin and angled it so their gazes met. "He's capable of many things, but not that. And to know that you were together as children, perhaps he could shed some light on the missin' years for both of us. This is wonderful."

Of course it was wonderful, Serra admitted, a giddy feeling bubbling within her. Yes, it would all work out for the best, for all of them. She turned to Dr. Chelsey—her mentor, her provider for so long—wanting so much to include him in her newfound joy.

But Chelsey refused to acknowledge her or her happiness. "Are you refusing to heed my advice, sir?" he asked, a scowl distorting his features.

Langston shrugged. "I've heard what you had to say. I just don't happen to agree." He gave Serra a confident hug, as if he figured the subject closed.

"You know, Langston, if I don't like the way you treat this child, I have the power to take her away." The doctor reached out and clamped Serra's wrists. It was as if he shackled her with his cold, biting strength.

She caught her breath and held it for so long it pained her. From somewhere deep inside her, a terrible panic erupted in her chilled veins.

"Just what are you suggestin', Chelsey?" Langston demanded in a low, even voice, his arm tightening protectively about her shoulders. But Serra suspected even that wouldn't be enough to protect her from Chelsey's powers.

Fumbling with his coat, the physician pulled out a scrolled paper from an inner breast pocket and waved it in the air. "This, I am her legal guardian, or have you forgotten that? And no one, not even you," he declared, shoving the document under her father's nose, "can take that away from me. I want Mr. Ramsey out of here now," he ordered, "or Serenity will be going back to New Hope with me."

The earth began to shake beneath her . . . or was it that she trembled? Serra couldn't be certain. Oh, God, she had spoken too soon, been too confident. Dr. Chelsey was more than capable of flipping her world upside down and taking away everything she found important — her home, her family, Ty.

For a fleeting moment she had freed herself from Chelsey's influence over her, had discovered she was quite capable of making decisions for herself, and had liked this new inner strength she had found. But now it looked as if he was the stronger after all. There was nothing she could do to keep him from tearing her world asunder. Nothing.

Or was there?

Her heart picked up speed, like a mighty steed discovering the feel of independence. Whirling in place, she jerked her arm from Chelsey's grip and faced him like a young lioness flexing its claws. "No. You can't force me to do anything or go anywhere if I don't wish to, ever again," she announced quietly.

With that, she rushed out of the room and down the hallway to the bottom of the stairs. Picking up her skirts, she gathered her aplomb, knowing exactly what her next move must be.

Chapter Nine

Ty entered Langston Mining and Smelting Company sporting a full-fledged chip on his shoulder. Although they shot him secretive looks, not one person uttered a word as he plowed through the front office, not even Mr. Murrow, sitting mouselike near the rear of the building, his stacks of papers neatly arranged on his desk as usual, his balding head coated with a sheen of perspiration that he ever actively swiped at with the handkerchief he kept in his breast pocket for just that purpose.

Fingering the cut in the corner of his mouth as he zigzagged his way to the rear of the building, Ty knew what the employees — all of them — were thinking. The "old man" had been at it again, and he had taken the brunt of Langston's renowned anger. Well, let them think what they would, as long as they held their silence.

For the last two years he had run Langston Mining, for the most part, the "old man" rarely showing up except on token occasions, and Ty figured he'd done a damn fine job of it.

Reaching his own office, tucked away in a separate room at the back of the building, Ty stripped off his coat, revealing his shirt with the sleeves already rolled up, ready to delve into the mounds of work he knew awaited him. Not that he particularly enjoyed office work. He much preferred the freedom of the mines and the smelters, but he had plans . . . grand plans to expand the already-profitable company. Sitting down at the desk, which overflowed with paperwork, he opened the report books to check productions during his short time away.

"Excuse me, Mr. Ramsey."

"Yes." Ty glanced up, acknowledging Mr. Murrow, his secretary.

"There's some correspondence here I think you need to be made aware of." The older man took out his handkerchief and mopped the top of his head.

Ty signaled the employee to enter, sitting back in his chair and lacing his hands across his stomach, ready to listen to what Murrow had to say.

The secretary shuffled his papers as if organizing them, then cleared his throat. "One of the miners, a Jack Handley," he said, glancing at a notebook, "apparently suffered an injury in tunnel number twelve."

"Is he back on the job?" Ty asked matter-of-factly.

"Well, no, sir. It seems he broke his leg," Murrow answered.

"Was it his fault or ours?" Ty hunched forward, planting his elbows on the desktop.

Murrow studied his report. "Apparently, Mr. Handley was inebriated at the time and tripped over a car rail."

"Then dock his pay until he can return to work," Ty ordered with Solomon-like ease. "And warn him if he's ever caught drinkin' on the job again, it will be his last day."

"Yes, sir, already seen to," Murrow replied.

"Then what's the problem?"

Murrow wiped his hairless pate again. "He has a wife and a passel of small children, Mr. Ramsey."

"I see." Tyler sat back once more. He was not one to allow guiltless women and children to starve because of the stupidity of another. But, then, Mr. Murrow knew that, and he could tell from the look on the little man's face that he expected a fair judgment. "See to it groceries are taken to Handley's missus once a week. And rent money if she needs it, but I don't want Handley using it up on drink. He needs to learn a lesson. Is that understood?"

"Yes, sir," Murrow said with a nod, apparently satisfied with Ty's generosity. "Thank you, sir."

"What else?" Ty laced his fingers on the desk in front of him and waited, knowing the secretary would have more.

Murrow handed him a stack of correspondence. "I think the top one will interest you the most."

Ty read the letter, and his heart quickened. At last. He'd been waiting more than four months for this news . . . waiting long before this situation with Serenity Langston's supposed return. Earlier, he would have been ecstatic over the letter's contents, but now . . . he wasn't so sure.

How quickly priorities change.

"Who else knows about this?" Ty asked the other man.

Mr. Murrow's perplexity was obvious, but he answered, "Nobody."

"Not even Mr. Langston?"

"No, sir. I figured you would want to see it first."

Ty knew he could trust the secretary's vow of discretion. Taking the letter and folding it up, he slipped the envelope into the breast pocket of his shirt. "Thank you, Mr. Murrow," he said in a tone of dismissal.

The secretary backed toward the door but hesitated to leave. "Is everything all right, sir?"

Ty wanted to shout, Hell yes, everything is all right if one took into account that his life had gone to the devil in a hand basket. Nothing he'd taken for granted for so long was viable anymore—the state of his future, his fortune, and his heart. But instead, he gave the other man a steady look.

"Everything's fine, Mr. Murrow. Just keep up your good work," he said, patting his pocket for emphasis, "and continue to keep this information to yourself."

The moment he was alone, Ty slipped the letter from his pocket to read it again. So, at last it had happened. A superior method of extracting zinc from the useless, discarded jack taken from the lead mines, and he was being given the first opportunity to acquire the know-how.

A man could make a fortune setting up the proper smelting facilities and buying up the discarded jack for practically nothing. His own fortune. Not John Langston's. In fact, he could make them all sit up and take notice—Moffett, Granby, Murphy, his competitors who were unaware of the newest technology. Ty smiled to himself. This could rate right up there with any bank job the James boys had ever pulled off.

Then he frowned with deep-rooted concern. This opportunity belonged to him, didn't it? He had found it; he had the right to claim it for himself.

Ty dropped his face into his open hands, torn in his decision.

Serra threw on an appropriate outfit—a simple muslin skirt and jacket, with a plain high-collared cot-

144

ton blouse that stopped just under her chin—and located the sturdiest shoes in the wardrobe. She must track Ty down and confront him, make him see how wrong he was in the way he treated her . . . treated all of them. Make him realize she was no threat to his security. Make him accept how she felt about him.

She loved him. God help her. Heart, body, and soul. And she supposed she'd felt that way since their days together at the orphanage, only she'd been too young and immature to understand her emotions.

But now. That day together in the isolated stone cabin had changed all of that. It needn't be a contest between them.

Racing back down the stairs, she headed out the rear to the carriage house, tying the ribbons of a leghorn straw bonnet beneath her chin. She was Serenity Langston. The servants would deny her nothing, especially if she demanded it.

Swallowing down the trepidation, she quickened her steps. She could make demands. She could if the need arose.

By the time she reached the outbuildings, she had her apprehensions under control. Pulling herself up to look as haughty as she could, she demanded of the first person she saw, "I would like a vehicle. Now." She studied the stableman and read the reservation in his eyes. "Please," she added, hoping he would respond favorably and not find reason to doubt her authority.

For a moment the man held her in a staring match, then he finally conceded, "I suppose you could handle the lightweight trap."

Fifteen minutes later—fifteen minutes that seemed more like an hour to Serra—the servant brought around a two-wheeled carriage. He handed her into the seat and draped the reins into her gloved fingers.

Serra stared down at them. Dear God, she had never driven a carriage before and had no idea what to do.

The stableman reached up and released the brake beside her boot heel. "Don't forget to set it when you get where you're goin'," he instructed.

With a nod, she tentatively snapped the reins across the horse's back and clicked at it the way she had seen Dr. Chelsey and her father do before. The carriage jerked forward and they were off, rolling down the drive to the street.

That's when Serra realized she had no idea which way to go, but she was not about to turn around and ask directions from the stablehand now; he might hesitate to let her go again. She would simply have to inquire along the way how to get to the Langston Mining offices, where she was confident she would find Ty.

Fortunately, the stableman had chosen her horse wisely. Serra managed to bring the trap to a stop at a busy intersection in the middle of town so she could ask directions. Then they were wheeling down the street, the little mare trotting along, bobbing her head as she snorted, and before long Serra was having the best of times.

Several people nodded her way, men doffing their hats when they recognized the Langston trap. One couple she passed even lifted their hands and called out, "Welcome home, Miss Serenity."

Thrilled by her acceptance in the community, she gaily waved back, feeling most daring when she handled the reins with only one hand.

But once she reached her destination, her heart began to hammer against her chest and she wasn't so sure of herself anymore. What if Ty refused to see

146

her? What if he made a scene or treated her with spitefulness? Perhaps she shouldn't have come here but instead waited to confront him at home.

No. No. It was important that she make him understand about Dr. Chelsey. The physician meant no harm; he was just trying to protect her the only way he knew how.

She stopped the trap on the side of the road and, not knowing what else to do, left the reins dangling over the footboard in front of her. The horse stood quietly, so she felt confident it would go nowhere. Scrambling down from the high seat as best as she could, she grabbed her reticule in her gloved hand and patted the animal's forelock as she passed in front of it.

"Stay here," she instructed the placid mare, regathering up her skirts and moving hesitantly toward the entrance of the nondescript building with the plain hand-lettered sign on the front proclaiming Langston Mining and Smelting Company.

She stared at the name Langston for one long moment. "Langston," she whispered almost reverently. Then she entered the front doors, confident that she belonged there, the sign itself declaring she had every right to enter. Every right.

Several men occupied partitioned cubicles, their desks dwarfed by the stacks of paperwork cluttering their surfaces. At first no one seemed to notice her, or if they did, they didn't acknowledge her arrival. Then as she began to draw her gloves from her fingers, a balding little man emerged from the rear of the building, mopping at his hairless skull. Her very presence appeared to confuse him.

"Y—yes, m—miss?" he stuttered his questioning greeting.

147

Serra twisted her fingers in the strings of her reticule. "Mr. Ramsey," she blurted out with a great rush of air. "I would like to see Mr. Tyler Ramsey."

The man frowned. "Is Mr. Ramsey expecting you?"

The last thing she suspected Ty expected was to see her. "No, but tell him Miss Langston is here."

"M—m—miss Lang—ston?" he repeated, his gaze sliding up and down her with bulging-eyed surprise. "Miss Serenity?"

She gave a stiff nod and he was off like a stray bullet, weaving a comical course back the way he had come.

Serra glanced about uncomfortably, wondering how long she would have to stand there. Would the little man come back and tell her Ty refused to see her? Would Ty confront her and demand that she leave?

She glanced down at her hands, realizing she had twisted the strings of her purse so tight about her forefinger that it was numb. Unwinding them, she contemplated the red marks and puckers on the column of her finger, trying hard to ignore the underlying buzz of voices in the office, which grew steadily louder, and the sly, darting stares directed her way.

Then just as quickly as the sounds had begun, they abruptly ended. Serra lifted her chin, and that's when she saw him striding toward her in those long, confident steps—the Ty of her youth, the ominous stranger in black, the gentle, patient lover, the belligerent opponent . . . all of those personalities rolled into a single entity.

Swallowing so hard the knot of apprehension stuck in her windpipe, Serra clutched her throat as if trying to hold back the confusion, the welling emotions, the need to turn and run before Ty reached her. But like a frightened deer caught in the beam of a jacklight, she

148

held her ground, swaying toward him then away from him, her amber eyes unable to tear away from the deep blue penetration of his as her lungs sawed in and out.

Then he was upon her, towering over her, so tall she had to tilt her head back to maintain the eye contact. Was he angry? Was he glad to see her? His face revealed not one emotion, good or bad, as he stood there, staring down at her. Would he never stop looking at her so? She knew she would never get enough of watching him.

"Ty," she choked.

As if her simple utterance unleashed a floodgate, his face became animated, his brows furrowing, his eyes narrowing, his mouth — his beautiful, giving mouth — sloping downward. "What are you doin' here, Serra?" he demanded.

A terrible pain banded her arm just above her elbow, and she glanced down to see his fingers, white knuckled and strong — memorably so — digging into her tender flesh. Then he was pulling her along, past the bald man standing there mopping his head, his lower jaw dropped as if in shock, past the other occupants of the room who now stared in unabashed curiosity.

Where was he taking her? Panic whipped her pulse into a raging storm and she began to struggle, her gloves forgotten and dropped along the way, her reticule bouncing between them like a ball, hitting against her thigh and then his.

But her paltry resistance didn't slow him down — not one bit. He dragged her into a room and slammed the door before she had barely cleared the threshold. Then forcing her back against the hard, unyielding slab, he pinioned her between his arms, the flats of his palms slapping against the barrier as if to emphasize the fact that he was angry, yet in control.

"Tell me, Serra. Come to stake your claim on Langston Mining?"

If she could, she would have shrunk against the door, but try as she might, there was nowhere to go, no way to escape his warm breath skimming over the flesh of her face like skippers over the still waters of a pond, the smell of him so manly, the heat of his body radiating through her.

"No, Ty, it's not like that," she tried desperately to explain.

His gaze raked insolently over her—over her stomach that fluttered with a hodgepodge of emotions, over her breasts she couldn't keep from rising and falling no matter how hard she tried to control the movement, along the column of her neck to lips so dry she felt the need to moisten them. But she didn't dare make such a move; he might make more of the gesture than she'd intended.

From the corner of her eye, she saw his elbows begin to bend and knew he was inching toward her, crowding her, bullying her with a show of his superior strength.

She gasped, her tongue darting out before she could stop it, swiping at dry lips in a movement as automatic as blinking. Though she angled her face away, he pressed closer, his hips hot and pulsing against hers even through the many layers of petticoats. Then he hunched forward, towering over her as if staking his claim, his broad shoulder filling her line of vision, all dominating male.

He held her pinned that way, his hand reaching down to trap her unwilling chin in his strong grasp. Forcing her face back around, he stared at her, his mouth so near that had she leaned into him even slightly, their lips would have touched.

"Here, Serra," he said, his moving mouth all that she could focus on, "I'm in charge. And I'll be damned if I'll let you change that."

As quickly as he'd pressed against her, he stepped back, leaving her feeling naked and exposed. Had the door not been behind her lending support, she would have crumpled to her knees. Oh, God, though she didn't want to admit it, she missed his warmth, and though she tried to deny it, she wanted to reach out and beckon him return, wanted him to sweep her up into his arms and kiss her.

Crazily, her gaze darted about the room, as if the answer to this unexplained insanity that gripped her lurked out there somewhere. "All I want is a chance to talk with you, Ty," she choked, the lie somehow managing to stabilize the spinning world about her.

"Talk's cheap," Ty snapped, his blue eyes narrowing with suspicion. He leaned against the desk, perching one hip on the edge, his arms crossing over his chest. "So talk," he insisted.

All of the carefully phrased explanations she had invented on the ride over deserted her, vanishing like phantoms to the morning light. The only words that remained were "I love you," but with the contemptuous way he eyed her, she knew that if she expressed her deepest feelings, it would be for naught. He would never accept such a confession in the spirit it was given, not Ty. He would instantly doubt her motives.

"I don't want to take away anything that belongs to you. I didn't realize until this morning just what you mean to my father."

He snorted his disbelief. "Just what do you think I

mean to John Langston?" Still, he refused to acknowledge the truth of her identity.

Remembering how Langston had followed Ty's exit from the dining room with caring eyes, she allowed a small, hopeful smile to bow her lips. "Why, it's quite obvious he cares for you very much." If she didn't dare reveal to him her own feelings, she could point out how others felt.

"Yeah," Ty snickered derisively. "He cares so much, he's willin' to listen to the lies of that old charlatan Chelsey. Tell me"—his cold blue gaze flicked over her again, assessing and apparently finding her wanting—"did he agree to kick me out of the house?"

Serra caught her breath in surprise. Ty must have witnessed the terrible scene between her father and her guardian. "Oh, Ty," she pleaded. "You shouldn't judge the doctor so unkindly. He doesn't mean any harm. All he's trying to do is protect me the only way he knows how. I don't want to leave, Ty."

Pushing off his perch on the desktop, Ty spun away.

Serra reached out and grasped his arm before he could go too far. "But it is not my intention to cause you to be sent away, either. Can't you see there's room for both of us?"

He glared down at her restraining hand, but he didn't pull away. Staring at the chiseled profile of the face she dearly loved, Serra was only too grateful for even so small a concession.

"Woman, you're a fool if you honestly think that." He whirled about to confront her. "I'm not like some buzzard skirtin' about the edges, willin' to snatch any tidbits overlooked by the wolves."

"Are you saying I want it all?"

"Don't you? Isn't that why you came here in the first place . . . to lay claim to the Langston name?"

"The name, yes, Ty, but not the rest . . . not the money." She swept her arm in a wide arc of denial. "Nor this mine. I wasn't even aware of all this until this morning. You can have it," she exclaimed, thinking to call an end to the conflict here and now.

Apparently, Ty didn't see it that way. His lip curled in a snarl, his teeth clamping together so hard she could hear the sound of them grinding.

"So it's yours to so generously give away, is it, Miss Langston?"

"No," she retorted in frustration. But then confusion set in, and she pressed her fingers to her temples. Did such a disavowal negate her claim to the Langston name in his eyes? Did it amuse him to see her so flustered?

"Yes," she changed her declaration, notching her chin. Oh, why did he try to twist her up? Why must he be so damn bullheaded? "Does it matter?" she cried in frustration.

"Yes, Serra, it matters. To me, to John Langston, and especially to your dear Dr. Chelsey."

"He's only trying to protect my interests, Ty. Can't you see that?"

"Protect yours or his own?"

Serra blinked and drew back, unable to understand just what he meant by such a blatant accusation. "Just what are you insinuating?" she demanded angrily.

For the longest time, he simply stared at her. A kaleidoscope of emotions moved across his face—righteousness, betrayal, helplessness, and finally resignation. "Nothin', Serra. It didn't mean a damn thing."

"Ty," she whispered, stepping toward him, seeking reconciliation.

He lifted his hands in the age-old sign, indicating

153

she should halt. "Just go home, Serra," he ordered softly.

Home? Did he mean return to the Langston mansion, or for her to go back to New Hope? Serra couldn't be sure, but regardless of his intentions, she couldn't let it lie between them like this. Ignoring the barrier his raised palms created, she rushed forward, brushing past his hands to press herself against his chest. "Ty, please," she pleaded. "Try to understand."

At first he held his arms out stiffly, refusing to allow them to drop against her shoulders. But finally he lost the battle raging within his soul and he draped his arms about her back, drawing them tightly around her. "I do understand, Serra. God knows only too well."

She tilted her head to look up at him, hoping beyond hope that he might . . .

His mouth descended, molding against her lips with a gentleness that made the strings of her heart sing like the finest Stradivarius. Pushing up to stand on the tips of her toes, she threw her arms about his neck, so willing, so eager to let him know how his caresses stirred her, how much his surrender meant to her.

Deepening the kiss on her own initiative, she opened her mouth beneath his, her tongue darting out in invitation, one he made no attempt to resist. His tongue dipped, exploring, soft and exciting. Then his hand moved up to grasp the leghorn nestled in her flame-colored hair, and he gave it a gentle tug.

The hat pins pulled at her scalp, but the pain seemed incidental to the pleasure washing over her. At last the bonnet tore free, and her hair tumbled down her back like copper filigree. His fingers weaved into the mass, clutching, almost desperately, forcing her head back, revealing the column of her neck in open vulnerability.

His lips lay claim to her convulsing throat, the familiar brush of his beard sending a shudder coursing through her. The idea that she might resist never crossed her mind. Instead, she clung to his shoulders, her head thrown back, offering up the vital pulse in complete trust.

There was remembered gentleness in his roving mouth, yet a familiar urgency in the way he gripped her, in his groans of excitement laced with despair as he worked his way to the high collar of her blouse. Releasing her hair, his hand fumbled with the trio of buttons that held the band primly about her throat. Then he pushed the material aside to press his kisses on her exposed flesh.

But still it wasn't enough. His hand trembled as his fingers grasped the fasteners on her bodice.

She should stop him here in this public place. Someone could walk in and find them so compromised. His fingers freed the first one, and his lips brushed against her exposed collarbone, warm and wet. She would enjoy only this little bit, she relented with a sigh, but no more.

Yet when he tackled the next button, she found herself reasserting her determination to call a halt to this madness, with the same results. Only this one, no farther, she compromised with her thundering heart. His mouth caressed the beginning swell of her breast, his swirling tongue causing gooseflesh to thrill across her chest.

Just one more. Then she *would* stop him, she vowed, closing her eyes in order to savor the momentary pleasure. The third button gave way, along with the bow at the top of her chemise. Then his hand was inside her clothing, covering her breast, the palm

155

warm and soothing to her swollen nipple, which was puckered so hard that it ached.

"This is wrong," she at last managed to stammer aloud, unable to open her eyes or lift her head, unwilling to push him away.

"I warned you, Serra, didn't I? I told you to go home, but you just wouldn't listen." Round and round his palm massaged the hardened nodule of delight, stirring the ache inside her as if it were waves radiating from a pebble tossed into a pond. Bigger and bigger her need grew, until it encompassed all of her, mind and body . . . moral resolve.

Her knees trembled and she felt herself slipping, but Ty held her upright with one strong arm, his exploration never faltering.

Floundering in the feelings he ignited, she gave up the pretense of being in control of the situation. She would do whatever he wanted, wherever he wanted, for as long as he wanted. Arching her back, she groaned, knowing herself lost and wanton, a woman with no moral backbone — at least not when it came to Tyler Ramsey.

Even when he brushed aside the stacks of papers littering his desk and draped her across the cleared surface, she looked up at him in trust. If this was how he really wanted it to be, then she would agree. Yet as she lay there, the front of her blouse gaping open, the exposed swells of her breasts rising and falling against his warm palm, Ty suddenly paused and stared down at her, at the way she arched against his hand, and he frowned.

Her heart caught in her throat, stifling the unrestrained moans of enjoyment she made. For some reason she couldn't comprehend, she didn't please him.

"Oh, Ty," she murmured, closing her eyes, thinking

to make right whatever was wrong. "Don't you realize I would give you my all just for the asking?"

Her whispered confession hung potent in the silence between them. Then to her utter surprise, Ty's hand hastily withdrew from her clothing, and the next thing she realized, he was fumbling with the ribbon of her underclothing, attempting to reconstruct the bow she had tied earlier that morning.

"Ty?" she questioned his unexpected actions, her eyes flying open, her hand moving up to cover his.

"Be quiet, Serra," he muttered, finishing a lopsided bow and concentrating on the buttons that seemed incapable of reaching their fasteners. The minute he completed the difficult task of restoring her modesty, he scooped up her discarded hat and reticule from the floor and pressed them into her hands as she sat up.

Tears of embarrassment welled behind her eyes. It was only too obvious he had changed his mind about wanting her. When her bottom lip began to tremble, she snagged it with her teeth, refusing to let him see her disappointment, her weakness in the face of his rejection. Snatching the accessories from his grip, she stood and made a move to push by him without saying a word.

But that he wouldn't allow. Catching her by the shoulder, he cupped her chin in his fingers, gently yet firmly.

"You were right, Serra. This is not the time nor the place—not with us. Now go home before I change my mind and do something we might both regret."

She rushed from the confinement of his office, finding more privacy in the crowded outer room, even though her face was flushed, her hair falling in loose ringlets about her shoulders, her hat and purse clutched to her chest where the buttons of her bodice sat askew. At the moment, she cared less what the employees of Langston Mining thought of her. Only Ty's opinion mattered.

All she wanted to do was escape the building, climb back into the carriage, and get home as fast as she could. Once there, she could crawl into bed and hide the shame and humiliation crimsoning her face beneath a pillow. How could she have been such a fool to venture out like this in the first place? Why had she thought she might resolve things between herself and Ty? All she had managed to do was make matters worse. No doubt, now he thought of her as just another loose woman.

Reaching the outside, she paused on the front steps and glanced about, blinking like a confused owl. She could swear she had left the horse and trap right here in front of the building.

But the vehicle was nowhere to be seen. As much as she dreaded the prospect, she had no choice but to go back inside the mining office and ask one of those gawking men if they knew what had become of her vehicle.

Muttering her malcontent, she spun about and crashed into something as solid as a wall.

"Lose somethin', Serra?"

Her gaze climbed upward and met with blue-eyed sarcasm. *Yes,* she wanted to shout. *I've lost plenty. My heart, apparently my mind, and now it seems I've most certainly lost the last of my faculties.* "My carriage seems to be missing," she replied in a voice so calm she prayed he wouldn't suspect how upset she was.

Ty stepped out onto the stoop with her and took a long look around. "Perhaps the driver merely took the carriage around the block," he surmised. "He'll be right back."

"I didn't have a driver," she explained.

"No driver? You mean John turned you loose on your own?" Ty looked at her dubiously, one brow lifting in surprise.

"Well, not exactly. I took it upon myself to arrange a vehicle." Discovering that she was leaning toward him, ready to confess how desperate she had been to track him down, she straightened, attempting to look as dignified as she could under the circumstances. "I see no reason to explain my actions to you."

His eyes narrowed at her flippant remark, but he said nothing as he knelt at the edge of the road and seemed to contemplate the dust. But when he rose, he clutched her by the arm unexpectedly and started walking away from the building, down the street, forcing her to go with him. "Tell me, Serra, do you do much drivin' about on your own?"

So he thought to find further moral fault with her actions, did he? Well, she'd show him. "Often enough," she lied, jutting out her chin in haughty determination to prove she cared less what he thought about her. "Dr. Chelsey gave me access to his buggy anytime I wanted it. Anytime," she stressed, stumbling over a rock in the road. Ty didn't pause but just jerked her along, forcing her to match his longer strides.

Down the hill and around a corner they went, Serra practically running alongside him in order to keep up.

"All the time, you say?"

"Yes, whenever I wanted," she declared once more.

"Then if you're so damned experienced," he asked, stopping in the middle of the road to face her, "how come you forgot to set the brake?" He lifted his free hand and, like a cigar store wooden Indian, pointed down the street.

Serra's amber gaze followed his finger, and her face

turned a shade of deep scarlet. Just ahead she saw the trap moving aimlessly alongside the road, the little mare grazing on clumps of quack grass. Finally, the animal came to a halt before a flower bed, and snagging giant bites of daisies, it chewed contentedly as a crowd gathered to watch the spectacle.

"Set the brake?" she mouthed slowly. Her pride plummeted to the bottom of her stomach. How could she have forgotten something so fundamental? The stablehand had even reminded her of the necessity, but in her haste to confront Ty, the last minute directions had simply slipped her mind.

He would know that she had lied to him about her driving experience and would probably use that knowledge to assert she did the same about everything else. Well, at the moment, there wasn't much she could do to alter his opinion.

Stiffening her spine to stand as tall as she could, she marched down the small incline, ignoring the titters of amusement about her, refusing to look back and see Ty laughing at her as well.

Bending, she grabbed the bridle straps along side the horse's head and gave them a jerk, forcing the animal to abandon its late morning snack. Then she headed the mare in the direction of home, not trusting her abilities to turn the vehicle about once aboard. Tossing her paraphernalia onto the seat, she climbed into the trap, all to the gathered crowd's entertainment. With a lift of her arms, she snapped the reins over the horse's back and they started up the hill, headed directly toward Ty who stood in the middle of the lane.

You had better move, Tyler Ramsey, or I swear I'll happily run you down, she railed inwardly when he acted as if he had no intention of getting out of her way. Then at the last moment, he stepped to the side of the road, allowing the vehicle to pass.

"Good day, Miss Langston," he called, doffing his black felt hat as she whizzed by. His laughter followed her clear to the top of the hill and down the other side.

"Ya-ah," she cried, snapping the reins once more along the little mare's sweating spine. Racing back to the Langston mansion, she made a vow. Somehow, someway, she would rub Tyler Ramsey's nose in humiliation. Then she would laugh as he choked on his slice of humble pie, just as he had at her.

Chapter Ten

Ty watched her go, hell-for-leather, the little trap careening to one side as it crested the next hill. The cocky grin that creased his face faded. His hand, still resting on the brim of his hat, pushed it back off his forehead, and he scratched his hairline in total perplexity.

Women. They were so damn hard to figure out. Then he frowned, pulling his hat back into place. And it just seemed to be in their nature to lie—about everything—almost as if they couldn't help themselves. Just like poking their noses where they didn't belong. Well, he sincerely doubted *she* would come snooping around Langston Mining again.

With an unconscious effort, he slid his open hand down the side of his pant leg, trying to erase the feel of her warm, aroused breast, which still seared his palm. And though he scrubbed at his flesh, the tingle intensified, as if he'd been branded. Serra Paletot, Serenity Langston, whatever name she chose to use . . . she had left her mark on him in ways he could never forget. And even if he could, he wasn't sure he would want to.

Balling his hand into a fist, he pressed his mouth

into a grim line and spun about to face Langston Mining and Smelting. His heart might be ruled by his nether region, granted, but his mind was something altogether different.

He knew then and there what he had to do. If Tyler Ramsey was to survive this fiasco intact, then he must by necessity strike out on his own.

It was time to take a little trip to Chicago. Ramsey Smelting. Patting the breast pocket of his shirt, which still held the letter he had received that day, he smiled to himself. The name had a damn fine ring to it.

Once back at the mansion, Serra scrambled down from the seat of the trap and turned the vehicle over to the stableman with relief.

"How was your outin', miss?" he asked.

Serra merely nodded and rushed from the carriage house, only too glad to get away. It wouldn't bother her one bit if she never again took reins in hand . . . if she never had to come face to face with that irascible Tyler Ramsey.

Gathering up her skirts, she hurried back into the house with a determination contrary to the one she had left with earlier that morning. But her plans to escape and bury her head under the pillows of her bedding were not to be.

"There you are, Serenity, dear." Dr. Chelsey spoke loudly, dramatically. Then he clasped her by the arm and, taking in her disheveled appearance, hissed in her ear so only she could hear, "Where have you been? Your father has been concerned about your apparent willfulness for the last hour. He was ready to organize a search party."

Serra's face reddened, remembering how just a

short while before she had been sprawled across an of-fice desk, wantonly wiggling beneath Ty's caresses. She could just imagine her father again barging in on such a compromising scene between them. At the mo-ment, she was only too glad Ty had changed his mind about wanting her, even if the thought still rankled deep inside. "I went for a drive."

"A drive?" Doc rolled his dark eyes. "Dumpling, you must be very careful. Otherwise, you might call un-due attention to your behavior. Serenity Langston," he whispered, "would never do something so . . . socially unseemly as to disappear without letting someone know beforehand where she was going."

Serra cocked her head and stared at the physician strangely. *Just what does he mean by that? I am Serenity Langston, and whatever I do is exactly what she would do,* she wanted to retort in her own defense, feeling as if Doc was suddenly deserting her and she had no one to believe in her anymore. Surely he didn't doubt her identity, did he? "I'm sorry," she murmured, thor-oughly shaken by such a frightening possibility.

He shook his head as if her admission of guilt wasn't enough. "You know, I won't always be here to guide you, child. In fact, I must head back to New Hope tomorrow."

"So soon?"

"Not to worry, dumpling. Now that that terrible Mr. Ramsey will be leaving, you will have no trouble mak-ing John Langston depend upon you. You just have to stand up and claim what rightfully belongs to us . . . to you."

Serra forced her feet to a standstill. Her father couldn't have agreed to send Ty away. Why would he do that? She had thought him strong enough to never succumb to Doc's ridiculous demands. Grappling with

Chelsey's fingers, which dug painfully into her upper arm, she refused to meekly allow this to happen. Why did Chelsey feel so threatened by the younger man's presence? Ty had never tried to claim the Langston name, and that was all she wanted — the name, together with the love and security that came with it. "You mustn't make him leave," she exclaimed, still struggling to escape.

Doc paused in the front hallway and turned to stare at her, gripping her arm tighter than ever. "Why not? He's constantly challenging *your* claim, trying to make *you* — and me as well — look bad in your father's eyes."

"That might be true, but the legitimacy of my identity can withstand a challenge . . . can't it?" For one fleeting moment, she remembered the way Ty had repeatedly studied her with disbelief and disgust, as if he knew something she didn't. She pulled away from Chelsey's grip, pressing the flats of her hands against her temples to alleviate the unsettling questions pounding in her head. No. No. She must never doubt herself. There were the childhood memories . . . so clear. And the way her father looked at her. He believed in her; she could do no less.

"Calm yourself, Serra," the doctor ordered. "If you just remember everything I've taught you over the years, you'll do fine."

Of course, she would. Why think otherwise? Forcing her pulse to slow down and her mind to think calmly, she gnawed at her bottom lip. Then the tinkling of feminine laughter trickled into her jumbled thoughts. Serra raised her head in curiosity and alarm. "Who is that?" she asked, as if she feared it might be someone else come to deny her her rights.

Chelsey patted her hand in reassurance and clucked his tongue upon seeing her so rattled. "Why, Serenity, dear, nothing to be alarm about. You have guests. The Stokes—your neighbors, remember?—have come to call and welcome you home." His soothing words washed over her like the calming waters of a gently running brook, sweeping way the momentary doubts and fears that had gripped her. He believed in her . . . of course, he did. Why would it be otherwise?

With relief, she flashed him a smile, glad that the situation was returning to the way it should be between her and her mentor. She would miss him once he left, but he was right. The time had come for her to settle into her home and family. Just as they had prepared for over the years. And as far as Tyler Ramsey, she assured herself, she would talk to her father later in private, before Ty had a chance to get home, and make Langston see it was wrong to send him away. His unfounded threats and innuendos were best ignored. With time they would cease, and Ty would come to accept her. Just as her father had suggested earlier.

Confused by her defense of Ty to others, she tried to make sense of her conflicting emotions. After the way he had ridiculed her and her rightful claim to the Langston name, why should she care what happened to him? Then her eyes narrowed with conviction. If he were gone, how could she extract her justified revenge?

But her formulating plans to make Tyler Ramsey pay for his insolence must wait. At the moment, she had guests to receive, her very first since arriving in Joplin. Excitement laced with apprehension fluttered her pulse, and she smoothed out the wrinkles in her skirt, wishing her outfit was something a bit more showy. Her fingers jumped to the cascading curls that fell about her face in a coppery mass. If only she had time to smooth down her hair. Forcing her hands down to her sides, she pushed back her shoulders. Regardless of Dr. Chelsey's warning about watching her step, she was Serenity Langston, and no one but Tyler Ramsey would dare criticize her actions.

Placing her bonnet and reticule in the waiting hands of the butler, who miraculously appeared as if on cue, she sneaked a quick glance in the foyer mirror as she passed it by, entering the front parlor with the practiced grace of royalty.

Her father rose to greet her, beaming with pride as he took her by the elbow and led her toward the sofa where a young man and woman sat. The man stood as protocol demanded, tall and handsome in a refined sort of way, his blond hair slicked back to perfection, his face clean-shaven except for his stylist mutton-chops. Nothing like Ty, with his dark brooding appeal. And though this man's eyes were blue, they were washed out compared to Ty's cobalt ones.

Yet when he smiled, her pulse quickened unexpectedly, realizing the greeting was meant only for her as he studied her intently. Before Ty, she had never interacted with many young men, Doc having said she had more important matters to attend to. And Serra had never argued, never having had a desire to experience the wonders of courtship.

But now . . .

She flashed this young Mr. Stokes a most engaging smile of her own. Her finest one, she hoped, realizing her lashes fluttered with a natural coyness she'd never known she possessed, her pulse with a heretofore unknown giddiness that made her feel like an innocent schoolgirl.

"Serenity, dear," her father spoke up. "May I present Miss Amanda Stokes and her brother, Monte."

"Mr. Stokes," she acknowledged the staring young man, then with a calculated tilt of her head that she hoped made her look to her best advantage, she turned to the woman.

If she had thought Monte Stokes stylish, then she wasn't prepared for his sister, Amanda. The young woman, who couldn't have been more than a year or two older than herself, looked as if she'd stepped out of a fashion plate from *Harper's Bazaar*.

There was nothing girlish about the way she was dressed, her angel-blond hair swept up and crowned with a confection of feathers and ribbons that would make any woman's mouth water. And even though she was sitting, the blue poplin of her skirts that matched her eyes to perfection spilled across the patterned roses of the damask couch, Serra could tell she possessed the tiniest waist below the loveliest expanse of feminine bosom she had ever seen. Wasp-waisted, the magazines called them. She had read about such lucky females, and she felt frumpy and downright plump in comparison. But she hid her lack of confidence, as well as what she supposed was a touch of envy, behind a gracious smile.

"Miss Stokes," she said with a dignified nod, wishing now more than ever that she had changed her wrinkled clothing before receiving her guests.

"Amanda, please," the woman replied, reaching out her ungloved hand to accept a cup of tea from Serra in a gesture of friendship. "And may I call you Serenity?"

Serra smiled, warming to the beautiful young woman. "Serra," she gushed, sensing Amanda's kind nature beneath her perfect beauty. "My friends and family call me Serra."

"Then Serra it shall be." Amanda laughed, that same soft, feminine tinkle of amusement Serra had

168

heard earlier from the hallway. "And if I'm permitted to call you by your nickname, you must reciprocate. Call me Mandy, but only in private," she warned, shooting her handsome sibling a squelching but loving look. "If that's your preference as well, Serra, you had better inform my brother now. He has this exasperating habit of saying the wrong thing at the most inopportune time."

Serra cast a shy, wide-eyed look at Monte Stokes, aware, almost enviously, of the friendly banter between brother and sister. "Oh, no," she replied breathlessly, blushing in confusion when she realized Monte still stared at her, "Serra is fine—anytime."

A moment of potent silence filled the room, and Serra knew that as the hostess, she should be the one to pick up the conversation, but for the life of her, she couldn't think of a single thing to say.

Her father cleared his throat and rose.

Bless you, Father, she thought, shooting him a grateful glance, to find that he was smiling at her in a most inane way.

"Come, Monte, Dr. Chelsey. I think we should leave the ladies to get better acquainted."

"By all means. I think brandy might even be in order, wouldn't you say, John?" the physician answered, his smile sparkling with the same pleasure as her father's. It was as if the two of them enjoyed her uneasiness, her awkwardness.

"Y—yes, of course, s—sir," Monte stammered. With reluctance, he followed the older men out of the parlor, his gaze lingering on Serra up until the very last second.

The moment the two girls were alone, Amanda giggled, covering her perfect bow-shaped mouth with one hand. "I believe my dear brother is dumbstruck by your charms."

"With me?" Serra queried, turning in surprise to Amanda and pressing her hand over her heart.

"But, of course, Serra. You have such a natural innocence about you, what young man wouldn't be enamored?"

"Innocence?" Serra again flushed a color to rival her flowing tresses, remembering only too well just how her virtuousness was lacking. Thanks to Tyler Ramsey.

She took a breath and held it deep in her lungs, to keep a groan from escaping her clamped lips. For the first time, the full implications of her situation, of what she'd done without considering the consequences, struck her. It would be accepted, expected, that Serenity Langston be a woman of moral fiber and unsullied virtue. A sickening feeling balled in the pit of her stomach. What would someone like Monte Stokes think if he only knew the truth? And Amanda? she worried, casting a sidelong glance at her smiling guest. Would she shun their budding friendship if she were to discover that Serra was a fallen woman?

"But, of course, you silly goose," Amanda answered.

For one frightening moment, Serra just knew the girl had read her thoughts.

" 'Tis an unmarried woman's most important asset, and you display it so well," Amanda continued, situating herself on the sofa so she could pat the seat beside her. "Come, you must share with me all of your experiences since your disappearance." She leaned forward, taking Serra's hand, encouraging her to join her on the cushion. "You must have had quite an adventure." She stared up at Serra dreamily, expectantly, so trustingly.

If only she knew the truth.

170

"I — I suppose," Serra replied, succumbing to the pressure of sitting down beside Amanda, somewhat bewildered by the other girl's enthusiasm and her interest in what she had always considered a most unexciting existence.

"I've read all the great classics — *Camille, Anna Karenina* — and once while in Chicago at the School for the Development of Young Ladies," Amanda whispered, leaning forward in a confiding manner, "I actually saw a production of Ibsen's *A Doll's House.*" She sat back as if saying, "What do you think?"

If Serra was supposed to be impressed, she wasn't. Not that she hadn't heard of the great romances of which Amanda spoke and of the great dramatist Henrik Ibsen. It was just that she had woven her young girl's dreams about the finding of her family, not about the capturing of young men's attentions. That hadn't seemed of much importance at the time. Besides, she had been waiting — foolishly, she realized now — for Ty to come back for her. There had been no need for romantic interludes. "I don't want to disappoint you, Mandy, but my days were nothing like you might imagine. Once Ty and I were separated on the orphan train . . ."

"Tyler Ramsey?" Amanda's eyes widened, melting like blue paraffin in the heat of a flame. "You knew him from before?"

Serra chewed her bottom lip. She hadn't meant to mention Ty. The comment had just slipped out — naturally. "We were only children then," she explained, trying to make light of what the other girl seemed to think was monumental.

Amanda leaned forward. "You knew him as a little boy? Tell me, Serra, what was he like then?" she pleaded prettily, clapping her hands in delight.

171

At that moment, she realized Amanda's interest was more than simple curiosity. Did Ty return the . . . attraction? Was Amanda Stokes the reason Ty had never come back for her? A full-blown streak of jealousy coursed through Serra. She had realized there were many obstacles separating her and Ty, but the possibility of another woman . . .

An image of Ty as a little boy—so young, not much more than seven or eight—flashed across her mind, so vivid, so real as he lifted his arm to allow her to crawl under the covers with him. "I remember," she began, then bit off the rest of her sentence. That was impossible. Ty had been at least eleven when she had arrived at the orphanage. She had no way of knowing what he had looked like earlier. Somehow, her mind was being most inventive. "I'm sorry, Amanda," she murmured, her heart hammering fearfully in her chest. "I don't really remember much about him."

As if the woman sensed her reluctance to talk about the past, about Ty, she rose abruptly. Just as Serra suspected, Amanda had the most perfect figure. Beautiful and most likely virtuous as well.

"I didn't mean to pry," Amanda said somewhat stiffly.

"Oh, no, you weren't prying, Mandy," Serra blurted out, grasping the other girl's arm. For the first time, someone who was her contemporary had offered a hand in companionship, and she didn't want to lose the chance to make a friend. Choking on her own lack of qualities, Serra held on tightly to Amanda's wrist to keep her fingers from showing her nervousness, her self-doubt, to hopefully prevent the other woman from leaving.

A look of understanding floated across Amanda's beautiful features, and she smiled. "I'll tell you what," she offered, reaching out to squeeze Serra's restraining hand in understanding. "We'll just forget all about Mr. Tyler Ramsey—past, present, and future. That would probably be the smartest thing any woman could do."

"It's nice to know I can be so easily dismissed."

Serra glanced up from the settee and Amanda swung about, both girls gasping to discover the subject of their conversation leaning in the parlor doorway, his hat pushed rakishly back on his head, those incredibly blue eyes giving both of them the once-over with a slow, insolent sweep.

"Ty," Serra blurted out before she could stop herself. What was he doing here now? She'd yet to find a chance to speak with her father.

"Miss Langston," he acknowledged, touching the brim of his black felt hat with his fingertips in a formal way that suggested nothing less than proper had ever passed between them, that this very morning had never occurred. Then he dismissed her just as quickly. "Miss Stokes." He studied the other woman with undeniable interest.

Feeling as if her spine had sprouted porcupine quills, Serra glanced jealously at her new friend. Was Amanda's heart pounding as viciously as her own? If the look of rapture on the blonde's beautiful face was any indication, then it was.

"Why, Mr. Ramsey," Amanda began, gathering up her aplomb and turning on the charm that Serra knew came as naturally to her as swarming did to honeybees, "how perfectly delightful to see you again."

He eyed her with what Serra interpreted as cool caution. "I'm delighted you're delighted, ma'am." Then his dancing blue gaze slid to Serra. "Are you delighted, too, Miss Langston?" he asked, his voice reeking with sarcasm.

173

After the way he had acted earlier that day, she was anything but pleased at his sudden appearance, but she smiled and sat as straight as she could on the sofa. "Delighted couldn't begin to describe how I feel, Mr. Ramsey." She glared back at him, her amber gaze refusing to be daunted by either him or his flagrant show of flippancy.

Amanda darted a glance between the two of them, but neither flinched nor uttered another word. They just smiled at each other, each refusing to be the first to look away.

Finally, one corner of Ty's mouth lifted in a silent snicker, and his hooded gaze returned to Amanda.

She had won, Serra thought deliriously, congratulating herself. Then she began to chew her bottom lip. Just what she had won by outstaring him wasn't clear. Then when his eyes raked over her once more, it became obvious she had gained absolutely nothing as far as he was concerned.

"Ladies," he stated, stepping backward and nodding his head in dismissal, "it's good to find you both doin' all right."

It was only too obvious to Serra why he was there. He felt the need to check up on her, to make sure she'd made it back to the house without incident after that fiasco at the mining office. His interest — she refused to call it concern — pleased, yet oddly enough irked her at the same time.

"Mr. Ramsey," she heard Amanda summon, echoing her own desperate desire to call him back, to demand a reason for his "interest" in her well-being — perverted or not.

Ty turned, ever so politely acknowledging Amanda's appeal. "Yes, ma'am?"

"I'm curious to know if you plan to attend the Con-

174

gregationalists' charity dance next week?" she asked on a great rush of air, leaning toward him in sanguine expectation.

Ty looked the anxious girl up and down in that manner of his that Serra knew all too well, as if he enjoyed the womanly display yet dismissed her inquiry as trivial. "To be honest, miss, I'm not much on dancin'."

Amanda laughed in a rich, attractive pitch that Serra envied so. "Oh, bosh, Mr. Ramsey, that's no reason not to take a little time for pleasure. Besides, if it's instruction you're lacking, I'd be more than pleased to teach you the latest steps."

"Your offer is temptin', Miss Stokes." He grinned, knowing just as Serra did that the intentional expression always affected females.

Amanda Stokes was no exception. Her lashes fluttered like the frantic wings of a spider-trapped moth, eagerly anticipating his acceptance of her sincere offer.

Serra rolled her eyes in disgust. Couldn't Amanda see that Ty toyed with her for his own amusement? Then she found Ty's gaze had settled on her, and they shared a private moment like so many others from their youth.

Silly female, his gaze indicated about the simpering Miss Stokes.

But Serra found herself no longer on his side—like when they were together at the orphanage. He simply trifled with another's emotions, and she didn't think it very nice, especially when she realized he was about to turn down her newly acquired friend without thought to how it might wound the girl.

"I think, Amanda," she butted in, "you'll find Mr. Ramsey has two left feet and absolutely no rhythm. It would be like trying to teach a barnyard rooster how to swim."

Ty's brow lifted at her unkind assessment of his lack of physical agility. He straightened abruptly, apparently tiring of the cat-and-mouse game he played with the unsuspecting Amanda. He jerked his hat low over his face, and if a man could imitate the growl of an angry bear, he did so quite proficiently. "Miss Langston, no doubt, is right. Besides," he continued, his cold, penetrating gaze impaling Serra like a butterfly at the mercy of a collector's straight pin, "I'll be headed for Chicago by then, anyway."

Before she could utter a single protest, the parlor door closed with a decisive click.

Chicago? That was so far away. *Ty, no,* her heart cried out. *Don't leave me again.*

For if he did, this time there would be no vows to return, whether sincere or not. She made a move as if to follow, to make him confront her.

Then the gentle pressure of Amanda's hand curved about her upper arm. "Wait," she declared.

"But," Serra protested, attempting to pull away, "you just don't understand."

"Don't I?" Amanda replied quietly.

Horrified that her inner feelings had at last been exposed, especially to someone she had only met today, Serra spun about to issue a denial. But to her surprise Amanda's face, animated with enlightenment, also held gentle compassion.

"Mandy, I'm truly sorry," she murmured, knowing the other girl harbored her own feelings for Tyler Ramsey.

"Sorry?" Amanda's laughter trilled pleasantly. "Oh, Serra, don't be a ninny. He's such a rogue. A handsome one, I'll admit, but I'm thinking . . . better you than me." Then her countenance turned serious. "He

176

means an awful lot to you, doesn't he?"

"Yes." Serra covered her betraying mouth with her hand. "No," she insisted. Then an overwhelming need to share her feelings with someone gained the upper hand. "Oh, Mandy, I can't let him get away again."

Amanda lifted one perfectly arched brow in comprehension, and she released her grip on Serra's arm. "I see. This is quite an on-going thing between the two of you."

Reluctantly, Serra nodded, guilt assaulting her under the other girl's scrutiny. Yet when she tried to open the parlor door, the blonde stopped her once more.

"You know, Serra, there are plenty of ways to snare an uncooperative maverick." As if deep in thought, she tapped the side of her mouth with one tapered finger. "If you intend to put your brand on him, it's best to make him come of his own free will."

"What do you mean, Amanda?"

Her new friend simply smiled, so deceivingly sweet yet so self-confident, that Serra wondered if the other woman was a bit more knowledgeable about men than she had first assessed.

"Trust me." Taking Serra by the hand, she led her back to the sofa. "Mr. Tyler Ramsey won't know what hit him." She giggled. "And by the time he does, it will be much too late."

Serra stared for one moment at the closed doors, then smiled to herself. What Amanda was saying sounded most tempting. With a sense of satisfaction, she followed her new friend's lead. What better revenge, she decided, than the sweet, unexpected kind?

Chapter Eleven

Sitting in the middle of Serra's big canopied bed, Amanda Stokes tucked her stockinged feet underneath her well rounded derriere and thumbed through the precious copy of *La Vie Parisienne* until she found what she was looking for.

" 'With trembling hands, your husband happily unlaces your stays with a certain clumsiness. You laugh, blushing prettily, certain that his fumbling has nothing to do with his inability to untie a knot or his inexperience, but that the sight of your tightly bound beauty, your bosom spilling forth from the lacy froth of your Enchantress corset, has put him in a state of high excitement.' " Amanda paused in her recitation and peered over the rim of the magazine, giggling like a young girl. "See," she announced, tapping the page with her finger. "That's what the experts say right here. That's what the sophisticated man will do."

Standing in the middle of the bedroom in nothing but her chemise and laced corset, Serra frowned, remembering that one glorious assignation with Ty so long ago—or so it seemed now. She had to admit there was some truth in what Amanda had read to

178

her. Ty had been in "a state of high excitement," but she had not been tightly laced.

"Mandy, where did you get a risqué magazine like that?"

Amanda clutched the periodical to her own high, full bosom, as if she feared Serra might try to snatch it away from her.

"All the girls at the School read them. How else were we to be properly prepared for the social graces and . . . the marital bed?" As if she feared lightning might strike her dead if she spoke the words out loud, she merely mouthed the last of her statement.

Serra sighed and dropped her fists on her gently swelling hips. The reading of racy literature didn't seem so proper to her, but she had to give Amanda her due. Everywhere they had gone together over the last few days, the men of Joplin had swarmed about her friend and her hourglass figure, vying for a moment of her time. With Serra, they had smiled and been most polite, some even somewhat interested, but their response to her was nothing compared to what the vivacious Amanda Stokes commanded.

And as far as Ty . . . . well, he made it a point to ignore her completely, but he had given Amanda her fair share of time. And though her father had agreed not to send him away, apparently Ty had plans of his own, and he had moved into the Joplin Hotel. In two days he was scheduled to leave on this mysterious trip to Chicago that no one, not even her father, seemed to know anything about, and there was no indication that he would be back anytime soon.

Two days. That didn't give her very much time.

"Come on, Serra. One inch." Amanda lifted her

hand to indicate how small the distance was between thumb and forefinger. "I know you can do it." Moving off the bed, she stood, placing her hands about her incredibly tiny waist in emphasis and encouragement, and whirled about like a child's top. "It will make all the difference in the world — especially to Tyler Ramsey." She lilted the name, dangling it like a carrot to entice acquiescence.

Exhaling through lips clamped in resignation, Serra emptied her lungs. She would try just about anything if it would make Ty stay . . . make him take notice of her . . . simply give her the time of day. Grasping the strings of her front-laced corset, she gave them a mighty tug. Amazingly, her waist contracted. But, oh God, she felt as if she couldn't breathe, as if someone had secured her lungs under lock and key.

"Slow and shallow," Amanda directed, taking the stay ribbons in hand and knotting them against Serra's bound rib cage without a show of mercy. "You'll get used to it," she assured. "In fact, as soon as you lace a little tighter, it's such a rush, that light, heady feeling it's pleasant, really, it is. You'll see."

"Tighter?" Serra squeaked. "I couldn't possibly take it any tighter."

"Of course you can. You know," Amanda leaned toward her conspiratorially, "if you said something like that at the School, you would be instantly laced by the instructors another two inches and made to wear your corset day and night until you recanted such a sacrilege."

"You would be punished?" Serra asked, horrified. Growing up in the orphanage in New York, she had always thought the pampered daughters of the wealthy never suffered anything worse than an occasional broken fingernail. She had dreamed about what it would be like to live in security on the Upper West End. But now such a prospect didn't seem so blissfully wonderful.

"Punishment? Not at all, you silly ninny," Amanda declared. "Enlightenment, that's what the instructor called it. Only the girls who persisted in their resistance were punished." At this, the blonde plopped back down on the bed, encouraging Serra to join her on the plumped pillows. "There was a Miss Flora Case from Arkansas. She had run wild, wearing pants until she was fifteen. Can you imagine that?" Amanda giggled and rolled onto her stomach, propping her chin on her fists, her eyes glittering with excitement. "Flora refused to be put in a corset, much less be laced tightly. The school mistress took her away, and when she returned four days later, not only was she in a corset with a lock and key, but her waist measured a mere fifteen inches — an inch for each year of her freedom."

"They forced her?" Completely caught up in the story, Serra waited, somewhat perversely she admitted, to hear the details.

"Not only did they force her, but Flora insisted they strapped her to the 'horse' and whipped her across the backside into submission."

Serra furrowed her brows, sinking down on the bed beside her friend, her imagination conjuring up a picture of a helpless girl bound and thrashed with a cat-o'-nine tails. "You mean they scarred her?"

"Oh, no," Amanda replied emphatically. "There wasn't a single mark upon poor Flora. Apparently, her corset protected her skin, but she nonetheless

181

suffered for her resistance."

Flopping back against the bolsters, Serra found herself a bit skeptical that such medieval practices still persisted. How could such a terrible thing happen in this modern day and age? It sounded more like fantasy than reality. Shaking her head, she voiced her doubt. "How can you be sure this Flora Case was telling the truth?"

"Oh, she was," Amanda insisted, pushing up on her elbows to meet Serra's skepticism head-on. "Why would she lie?"

Serra could think of a million reasons why some rich, bored girl might make up such fantastic stories. But what if the horror tales were true? She contemplated that possibility for a moment.

"If you don't believe Flora, then I'll tell you about Miss Amelia Hartshorne." She glanced about the room, as if looking for spies in the corners. "She wore breast rings," she whispered.

"What?" Serra's amber eyes widened, an image of some terrible steel band encasing a woman's tender flesh flitting across her mind.

"Breast rings," Amanda said a little louder, carefully enunciating each word in emphasis. "You know," she insisted, touching the small gold loops in her earlobes, then sweeping her hand down across her bust line. "Amelia spent two years at a fashionable French academy before arriving at the School. Apparently, it was all the rage in Paris to go down to the jewelers on the Rue St. Honoré and have it done."

Serra had no idea what the significance of this Rue St. Honoré might be, but having one's breasts . . . She swallowed hard and shivered in disbelief.

"No woman would do that!" she cried in a hoarse whisper.

"I saw them, Serra. Amelia showed them to me. She insisted that they actually made her bust line grow, and when she told her beau about them, he became extremely excited and proposed to her right then and there." Amanda rolled her eyes and sighed with romantic delight as she drifted back down against the pillows. "Some of us at the School thought about having it done, but we couldn't locate a jeweler willing to perform the procedure."

Totally bewildered by Amanda's fanciful stories, Serra didn't know what to think, what to believe. Were truly sophisticated women willing to go to any lengths to capture their man's interest? Was that what it would take to enamor Ty? Serra swallowed hard, her hands moving up to protect her bosom, which thrust against the lace of her chemise due to the rigidness of her corset. She wasn't sure she would go so far—even for Tyler Ramsey. But what if that was what he wanted? What if he simply found her too plain, too common and uninteresting?

Amanda began to laugh, screwing up her face to mimic Serra's perplexed expression. "See, silly, just as I promised you would, you've forgotten all about how tightly your stays are laced."

And she was right. Serra had completely forgotten, so caught up in the wild tales her friend had spun. She glanced at Amanda, gnawing on her bottom lip. They were just fabrications, she told herself. And though she wanted to confirm her conclusion, she didn't dare, afraid the other girl would ridicule her for believing such nonsense or perhaps, on the other hand, for questioning her integrity.

183

"Now," Amanda declared, bounding from the bed, "let's get you dressed and put your new figure to the test. We'll get Tess to nip one of your gowns in at the waist while I do something special with your hair."

Serra pushed up from the bed, but not with the spring Amanda displayed. Feeling as if her torso had been splinted and bandaged, she eased into the dainty chair of her lace draped toilette table.

The blonde stepped behind her, sweeping up her long coppery tresses and twisting them into a flaming mass, situating them this way and that on top of Serra's head. She clucked her tongue and sighed. "Your hair is just so . . . red. What a shame." Then allowing those vivacious locks to fall down Serra's back, Amanda smiled and patted her on the head. "With your sweet mouth, I think a soft Grecian style would do best, don't you?"

Sweet mouth? Serra contemplated her friend's reflection in the mirror. Was that statement intended as a compliment or an insult? Then she scrutinized her own image. Her hair was awfully red and so wild, springing from her head in uncontrollable curls. Puckering her lips, she swiveled her head from side to side, studying her mouth from every angle. Sweet? To her it looked more like an out of place gash across her face. Leaning forward, she ran a fingertip across her cheek and over the swell of her nose. And those awful freckles. Even though they weren't as noticeable as when she was a child, she could still see them. Glancing back at Amanda's flawless beauty, she felt truly unattractive in comparison. "I suppose."

A half hour later, she peered into the mirror once

more and was amazed at the transformation. Her hair, even though nothing could be done to disguise its outrageous color, looked like something from a fashion magazine. It was swept high on her head and held in place with several pearl tipped combs, a tamed, tubular swatch cascading down the back of her neck in an intricately interwoven pattern. But what delighted her most were the profusion of tiny curls Amanda had snipped to frame her forehead and temples.

"Close your eyes," the blonde commanded, turning Serra around to face her.

Willingly, she obeyed, feeling the brush of a soft puff glide over her face. Amanda spun her back around.

"Now, what do you think?"

Serra opened her eyes and voiced her surprise when she stared into the mirror once more. The faint discoloration of the unsightly freckles was gone, her complexion glowing as pale and as flawless as her friend's. "Oh, Mandy," she exclaimed, reaching up to pat her face. "How did you do—?"

"Shhh," the blonde sibilated, slipping a small velvet sachet back into her reticule. "Rice powder, but don't dare tell anyone."

"Rice powder? But that's cosmetics. Only women of questionable reputation use—"

"Only women who are *caught* using it are questionable." Amanda drew the purse string tight. "And the secret to not getting caught is knowing what you're doing."

"You mean *you* use—"

"See, you can't tell, can you?"

Serra had to admit she would never have guessed

that Amanda Stokes resorted to such artificial means, but then what was she saying? She wondered just how trim the beautiful blonde really was without her tightly laced corsets.

At that moment Tess entered the room, a leaf-green percale walking dress draped over her arm. "The alterin's done, miss," she announced with a curtsy, her curious eyes taking in the transformation that had taken place during her short absence.

"Good," Amanda stated, taking the costume from the serving girl's arm, shooing her from the room, and closing the door in her face.

"You needn't be so short with Tess. She's been very kind to me."

"Kind? Oh, Serra, it's her job to be there when you need her. Besides, we don't want rumors to start flying about, now, do we?"

"Rumors?"

Amanda clucked her tongue and sighed. "Don't you know anything? Your servant sees something," she explained, dropping the dress onto the bed, tip-toeing toward the door, and placing her ear to the barrier, as if listening for activity on the other side, "or hears something." She straightened, apparently satisfied no one was eavesdropping. "Your girl tells her friend who works down the street, who tells her mistress, and before you know it, everyone in Joplin has heard about what we've been up to today."

Gossiping servants, boudoir secrets? Serra pondered this new information, reaching for the gown to put it on. She had never even considered that such things took place. There was so much she had to learn about being a Langston, about the ways of society, that she wondered if she would ever absorb it all.

Gathering the material of the flowing skirts to put it over her head, she raised her arms. But before she could wiggle into the gown, Amanda grabbed the ties of her corset and cinched them tighter, so tight that Serra squeaked a protest. But her rib cage was so squeezed she couldn't put up much of a resistance. Then the blonde helped guide the dress over her carefully coiffured hair and down about her hips.

"There," she murmured, spinning Serra about to fasten up the back of the dress with quick, experienced fingers.

On the verge of declaring her discomfort, of insisting she'd changed her mind and no longer wanted to do this, she caught a glimpse of her image in the long cheval mirror. The altered costume fit her like a glove, outlining her new slimness, which was accentuated by the vee inset at her waist and the gentle flare of the skirt. Amazed at how unbelievably tiny her waist appeared, she angled herself to better view the way her breasts filled up the bodice.

Amanda reached up under her skirts, grabbed the tails of her chemise, and pulled them through the opening in the back of her knee-length knickers, creating a puff of material over her derriere that made the rear of her skirts stand out even further, but with a much softer, more natural effect than the cumbersome bustle that the older, stauncher women wore. That accentuated her tiny waist and swelling bosom even more. And though she felt as if she couldn't catch her breath, she had to admit she did indeed look as fashionable and almost as beautiful as her friend. How could any man resist her? How could Ty possibly ignore her now?

Whirling about, she placed her arms around Amanda's shoulders. "Oh, Mandy, how can I thank you," she declared, appreciative of the way the other girl had shared her beauty secrets with her when she didn't really have to.

"Just make a vow you won't steal all of my admirers away from me."

"Oh, I wouldn't," Serra assured her, leaning backward in the other girl's embrace, "Not ever. Only one."

And they broke out in peals of laughter, both knowing of whom she spoke.

"Like I promised you, Mr. Tyler Ramsey won't have an inkling of what has happened to him before it's too late."

With that corroboration, the two girls sailed from the bedroom, arm in arm, and down the stairs to the Stokes carriage, which waited in the front drive for their entertainment.

From the entrance to the Joplin Hotel, where he'd just finished lunch and had been staying the last few days, Ty saw them coming. Thick as beggar's lice on a hound dog, those two, he thought. And about as compatible as burlap and Belgian lace. Yet, Serra and Amanda Stokes were inseparable. He snorted. The prancing, hoity-toity Miss Stokes with her pretentious airs, whose mother waited like a trap-door spider to snare some poor, unsuspecting male in her silk-lined nest to marry her daughter, and Serra, who of late seemed to have lost every bit of common sense she'd ever possessed, traipsing after Amanda like a shadow.

Cocking his black felt hat to ride on the back of his head, he watched the carriage cross in front of the hotel and roll on down Main Street. Just what were the two of them up to this afternoon? Whatever it was, he doubted it was something worthwhile. That Amanda Stokes possessed a bottomless tote sack of antics. And he knew darn good and well that Serra would be in the thick of it, even though she just wasn't the type to do empty-headed things on her own. At least not the Serra he was familiar with and cared about.

Regardless of how he'd made a point of ignoring her since that day she'd foolishly come to visit him at the mining office, he did care about her . . . deeply. It just seemed best, now that he'd made up his mind to leave, not to stir up the mud in the bottom of the pond. Apparently Miss "Langston" was having no trouble fitting in.

And taking over.

He'd never forget that meeting with John Langston and the smug Dr. Chelsey. No word had been mentioned about him vacating the house, and yet it had been implied. Langston had informed him quite casually that he was having his will changed. Everything he owned would now be passed on to his miraculously resurrected daughter. He understood, didn't he, why Serenity must have the best of everything, so she could attract suitors with good family names? Langston had asked, hoping Ty would stay on as manager of the mine, with a promise of adequate compensation to see that the operation went smooth.

He understood all right. He understood he wasn't

considered good enough to mix with the Langston name, that the years he'd worked so hard to make the mining company what it was today had all been for naught. An imposter would reap the benefits. And if the look on Chelsey's face had indicated anything, the old charlatan wouldn't hesitate to dip his paw in the Langston till as well.

Respectfully, he'd declined John's offer, and the same day he had moved out of the Langston mansion on his own accord. And so to put his conscience to rest, he'd agreed to tie up any loose ends at the mining company. But in exchange, he'd not hesitated to conceal the information and opportunity offered in the letter from Chicago. Why shouldn't he keep it for himself? It was the least he deserved under the circumstances.

And after his trip to Chicago . . . maybe it was time to find out what he could about the good Dr. Chelsey. For Serra's sake, of course, he rationalized. Though he had to admit he would gladly rub her nose in it if he found out anything contrary about her beloved guardian. If he uncovered even the slightest evidence that Chelsey planned to line his own pockets with Langston money, he wouldn't stand by and allow it. Serra was one thing. Let her have it—perhaps she even deserved it for all the hard times she'd suffered—but not Chelsey, not if he could stop it.

Still standing in the front doorway of the hotel lobby, he spied them again, the two fashionably dressed females with the most ridiculous hats he'd ever seen perched on top of their heads, emerging from the Stokes highfalutin carriage and stepping up on the sidewalk, coming his way. Apparently, they had plans to take a late lunch at the time of day when many of the upstanding male citizens met to do social business. Knowing Amanda for her conniving ways, he suspected she had socializing plans of her own.

He could avoid them; he supposed that was what he should do. All he had to do was turn and walk the other way down the street, but he wanted to see her again, wanted to take a whiff of her sweet smelling hair, maybe even see a hint of a smile crease her pretty mouth, take a fresh memory of her naturally glowing beauty with him.

So he ducked back into the lobby to await their arrival and make his plans to see that the meeting appeared accidental. Didn't want her thinking he missed her. But, oh God, he did. Now that he had found her again, he felt as if a little piece of himself withered and died every day they weren't together.

Posted behind a potted palm tree, he watched their entrance, noting the way several local gents dressed like city slickers paused in their conversation to watch as well.

From his concealment, he frowned. What was happening to Joplin? Not so long ago the mining town had been one of the roughest jumping-off places west of the Mississippi, having a nationwide reputation for its bars and brawls, having accommodated notorious outlaws like Jesse James. But now look at it, with its parlor palms. Disgusted, he batted at the plant in front of him. And its gas street lamps, and those newfangled goer-asker, teller-and-comers invented by Mr. Bell, which were being installed everywhere. For the most part, the men of Joplin had gone soft in the middle. And the women

191

. . . like Amanda Stokes. He rolled his eyes as her artificially created hourglass figure moved toward him.

He preferred the tried and true days when men were men, and the old ways of a pioneering town when women's curves were soft and natural . . . like Serra.

Serra?

Ty pushed a palm frond out of his way and strained to take a better look at the vaguely familiar woman walking toward him. What in the hell had she gone and done to herself? She looked as trussed up as Amanda.

Then his view was blocked by a group of men — he knew each and every one of the sons of bitches — that flocked about the two women like strutting cockerels in the hen yard. Catching a glimpse of her, he saw her lift her gloved hand and laugh. No titter would better describe her reaction to something Monte Stokes, the pompous buffoon, said to her. Look at the way she blushed when he bent over her hand and pressed his lips to her knuckles . . . the way she accepted his arm when he offered it to her.

Apparently, she was enjoying herself immensely as she fluttered her lashes and oohed and aahed over that overdressed jackass. He glanced down at his simple, rough attire — corded jeans, work shirt, boots — and suddenly felt inadequate, slipshod in comparison.

Were men like Monte Stokes what she found attractive now that she'd gone all sophisticated?

Then he narrowed his cobalt-blue eyes. Turned silk stockinged or not, he remembered how she had melted under his caresses, how she'd been more than willing to accept his advances. He had been the one who had called it to a halt, the one who had considered her blasted reputation, the one who had ached for the rest of the day wanting her . . . like now.

So this was how she went about paying him back when he wasn't looking.

Ty knew he was being somewhat irrational, acting like a jealous lover, but he couldn't help himself. Serra might be embroiled in an attempt to fleece John Langston, she might be caught up with the likes of Amanda Stokes. He was willing to overlook that. But when it came to her involvement with other men, he just couldn't stand by and watch. Deep down, she was still his responsibility.

Perhaps little Miss Fancy Pants needed to be reminded. Spinning about, he marched the opposite way the trio of Amanda, Serra, and Monte went. Convincing the serving girl, Tess, to admit him in to the Langston house tonight would be easy. Then Serra was in for a lesson she would never forget.

"Did you see him?"

In response to Amanda's query, Serra slid her gaze to her friend, then to the potted palm and back. Nodding, she took a deep breath — at least she tried to, but wasn't very successful. She had seen Ty all right, positioned behind the plant, watching. It had been so hard not to stare back, but Amanda had insisted she ignore him completely.

And so she had, making an effort to look as moony eyed as she could at Amanda's brother. And Monte had been such a good sport about it, willingly going along with their plans — in fact, encour-

193

aging them.

"Look at me like I'm a long lost love," he'd insisted, making a funny face at her.

Serra couldn't help herself. She had laughed at his antics, attempting to stop herself by covering her mouth with her hand, but Monte had stuck out his tongue at her, and she just couldn't control herself.

Then when he had offered her his arm, she had linked hers with his willingly. Monte Stokes was a true gentleman and friend.

As they entered the dining room of the Joplin Hotel, Serra saw Ty striding through the lobby and out the front door. She couldn't help the way her heart lurched, wanting more than anything to call him back, but she held her tongue.

"Well, what do you think?" she asked Amanda, forcing her shoulders to relax and slipping her hand from Monte's crooked arm.

"I think Mr. Tyler Ramsey has just caught wind of the baited trap."

"And you'll be there to happily spring the lid. You truly enjoy this, don't you, sis?" Monte interjected with a hapless snort.

Amanda just laughed in response to her brother's bantering criticism.

"Well, I must admit," Monte declared with a shake of his head, "if any man needs to be taught a good lesson, it's Tyler Ramsey." Then he turned to Serra and gently captured her chin between his thumb and forefinger. "I'm just not sure you deserve to be used as a lure to catch such a low-down skunk."

"It's what I want," Serra declared, notching her chin in pride.

"Truly?" he asked with what she interpreted as sin-

194

cere disappointment.

After only a moment's hesitation, she nodded.

Exhaling in defeat, Monte smiled his acceptance like the gentleman he was. "Very well, then. All I can say is good luck. I have a feeling you'll need it."

Chapter Twelve

Late that evening, sitting at the toilette table in the solitude of her bedroom, Serra awaited Tess's return with her favorite lawn bedgown from the laundry. Dressed only in her underclothing, she ached to escape the confines of her stays after the long day, yet at the same time she was fascinated with the mirror image that reflected the transformation from orphaned waif to Vanity Fair.

Straightening her spine and angling this way and that so she could better study her corseted torso, she wondered if Ty had truly found the new her as irresistible as Amanda had assured her he would. The fact that he had marched out of the hotel without a word to her, without looking back, left her to wonder. But no. Amanda had said she'd seen the glint of jealousy in Ty's gaze as he'd watched her with Monte.

If only she would hear from him. Tomorrow, she asserted. He would come to call tomorrow or else. Or else what? She couldn't go after him again. Not after the other day at the mining office. But, oh, she just couldn't let him leave.

Releasing a frustrated sigh, she returned to her

self-scrutiny. She had to admit her figure, her bosom, did look so much more becoming. He wouldn't be able to resist her, she decided.

"Oh please, God," she whispered, her bolstered confidence turning to supplication, "let him be unable." Over the last few days, she had to admit that her desire for revenge had melted beneath the heat of his rejection to a need to just be near him. It was important that she be strong and not allow him to see how desperate she'd become. But, oh, she would do just about anything—if only he would find her irresistible.

Twisting, she lifted the lid of her jewelry box and stared at the contents as if she thought to find the answers in there. So many beautiful pieces to choose from. She reached inside, took out a necklace of perfectly matched garnets, and draped them about her bare throat, allowing the teardrop of gems to dip into the deep décolletage of her chemise.

With trembling hands, your husband will unlace you, she recalled the magazine article Amanda had read to her earlier that day. Closing her eyes, she could vividly imagine Ty doing just that. Then she remembered the other thing her friend had told her about. Breast rings. Did men really find them titillating?

Bending over the jewelry box once more, she spied a pair of simple gold ear loops. She took them out and held them up for inspection, wondering . . .

Taking an earring in each hand, she held them up to the tips of her breasts, concealed beneath her underclothing, and tried to imagine how they would look attached to her bare skin. But somehow over the fabric it just wasn't the same.

She glanced behind her at the closed door. Tess would knock before entering, as was the servant's custom. Besides, it would take the girl a few more minutes to retrieve the nightdress from the laundry. What harm could there be in a little innocent experimentation?

Pushing down the neckline of her chemise, she took up the earrings once more and dangled them in front of her bared breasts, but still . . .

Then she had a brainstorm. Pulling her chemise back into place, she pinned the earrings into the fabric with precision. Then she pushed the fabric back down so the tiny gold loops gave the illusion she wished to achieve.

"Oh, my," she murmured, and then couldn't help the giggle that escaped as she watched the baubles swing and glint in the candlelight. Was it possible that Ty might find them as tantalizing as Amanda had attested?

Even though evidence of the arrival of spring was all about him, Ty scrunched his shoulders and wrapped his jacket collar about his neck. It was damned cold standing on the back stoop of the Langston mansion, hovering about the perimeters as if he were a stranger, unwelcome, which it now seemed was the case, anymore. As unwelcome as a late season snow.

Cupping his hands about his eyes, he pressed his face against the glass pane of the window in the downstairs service porch, which doubled as a back entrance to the house as well as a laundry-storage area. To his disappointment, the room was empty and dark, with no sign of Tess. And the door was locked. Apparently, John Langston felt it necessary with his precious daughter inside.

Pushing off, he retreated down the steps and skirted around the back of the house until he reached the south end, where the serving girl had a small room on the third floor. He'd been there enough times to know which window was hers. Then he bent, scavenging for small rocks on the ground. A few steps farther back and he took careful aim, sending one of the pebbles flying to tap against the glass.

Then he waited, shifting his weight from one foot to the other, for Tess to respond.

But nothing.

"Damn it," he grumbled, dropping another stone into his right hand and sending it flying along the same path as the first. This time his aim was not as sure, and the missile smacked against the window ledge rather loudly. Oh, hell, he wasn't trying to awaken all of the servants. Hunching forward, he took the corner and flattened himself against the house, waiting.

"Tyler Ramsey, are you tryin' to wake the dead?"

Ty twisted his head at the whispered query, whistling his relief when he found Tess standing on the stoop, her hands planted on her hips. Leaping forward, he joined her there, taking her by the arm.

"Thank God," he answered, commandeering her toward the door. "I want to get in the house, and I knew I could count on your help."

"Just a minute, mister," Tess objected, prying his fingers from her arm. "Why should I let you in? The word is you're not supposed to be here."

Turning, he slid his hands up her bare arms in a familiar gesture. "Just a misunderstandin', Tess," he cooed in his most persuasive voice, "and a temporary one at that," he assured her, using all of his wiles to

199

convince her.

She responded by sidling up against him. "Were you comin' to see me, Ty?" she asked huskily.

Damn it, he knew exactly what she meant, and it wasn't the response he wanted. Dropping his hands from her flesh, he stepped away. "To be honest, Tess honey, not really," he admitted, fishing in the pocket of his jacket and pulling out a small box with a strip of pretty ribbon tied about it. "But I did bring you this." He offered her the box, glad he'd thought to come prepared.

Tess ogled the gift suspiciously, then she begrudgingly accepted it. "You shouldn't've," she said with a pout.

But Ty knew she didn't mean it. Not Tess. If he hadn't brought it, she probably would have refused to help him. He grinned at her, crossing his arms over his chest and waiting for the girl to open the present. "Thought it would look nice with your pretty green eyes."

With eager fingers, she stripped off the ribbon and lifted the lid, unveiling a silk scarf he'd picked up from the mercantile earlier.

"Oh, Ty," the girl murmured, scooping up her prize and rubbing it against her face. "It's real silk, isn't it? It's so beautiful." With the scarf threaded through her pudgy fingers, she circled his neck.

Draping his arms about her waist, he bent down and whispered in her ear, "Think you can find it in your heart now to let me in?"

She giggled when the brush of his beard tickled her neck. "Wel—l—l—l, I suppose I could—this once." She pushed him back, playfully slapping his chest. "But only this once, Tyler Ramsey. You be understandin' me?"

200

He chucked her under the chin and released her. "Fair enough. Once should do it." He grinned at her, but mostly to himself.

Tess took his hand and led him onto the service porch. There she stopped and gathered up a lacy lawn nightgown, folding it carefully.

"Since when have you started wearin' such expensive nighties?" He frowned. "You got some other man givin' you gifts?"

"Of course not, silly. It's Miss Serenity's. It's her favorite, and she be waitin' for me to bring it to her right now."

"Miss Serenity's, huh?" Confiscating the garment, Ty trapped the girl's groping hand when she tried to snatch it back from his grasp. "Don't worry, I'll deliver it to Miss Serenity personally." He could just see her now, standing in the middle of her bedroom, tapping her bare foot, stripped and waiting for her favorite bedgown to be delivered by her servant. How easily one forgets his or her humble beginnings.

"Ty," the girl squealed, jumping up. "Give it back. You'll be gittin' me into a peck o' trouble."

He chuckled, holding the gown above the girl's short reach. "I think not, Tess. Just go on to bed, I'll see to it Miss High-and-mighty Langston gets her gown and keeps her mouth shut."

Tess's brows knitted in a small frown of uncertainty. "Are you sure?"

"Of course. Have I ever let you down?"

She shook her head.

"Then scoot." He smacked her bottom teasingly, and watched the girl scurry toward the kitchen and the stairway that led to her quarters.

Tucking the folded gown under his arm, Ty veered

toward the main stairway. He just hoped Serra was as receptive as he'd figured. Otherwise, Tess had no idea just how right she would be. They'd all be in a shit load of trouble.

The rat-a-tat of knuckles sounded on the door.

Still caught up in her self examination, Serra squeaked in surprise. Tess. Back so soon?

"Just a minute," she called, grabbing at her lowered chemise and frantically attempting to remove the gold loops from the material. But her fingers trembled so that the first earring jammed, the backing catching crookedly on the post and refusing to budge. Guiltily, her heart hammered against her chest. Fearing she might get caught doing something so outrageously unacceptable, she flew from her seat at the dressing table, nearly knocking over the jewelry box stand in her haste to reach the door before the girl could enter.

Oh, God, what would Tess think when she saw the strategically pinned jewelry? Serra placed her fingers over the gold loops in an attempt to hide them, the weight of which made the chemise sag low across her cleavage. "Oh, that won't work," she muttered, realizing how foolish she must look with her hands plastered against her breasts.

What was she going to do?

"Tess?" she called, her voice sounding strained and guilty—oh, God, so guilty. "Just leave the gown outside the door. I won't be needing you anymore tonight."

She waited for a response, her blood racing so hard she could feel her pulse throbbing at the base of her throat and against her palms pressed over her

202

heart.

But there was no reply.

Perhaps the serving girl hadn't heard her.

Spinning about, she placed her mouth as close to the door as she could. "Tess?" Then she fitted her ear against the wood, listening.

Silence.

"Are you still out there, Tess?"

Nothing.

Maybe the servant had heard her after all and had already followed her instructions. Hesitating for a moment, Serra cracked open the door and peeked through the tiny slit to the hallway beyond.

The corridor was darkened, the faint glow of a wall sconce farther down creating a dim semicircle of illumination. There on the floor a few feet from the doorway she spied the nightgown, primly folded.

Serra released a sigh of relief. "Thank God," she whispered, opening the door a hair more in order to retrieve the gown. Still somewhat unnerved, she stuck out her arm, her fingers inching like a crab across the floor, but the garment was just out of her reach.

She widened the gap, and on her knees, one hand scrunching up the fabric of her undergarment to conceal the dangling earrings, she draped herself across the threshold and stretched into the hall.

As her fingers grasped the nightdress, a booted foot pressed gently over her knuckles, not painfully, but just enough to stop her from reeling in her booty.

"Serra, what do you think you're doin'?"

Caught by complete surprise and feeling most foolish, she shrieked, a tiny mouselike sound, and released the clothing, both the nightgown and her chemise, attempting to scoot backward into the safety of her bedroom and slam the door as fast as she could. But before she could accomplish her goal, the black boot followed and wedged its way into the opening.

"Serra, let me in."

Sitting on the floor with her back against the barrier, she felt him put his weight against the door and push.

"I can't," she squeaked, reaching up to tear at the earrings still attached to her chemise. The thought of being caught by Tess had been bad enough, but Ty? . . . She couldn't imagine a worse disaster.

Then her hands stilled against her bosom. A disaster, or perhaps a golden opportunity? He *had* come just like Amanda predicted, even if it wasn't quite the way or at the time she'd expected.

With trembling hands, your husband will unlace you. That promise of utopia reverberated in her head and sent an undeniable thrill coursing through her.

"Ty?" she asked, as if surprised. "What do you want?"

"I want you to let me in, Serra. I need to talk to you." He leaned a little harder against the door, as if testing to see if her resistance had subsided.

A need to talk, was it? She smiled to herself as she braced her feet on the floor to counteract his increased pressure. "I don't know," she responded coyly. "It's so—o—o late. Besides, you're not supposed to even be here."

"Please, Serra." He relented his pushing, and he did ask so nicely.

"Well . . ." Her heart pounded as she decided to let him stew a bit longer. Don't give in too easily, Amanda had warned her.

"If I'm caught outside your door, we're both in trouble, you know." The pressure resumed. Apparently, he was losing patience—not that Ty ever had that much.

"I won't get in trouble if I continue to deny you entrance, Tyler Ramsey . . . only you," she corrected, trying unsuccessfully to suppress an urge to giggle.

"Damn it, Serra, let me in." He hit the barrier with his shoulder. "Don't make me force the issue," he threatened.

Smothering her laughter with her fist, she slid her back up the door to stand. It would be accurate to say Ty was primed and ready. "Do that, and I swear I'll scream," she warned, trying hard to sound sincere.

Then when she knew he was pushing the hardest, she stepped away and let the door swing open.

Ty came crashing into the room, nearly falling at her sudden compliance with his demand. She whirled about, attempting to make as pretty a picture as she could, her chemise dipping down provocatively, her breasts so full, her waist so tiny. She took several quick breaths, conscious of how the movement accentuated her newly acquired curves.

Touching her fingertips to her throat dramatically, she murmured, "You shouldn't be here."

Once he regained his balance, his gaze slid like silk over her figure, taking it all in. "Serra, why are you dressed that way?" Though he frowned, she noted with satisfaction that he never took his eyes from her breasts, so round, so enticing . . . so accented by the earrings.

She glanced down at herself, then back up at him, trying to appear as suggestive yet as innocent as she could. "I wasn't expecting a visitor." She dropped down on the bed and postured, lifting one knee and placing her hands behind her head like the picture Amanda had shown her in the magazine.

The effect on him was only too obvious. He stared, his mouth opening to allow his tongue to take a swipe at his dry lips. "Could have fooled me," he mumbled. Then he strode across the room to stand directly over her. His gaze as hard as arctic ice raked over her form and paused once more upon her breasts, so near to spilling from her chemise she didn't dare inhale again.

His hand reached out and she closed her eyes, anticipating his caress.

"What are these?"

The chemise whisked against her skin.

Her eyes popped open to find that he carelessly flicked at the earrings in her clothing. Cocking his head, he grinned at her.

Lowering her arms, she felt her confidence take wing. Didn't he find the strategically placed jewels exciting? Then when he flicked the bauble again and lifted one brow at her in curiosity, she realized that not only didn't he find them enticing, but he was amused, laughing at her as if she were a little girl attempting to play grown-up in an oversized dress and shoes.

"Nothing," she declared, brushing away his hand and rolling to her stomach to hide her welling embarrassment. Oh, God, she wished now that she'd never let him come into her room. What had she been thinking?

The bedsprings squeaked as he sat down on the edge of the mattress beside her, his hands sliding over her shoulder blades and down her bare arm.

"Serra."

Not some silly little child for him to console, she jerked away from his touch. "Get out, Ty." Her demand was muffled by her pillow, which was squashed against her face.

"Serra, listen to me. I didn't come here to . . ." His voice trailed off.

Lifting her face from the bolster, she sniffed, refusing to roll back over. "Didn't come here to what? Make sport of me?"

His features contorted, wiping away the amusement and leaving a strained expression in its place. "Look, Serra, I'm not sure now why I came, but you know as well as I do that we need to talk."

"What is there to talk about?" She swiped at her nose with a knuckle.

"You . . . me. Everything that has taken place—and will eventually happen."

"Well, whatever has happened won't happen again," she vowed. Never again would she try to act the coquette. That tactic might work for someone like Amanda, but she was no Amanda Stokes no matter how she tried to fool herself not by any means. She buried her face back into the pillow.

Then he gripped her shoulders and physically rolled her over. She crossed her arms over her chest to conceal her bosom, as well as the earrings she'd so foolishly thought might impassion him. He pushed her arms away, and instantly his fingers tugged at the ties of her corset. Working his way down the crisscross of ribbon, he slowly released her bound torso.

"What do you think you're doing, Tyler Ramsey?" Plucking at his busy, determined hands, she tried to stop him.

207

"You don't need this, Serra," he insisted, jerking out the last lace and dividing the two halves of the stiff, uncomfortable corset.

She took a deep, cleansing breath, the freedom from the tight lacing so wonderful she just kept taking them, savoring the feel of air rushing deep into her starved lungs.

Twisting a finger in the top of her chemise, he dragged it down.

She jumped, unsure of what his intentions were.

"And these baubles," he announced, indicating the gold loops still attached to the fabric. "I'm not sure what you thought you were doin', but your breasts are so beautiful without adornment, without—"

She watched his throat convulse what seemed almost painfully as he swallowed, his hand covering the swell of her feminine flesh and gently kneading.

"—anything." His cobalt-blue gaze intensified, deepening with desire as her flesh reacted to his touch, tightening into a nubbin. "When I saw you talkin' with Monte Stokes today, I thought my blood would boil." The tips of his fingers met and peaked on her hardened nipple.

"Monte was a perfect gentleman," she rasped, finding herself arching as if his hand controlled her with puppeteer strings.

"Tell me, Serra, if he's so perfect, can he do this?" His hand slid down, parachuting around her breast until the heat of his palm grazed the aroused tip, circling.

She bit her tongue to silence the whimper and the confession that only he made her feel this way—so wanton, so willing—to hold back the admission that it never crossed her mind to allow Monte such liberties . . . that all she thought about of late was the

208

feel of his own caresses.

Ty's hand drifted over her belly and down her chemise-covered thigh, until he found the hem about her knees. With confidence and familiarity, he worked his way beneath the material. Like ice touched by the flare of fire, she felt herself melting, willing his caress to move higher, more intimate.

Perhaps his fingers had not trembled when he had unlaced her, nor had they been clumsy, not by any means. Maybe she hadn't laughed or blushed prettily, but she did feel the electricity that crisped the air between them, leaving him as well as her in a high state of excitement.

"And this, Serra, does your perfect gentleman begin to know how to do this?" His mouth descended, circling her breast at the same moment his fingers touched her there in that secret place no one had ever caressed except Ty.

Even though arrows of desire ricocheted through her, she held her tongue. She wouldn't confess to him, she wouldn't, she vowed to herself.

But then his mouth was against her ear, his warm breath and soft beard that caressed her neck sending shivers down her spine, undermining her determination, weakening her knees, unsealing her soldered lips. "Oh, Ty," she murmured.

"Just how perfect is your gentleman now?" He nuzzled her throat. "Which do you prefer — Monte Stokes or me?"

There was no contest, and she knew it. "You," she admitted. "Only you." Circling his neck so her fingers could weave through the thick black hair that curled against his collar, she sighed, giving in to the desire that clutched her so fiercely. "No one but you, Ty." And God she meant it, heart and soul.

As if he doubted her honesty, he captured her face in his hands, brushing away the wild array of burnished tresses that framed it. He looked at her hard, his gaze never releasing hers. "Promise me, no one else, ever."

Serra heard his request, and she put her own meaning to what he asked of her. "No one else, ever," she vowed, thrilling in the union, the binding of their love at long last. She didn't need his verbalization to know he made a commitment. He loved her, she loved him, and they would always be together, sharing their prosperity, sharing their dreams.

A joy so pure it made her gasp, washed over her like a tidal wave. For Ty . . . anything.

To seal this mental avowal, she urged him down on top of her, fitting his beloved body between her thighs and against her racing heart so filled with love. Then lowering her lashes, she kissed him, softly, yet urgently, sweetly, yet full of passion and knowledge.

His desire blossomed beneath her simple embrace, and he moved against her in that manly way she found so exciting. Molding against his long, lean form, she gave in to the power he exuded, gave in to her own longing to be loved by him once again.

Forgotten were her devious plans to ensnare him, to tame him, then teach him a well-earned lesson. There remained only the need to give, to be an intimate part of him.

He pushed aside her chemise, freeing her arms and bunching the garment about her waist. His mouth, so tender, so loving, again claimed her breasts, drawing one and then the other between his lips until she lay, head thrown back, spine arched as if he didn't give—or perhaps it was take—enough. Her hands urged him on, plucking at the buttons and fasteners of his shirt and pants.

"Easy, Serra," he whispered against the valley between her moisten-tipped breasts, reaching up to stop her and go about shedding his clothing for himself. "I want this to last me for a lifetime."

A lifetime, she sighed inwardly, impatiently. Their love would last much longer than that, she vowed, watching him divest himself of all pretense, all covering. She would make sure of it.

Returning to her side, he took her in his arms, his mouth moving lower, nipping at the ridges of her rib cage. Then his tongue traced one of the red welts and indentations the tightly lace corset had embossed on her pearl-sheened skin. "Promise me, Serra, you won't do this again. Don't mar your natural beauty like same frivolous fashionmonger."

"If you don't want me to," she agreed, her fingers combing through his dark hair. But then there was nothing she wouldn't agree to do for him at this moment if he asked her.

But he grew silent, the only demand he made of her being to feel, to revel in the delicious pleasure that he ignited throughout her trembling body.

And enjoy she did. The brush of his face against her abdomen, her inner thigh, and then . . . He loved her in ways she'd never imagined possible, the rising waves of sensation his mouth wrought carrying her to such rapture-filled planes that she found herself urging him on, not only with her hands but with her unfettered words.

"Oh, yes, yes. Whatever you want," she cried out her desire, opening to him completely and unabashedly.

But they both knew it was what she yearned for, strove for as well.

As if he played a rhapsody on ivory, he took her higher and higher, until she thought her heart couldn't survive the battering undulations of ecstasy. And then when she reached the pinnacle and teetered on the very edge of fulfillment, he held her there, drawing out the chords of love, a master of sostenuto, prolonging her pleasure beyond imagination, finally allowing her to plunge to her culmination.

With the grace of a dying wind eddy, she spiraled back to reality. Hovering over her yet not touching her, his hands planted on each side of her waist, he waited for her to surface. "Serra, love," he whispered, encouraging her to open her eyes as he brushed his lips over the petal-soft lids, one and then the other.

The moment her lashes fluttered and parted, his mouth covered hers with such sweetness that the wondrous thundergust began all over again, churning in the pit of her stomach and radiating outward. Yet he took his time, his kiss slow and sensuous, his tongue exploring unhurriedly as he staked his claim upon her not only physically but spiritually as well. Slaking his undeniable thirst, he savored her growing passion as if each step, each drop, were precious.

And they were precious to her as well, for even as he ended the kiss, his lips lingered on hers as if he couldn't get enough. Their mouths a mere hairsbreadth from each other, he murmured, "Serra. My sweet, li'l Serra."

"Ty," she replied, her lips parted and moist. Reaching up and arching toward him, she needed to feel him, wanted more, so much more, wanting all of him.

With the decisiveness she knew so well, he complied to her demands. Dropping down against her, he pressed his hips intimately to hers. The moment she opened to him, he thrust against her, filling her, fulfilling her need to be joined with him. With slow, tentative movements, he rose and fell within her. Meeting his rhythm with eagerness, she urged him on. Soon they were caught up in the age-old ritual of love, climbing the cliffs together, hand in hand, heart to heart. Once they reached the top, he guided her over the edge, cradling her gently, crooning his encouragements, his mouth covering hers to merge her cries of delight with his own.

Thoroughly spent, she savored the feel of his heat and weight blanketing her, his dark hair feathering her neck and chin, his thundering heart that mimicked her own as they both eased back to a normal rate. They lay there, still entwined, breaths mingling, eyes fluttering open at the same moment.

Curling her arms about his neck, she gave him a languid smile followed by a gentle sigh of satisfaction, and he kissed the tip of her nose in silent adoration. Then to her disappointment, he pushed himself up and rolled to his side, taking her with him.

There she nuzzled in the crook of his arm, her face pillowed against his muscled shoulder.

And it was there that she drifted off to sleep, her last blissful thoughts being to remember to tell her father tomorrow that she wanted to make sure Ty shared any inheritance planned for her.

Share. Confident that he would never leave her now, she bowed her lips in pleasure and brushed the knob of his shoulder with a kiss, one that proclaimed him hers in every way. Just as she belonged to him. From this moment forward, they would share everything—their pasts, their presents, and their futures.

There would be no more schemes, no more need for them, but most of all, nothing would separate them again.

Chapter Thirteen

Morning mushroomed like an iridescent bubble, shimmering and quivering, full of color and excitement enveloped in a wondrous sense of expectation. Still half asleep, Serra wiggled toward the middle of the big canopied bed, seeking the masculine warmth she anticipated would be there, for some reason needing to feel the familiar curl of his arm about her.

Her lashes fluttered open. How strange. It was as if awaking to the rising sun with him there to protect her was not unusual. But how could that be?

It couldn't. Even though they had been together all those years in the orphanage, they had still been separated in the evenings, the girls from the boys. She would never have had the opportunity to spend an entire night with him.

"Ty?" she whispered. Her voice, edged with confusion and a sudden sense of urgency, was still husky with sleep. She moved again, flipping over to reach out and wake him. Instead, her fingers touched nothing but the cold indent that suggested he had ever been there at all.

Fingers curling on the nothingness, her heart

215

about a hollowness, Serra wondered if perhaps she had only fantasized the nocturnal experience. But no, it had been real, so very real. But just as undeniable was the fact that Ty had disappeared — without even bothering to say good-bye.

"Mornin', miss."

The bright, cheery salutation caught her by surprise.

Tess bound into the room, as was the servant's custom, to waken her mistress and help her select her wardrobe for the morning meal. As she entered, the girl stumbled over something on the floor and paused to look down.

Serra sat up, blinking, flustered, hurt, yet relieved to find herself alone. Then noting the bed's state of disarray and her own undress, she turned crimson and snagged the covers, draping them about her nudity, trying to smooth them back into place.

"Miss Serenity?" The query conveyed a sense of surprise to discover her so.

Serra glanced up somewhat sheepishly to find Tess contemplating her with serious intent, her mouth flopped open. Recovering, the girl stooped, picked up the nightgown at her feet, and shook it out, revealing the fact it had never been worn.

"It was . . . awfully warm last night," Serra stuttered her lame excuse for being found naked, the covers mussed on both sides of the bed, the pillow still showing the indent where Ty had lay his head. She pulled the coverlet higher up under her arms and looked away, unable to confront Tess's shocked gaze.

"Ay, I suppose," the girl replied finally after a long, embarrassing pause. Carefully folding the garment,

216

she carried it to the wardrobe, where she deposited it in one of the drawers. "I'm surprised, miss, that your room was so uncomfortable. Mine was quite cool last night with the window cracked a bit."

"I tried to open the window, but it wouldn't budge," Serra babbled on, latching on to the flimsy reasoning, wanting more than anything to get up but not daring. All she could think of was what Amanda Stokes had warned her about. Servants gossip among themselves. Just what did Tess suspect might have happened last night? Her eyes narrowed. What did she actually know about Ty's clandestine visit?

Tess moved to the window and clutched the sash, tugging, testing out Serra's assertion. Of course, the window slid up easily. "Seems to be workin' fine this mornin', Miss Serenity. You should have called me if you were havin' so much trouble." She slammed the window shut, but before she did, a cold draft swept into the room. Serra couldn't decide if the servant was being sincere or not.

"Yes, well, last night I couldn't open it even a little bit, and I didn't want to wake you. And it *was* warm in here—very much so."

Tess glanced at her and smiled. "If you be sayin' so, miss. I'm not one to be arguin'."

Oh, God, Serra agonized, Tess knew. Most likely she'd even had a hand in seeing that Ty got into her room undetected. Serra could tell by the way the girl's eyes glistened mischievously whenever they swept over her.

It was essential she take charge of the situation and make sure Tess realized that she, Serra, was the boss here, not the other way around. So straighten-

217

ing her spine, she changed the subject. "Please, Tess, bring me my chemise."

Though she tried not to, she darted a glance down at the one Ty had stripped from her and tossed in a ball on the floor last night. Looking up, she found Tess staring at it, too.

"A clean one, please," she insisted hurriedly, remembering only too well that the earrings were still attached to it.

"I know, miss . . . that unbearable heat durin' the night." The girl brought Serra the underclothing and waited while she slipped it on.

All Serra wanted to do was to get dressed and escape the bedroom with its fresh, lingering memories . . . the knowing, accusing eyes of the servant. Scrambling from the bed, she selected something to wear without fanfare, a sedate morning gown void of frills that she would have normally passed over. But the dress was easy to don, and the sooner she could send Tess away, the better she would feel.

Finally alone, the first thing she did was to tackle the earrings still attached to the chemise. It would not do for anyone else to find them. Hopelessly stuck, she finally had to rip them from the garment. Returning the jewels to the safety of their box, she caught her reflection in the dressing table mirror, noting every line in her face, the dark circles beneath her eyes. There seemed nothing left of the girl who had foolishly thought to work her wiles on a man like Tyler Ramsey. With an angry sigh, she turned away from her image and headed toward the door, not sure what to expect once she left the protection of her room.

* * *

In grim-faced silence, Ty boarded the early morning train to St. Louis, the first leg in his journey to Chicago. Gripping his satchel as if it contained the future—not only the anticipation, but the regrets as well—he worked his way through the car to a seat near the rear exit and dropped down on the hard, uncomfortable bench. Then situating his bag next to him, he stretched out his long legs and slouched against the backrest, tilting his hat to cover his blue eyes and crossing his arms over his broad chest, hopefully giving an air of unapproachability.

That was what he wanted: to be left alone. No one trying to pump him for conversation, nothing to make him possibly change his mind. He didn't feel like talking. In fact, he didn't feel much like thinking, but there seemed no escape from the images that lurked in his brain like hants looking for a dark corner to occupy and fester.

However, they were the sweetest of memories, he had to admit, still so fresh in his mind he could almost touch them. His nostrils flared, smelling them, living them all over again. Serra, her burnished tresses spilling over the snow-white pillowcase, across his arm in all of their lavender-fragrant splendor. A flame to kindle a spark of warmth even in the coldest of hearts.

And that's what he figured himself. A coldhearted bastard. Wanting hadn't kept him there—in her bed, in her arms, in her life. Instead, he had slipped from her embrace and, like a thief, stolen away from the Langston house.

Shame dogged him like the pungent odor of a polecat that was impossible to shed once it found its mark. All he could do was wait for the stink of self-condemnation to fade with time. But, God, it would be hard to forget the way she had looked . . . tasted . . . felt beneath him. The way she had given to him with such trust, when he had been there to make her regret her flagrant display of coquetry in public, to remind her that the Langston name didn't lift her above it all. Perhaps she needed to be taught a harsh lesson, but his motivations had been all wrong. The only reason her harmless flirtations had infuriated him was because they had been directed at Monte Stokes, the son of a bitch.

Ty snorted in self-disgust beneath the protection of his black felt hat. Jealousy—pure and simple—that's all it was. To call his justifications anything else would be lying to himself. How had he managed to sink so low? Damn it, his well-laid plans didn't include such sentimental hogwash.

He should have avoided her, should have left for Chicago another day earlier than he'd planned, should have never made love to her. For regardless of his intent last night, that was what he had done—unleashed up-until-now-buried passions, relinquishing his heart to her safekeeping.

But there were more important things at stake here than just his hapless heart. He had stolen away like the lowest of scoundrels in order to salvage what was left of his ambitions. And he'd like to think that he had deserted her for her own good as well—to save her dreams. If he'd stayed around, he would have eventually unveiled the secrets of her past and his own. Serra was happy in her delusion; who was he to destroy it?

So he'd been smart, he convinced himself. Gotten

out before she could open those persuasive amber eyes of hers and lock them on him, turning him into a batch of jelly made from fruit left too long on the tree—watery and soft. Gotten on the train determined not to look back, not to regret his decision. Left with no plans of returning—at least not any time soon.

But no matter how he denied it, the regret was there. All he could do now was learn to live with it.

Like an ancient war machine left idle too long, the floor beneath his feet began to tremble as the train worked up steam, its driving wheels straining to set the connecting rods in motion and grip the rails beneath them, as if his reluctance to depart had seeped into the iron and steel that enveloped him.

Ty sat up and pushed back his hat to stare out the window as the last of the neatly laid-out town rolled by, slowly at first, then picking up speed as the scenery changed to grassy hills and valleys.

Trains. It always seemed these heartless monsters took control of their destinies—his and Serra's—tearing them apart, pushing them together, now separating them again.

But it was best this way, he told himself, hunching back down in his seat and draping his arm over his satchel, which contained a couple of changes of clothing and the letter that would open the door to his future. The Missouri Pacific railcar rolled out of Joplin, away from the multitude of responsibilities he'd never asked for but had somehow been thrust upon him. Shrugging his broad shoulders, he shed them like water from a duck's back. No more. From now on, there was only Tyler Ramsey and Ramsey Smelting to be concerned about.

By damn it, if he had a brain in his head, he would vow here and now never to return to Joplin at all.

As hard as she tried to maintain her calm resolve, by the time Serra reached the dining room, served up a meager plate of breakfast from the sideboard, and sat down, she could feel the anger, the humiliation gathering behind her eyelids like floodwater, threatening to leak, to betray her.

Fidgeting in her chair at the table where she sat alone, she contemplated the egg that stared back at her like a one-eyed ogre, analyzing the hollow feeling that resided between her breasts. Not pangs of hunger, but of hurt. There was no denying Ty had intentionally betrayed her.

Yes, betrayed best described how she had felt this morning upon arising and discovering he had sneaked out of her room, out of the house sometime during the night. He was probably still laughing at how easily she'd succumbed to him. This must surely be the worst day of her life.

"Little fool," she mumbled, directing her criticism to the bug-eyed egg, wondering just what she would say to him, he to her, when next they met. Oh, God, what was she going to tell Amanda? Would she confess the sordid truth to her friend or keep it to herself?

Without a doubt, a fool. That's exactly what she had been. A brazen little nincompoop. Stabbing her fork into the yolk, she watched the yellow ooze forth onto her plate from the infliction. Just like the pain residing in her heart, and he had so callously pierced it to puddle behind her eyes, threatening to spill. And here she had thought to share with him, she chided herself with a self-indulging sniff.

To share, damn it. She jabbed the egg once more, then threw down her utensil in disgust, not only with Ty, but with herself as well.

"Not to your satisfaction, girl?" From the doorway, John Langston grinned at her in parental interest.

Serra glanced up at her father and tried to reciprocate, but found it impossible. "Not at all," she replied, feeling guilty that she had done something so awful as to allow a man—especially Ty—into her bedroom here in her father's home. What would he say if he knew? What would he do if he found out they had again disobeyed his desires.

Sliding her eyes away, she feared he might decipher the truth from them. She'd never been very good at lying. The fiasco this morning with Tess was a good example.

To her relief, Langston presented his back and dished himself up a hearty breakfast. Then he sat down opposite her, taking up his silverware and delving into the pile of food. "Eggs are kinda like ambitions. I always say, if it ain't right, throw it away and get another one." He popped a forkful of the same into his mouth.

She glanced up, somewhat taken aback by his intuitiveness. "It's not that easy, Father," she declared, pushing away her abused, but otherwise untouched meal.

Chewing slowly, his fork poised over his plate, he cocked his head at her. "Sure it is. Trust me." He lifted his cup and took a big gulp of coffee. "Hell, girl, I'm older than dirt. I know about these things.

223

If somethin' ain't to your likin', then change it."

Serra sat back, blinking. Her father made it sound so simplistic. If only things could be that way. If only she could change it all. God, she would, from that very first day Ty had abducted her from the train. If she could do it all over, she would put up a fight he would never forget. And last night, she should have sent him packing. Never should she have gone along so willingly, so innocently with his devious plans of seduction. "Tell me, Father, how do you change something that has already happened?" she asked in soft earnestness.

As if sensing her seriousness, Langston deposited his utensils beside his plate and templed his hands in front of him as he swallowed the last of his scrambled eggs. "Guess you can't really change that, but you can see it never happens again," he replied.

Though there was parental concern etched on his lined face, he never questioned her, never demanded an explanation, just tried to help alleviate her pain in blind trust. From somewhere deep inside, a seed of pride, of sincere affection for this man—her father—took root and began to sprout into full-fledged love.

Serra rose and skirted about the table until she stood behind him. Throwing her arms about his neck, she embraced him, planting a kiss on his weathered cheek. "Oh, Father, how did I ever manage without you for so long?"

He reached up and patted her arms crossed over his heart. "The same as all of us do, I suppose, girl, takin' it one day at a time."

Her father was so right. She had focused on the wrong objective since her arrival in Joplin. It was time she took charge of her own destiny. For so many years she had been driven by the desire to be reunited with her family. Once she had obtained that goal, she had squandered her precious days worrying about Ty—about what he wanted, what he thought—attempting to make their lives mesh when it was obvious there was no way to create harmony. She owed him nothing, and it was time to stop trying to indulge him and make the effort to please herself, her father, to go on with her life—with or without Tyler Ramsey, whatever suited him. No, whatever suited *her*, she corrected her thinking.

"I'll tell you what, girl," her father piped up, twisting in his seat to face her. "It's Saturday. Why don't you and I make a day of it? Just father and daughter."

She pulled back and looked at him questioningly. "Doing what?"

"Why, child, Joplin is quite a mecca of entertainment. There is Schifferdecker Gardens, with bowlin' greens cut in the meadow." He smacked his lips appreciatively. "And the coldest, mellowest beer you could ever taste." Then he cleared his throat, as if remembering this was his daughter he was speaking to, not one of his cronies. "Not that you'll have a chance to taste it, mind you."

Serra clapped her hands with delight and laughed, gay and tinkling, savoring the prospect of spending such a wonderful day with her father, a day she had merely dreamed about before now.

"And then there's the Exposition, with the art and floral hall . . . the observatory," he added soberly. "A most appropriate pastime for a young lady of your stature and reputation."

"How soon can we leave?"

"Well, I suppose as soon as you get all gussied up."

Serra waltzed out of the dining room, humming to herself, wondering what it would feel like to spend a day—just think of it, an entire day—with her father. Her very own father. She laughed, her mind churning up daydreams. Perhaps Ty would be there. Perhaps he would . . .

No. She wouldn't ruin her day thinking about him. But should they cross paths, she would let him spend his time worrying about her.

By the time the train reached St. Louis, Ty had grown completely disgusted with his own company. The more he'd thought about it—and he'd had plenty of time to do just that: think and sweat in that stuffy, uncomfortable train car, and then think some more—the more he realized he just couldn't let matters lie the way they were between himself and Serra.

The call to detrain broke into his thoughts. Ty rose, stretched his aching muscles and, repositioning his hat, snapped up his satchel and hurried from the railcar to find the way to his connection.

He would go on to Chicago. He'd not come this far to turn his back on such a golden opportunity. But once his business was concluded, he would deal in his own way and time with Serra.

The first thing he must do was to gather as much information as he could about her and that damnable Dr. Chelsey. He'd suspected that man from the beginning, and in his heart perhaps he had never

226

completely trusted her. The place to begin his search was in New Hope, where it had all started so long ago.

Stopping at the ticket counter he made arrangements for a wire to be sent back to Joplin with instructions for Cochise to be taken to New Hope and boarded.

Ah, Serra, love, he thought to himself. *I'll get to the bottom of all this, and if you're as innocent as I pray you are, then I can only hope you have it in your heart to understand and forgive.*

But until he had answers, he would find the strength to keep his distance.

Sitting on a native rock bench, the full skirt of her day gown fanned about her like peach cobbler, Serra clapped her hands as her father took careful aim at the triangle of pins situated on the far end of the grassy bowling lane.

"Now, watch, girl," he bragged, doffing his felt hat toward her and several other women who were observing the game, "and I'll show you how an expert does it." He moved forward, releasing the ball with deadly force.

As the pins teetered and fell, Serra jumped up in excitement. "Oh, Father, please let me try," she pleaded so prettily that several of the other bowlers, mostly gentlemen, gave her interested, if somewhat condescending, looks.

John Langston strutted forward, so proud of himself and of his daughter, Serra assured herself. Just as she was so proud of him. Signaling for her to join him, he took up another bowl. Then standing behind her, he demonstrated to her how to palm the sphere, which was surprisingly heavy for its size.

"Like this, Serra, girl." He clasped her hand from underneath, and showed her how to swing her arm and flex her knees at the same time. "Now, let it go."

She released her uncertain grip on the ball and watched it wobble in an arc across the green to miss all of the pins.

"Oh, it's so much harder than it looks," she exclaimed with disappointment.

"You didn't do all that poorly. Like most things, it takes time and practice to be good at somethin'."

Serra looked up at her father, his eyes so brown and sincere, and a special feeling was shared between them. Of course. Just like learning to be someone's daughter or father all over again. It simply didn't happen overnight. Her heart full of joyous discovery, she smiled.

"I hear tell back east," he informed her, picking up another ball and turning her about to try again, "they're makin' these things with finger holes in 'em, now."

"Really? That must look strange," Serra replied, trying hard to concentrate on the way she held the ball and on her angle on the green. When at last she sent it rolling toward its goal, she was pleased to note that her aim was much straighter this time. She actually managed to knock down several of the pins. Clapping her hands, she did a little dance around her father and couldn't wait for another turn.

Hours later, they were the talk of Schifferdecker Gardens. Sipping iced tea, her father savoring one of those famous brews he had mentioned earlier that morning, Serra beamed with delight as people stopped by their table to introduce themselves and lavish her with compliments on her abilities on the bowling green. She met so many that she couldn't begin to remember their names, and soon her head was spinning, deliciously so, from all of the attention given her.

At one point, her father reached across the table, gathered her hand in his large, calloused ones, and gave it a squeeze. "Don't know if I've told you or not, girl, but it sure is good to have you home again. I can't tell you how proud of you I am, how you've grown up so pretty and mannered, such a fine young lady. Your mother would have been pleased, too."

A twinge of guilt nipped at her conscience. From now on, she would measure up to his expectations — in every way. A beam of sunlight danced across his face, and for a moment he looked so frail, so vulnerable, but it was just the play of light, she convinced herself. Her father was much too robust to consider sickly-looking.

It was just as hard to believe that this man, with his kindness and his generous nature, was the same one who had been so harsh with Ty at the cabin. But, then, Ty had a way of bringing out the worst in people. Look what he had done to her. Never again, she vowed. She wouldn't disappoint her father.

Serra sighed, lacing her fingers through his. Bringing his hand to her lips, she kissed the rough, scarred knuckles, for the first time noting the way his flesh seemed too abundant yet his bones stood out, prominently defined.

"I love you, Father," she stated, realizing that was the very first time she had ever said those words aloud to anyone. It felt good, so very good to belong.

Langston smiled, and depositing his mug on the table with a thump, he stood. "Come on, Serenity. There's a whole Exposition to explore together."

As they started from the Gardens to the carriage that would take them to the Exposition, Serra heard her name called.

"Serra. Serenity Langston."

Her hand cradled in the crook of her father's arm, she turned to see Amanda Stokes hurrying across the grounds.

"Amanda," she called back gaily, yet somewhat reserved. If it hadn't been for the other girl's encouragement, she would never have run across Ty yesterday at the hotel, would never have resorted to tight lacing, would never have pinned those ridiculous earrings to her clothing, would never have been caught unawares by Ty. And though in her heart she knew she was being a bit unfair with her friend, she still held back. She didn't want the glamour, the social stimulation Amanda needed to be happy. The things that were important were already hers: a family.

John Langston greeted the girl warmly, tapping the brim of his hat. "Why, Miss Stokes, so good to see you. Is that brother of yours around?" He craned his neck to look over the grounds, seeking the younger man.

Serra cocked her head, studying her father, noting the way the weathered skin of his neck seemed to sag loosely. Why would he be so interested in Monte Stokes?

"He and his friends are somewhere about,"

230

Amanda replied, waving vaguely back toward the Gardens. "The last time I saw them they were hovering about one of the beer kegs."

"Would you mind too much, Serra, girl, if I took a minute?" Langston asked.

She frowned, sensing that the magic of the moment had been broken. Wanting more than anything to reclaim it, she shrugged. "I suppose—"

"Oh, Serra doesn't mind," Amanda piped up, taking her by the arm and leading her toward the pavilion. "We have some talking to do, too. Take all of the time you need, Mr. Langston."

Without a doubt, Serra knew what her friend had on her mind. Reluctantly, she allowed the blonde to take charge. Oh, dear, what sordid gossip had she heard?

Just as she predicted, the second they were alone and seated at one of the small tables Amanda peered at her glowingly. "So, tell me, what happened?"

"Happened?" Trying to appear as if she didn't understand, Serra blinked rapidly. "I can't imagine what you're talking about."

Amanda's face clouded with hurt. "Oh, come on, Serra. You weren't going to keep secrets from *me*, were you? My servant, Lizzie, got it from Tess that she let *him* into the house late last night." On the word *him*, her voice warbled, and she darted her eyes about, looking for someone to be eavesdropping on their private conversation. "Did you—?" She paused, waiting for Serra to fill in the blank.

If she could, Serra admitted to herself she would gladly keep Amanda Stokes in the dark, but she doubted the other girl would accept much less than the truth. Pressing her lips together to keep the facts

231

from blurting out, she looked down, brushing at imaginary specks of dirt on her gown. "It's not what you think. Ty and I have known each other for so long; we've been through so much together."

Amanda made a sound of exasperation. "Are you trying to tell me nothing happened?"

Serra nodded vigorously, still unable to look up, a sense of relief coursing through her.

"Do you honestly expect me to believe that a virile man like Tyler Ramsey came into your bedroom last night and left without doing *anything?*"

She had to admit such a claim did sound most unlikely when it came to Ty. Oh, Tess. She could just kill her for having such a big mouth. When she got home, she was determined to sit that girl down and tell her a thing or two about discretion and loyalty, but for now there was no way she was going to skirt about the truth with her friend. "Oh, Mandy, I didn't mean for it to happen," she blurted out. "He caught me by surprise, and there I was with those darn earrings pinned to my chemise."

"Chemise?" Amanda gasped. "He actually saw you in your underclothing?" A look of absolute disbelief colored her pale face. "Oh, Serra, you mean *it* happened?"

With a sinking feeling, Serra realized she'd confessed to more than she'd meant to or needed to. "I didn't say—"

"Oh, yes, you did," Amanda insisted, leaning so close that Serra could see the telltale signs of rice powder on the bridge of her nose. "You didn't mean for *it,* you said. Oh, Serra," she demanded breathlessly, "what was it like? What did he do? Was it as wonderful as the books and magazines suggest?"

232

Serra didn't know quite how to handle her friend's rapidfire questions. She'd assumed Amanda knew all about what men and women did in the bedroom, but apparently she was mistaken. Glancing about guiltily, she sought a means of escaping. How had this situation managed to get so completely out of hand? "I think maybe we should end this conversation here and now." Serra started to rise from her chair.

The other girl caught her by the arm. "Not until you tell me exactly what happened, Serenity Langston." There was earnest appeal on her face. "I'm dying to know."

Serra had to admit it would be nice to talk to someone about the whole affair, from that day she'd gotten on the train to come to Joplin. For a moment she swayed in indecision, pulled between her conscience and her heart's need to alleviate its burdens.

"Serra, you can trust me," Amanda assured her. "I won't tell a soul. And if I do, look at all you have on me."

Serra glanced down, assessing. There was validity in what the other girl said. The magazines, the episodes at the finishing school in Chicago. Amanda had shared those things with her, completely, trustingly. Could she do no less?

Sinking back down in her chair, she began, hesitantly at first, but then the story tumbled from her lips like spring floodwater cresting an earthen dam: Ty's long-ago promise to come back for her, the abduction, the hours alone in the cabin, her father's terrible reaction when he had found them. And last night the fiasco with the earrings, the wonderful giving and taking, and the heartbreak of finding him

233

gone without a word of farewell, without a renewal of his promise to return. How should she act when she saw him again? How should she expect him to react to her?

When at last she finished her oration, Serra turned to Amanda for answers. But for once the other girl sat stunned, speechless, looking at her with a mixture of awe and pity.

"Mandy, please tell me you don't hate me for what I have done."

"Hate you? Oh, Lord, no. I just don't know how . . . to tell you."

"Tell me? Tell me what?" A small frown knitted Serra's brows.

Amanda glanced sideways, working her bottom lip between her teeth. "Your father has apparently been speaking to Monte about you."

"Your brother?" Serra's amber eyes slid to where the two men stood talking, gesturing, in comfortable camaraderie. "Whatever about?"

"It seems . . ." Amanda stumbled over her words and, sitting back, gnawed at her bottom lip before beginning again. "Your father is making plans for you. Big plans."

"Plans? What kind of plans?" Serra was sincerely perplexed.

"He has designs on you . . . and Monte."

It took a moment for the meaning of the blonde's statement to sink in, but when it did, Serra was aghast. "You don't mean to say—"

Amanda's head bobbed in affirmation.

"Oh, no." The bubble of innocent happiness shattered into a million soapsuds of horror. "It's not that I don't like your brother," she assured her.

"I realize that."

"But it's just what will Ty say . . . do, when he learns about Father's newest betrayal of his trust?"

Amanda cleared her throat, waiting for Serra to acknowledge her. "That's the other thing I don't know how to tell you."

A strange feeling of dread cut through her. She didn't want to ask, but she had to. "What other thing?"

To avoid answering, Amanda began to fidget, first with her purse strings, then with her hair, and finally with the collar of her dress.

"Amanda, what is it!?"

A long, potent moment hung in the air, their gazes locked, neither one breathing.

"Tyler's gone," the blonde replied quietly.

"Gone?" Panic shot through Serra, but she battled it down. Ty came and went all the time.

"It seems he left this morning on the train to St. Louis."

A sound of relief whistled passed her pursed lips. "We knew he planned a trip to Chicago."

"Yes, but we didn't think he would give up his room at the hotel and—"

"And what?" The frown returned.

"He even got rid of that black beast of his."

"Cochise?" Serra gave a little titter of nervousness. "Oh, no, you must be wrong. Ty would never give up that horse, not unless . . . unless . . ." Serra paused to swallow, unwilling to face the obvious.

"Word has it, Serra"—Amanda reached out and took her hand, squeezing it— "that Tyler Ramsey doesn't plan to ever come back to Joplin."

Chapter Fourteen

Chicago, Illinois

Ty stood ramrod straight in the tiny, ornately paneled box as it zipped upwards, leaving what felt like his stomach and his heart several floors beneath. This was his first ride in a mechanized elevator, much faster than the hand-hoisted mine lifts. Now he wished he'd just taken the damned stairs like he'd wanted to do in the first place and ignored the black man who operated the contraption when he'd asked, "What floor, sir?" encouraging him to step aboard.

The couple sharing the experience with him, obviously old hands at elevator riding, gave him strange looks, especially the woman, who boldly judged his masculine attributes beneath his travel-wrinkled jeans, leather jacket, and black cowboy hat, his pistol strapped low across his hips. Her gaze, which seemed permanently attached to the front of his pants, and the way she sniffed, said it all: "Interesting, but a bit rustic for my taste, darling."

Ty eyed her back just as brazenly, his mouth twisted in a sneer. For someone who had spent more than half of his life surviving the streets of New

York City, he had never thought to be judged a country bumpkin. His gaze slid over the gentleman, dressed in his fancy silk suit, noting the way the cutaway coat fell open, revealing his wallet.

For a split second, Ty wondered if he still had the knack. Six or seven years ago he could have picked the bastard's pocket while smiling at his lady. But now, look at him. He glanced down at his dusty attire and grimaced. A Missouri hayseed if he'd ever seen one.

The "big city" and its newfangled progress — buildings as tall as mountains, ten stories high and more, elevators, telephones, electric lights — it all bewildered him now. Rubbing his sweating palms down his pant legs, he flexed the fingers of his right hand the way he used to long ago. The woman still watched him, still sized up his manliness as if he were the main attraction of a wild West show, and her arrogant manner irritated him. She wanted cowboys and Indians, did she? Well, he'd see she got just what she begged for.

Whipping his pistol from its holster, he cradled it in the palm of his hand, most casually.

The couple apparently didn't see it that way. They moved as one to crowd against the far wall of the elevator, the woman emitting a little screech of alarm as she pushed against the operator, whose dark eyes seemed to bug out of their sockets.

With a sense of smug satisfaction, Ty watched them all squirm, the way Mr. Fancy Pants pushed his lady behind his back when his eyes suggested he would much rather to do otherwise.

But Ty ignored the gentleman, judging him no threat at all. Probably if he pointed the weapon at the man, he would disgrace himself. Instead, he leveled his dancing blue gaze on the woman, who peered around her escort in fear, yet still somewhat fascinated. Extending the weapon toward her, he grinned, thoroughly enjoying himself, knowing the effect that look had on women, no matter who they were or where they came from.

"The way your interest was latched onto my crotch, ma'am," he drawled ever so politely, "I figured my gun or my"—he jiggled his brows suggestively—"fascinated you. I'd be glad to show you my gun, but we'd have to find somewhere a bit more private for the other."

The woman shrieked. "William, did you hear what that man said to me?"

The elevator came to a squeaking halt on the third floor.

"Shut up, Agnes. If you'd learn to keep your eyes where they belonged, things like this wouldn't happen." Without looking at what he was doing, the gentleman pushed the operator out of the way and pulled the lever to release the door, which slid open. Mute, the couple scurried out of the structure, then turned and began running down the hallway as if a mad dog snapped at their heels.

Ty stepped halfway out and laughing, called out to their retreating figures, "Didn't mean to offend, ma'am. But I never was one to say no to a lady's show of interest."

Once they were gone, he lowered the gun to his side and stepped back into the car. As silent as a mouse, the dark-faced operator watched him, obviously unsure what he should do—stay at his job or run—his hands shaking so that Ty felt truly sorry for

238

the little man.

"Seventh floor," Ty reminded him calmly.

"Seventh floor, y—y—yes, sir," the man squeaked, but his hands never moved to pull the door shut, his eyes glued to the pistol in Ty's fist.

They both stood there, staring at each other.

"She got what she deserved, you know," Ty declared matter-of-factly, jerking his head toward the corridor where the man and woman had disappeared. Giving the revolver a quick once-over, he slipped it back into the holster.

"Oh, yes, sir, she sho' did," the elevator operator blurted out, relief brimming in his dark gaze.

Ty stared pointedly at the levers. "Then, if we're in agreement, do you think you could get this contraption movin' along?"

"Oh." Hands still trembling, the operator pulled the door closed and started the elevator in motion.

The steam-driven hoists rumbled. There was that terrible sinking feeling again. Ty braced himself against the wall, willing away the queasiness.

"After a few times up and down, you get used to it."

Ty looked up to see the other man grinning at him. "Yeah, I suppose, but I don't plan on bein' around long enough to get used to anything about this godforsaken town."

"Just visitin', then?"

"Here long enough to make my fortune." Ty patted his shirt pocket, which held the letter written by the inventor of the new method of zinc extraction.

"That's good, sir. Your kind o' man wouldn't make it long here in Chicago, anyway."

"My kind of man?" Ty asked, curious what the fellow meant by that. "Just what kind is that?"

"The kind that demands things be done his *own* way." The elevator came to a halt, and the operator reached out and opened the door, revealing a corridor identical to the one on the third floor.

Ty stared down the long, austere hallway. "Mister," he said with a sigh of fatalism, "if things were goin' the way I wanted them to, I wouldn't be here in the first place." He shuffled out of the elevator, knowing that once he took this final step to sever his affiliation with Langston Mining, nothing would ever be the same again.

Security enveloped her, comfortable, protective, familiar. So much so that the last thing Serra wanted to do was acknowledge the world around her. Reality wasn't so wonderful. She fought the intrusion, squeezing her eyes shut.

"Go away," she mumbled into the pillow created by her bent elbow, which was propped on the sill in the window seat where she sat.

"Miss Serenity." The hand shook her shoulder again. "You can't spend another day just sittin' here, starin' out the window. Your father is very concerned about your lack of interest in—in anything. And Miss Amanda is downstairs to see you again."

That was the same thing Tess had said yesterday, but she'd ignored the servant then, and she'd do the same now. "Tell Amanda I'm indisposed."

She wanted back her dreams. Ty was there. And though they were somewhat disturbing, they were still better than the light of day.

In her visions, Ty cared for her, shared his

240

warmth, his arms wrapped about her, his verbal assurances so soothing. Not that that was so particularly unnerving. What bothered her was that they were children again, so young, younger than she'd ever recalled before. A past that had escaped her until now. A past that could never have existed before those days together in the orphanage.

The dreams had to be illusions, but, oh God, they seemed so real. More realistic than the images of a childhood here in the Langston house. And though the nighttime recreations left her bewildered, they were comforting at the same time.

Oh, Ty. Ty, she cried inwardly, reburying her face in the crook of her arm. If only he were here to explain. He would clarify her confusion. Make everything all right again.

Just like he used to do when they nestled together beneath the stairwell in the tenement, listening to the wretched men and women who rented the squalid rooms, her own parents . . .

Serra sat up, pushing from her eyes the tumbled copper tresses she'd not brushed in days, shoving away the memories—false ones, damn it; they had to be. She was Serenity Langston. She was. These crazy mixed-up images were driving her insane. Her past here in this house was too vivid to be a lie. . . .

Oh, God, she didn't know what to think anymore.

Pressing the heels of her hands against her temples, she took several deep breaths, willing her pounding heart to slow down, the pain trapped in her throat to subside.

"Miss Serenity, are you all right?"

Serra could hear Tess, but the serving girl sounded so far away.

"Please, miss, answer me."

Lifting her head, Serra tried to smile reassurance but failed miserably. She wasn't sure about anything—not anymore. "Didn't I just tell you I'm indisposed?" she snapped, ignoring the servant's pained expression.

Why was she having these strange visions? Why, now, when she had at last found the loving family she'd always dreamed of, did doubt have to rear its ugly head?

She narrowed her amber eyes and sniffed defiance. This was all Ty's fault—with his denial of her rightful place in her father's house, his life, his legacy.

First, he'd planted these seeds of uncertainty, and then he'd had the gall to turn his back on her.

"Damn you, Tyler Ramsey. Damn you." She balled her fist and slammed it against the windowsill.

"Miss!"

Serra looked up at the servant, her youthful face lined with confusion and shock at her mistress's sudden, unprovoked outburst.

"Please, Tess." she moaned. "Go away, will you? Leave me alone. And tell Amanda I don't want to see her."

Moments later, Serra realized that she'd gotten her wish. She was alone. And just as lost as that day long ago when she'd stepped from the train car in New Hope, a frightened little orphan girl clinging to childish delusions that finding her family would cure all of the ills of the world.

Would happiness never find her?

She lifted her chin, a tremor of that long-forgotten emotion, hope, fluttering in her heart. New Hope. Of course. Why hadn't she thought of it sooner? Dr.

Chelsey would know why these terrible nightmares plagued her and what they meant. She would confront him and insist he supply her with a feasible explanation. And then if there was any truth to be found in the dreams, well then . . . then . . .

She wasn't sure what she would do then.

The deed was done. Tyler Ramsey now possessed the sole rights to the new separation method call froth flotation. It was up to him whether he chose to share the idea with others, including John Langston, or whether he kept it strictly for his own use — and profit.

The process was so simple, he was amazed he'd not thought of it himself. By crushing the jack into small particles and agitating it in aerated water, the gangue, or earthy constituents, succumbed to the moisture and sank, while the mineral portion clung to the bubbles and rose to the surface as a foam. At first he'd doubted the validity of the method, and only after watching it put to the test over and over had he finally become a firm believer.

The most amazing part of it all was that the equipment needed was relatively accessible, even if it was a bit expensive. He could be up and running in less than a few months, lining his pockets from the piles of jack that the other mining companies tossed away as worthless.

Which led him to his next decision. Where to set up his operation. The day he'd departed from Joplin, he'd intended to never return. He'd made a vow to stay away from Langston Mining, away from Serra. There were other mining towns where he could go, live, and make his fortune. But after his ordeal in Chicago, he didn't want to go anywhere else. Joplin, Missouri was his home.

He'd never thought he'd feel that way about any place. But the wild, crowded community was where he wanted to be. And, God help him, he missed Serra so much a physical pain knifed through his insides.

But there wasn't room for the three of them—himself, Serra, and the damnable lie that hung between them like soiled sheets. Serra Paletot had never been and would never be Serenity Langston. If John Langston would only take the time to think about it, he would realize the absurdity of her claim. But the old man had his reasons for grasping at straws, reasons Ty could sympathize with, even if he didn't agree with them.

What would John do if he brought him proof of the deception being played on him? Ty paused, his heart thundering in the prison of his rib cage. Didn't he deserve to know the truth before . . . before? . . .

Didn't Serra deserve to know as well?

Not sure whether his motives could be labeled self-centered or sacrificial, Ty walked up to the ticket window of the train depot. If he planned to expose the fraudulent claim for what it was, then the best place to begin was where it had originated: Dr. Lionel Chelsey.

"One way to New Hope, Missouri."

The stationmaster gave him only a perfunctory glance and made out the necessary documents.

"New Hope, Missouri," the man repeated, shoving the paperwork under the grill and accepting the money Ty offered in return.

244

His own future, Ty concluded nobly, taking the tickets and gathering up his satchel, could be put on hold while he went about the business of . . . of . . .

Oh, hell, there was no denying that in his quest for the truth, he would be destroying Serra's hopes and dreams. And in the process, he most likely would wreck any chance they had of making it together.

Ty boarded the train. This time the iron monster of fate would push them so far apart that he had no doubt of what the outcome would be.

"I'm sorry, Serra," he mumbled. "But there's no other way."

"Serenity, what do you think you're doin'?"

Her hands full of clothing and toiletries, Serra spun about to confront her father. After a potent moment of silence, she replied in a calm voice, which belied her true state of high emotions, "I've decided I'm going to visit Dr. Chelsey for a while."

A look of hurt crossed Langston's thin, harried face. Oh, dear, had she done this to him? He looked as if he'd not slept in days. Serra wanted to retract her statement, but she couldn't do that. Instead, she dropped her packing and rushed to his side.

"Please, Father, try to understand." Oh, God, did she have the right to call him that?

Langston frowned and curled his arm about her slim shoulder. "God knows, girl, I'm tryin'. I really am. But you mope 'round here for days, refusin' to see anyone, refusin' to eat anything. And now you make plans to just rush off. You weren't even goin' to talk to me about whatever is botherin' you, were

245

you?"

Serra hung her head guiltily. She'd wanted to talk to him. Truly, she had. But she'd just felt he was too involved in the problem. And there were the dreams. How could she possibly confess to him about the nightmare-fantasies that contradicted her very reasons for being there? "I'm sorry," she murmured. "I just thought—"

"That's your problem, girl," Langston said, taking her face in his hands, forcing her to look up at him. "You think too damned much. Try feelin'."

"Wh—wh—what do you mean?" What did he know or suspect? Her mind fluttered about like a trapped butterfly seeking a means of escape. Oh, God, what had Tess told *him?*

"I know it's that boy who's got you so wound up."

"Boy? I don't know who you mean."

"Don't you think I have eyes to see? Tyler Ramsey. He stirs you up like a hornet's nest, doesn't he? It's his leavin' town that's got you in such a dither."

Serra pulled away and presented her back, unwilling to admit to the simplistic truth. Tyler Ramsey tugged on her strings, and she danced like a mindless puppet.

"Serra, girl." Langston's hands covered her shoulders, consoling. "I thought his leavin' would be the best thing . . . for you. There's so much I want for you, and I don't think Ty with his wild, ruthless ways is the man to give it to you."

Unbidden tears welled behind her closed eyelids, acknowledging that what her father said was probably true. Someone like Monte Stokes would be better for her, yet there was no denying how she felt about Ty. She glanced over her shoulder at this man

246

who was willing to take her at her word that she was his daughter, completely trusting, and she sensed he would never understand or approve of her love for Ty. She wasn't so sure she completely understood it herself. "I know you've done what you thought was best," she replied earnestly.

"Give my way a chance, will you? And then if you're still not happy, I won't force you to do somethin' you don't want to do."

"Thank you, sir," she whispered, knowing his concession and her own were not enough. If only he knew of the terrible suspicions she harbored. If only she dared to share her doubts and fears of her identity with him.

"If you want to go and visit the Doc, then that's all right by me. But you have to promise that afterward you'll come home and give me—and Monte Stokes—a well-deserved chance."

Serra whirled about and pressed her face against the warm blue and white checks of his shirt. "Thank you, Father," she sobbed, wanting more than anything for this man to be her sire and to be proud of her. "I'll make it up to you. I promise." She'd make it *all* up to him somehow.

Holding her away from him, Langston grinned down at her. "And no more tears, you hear me?"

She nodded, giving him a wavering smile.

"And I want you to take Amanda with you. She's downstairs right now, determined to speak to you even if you do say no again."

She opened her mouth to declare that she didn't need a watchdog, not even a friend like Amanda. And the blonde was a true friend, there was no denying that. She might even be her sister-in-law someday.

Langston laid a work-roughened finger against her lips. "No argument. I insist that you don't travel alone. John Langston's daughter doesn't do that."

"All right, sir," she replied obediently, accepting that Amanda's companionship might make the long train ride much more bearable.

"And pin money. Come to my office when you're ready to leave, and I'll see that you have plenty. Will you at least allow me to see you to the station?"

"Of course," she conceded. "I would be honored."

He gathered her face once more in his aged hands. "You wire me when you're ready to come home, and I'll pick you up at the station."

Serra hesitated. What if she found out she didn't have a right to come back?

"You hear me, girl? I'll miss you every minute you're gone."

"I'll wire," she promised.

The feel of his dry, hesitant kiss upon her cheek lingered long after he left the room.

"Please, God, let him be my father," she prayed aloud, her palm pressed against her face to retain the love his simple gesture represented. Then she returned to her packing, torn between her desire to cling to her dreams and her need to glean answers to her burning questions.

"Why, Serenity, dear, what a surprise!" Mrs. Chelsey's serene face greeted her at the door of the rambling old house on the outskirts of New Hope, which Serra had called home for so many years.

She tried to peer around the older woman, who

still maintained a portion of her fading beauty. "Is Doc home?" she asked hopefully.

"Actually, he's gone to Jefferson City for a few days and is due back on the afternoon train. Some sort of legal matter," the woman replied vaguely, her gaze darting about, unable to light anywhere in particular, especially not on Serra.

"Oh." The last thing Serra had anticipated was for the physician not to be there. "Do you think we could come in and wait for him?"

Mrs. Chelsey hesitated for a moment—or so it seemed to Serra. But then she swung open the door and stepped aside. "Of course, child. You're always welcomed."

Serra picked up her valise and stepped inside, a subdued Amanda trailing after her like a loyal entourage. On the long trip there, she had explained a little about her life before coming to Joplin—not everything, not the dreams—and Amanda had listened in silent awe to learn that Serra had been through so much.

"Oh, ma'am, this is Amanda Stokes, my friend," she introduced the other girl. She had always called the woman "ma'am," somehow their relationship never having gelled as it should have. Doc had been the one who had been there for her, guiding her, caring for her. Not that Mrs. Chelsey had ever been anything but nice to her, but it was as if the woman felt uncomfortable around her. If the truth be known, she'd been somewhat uneasy around the physician's wife as well.

She followed the woman down the familiar central hallway to the tiny bedroom in the rear of the house near the doctor's office, which she had called her own for nearly seven years.

"I'm sorry, but you girls will have to share."

The information surprised Serra, as she knew there was a second downstairs bedroom, much more spacious, that the doctor used for visitors and occasional patients. She had thought Amanda would be housed there.

"We have another guest who is scheduled to arrive this afternoon."

The insinuation didn't pass by Serra. A scheduled guest, whereas she was an unscheduled one. "I'm sorry, ma'am. I suppose I should have written first announcing my arrival," she admitted with chagrin. "It's just that I decided to come at the last moment. Doc told me if I ever needed him to not hesitate to come—" She almost said *home*, but it was apparent Mrs. Chelsey didn't think of this as Serra's home, not anymore.

And if this wasn't where she belonged and the Langston mansion wasn't home, either . . . Serra didn't want to think about the implications—not now.

"Of course, dear. You're always welcomed." The woman then whirled out of the room, closing the door behind her back.

"I'd say, Serra, that woman is either afraid of you or doesn't care much for you." Amanda pivoted slowly, taking in every aspect of the tiny bedroom. It was clean but austere, nothing like a young girl's room should be, filled with bright colors and frills.

Serra watched the other girl take assessment of what the past had held for an orphan girl who had known very little about love and family, who had been more than willing to accept even the meager

250

crumbs of what life had offered and had been happy. At that time, she'd never put much stock in Mrs. Chelsey's behavior, but Amanda was right. There was something definitely amiss in the aloof way the doctor's wife treated her.

But just as wrong was the way she, herself, had acted of late. Now that everything she could possibly want was there for her, she had lost the one thing she possessed—her ability to be happy.

It didn't make much sense. None of it.

Then it was as if she floated high above the room, over the house itself, staring down at herself and everyone about her, seeing her life from a different perspective, perhaps through the eyes of her friend who had known nothing of struggle, or loss, or abandonment.

Maybe she'd made a terrible mistake coming back to New Hope. She was no longer so sure that finding the answers to her questions was the solution to her problems. What she wanted was to be happy with the blessings God had been gracious enough to bestow on her. Why did she allow the accusations Ty had made about her take root and grow? If John Langston was willing to accept her without reservation—surely the man would recognize his own daughter—why couldn't she do the same for herself?

Frowning, she plopped down on the overstuffed chair by the one small window the room possessed. Now that she had come all this way, she would wait for Dr. Chelsey to return. Once he explained away these nightmares she'd been having of late—and she had no doubt he would have a good explanation—she would go home. Then she would cast out all the demons, including Tyler Ramsey, and happily be the

251

perfect daughter John Langston believed her to be.

The scheduled guest Mrs. Chelsey had spoken of
arrived as planned. The rather large woman, toting
her valise in one hefty hand, her purse in the other,
her straw bonnet centered most unbecomingly on the
top of her head, making her face look even rounder
than it was, took the house by storm, as if visiting
the Chelseys was an everyday occurrence. But Serra
never recalled meeting her during her six-year stay
in the house, yet there was something distinctly rememberable about her. She was sure she'd seen her
somewhere before.

Confirming her feelings of familiarity, when intro-
ductions were made that afternoon over tea, Mrs.
Babison stared at her as if she were seeing a ghost.
So unnerving was the way the woman watched her
that Serra found it impossible to enjoy the little petit
fours Mrs. Chelsey served. But, then, she wasn't all
that hungry, anyway.

Slipping her teacup into its saucer on the table beside her chair, Serra smiled at the rotund woman,
who immediately glanced down at her own plate of
food and began consuming it at so rapid a rate
Serra could see why she was so large.

"Mrs. Babison," she began the usual idle teatime
conversation on a forward note, "have we met somewhere before?"

An exchange of subtle glances between the woman
and the doctor's wife didn't go unnoticed amongst
the rattle of china in nervous hands. It was also obvious she struggled to form an appropriate answer.

"Oh, my dear," the woman began, "I think perhaps—"

The opening of the front door provided a convenient interruption.

"Oh, it must be Lionel," Mrs. Chelsey announced with obvious relief, rising and rushing from the room.

Her lips tightly sealed, Mrs. Babison continued to scrutinize Serra, but she didn't bother to finish her answer to the pointed question put to her.

Then the doctor swept into the room, and for Serra all else ceased to exist. Her heart began to race, and she suddenly wanted to get up and run from the room. She didn't want answers, didn't want to know the truth. She didn't want her family taken away from her. Then his dark eyes that had first settled on Mrs. Babison swiveled to her, and she caught the flicker of a frown just before he smiled at her.

"Serenity, dear." He stepped forward, reaching out his hand. "What an unexpected surprise."

Serra rose to greet him, unable to expel the rush of uncertainty that coursed through her. Was he only mildly surprised or irritated at her arrival? "Doctor," she rushed into her statement of defense, "I've needed to speak with you. Perhaps later you could give me a few moments."

"Of course." He placed his arm about Serra and steered her toward the door.

This was happening a little faster than she'd anticipated, and she fought the urge to pull back. But this was what she'd wanted, she assured herself, a chance to confront the doctor, to know the truth. She clamped her mouth into a tight bow. The sooner, the better.

253

"I'm sure you ladies don't mind. Go on with your tea while I take Serenity to my office for a little counsel."

As he led her down the well-remembered hallway, his hand pressing against her spine, he asked somewhat disinterestedly, without a hint of alarm that she could detect, "Everything *is* all right at home, isn't it, dear?"

"Oh, everything has been wonderful," she assured him. "It's just—"

At the threshold of his office, he paused, turning her to face him, clutching her shoulders most painfully. "What is it, Serenity? That nasty Tyler Ramsey hasn't been pestering you, filling your head with nonsense again, has he?"

"No, no," she denied, unprepared for the venom of his attack that found its target so easily. "It's not Ty," she lied. "It's just that I've been having these strange, unexplainable dreams," she blurted out. This wasn't going the way she'd envisioned. She'd wanted to ask him certain questions about her past first, without revealing where the information had come from.

"Dreams?" Firmly, he took her arm and led her inside his private study, sitting her on the green and white sofa she had spent many a morning perched on while they discussed her past. "What kind of dreams?" he demanded.

She hesitated to reply. How had the physician managed to reverse their roles so neatly? Her stiffened upper lip began to tremble, and she sucked it between her teeth to still it.

"Dumpling, how can I help you if you won't even tell me what the problem is?"

She so did want . . . need help. The words spilled forward like an unleashed dam, the images of she and Ty together as children that contradicted everything the doctor's guidance had led her to believe verbalizing themselves. "I just don't know what the dreams mean nor how to make them go away," she finally concluded after the long, uninterrupted oration.

"You did the right thing coming to see me, Serenity," he told her, his words, the familiar strumming of his fingers, oddly enough giving her comfort and relief like nothing else could. "Anytime you're not sure, you are to return to me immediately. Do you understand?"

Rebellion roiled within her, and she opened her mouth to protest the way he ordered her about. But then his shiny gold pocket watch appeared as if from nowhere. He began swinging it, and Serra was helpless to do more than watch it, to accept the sapping of her determination and willpower. But, then, wasn't this exactly what she'd come here for—relief?

"Dreams are strange phenomena, Serenity. Usually they're not at all what they appear to be. Instead, they're the manifestation of our fears and apprehensions, nothing more, and rarely represent the truth. Do you believe me?"

Feeling as if her very soul had been sucked from her body, she clutched at his explanation, wanting more than anything to believe him. She nodded her head, the familiarity of his voice soothing away her distress.

"Good girl. Now, Serenity, when I snap my fingers, you will awaken and these false dreams will haunt you no longer. You will once more be the willing, obedient daughter of John Langston."

Oh, I will, I will, Serra acknowledged with an overwhelming sense of relief. Once again, she was free to be Serenity Langston.

She paused for a moment, blinking her eyes to clear her vision. It was freedom she'd gained, wasn't it?

But of course, it was.

Remembering her father's request that she accept his plans for her, she suddenly found the prospect of Monte Stokes no longer so farfetched, in fact rather stimulating.

At last having found the peace of mind she'd come seeking, she was ready to go home. She would send her father a telegraph right away this afternoon, then catch the morning train back to Joplin.

Chapter Fifteen

New Hope was exactly the way he remembered it being nearly seven years before, a sleepy little farming community with no need to grow bigger, no need for progress, yet no threat of diminishing for its lack of foresight. Ty wondered what would have happened to him, to Serra, if he'd never run away from the orphan train and the dauntless Reverend Millboone and his wife. Would he and Serra have grown up side by side and gone on to marry — he a farmer, she a farmer's wife? No conflicts, no ups or downs in their existence? . . .

No, not the wild boy he'd been. He smiled, remembering all too well what he'd wanted from life then. Just like Jesse James and Billy the Kid, he'd vowed. And in a sense that was what he'd become — a social outcast, struggling to make the best for himself the only way he knew how.

Fortunately, he'd had someone like John Langston to ride his flank instead of a Quantrell, someone to teach him a true sense of right and wrong.

Ty gritted his teeth and walked away from the train depot. Regardless of how things turned out between the two of them, he must admit he did owe

Langston a debt. He only hoped the way he planned to repay the man would be accepted in the spirit given.

Stepping upon the wooden sidewalk of the town's main street, he passed the opera house where Serra had stood up for him when he'd refused to participate in the orphan performance. He smiled, thinking of how she'd moved center stage and covered up his defiance by declaring him shy. Shy? Hell, he'd been anything but shy.

Li'l Serra, always taking it upon her slim shoulders to defend his welfare and honor until . . .

Until he'd given a damn about either one of them.

That's when he saw her coming out of the New Hope Mercantile/Western Union Office, and he couldn't believe his eyes. Serra? What was she doing back here? Pausing behind the protection of a porch post, his Stetson drawn low over his face, he watched her sashay out the door, followed by a chattering Amanda Stokes.

What were the *two* of them doing in New Hope? For one moment, Ty's belief in Serra's innocence wavered. Especially when the pair climbed into a waiting buggy occupied by none other than Dr. Chelsey himself.

Dr. Lionel Chelsey. The man he'd come looking for. Self-proclaimed healer through the rejuvenescent powers of the mind. The train had made a stop in Jefferson City, and on impulse he had gone into the city and checked state records on the man. He'd discovered the old charlatan had no license to practice medicine, at least not in the state of Missouri, but then there were no set regulations for his kind of doctoring.

Ty had then had this brainstorm. Licensed or not,

didn't all physicians keep confidential records about their patients? Chances were he would have just such a file on Serra. Maybe, just maybe, he could find the proof he sought right under the old quacksalver's nose.

Serra's unexpected presence didn't change a damn thing. He had come for answers, and he would stop at nothing to get what he wanted.

With that in mind, he watched the buggy disappear around a corner. Then he continued on his way to the New Hope Hotel, to take a room and to wait for the sun to set.

Serra lay in the darkness, listening to the soft, shallow breathing of Amanda in the bed beside her, unable herself to close her eyes. It was no longer doubt that kept her awake, nor fear of the dreams. They would haunt her no more.

What did disturb her was a vivid image of Ty. Every time she tried to envision what it would be like to kiss Monte Stokes, to allow him the liberties she'd gladly bestowed on Ty, somehow she just couldn't bring herself to do it, not even in her mind. Those things, those intimacies belonged to one man only, whether he particularly wanted them or not.

Lying still, she listened to Amanda mumble in her sleep, unable to make much sense of what the girl said. But, then, she didn't really understand what she was feeling, either.

Reaching out, she touched the other girl on the shoulder and shook her. "Mandy?"

The blonde muttered something about a fuchsia blouse needing ironing and to come back when it was done.

Serra smiled, knowing her friend thought a servant was attempting to stir her. "Amanda," she whispered again, "wake up."

The girl jerked awake, pushing up on her elbows in the bed and brushing her hair from her face. She blinked around, noting the darkness and the strange surroundings. "Is something wrong, Serra?"

"No, not really. I couldn't sleep."

"Oh, Serra," the blonde huffed in exasperation. "Whatever it is, can't it wait until morning?"

Serra ignored her friend's nocturnal protest. "Do you think it's possible to love and hate someone all at the same time?"

Amanda said nothing, and Serra turned over on her side to nudge the girl again. "Mandy?"

"I'm thinking," the girl muttered a protest at Serra's impatience. "When you say someone, whom do you mean? A man?"

"I suppose."

"Someone like Tyler Ramsey?"

Serra sighed. "Am I that transparent?"

"Tyler Ramsey is a man worth lying awake for."

"Do you think it's possible for me to want to both throttle him and—and—? Well, you know what I mean."

"I read once that love is a raging ocean of emotions. I imagine that hate could be in there somewhere." Amanda propped her head on her arms. "Whenever you think about him, which is stronger—the love or the hate?"

Serra considered the question for a moment. "Sometimes it's one and then the other. But when I'm with him, all I can think of is wanting him to kiss me."

"If he was here right now, what would you say to

him?"

Serra giggled at the turn of their conversation, then she grew serious. "Well, first of all I would tell him he was wrong and then—" She paused in mid sentence, stiffening, swearing she heard an unfamiliar noise. "Did you hear that?"

"Hear what?" Amanda asked sleepily.

The quiet thump sounded again.

"That?"

"Probably just a mouse in the wall. You'd tell him he was wrong and then what?"

"I'd tell him I loved him," Serra answered quietly, accepting the other girl's explanation of the noise, as well as her own heart's interjection.

"Really?" Amanda's surprise rang out in the darkness.

Serra's heart began to thunder, realizing, at last, that she'd vocalized her love for Ty. "Yes, really."

"Oh, Serra, what would your father say?"

John Langston wouldn't be pleased, yet he had assured her that her happiness was most important to him. But would he really accept her feelings for Ty?

The muffled thump sounded again, louder, closer, as if it were in the wall behind the bed. No rodent made that much noise.

"Oh, Serra, that was no mouse," Amanda shrieked quietly.

Serra sat up, tossing off the covers. "Someone is in Dr. Chelsey's office." She threw her legs over the side of the bed, gliding her bare feet into her slippers and grabbing up her night mantle.

"Serra, what are you doing?"

"I'm going to see what's happening."

"Oh, no," Amanda protested, reaching out to stop her. "What if it's a thief?"

261

But Serra was already out the door and down the hallway to the next room—Dr. Chelsey's study. She stood there in the corridor, listening, her ear pressed against the wooden barrier, her heart racing in apprehension as she tried to convince herself not to be alarmed. She heard the squeal of the file drawer opening. There was no doubt someone was in the doctor's office, going through his records. That someone must be Dr. Chelsey up late doing some work, that was all, she rationalized.

She knocked on the door. "Doc, is that you in there?"

Dead silence greeted her.

She tested the knob and was mildly surprised to discover it unlocked. Usually Doc secured the bolt within to assure his privacy while he worked. Slowly, she twisted the handle, then peered through the slit between the door and the sill. The office was darker than the hallway, which sported a low flamed wall sconce.

"Doc?" she called again, poking her head in the room a little farther.

The doorknob was ripped from her fingers, her wrist caught up in a viselike grip, and she was jerked unceremoniously into the dark office. Then before she could utter a protest, a hand clamped over her mouth and nose, rendering her helpless to cry out, to breathe. She clawed at the fingers to no avail, and only when the world began to spin and her knees grew weak did the pressure let up, just enough to allow her to fill her aching lungs.

Dragged backward across the room, she crashed her ankle against the protruding claw foot of the sofa. When she shrieked in pain, the suffocating palm pressed hard against her face once more, so

262

she swallowed the sound, making it a mere whimper.

Stationed beside the doctor's desk, she heard the whisper of gas as the jet on the reading lamp was turned up. Her lower face still covered by the large masculine hand, nothing but her wide, frightened eyes unobstructed, she stared up at her captor.

Her already raging heart accelerated—as much with joy as with fear.

Ty.

Though she said his name in her mind, the muffled exclamation erupted past her mashed lips.

His cobalt-blue eyes, hard and untrusting, traveled her length, raking over her rising and falling breasts beneath the thin layers of her mantle and nightdress. His hand, which held her arm twisted painfully against her back, seemed almost to caress her spine, sending a shiver coursing through her.

You're wrong about me. I love you.

Blinking back her surprise at the turn of her thoughts, Serra grew very still. The feel of his broad chest, expanding and contracting against the back of her head, his warm, hurried breath fanning across her face, oddly enough was comforting, and she willed her gaze to express her true feelings, her readiness to cooperate if only he would trust her and let her go.

His hand on her face relaxed just a little, the one on her wrist flexing. "I take it you won't scream."

She nodded.

He released her, then stepped back. When she spun about to confront him, he grinned down at her in that way he had that she knew so well.

In harmony to the hiss of the lamp, she exhaled in indignation. "What are you doing here?" she demanded, rubbing her sore wrist.

His gaze flicked over her. "I missed you so much I came lookin' for you, darlin'," he replied, his voice syrupy with sarcasm.

Oh, how she wanted to believe that, but she knew he was merely toying with her. But she also realized he was here for *something*. But what? Scanning the halo of thin light given off by the lamp, she noticed the open file on the desk, one of Dr. Chelsey's. Apparently, Ty had been reading it.

"That's confidential," she rasped, reaching out to gather up the physician's personal papers and protect them from prying eyes.

But Ty was faster, his arm longer, and he scooped up the folder, holding it just out of her reach. That's when she spied the writing across the front in Chelsey's familiar scrawl. "Patient: Serra Paletot, orphan."

Her gaze widened with shock and outrage. "That's about me." She jumped up, trying to snag the file from Ty's hand.

"Ah, no." He raised it a little higher. "Confidential, remember?" he taunted.

"But you read it, didn't you?"

Ty's mouth compressed into a slash across his face, and for a brief moment, she swore she witnessed a flash of compassion in his gaze.

"Didn't you!" she demanded.

"No, Serra. No, I didn't."

Their eyes locked, unwavering, hers with a question, his with a steadiness. Was he telling her the truth? She couldn't decide. She wanted to believe him, wanted to think she had interrupted him before he'd had a chance to read the doctor's private notations, for she had no doubt his intentions had been to do just that.

Notations about her. The thought was unsettling.

She'd not considered herself just another of Doc's patients, a specimen to watch and write comments on. What did the papers say about her? Her curiosity piqued, she stared up at the file, wishing she had the ability to see through the covering to the remarks beyond.

"Why did you want to see . . . to know about me?" Old, familiar suspicions took root and sprouted up within her. He still didn't believe she was Serenity Langston, she just knew he didn't; his look said as much. "You're wrong about me, you know." The claim spewed forth like a geyser. She swallowed hard. Having said the first thing, now there was only to say she loved him. And, Ty . . . I . . . I . . ." she stuttered, gathering her courage to continue and just say it. "I . . . I lo—"

"Oh, my goodness, whatever are *you* doing here?"

They both turned to discover Amanda Stokes filling the doorway, the back of her hand stuffed into her open mouth. Serra realized it was only a matter of time before the rest of the household awoke and came to investigate the strange noises issuing from the office.

She spun and splayed both of her hands across Ty's chest. "You have to get out of here."

He looked at her incredulously, one brow jutting skyward, but he didn't budge.

"Didn't you hear me?" She pushed him hard, urging him back toward the open window, which he'd apparently used to enter the house. "If you don't go now, someone else might find you."

"You really plan on lettin' me leave?"

Oh, no, I don't want you to ever leave me again, Tyler Ramsey, her heart declared silently. "Just get out of here, Ty, before I change my mind," she cried, knowing she would never alter her heart's desire, no matter what she might say aloud.

He looked back only once as he slipped through the window, the cool evening breeze billowing the curtains, and for a moment, she thought she'd only imagined, only dreamed his presence in the room.

"Serra, what was he doing here?"

She turned to face Amanda, her gaze sweeping over the top of the desk, and she realized the past few minutes had indeed been real. The file—her file—was missing.

Like a blind person, she scraped her fingertips over the uncluttered surface, as if such a ritual would perform magic, but she still came up empty-handed. Agony speared through her, the pain of betrayal.

"He came because he still doesn't believe me," she confessed to the terrible truth. Spinning away, Serra rushed from the room, her eye sockets welling with a blend of defeat and fatalism. "But it doesn't matter. There's nothing I can do to change the fact I love him and hate him in the same breath." The best thing she could do was to forget him and go on with her life as best she could.

Well, he'd gotten exactly what he'd come for. Answers.

Closing the file, Ty dropped his head back against the headboard of the lumpy hotel bed and shut his eyes, seeing the image of Serra as he'd known her then, a willowy little girl, so full of hopes and dreams. So filled with the need to find her place in life, to latch on to it and never, never let it go.

Not that he could blame her. God knew, what she

wanted wasn't all that unreasonable.

Damn.

He lifted his head and opened the folder once again, finding the page of notations he sought.

"July 29, 1881 — Serra has shown remarkable flexibility and responds readily to stimuli. Due to her apparent psychodynamics, over the last few weeks she has accepted the concept of being Serenity Langston with amazing gusto and gives classic response to heterosuggestion. Her ability to retain facts and events is most extraordinary."

Ty pressed the pages together, his fingers still dividing them. Stimuli, psychodynamics, heterosuggestion? He could barely pronounce the words, much less make much sense of their meaning. Just what kind of hocus-pocus had Chelsey performed on Serra?

He parted the pages again, flipping back to an entry several weeks before.

"June 27, 1881 — Serra Paletot, orphan, approximate age twelve, has displayed a limited amount of nervous reservations, however she shows a willingness to please that could be advantageous to the project. The subject responds to somnambulism now with only initial stimulus. This morning I experimented with the power of suggestion, showing her a photograph of the Langston household, circa 1773, taken just before the kidnapping. With only a limited hesitation, Serra regressed favorably, transforming into the Serenity personality with very little urging on my part. I am pleased with the subject's progress."

More of those highfalutin' words he didn't understand. But he did know Chelsey had done something to Serra to make her honestly believe she was Serenity Langston.

There in the file was the picture Chelsey had referred to. He picked it, studied it, recognizing John Langston as a much younger man, the woman and child beside him, obviously his wife and daughter, strangers. But the sour-looking woman sitting in the carriage? He studied the slightly out-of-focus face, reaching into his memory to place it, but he couldn't.

That was he Langston house all right, even though the wrought iron fence and gates were missing, along with the trees and flower beds, but it was the house he'd spent the last few years growing up in. And the little girl. God, if he didn't know better, she could be Serra. The resemblance was uncanny. How had Chelsey gotten his hands on this picture?

Frowning, Ty tossed the photograph back into the file. Why did the old quacksalver—and that was all he could call Chelsey now, not a doctor by any means—want to go to such extents to pull off this deception?

But no matter how hard he figured, he came up empty handed. What did Chelsey have to gain? He knew it had to be something, as the man was not the Good Samaritan type. Money was the only answer Ty could conjure up. Somehow he planned to swindle money from John Langston. But how? Bribery? Blackmail? He could imagine a dozen different ways.

Perhaps Chelsey's motives weren't important. He had the proof he needed to convince Langston that Serra wasn't his daughter—more than enough. Enough to set the records right and give him back those things that belonged to him.

Fisting his hand that still held the incriminating

evidence, his salvation, he laughed at the absurdity of it all and flung the file across the room, watching it hit the wall and scatter into a multitude of individual papers.

The photograph stared up at him, and then the pieces began to fall into place. Dropping to his knees, he retrieved the picture, focusing on the one face he'd not recognized until this moment. The woman in the carriage was older, much heavier now, but he had seen her entering the doctor's house yesterday afternoon. Whoever she might be, she was the link between Chelsey and Langston.

Excitement coursed through him as Ty realized he now had all the pieces of the puzzle before him. Maybe he didn't have the education, the know how to assemble them, but he had a good idea where he could turn for help.

Serra's nervousness was uncontainable. Ty had taken that file, of that she was certain, but what it said and what he planned on doing with it, she could only imagine.

Not that she was afraid the medical notations might indicate her claim false. Quite to the contrary. Doc firmly believed she was Serenity Langston, and it would only show the struggles she had gone through to regain her memory. But what right did Ty have to probe into her private affairs? And her father—and she was now again confident John Langston was just that. She didn't want him to know how difficult it had been for her. Of late he looked so frail and thin that she didn't want to cause him further distress. She'd done more than enough of that already.

She frowned, knowing she couldn't be so sure of what Ty might do. He was capable of anything, she realized now, to regain his lost position. Forcing a brilliant smile to bow her lips, she glanced at her father sitting in the carriage seat beside her and, without outward provocation, curled her fingers about his arm just below the elbow. Somehow, she had to protect him from whatever Ty had planned.

"Ah, Serra, girl. It's so good to have you back home." He patted her possessive hand with paternal gusto. "God, when you left, I actually feared you might not come back . . . that you were so unhappy here that you didn't want to return." He leaned closer to her. "That you might feel more affection for Chelsey than for me."

"That's silly, Father." She studied his concern-lined face. Had Ty already gotten to him? No, how could he have? She had taken the first train this morning to Joplin, and even if Ty had boarded it, too—and she was fairly certain he hadn't been in any of the other passenger cars—there would have been no time for him to talk to her father first, for John Langston had met her at the station as promised. From there they had dropped Amanda off at her house, and now they headed home.

"So much was happening at once. I just needed to clear my mind, that's all," she assured him, patting the sleeve of his jacket.

"And it's all clear now?"

She nodded.

"Good." He sat up on the seat and signaled for the driver to continue past the mansion and make a turn at the next corner. "Then I have a surprise for you."

"A surprise?" She turned giddy and clapped her

hands. "Whatever is it?" This was just as she had imagined it to be. Surprises and presents from a doting parent.

"While you were gone, I did some figurin' myself. I should have been better prepared for your arrival, Serenity, made more plans to integrate you back into society here in Joplin . . . into my life." He hung his head and took up her hand once more. "But I must confess, when I learned you were found, safe and sound and so near to home, I had my moments of doubt."

Serra's heart began to hammer.

"It just seemed impossible, after all of these years. I wanted it so much, yet I didn't want to be disappointed, so I held back."

"Oh, Father." Somehow, it was comforting to know he had had his reservations, too. That she had not been the only one to fear their reunion.

"But the minute I laid eyes on you"—Langston reached up and gathered a handful of her coppery hair in his hand and caressed it—"I knew you were my girl. And even if you weren't, it didn't matter," he said, choking with emotion. "God had given me a second chance before—before—"

She placed her arm about his broad shoulder and comforted him as if he were the child instead of her. Squeezing her eyes closed, she reveled in the feeling. It felt so good . . . so good to be wanted and needed.

The driver called to the horses "Whoa," and the carriage came to a halt before a house where several other vehicles were parked.

"Father, what is going on?" She glanced about, taking it all in.

"The Joplin League of Ladies is havin' their

weekly meetin' today. They have invited you to join them."

"A meeting?" Serra's gloved hand automatically reached up to her hair. "But I must look a sight." She frowned, glancing down at her wrinkled skirts dotted with soot from the long train ride. "Having been in transit all day . . ."

"You look beautiful, Serra, girl. You will represent the Langston name just like your mother used to do. She'd be so proud of you if she could see you now."

As tired and as grimy as she felt, she couldn't find it in her heart to decline; he looked so happy, so hopeful. But, oh my, the pillars of Joplin society would be at such a prestigious gathering. What would they think of her? How would they receive her, an orphan, a child of the streets of New York?

Then Serra paused, somewhat shocked by the turn of her thoughts. She wasn't an orphan nor a product of the slums. She was Serenity Langston, daughter of one of the community's wealthiest businessmen.

Langston swung down from his seat, and for a moment when he reached up to assist her from the carriage, she caught a glimpse of the person he once must have been, dashing and handsome, a man any woman would have gladly given her heart to.

Her mother? She remembered so little about her. What kind of woman had she been? It was obvious from the way her father spoke of her that they had to have been very close. Had they made mad, passionate love the way she and Ty did? But of course they had. How else would she be here now?

Accepting his hand, she allowed him to swing her down to the ground. "Don't you worry, Father. I'll see to it that the ladies of Joplin are duly impressed."

"As well they should be, girl," he replied, taking her arm and leading her forward.

Once at the front door, her courage and determination crumbled. And if her father hadn't remained with her, giving her his arm to draw moral support from, she would never have rung the bell.

The door was opened by a staid looking servant, who eyed them down the bridge of his long nose.

"Miss Serenity Langston here for the League meetin'," her father announced.

"Ah, of course, Miss Langston," the servant repeated. "Mrs. Tindle is expecting you. Please, won't you come in." Accepting their wraps, he led them through the front foyer.

Bless her father. He stayed right beside her.

"Do you know what I do when the thought of socializin' frightens me?" he whispered in her ear.

She glanced at him, expecting some profound words of wisdom. "What?" she whispered back.

"Why, I just imagine whoever it is I must confront in the privy with their pants down."

Serra gave him a surprised look, suppressing a spurt of laughter, but then they were ushered into the parlor full of women. Her heart began to hammer out her self-doubts, but then an image of each of them with their skirts flipped up, their drawers about their knees, filled her mind and made them not so formidable. She glanced at her father and she shared a private moment with him, knowing by the glint in his eyes that he was seeing the ladies of Joplin just as she did.

The rest was easy.

They came forward en masse, twittering like brightly plumed birds in a cage, all talking at the same time, taking her by the arm and separating her from her father before she could utter a single protest.

"Now, you go along, Mr. Langston," one large-boned woman who seemed to be in charge announced. "We'll take fine care of Serenity. Don't you worry."

Her father nodded his head, twirling his hat in his hands. "Thank you, Miss Lottie. I'll be back for her in a couple of hours."

"No need to rush, John." The woman smiled at him.

Then he winked at Serra. "Remember what I told you, girl," he reminded her just before he bowed out of the room.

And she would. But if the women were no longer intimidating, then the whirlwind of events was.

The League, all twenty of them, steered her toward a blue velvet-covered wing-back chair that was positioned suspiciously in the center of the room. Supplying her with a cup of tea and an assortment of finger sandwiches, they crowded about her.

Was she happy to be home again? Wasn't she surprised at how much Joplin had changed over the years? Did she remember when they used to visit her mother before her disappearance? Did she realize how much she looked like dear, sweet Laura Lee?

The bombardment of questions came so fast and furious that she couldn't begin to keep up with them, much less answer them. Her head nodded and shook until she was dizzy.

Then the big-boned woman, Lottie Tindle, clapped her hands as much in delight as to attract the other women's attention. "I know exactly what we must do."

The group turned, waiting as if it were Miss Lottie who usually came up with the ideas, and Serra found herself leaning forward in anticipation as well.

"We shall have a ball," Lottie announced. "A masked one."

"A ball, Lottie?" another woman asked.

"Oh, yes," Lottie informed her. "And we will ask Serenity here to be our guest of honor."

"But," Serra protested, "I'm not sure—"

"And we can have a competition for the best costumes, both ladies and gentlemen," added a third voice, drowning out Serra's objection.

"And the winners can be the recipients of a lovely prize."

Then it was as if a floodgate had been opened. Everyone was talking at once again, ideas flying about like confetti in a gale storm, discussed, accepted or rejected, expanded upon. Before Serra could say more, not only had it been decided that she would be the guest of honor without her input, but also what colors complemented her complexion best and would be used to decorate, as well as when the event would be held—two weeks from that day at the prestigious Joplin Hotel.

Finally, Lottie turned to her. "Have we forgotten anything, Serenity? Do you have something you might like to add?"

The ladies waited for her to reply.

She glanced from face to anxious face. What was she to say? That she'd never attended a ball before? That she didn't really think she would be very good at such an affair? Such reservation would be unmerited from someone like Serenity Langston.

Closing her eyes, Serra allowed her imagination to take charge, pushing away her doubts, swirling with her own envisionings of a gala like she'd only dreamed about before now. Ball gowns that shimmered and flowed to the rhythm of the music, spinning, waltzing couples, a starlit night, and stolen moments in the fresh air.

And Ty, giving her a courtly bow and leading her onto the dance floor.

There her fantasies came to an abrupt halt as she remembered the promise she had made her father—to give his plans for her and her future a chance. His plans didn't include Tyler Ramsey, but rather Monte Stokes.

She sighed, the vivid musing losing some of its color and excitement, wondering just where Ty might be and what he was doing. Glancing up at the expectant faces surrounding her, she smiled thinly. "I just hope someone will teach me how to dance."

Chapter Sixteen

"So why doesn't it work?"

His sleeves rolled up past his elbows, his arms coated with the black sludge from the jack, Ty wiped the sweat coating his forehead on his shirt and shot his engineer a squelching look.

"I'm not sure, Mr. Ramsey. All I can figure is that we're not getting proper agitation."

"By *proper*, do you mean not enough?"

The other man nodded.

"In other words we need more power, and more power means another engine."

Again the engineer agreed.

And more equipment means more money, Ty didn't say aloud, but they both knew that was where this conversation was taking them.

A dead end. There was no more available money. Somehow they had to make it work with what they had—or call the whole damn thing a loss.

To call it off meant admitting he'd failed.

Turning his back on the equipment and the expert who had warned him in the first place that the engine might not be powerful enough, Ty walked out of the building into the dusty street.

Just another little mining town eight miles northeast of Joplin, Webbeville stood far enough away yet near enough that he could keep an eye on Serra—if and when he decided he wanted to.

At the moment he would gladly welcome her, the Serra of his past who had shared the triumphs and the disappointments. Oh, God, how good it would feel to have her there to comfort him, to insist that he not give up, to look up at him with those big amber eyes of hers that spoke of her confidence in him. He would draw strength from her soft lips, her sweet body.

No, making this business venture succeed was something he had to do on his own. Then and only then could he go back for her, for then it would be for the right reasons. Nothing to do with John Langston and his money, nothing to do with Chelsey's devious manipulations, nothing to do with whether she was Serenity Langston or Serra Paletot.

But, oh, just to hold her again, even if for only a few moments.

"Mr. Ramsey, wait," cried a voice behind him.

Ty paused in mid stride and spun about in the street to stare back the way he'd just come. The young boy who worked in the telegraph office raced toward him, waving a sheet of paper over his head. Accepting the missive with eager hands, Ty tossed the lad a coin he dug out of the depths of his pocket.

He skimmed the message, then he read it again, carefully. Of course. It all made perfect sense now. The woman in the carriage: Annette Babison. She had been the real Serenity's nanny prior to the little girl's disappearance. Langston had let the woman go

278

without recommendation, accusing her of neglecting his kidnapped daughter. Her motive in all of this would be clear: revenge. And Lionel Chelsey. His part in the terrible scheme was clear now as well. By using his hocus-pocus, he was duping all of them, including Serra. He was not a man to be taken lightly.

Looking up, he eyed the building he had just stormed out of and acknowledged his choices. Stay here and do his damnedest to straighten out his own life and dreams; or go back and confront the public humiliation of failing on his own—all to save Serra from the ultimate devastation and disgrace she would surely have to face.

Serra. She had championed his causes so many times in the past that he couldn't begin to count them, a little red haired mite, abused, neglected, yet willing to stand up for him. Could he do any less for her?

Of course he couldn't. He cared for her above all else.

There was only one way he could see to stop Chelsey from realizing his goal to take control of the Langston fortune and to protect both Serra and John Langston from their own follies without telling them what was going on . . . without hurting them. Just like in poker, the ace of spades reigned supreme, and a husband's will overrode the desires of either a father or a guardian. He would save them all the only way he knew how. Through marriage.

Rolling down his sleeves, he purposefully retraced his steps. Just like Jesse James and Billy the Kid, he would murder, steal—or worse. He would do whatever it took, make any sacrifice, to see that Serra held on tight to her dreams and desires.

"One, two, three. One, two, three. Concentrate, Serra. Let him take the lead."

Who better to teach her the fine art of dancing than Amanda Stokes, her brother Monte the willing guinea pig. Serra closed her eyes and tried to do what her friend's lilting voice told her to do — glide her feet about as if she were on air.

"Ouch!"

Her eyes snapped open, and she came to a stumbling halt, backing away. "Oh, Monte, I'm so sorry."

He gave her a pained look, almost comical, limping the next few steps. Then he gathered her hand in his once more and held it up, his other positioned in the small of her back. "One, two, three," he began the count again, dragging her forward.

For the first couple of turns she followed, the Langston front parlor rotating about her as she pivoted, counting each step as she took it. But either she got ahead of him or he got behind, and then their feet were tangled once more.

Serra threw up her hands in self-disgust. "I can't do this."

"Yes, you can." Monte refused to release her, forcing her to stand still and resume the position. "Otherwise, we'll be here all day. Not that I would mind that so very much. I find holding you in my arms most delightful, Miss Langston, even if you do manage to lame me for life." He gave her a questioning, yet encouraging look.

Serra laughed; she couldn't help herself. She did like Monte — very much. How could she not? He had a way about him that made her feel so comfortable. There was no contest between them—like with Ty. No need to carefully pick each word she said to him, fearing that he would take offense the way Ty did. Monte Stokes didn't look for hidden meaning in her every comment, her every expression. She could relax and be herself. But at the same time, there was no pounding heart, no anticipation, no . . .

Absolutely no desire.

Perhaps she had it all mixed up. Were desire and love the same thing? Or was loving someone feeling . . . no competition? She looked up into Monte's faded blue eyes and found herself comparing even the color of his gaze with Ty's. Not as vibrant, exciting, demanding, but they were there. On the other hand, Tyler Ramsey might strike a wonderful image in her mind, but what good did it do her?

Monte believed in her, totally. He didn't question her identity, her abilities, her wants, her desires. Give it time, her father had requested of her. Closing her eyes, she let out a long, mournful sigh. She supposed she should do what he asked, but she doubted she would ever experience with Monte what she felt for Ty.

But Ty wasn't coming back. He had made that quite clear with his actions, if not with his actual words. Therefore, she must move on and make the best of what life offered her. Straightening her spine, she gathered up her sagging aplomb.

"Then I guess if you're willing to make the sacrifice, who am I to complain?" she replied, parting her lips in a bright smile, even if it was somewhat forced.

They began again, this time much slower, each

step deliberate on his part, carefully executed on hers. Then she recognized the difference. If it were Ty who held her so, she would revel in the feel of his arm about her; his hand covering hers would make her heart race out of control. She would feel his movement, anticipate it . . . savor it. Dancing was sort of like making love. She had to put her heart and body into it, her trust.

Lowering her lashes, she conjured up his image against the screen of her eyelids—brooding blue eyes, his hands warm and thrilling upon her flesh, his voice the one counting the beat, setting the rhythm, one she found easy to follow.

"That's it, Serra. You've got it."

She heard Amanda's encouragement and let her imagination whirl her away into a wonderland of her own making, where Ty danced with her until dawn.

The moment of reckoning arrived.

In shimmering white, the sprinkling of diamond-cut glass sewn to the tulle overskirt adding to the celestial illusion, Serra was a sylphlike vision, something from a fairy tale, a medieval lady awaiting her shining knight in armor. The ornate papier-mâché mask covered her face; the tall conical hat topped her hair. Her hair. Her pride and glory, Ty had once called it, and at last she understood what he'd meant by that statement. Nothing could disguise its coppery sheen spiraling down her back in riotous curls.

Everyone attending the gala recognized her and feigned ignorance. But then it was a social game they all played, pretending not to know who was behind the courtly mask of Hamlet, or Queen Victoria herself, or the demon in horns and tail.

Staring across the chandelier-lit ballroom on the first floor of the grand Joplin Hotel, Serra giggled when she spotted Amanda dressed as the notorious Egyptian queen, Cleopatra, the blonde's form-fitted gown so daring several people gasped. Serra wished she had the gumption to be so bold. Then she saw Monte, just as they had planned it, dressed in a midwestern rendition of chain mail, his mask the visor she and his sister had spent the last week designing and constructing to look like the real thing.

Monte Stokes was such a good sport, clumping forward in the overshoes they had cut from tin cans, coming toward her, just as they had prearranged that he would, taking a courtly bow and offering her his hand. From the corner of her eye she caught a glimpse of her father, looking so frail, dressed in street clothes like so many of the older gentlemen, yet beaming with pride as he followed her with adoring eyes. Serra dipped a well-rehearsed curtsy and, gathering up the long train of her sparkling medieval costume, accepted Monte's gauntleted fingers. Leading her out onto the dance floor, they began the festivities as the band struck up a fiddler's interpretation of a waltz.

"One, two, three," Monte counted under his breath for her benefit, leading her forward and making her look as if she had been born dancing.

And in truth she felt as if she had been as she spun about the room, realizing that the other guests held back, watching as the couple, the latest item in Joplin, made their public debut.

Serra knew she couldn't ask for more than Monte,

yet more was all she could think of. Tilting her chin, she studied her dance partner, the only object in the room that was stationary from her perspective. Monte Stokes represented everything a woman could want in a man—helpful, devoted, eager to go to any lengths to please her, including donning a stuffy, uncomfortable costume simply because she had asked him to. A woman should feel fortunate to find such a man willing to do what she wanted, to listen to what she had to say, to find worth in her other than as someone to manage the domestic environment and rear children, at least that was the consensus of the day. Too many men drank and swore and beat their women, treating them as if they were worthless. Yes, Serra should feel very lucky to have someone like Monte.

Ty swore, she reminded herself in an effort to find fault with him, and she supposed he drank as well, though she'd never actually seen him do so. And as far as beating his women, she knew if temper were any indication, he could be quite capable of violence if provoked. Yet despite it all, it was those same qualities—his iron will, his self-assuredness, his aggressive nature—that made her feel so—so alive and feminine. Ty had been there to protect her when she'd needed protection.

Yet as hard as she tried, she couldn't think of anything she needed protection from, not now—not unless it was from Ty himself.

She stumbled, and Monte covered for her beautifully, even though she knew she had managed to mangle his toes. And Serra was grateful. For whether he knew it or not, he served as a buffer, shielding her from her own impulsiveness. Otherwise, she would probably be foolish enough to throw herself into the lion's den and beg to be devoured.

Ah Ty, she repined as Monte Stokes once more spun her about the ballroom.

Poised in the darkened alley, Ty reached up and pulled the black bandanna up over his face and dipped his black hat low over his forehead, leaving nothing but his eyes exposed. Then he reached for his pistol cradled on his right hip. Using his thumb, he rotated the cylinder, checking the chambers for bullets. Satisfied, he eased the gun back into its holster and prepared himself, flexing his fingers with a calculated precision.

Just like Jesse James and Billy the Kid, he vowed to himself. He would take what he wanted . . . what was rightly his.

Glancing up at the brightly lit windows of the building, which cast its moon shadow over him, he cocked his head, listening for just a moment to the strains of fiddle music filtering through the open window. Then he moved forward, knowing that what he was about to do he should have done a long time ago — something strictly for himself.

The ballroom was alive now, every color in the rainbow represented as oddly matched couples swirled across the dance floor — a devil and an Indian princess, a biblical shepherd and an angel, Cleopatra and a mountain man wearing baggy overalls and a battered straw hat. Standing near an open window, Serra took a sip from the glass of punch

Monte had brought her and smiled as she watched Amanda waltz by in the arms of Amos Ledbetter. Of late, that was all her friend spoke of—Amos of the Ledbetter Mining Company. Amos was bright enough, reminding Serra of a loyal sheepdog, his long hair always falling into his soulful eyes. But he was good for Amanda and would most likely let the blonde do as she pleased should they ever marry.

She glanced over at Monte, his knight's visor lifted to give him fresh air, and she drew a parallel. Monte was good for her, too, she supposed, and most likely would never interfere with anything she wanted to do. But did that make him the right man for her? It was the same question she had asked herself time and again, but the answer was never clearcut in her mind.

Turning away from the festivities, she gazed out the open window which allowed a breeze to stir the stale air of the crowded ballroom. The moon, golden and round, peered back at her, mute, offering no solution to her dilemma; in fact, it seemed to mock her. Having everything she'd dreamed about—a family, a home, a position in society—wasn't enough. Ironically, the one thing she didn't have and wanted desperately was the one thing she'd possessed for so long and taken for granted would always be there. Ty.

"What's wrong, Serenity?"

The music came to a pause and Serra glanced up at Monte, deciphering the genuine concern animating his more-than-handsome features.

"Nothing." She said it too fast, revealing too much, and now she wished she'd taken her time to answer.

For a long moment he studied her masked face,

286

and his jaw began to work. The pain he experienced shot through her as well. He had wants and desires, too. Goals that seemed unattainable. An unrequited love.

How perfect and uncomplicated her life would be if only she could reciprocate. But she couldn't bring herself to give him what he asked for.

"Then I suppose," he said, his mouth crooking in an awkward attempt to smile, "we should do what we came here to do." He offered her his hand once more as the fiddler struck up a gay note to indicate the music would begin. "Would you care to dance, my lady?"

There was so much she could learn from Monte. About patience and kindness. How to be gracious when confronted by defeat. "Of course, my lord," she replied, allowing him to lead her back onto the dance floor.

As the music played and other couples joined them, she found herself wishing the night were over. The music was too loud, the press of bodies too confining. She wanted to escape, to find a quiet corner to sort out her thoughts, to come to grips with a solution and make her plans to follow through. It wasn't fair to lead Monte on. Not fair to him, or her father, or herself.

As always, whenever the turmoil reached this teetering edge of decision, the telltale pain began at the base of her skull and fanned out, encompassing every nerve in her body. Escape. Escape at any cost. That was all that Serra could focus upon.

Then the music broke off on a sharp note that turned sour as the fiddler dragged his bow over unfretted strings. A woman screamed and then another.

"Thieves," came a shrill cry.

Her left hand still resting on Monte's shoulder, her right one cradled in his larger one, Serra dragged her gaze upward and glanced across the room.

There he stood. Looking just as he had that very first time, confident, an image of power and control. The man in black. His face hidden behind his ebony bandanna, his gun drawn, he pinned her with a cobalt glare that made her throat constrict as much with fear as with excitement. Her heart accelerated, thundering beneath her fingertips pressed against the column of her bare neck.

"He's come back," she murmured, thrilled to see him again yet apprehensive of what his presence indicated.

"What?" Still holding her in his arms, Monte spun about so he could see whom she meant and came to a dead halt when he spied the gunman. Instantly, he tucked her behind his back. "Don't worry, Serra. I'll protect you," he announced with a courtly flare that befitted his dress.

"There's really no need . . ."

"Hush," he insisted. "Let me handle this."

Peering up at his tall figure, it dawned on her that Monte didn't recognize the intruder. Lighting on the faces of the other guests, she came to the same conclusion. None of them realized it was Tyler Ramsey holding them at gunpoint.

No one, that is, except her father. She saw his mouth screw down, his eyes narrow and turn steely, his countenance brighten with anger, his hands clench into fists.

"No, Father," she cried in a whisper as he took a step toward his ungrateful ward. Forgetting all else other than that she must put a stop to another confrontation between the two men most important to her, she attempted to dart about Monte's sturdy frame, unsure which of them she was most concerned about—her father or . . . or her lover.

"Don't be a fool, Serra." Monte stopped her, grabbing her by the arm.

Ty's gun was already raised and aimed at his benefactor, and Serra could only imagine what his intentions were. Had he come for revenge? Against her father? Or perhaps herself? Or did he mean to merely rob the wealthier citizens of Joplin, all of whom were represented at the affair.

A look passed between the two men, one of contest. "Don't try to stop me, John," Ty announced in a voice muffled by his mask. "This time I hold all of the cards, and you're neither a fool nor a desperate kid with no other alternatives."

For a moment she thought her father would ignore the warning but he held his ground, his fists relaxing only a minute amount as his jaws clamped tighter.

"I wouldn't be so sure about that, boy. Even old men have aspirations that they hang on to till the very end." He leveled his gaze on Serra. "She's everything to me."

"Then it appears we have somethin' in common."

Her father's shoulders slumped forward in defeat. Satisfied, Ty turned in her direction as well, and he sized up the situation. Her glittering costume, her masked face, Monte's. The way Stokes held her pinioned behind his back, a Don Quixote in his ridiculous get-up, willing to joust windmills to defend the honor of his fair Dulcinea.

He did it for me, she wanted to shout when Ty gave his rival a contemptuous look, *which is more than you're willing to do.*

Then he scrutinized her up and down once as if demanding, *Is* that *what you really want?*

No. Not at all, but she wasn't about to admit to the truth—not here, not now, and mostly not to him. She notched her chin in proud determination.

At her show of spirit, he smiled beneath his bandanna—either that or he grimaced, she couldn't be sure, but one side of the cloth lifted with his expression. "All right, Serra. If that's the way you got to have it." He slipped the gun into its holster and came toward her.

The moment his fingers touched her bare wrist, Monte reacted, knocking his hand away. "You have your nerve, Tyler Ramsey, showing up this way," he stated flatly, finally figuring out the identity of his opponent. "But, then, you never did have much breeding."

"It's all a matter of how you look at it, Stokes. Even swine have breeding." Ty reached again, handcuffing Serra's arm just below the elbow.

But Monte wasn't to be daunted. He clamped down on Ty's forearm.

They stood that way, a clover chain impasse, until Ty finally spoke. "Decide, Serra."

Said with confidence, there was no show of compunction in his demand, no regret that he pushed her into a corner and gave her no alternatives.

Decide? Here, now? Serra's amber eyes flashed and she swallowed hard, fully understanding the sacrifice he exacted from her. The choice was not just between himself and Monte. That selection she made easily, much too easily, for a pang of guilt speared through her when she glanced up at Monte's hopeful, yet confused face. But Ty forced her to choose between her loyalty to him and her father.

And that was not so simply done.

"Ty, please." She pressed her gloved hand on his broad chest, seeking a reprieve. "Don't ask this of me."

His eyes smoldered, blue and hard. "Just what is it you think I want?"

She knew very well what he wanted. He sought commitment without returning it. Sacrifice without mutual concession. He had promised her once to return for her and had forgotten—or worse, not cared. "More than I can give."

"Your love, Serra? Is that too much to ask for?"

"That you've always had," she answered. "Didn't you know?"

At her public confession, Monte released Ty's arm and stepped away. She hurt for him, only God knew how much, but she couldn't live a lie. That would do none of them any good.

No longer restrained, Ty drew her into his arms. "I know, Serra. I know. But what about your trust? Can you yield that so freely?"

She swallowed with uncertainty. "Are you deserving of it?"

"Serra. Sweet li'l Serra, I can be." He wove a finger into a strand of her coppery curls. "Marry me."

Reaching up, she pulled down the black bandanna from his face, not sure she had heard him right, wanting, needing to see his lips form the avowal she

291

could only hope he had made. Like a blind person, she closed her eyes and fingered the soft contours surrounded by the down of his beard and mustache, waiting to feel him speak once more.

"Marry me. Please," he repeated, his breath warm against her fingertips, his mouth forming a kiss against her flesh.

She glanced about, finding that all of Joplin watched her, waiting. There was Monte, wordless in his resignation. Amanda, her eyes dreamy and acquisitive. And her father.

He stood ramrod straight, his hands pressed to his sides as if prepared to march to the front lines of battle. He had said he would accept her decision if she gave his way a chance first. Well, she had done as he had asked, trying to make her heart conform to his wishes.

But hearts were funny things. One could bend them, wring them dry of emotions, force them into miscast molds, even break them, and always they rebounded, beating out their own tempo, making their own choices.

Their gazes touched, parent and child, so alike in many ways, two people who had suffered and dreamed and found fulfillment through the other. Working at it, Langston gave her a hint of a smile. It was enough to convey his acceptance if not his approval. But it was enough for Serra.

"Yes," she answered Ty's proposal in quivering excitement. "Oh, yes." She threw her arms about his beloved neck. "I'll marry you."

Amidst the cheers of approval, Ty tore away her mask, revealing her adoring face. Scooping her up, he twirled her about, his mouth claiming hers with

292

passion and commitment, with love spoken from the heart. His heart, alive and pulsating against the palm of her hand.

The fiddler struck up a merry tune, his arm sawing, his foot tapping, his head bobbing with the beat. Ty held her close, much too close to be considered proper, but then there had never been much proper about Tyler Ramsey. He had his own way of doing things, and she loved him for it.

Then her feet flew as if propelled by magic. Round and round they danced, the fair maiden of old and her dark clad outlaw. Not once did she stumble, so sure she was that she could follow his lead. One, two, three. One, two, three. The sound of her joyous laughter echoed into every corner of the ballroom.

He brought her to a halt in the middle of the room, the other dancers swirling on about them like colorful tops, surrounded, yet alone.

"Are you ready, Serra?" His eyes devoured her.

"Ready?" Did he mean to marry her here and now? His gaze suggested he planned to do something with her, something wonderful and delicious, and it would be best condoned beneath the canopy of matrimony. "But, Ty, I'm dressed for a costume ball, not a wedding," she protested.

"You're a vision in white. Isn't that what a bride is supposed to be?"

"Yes, but —"

"No buts." He smothered her protest with a kiss, long and lingering, creating a knot of anticipation deep within her. Yet she still couldn't ignore certain traditions.

"My father," she said in a low, pleading whisper.

293

"He will want to be a part."

Ty glanced up and stared out over the top of her head. "I want it understood here and now I'm marryin' Serra Paletot, not Serenity Langston."

"Is there a difference?" It was a question she'd asked herself so many times that she'd stopped counting. And the only one to ever doubt her stood before her, his guard down, his honesty shining through. Their future depended on his answer, on his acceptance.

"For me there will always be a distinction. It's Serra Paletot I loved, long before there was a Serenity Langston, but it will be Serra Ramsey who will be my wife. That's all that really matters to me."

And if the truth be known, it was all that really mattered to her. Ty had at last kept his promise. He'd come back for her, and she would follow wherever he led.

Chapter Seventeen

The marriage ceremony took place then and there in the gaily lit ballroom of the Joplin Hotel. Judge Tindle, at Lottie's insistence, stepped forward and took matters into his capable and judicial hands. Sending a hotel employee to his house to retrieve the proper documents and licenses, he set about organizing the festivities into a bona fide wedding.

The women fashioned a bridal bouquet for Serra from the floral decorations surrounding the punch bowl. Acquiring a piece of netting from one of the guest's costumes, they draped her conical hat to make her a veil. Even a boutonniere was stuck in the buttonhole of Ty's vest.

Bridesmaids and groom attendants were selected from among the party goers, the honors going to the best costumes. However, Serra insisted on choosing her maid of honor. That position went to Amanda, her dearest friend.

So attended by a gauze-winged angel, English royalty, and an Egyptian queen, Serra started down the makeshift aisle on John Langston's arm.

Her heart raced, her mouth went dry, and her hands began to tremble uncontrollably when the fiddler struck up the first notes of the wedding march. She clung to her father's arm feeling as if she sojourned in a fanciful dream. Yet when the marriage vows were put to Serra, her "I do" sounded clear and confident among the chatter of approval from the crowd.

And Ty. His loving gaze settled on her as she approached him and never wavered. With obvious pride, he claimed her as his bride both in words and in the sealing kiss once their troth was plighted.

Afterwards, the papers were filled out. With only a tiny hesitation, she signed her name, Serra Paletot-Langston, Judge Tindle assuring them that no matter which name she wished to go by, the union was legal and binding.

That seemed to satisfy Ty. For one fleeting moment, she thought to question him on his insistence that she use the Paletot name, but instead she held her tongue. She was too happy to spoil the beauty of a memory that would last her a lifetime, one that would go down in the annals of Joplin history as the most unusual masked affair to date. In a town that used any excuse to celebrate, what better than an impromptu marriage? Already, there were plans being made to organize a parade in the morning to honor the newlyweds.

But it was afterward that memories were made that would fill the last of the empty void within Serra's heart.

Ty led her away from the ballroom among shouts of good fortune and fertility. She tossed her bouquet, realizing it was with a conscious effort that she aimed it in Amanda's direction. But, then, what were friends for if she couldn't pass a little of her prosperity the other girl's way?

Finally escaping the crowd, Ty swept her through the front lobby of the hotel toward his room. Reaching the steps that led upwards, he came to a halt. Positioned at the foot of the staircase stood Monte Stokes, dressed now in much more somber street clothing, his knight in shining armor facade cast aside.

Well aware of his absence during the wedding, Serra had understood and had also been somewhat relieved. Now she feared a confrontation, and grasping her husband's arm, she tried to forestall such a happening.

"Please, Ty," she pleaded softly.

"Not to worry, darlin'," he assured her, grasping her uplifted chin between his forefinger and his thumb in a caress. "I have no intentions of spendin' my weddin' night brawlin' with a rival." He grinned down at her. "There are much better and more stimulatin' ways to spend my time."

Serra blushed and glanced at the floor. "He was never really a rival, you know."

"I know." He forced her to look up once more. "But I'm not sure he realizes that."

"Then let me handle this," she requested with simple straightforwardness, unsure what Ty's reaction would be.

She was somewhat surprised when he released her and moved back without protest.

His head bare, his hat held firmly in his hands, Monte stepped forward. "Hello, Serra," he said, his voice somewhat strained, and he paused to clear his throat. "I just wanted to tell you that I wish you the best." His gaze slid to Ty, but his face remained impassive. "Both of you."

"Thank you, Monte," she offered quietly, recapturing his attention by taking one of his hands in hers in a show of friendship.

"And I wanted you to know," he continued, darting another look at Ty, "nothing intended by the comment on breeding."

"No offense taken or given, Stokes."

Serra's gaze swept to Ty, and she read the guarded sincerity on his face. Relieved, she felt her heart swell with more love than she thought possible to possess, and she dropped Monte's hand.

"Then I suppose . . . I should let you be on your way." Monte stepped back, pivoted, and hurried through the lobby toward the front door.

Serra opened her mouth to stop him.

"Let it be, Serra."

Ty's gentle grasp upon her arm stayed her.

"Let the man leave with a little of his pride and dignity still intact."

Consenting to his appeal, she pressed herself against Ty's side. "Do you really think he understands?"

He shrugged. "I doubt it. I know if I was in his place, I wouldn't. But he accepts, which is more than I can say I would do. Hell, Serra." He squeezed her tightly. "If I had been him, I would have probably made an ass of myself. I would have never stood by and let him have you." One corner of his mouth curled upwards. "Maybe you made the wrong choice. Monte Stokes could be the better man."

"There was never a contest, Ty," she quickly assured him, rotating in his arms to press herself against his long, lean frame. "You're the only man I have ever wanted."

"That so?" His powerful limbs curled about her,

298

pulling her hard against his rising and falling chest.

"Cross my heart and hope to die," she vowed, and it was as if they were children again, making vows, sharing their secrets, their lives, their dreams.

And yet, it was oh, so wonderfully different.

Ty bent and swept her up into his arms, cradling her against his pounding heart. They posed that way for a short moment that seemed like an eternity to Serra. Then he spun about and took the stairs two at a time in his rush to get her alone.

It was with a giddy feeling that she clung to his neck. *My husband. Mine.* And she wanted him to hurry, also.

Carrying her into the darkened room, he knelt and placed her on the bed as if she were more precious than a cache of diamonds and rubies. Her arms were still locked behind his head and she held him that way, demanding a kiss before she would release him.

He eagerly complied, his mouth coming down to cover hers with such passion that the world could have spun to a shattering conclusion and she would have never known or cared. Without urging, she opened her mouth beneath his, meeting his tongue with her own, savoring the shivers of excitement coursing through her.

When he lifted his head, she groaned, wanting more, and never, never wanting to let him go.

"I only wish to light the lamp, love."

"What does it matter?" she demanded, feathering kisses along his jaw.

"I want to see you, Serra. I don't want to miss the passion in your eyes."

"You'll come back?" As innocent as the question seemed, it was spoken from her heart. She couldn't bear the thought of losing him again — not now, not ever.

"Ah, darlin', don't worry. I'll return as fast as my legs will carry me."

She released him and he moved away, the bed creaking and springing back into place at the absence of his weight. In the darkness she heard him strike a match, then smelled the sulphur that emanated from the flicker of light. The leaking hiss of the gas lamp filtered toward her just before the jets illuminated the room.

With the golden aura outlining his dark-clad body, he tossed off his hat and began unfastening his black leather vest. The white carnation someone had looped in the top buttonhole fell out and he stooped to retrieve it, placing the flower on the table beside his Stetson. "I imagine you'll want to press the petals between the pages of a book."

Making keepsakes and precious memories . . . it all seemed so magical, so unconceivable to her. But here she was, Mrs. Tyler Ramsey. She nodded.

Stripping off his vest, he reached for the gun belt still strapped across his hip. As he untied the holster thong about his leg, Serra's eyes slid downwards, taking in the pistol cradled there, remembering how he had literally held them all at gunpoint.

Ty followed the direction of her gaze. Flashing her a sheepish expression, he unbuckled the weapon and took it in his hand, spinning the cylinder and revealing the empty bullet chambers. Then he shrugged and grinned as he discarded the gun. "Like I told you long ago, I had no intentions of shootin' anyone, just robbin' 'em."

"Oh, Ty," she said in mock exasperation, opening up her arms in invitation.

And he came willingly back to her. Lying over her, his thighs pressed against hers, his heartbeat matching strides with hers, he propped himself upon his elbows and stared down into her trusting amber eyes. With one hand, he pulled off her hat and gathered up a fistful of her fragrant hair, letting it stream between his fingers as he buried his face into its coppery depths. "Ah, Serra, I wasn't mistaken in comin' back. Tell me I wasn't wrong."

His cry for absolution took her by surprise. Curling her arms about his neck, she pulled him closer, cradling his head as if it were a child's. "Never wrong, my love. You just should have returned sooner," she chided gently.

The need for words diminished, and Serra shut her eyes as well as all of her other senses to everything but the desire only one man evoked from her. The feel of his hands and mouth upon her flesh, his warm breath trickling along the column of her neck, his tongue, roughly textured yet soft, tracing the contours of her ear, left her mindless to anything else. And the beauty of it was that this was Ty, her husband, her beloved, and no one would dare to try to come between them or condemn them for whatever they did. Marriage bound them now as nothing else could.

Her heart swelled with the purity of their lovemaking, and she opened herself to him fully without reservation. Sensing it was the same for him, she sighed her contentment. There were no boundaries between them now, no secrets, no need for inhibitions.

Then she remembered what he had said about wanting to witness the passion in her eyes, and she parted her lashes to find that, yes, he was watching her as he slowly made love to her.

As he peeled away the layers of her clothing until she wore nothing but her long, loose fitting chemise, he reverently paused to pay homage to each part of her body he exposed—her fingertips, the sensitive crease in front of her elbow, the knob of her shoulder, the hollow at the base of her throat. Keenly aware of how attuned she was to him and he to her, soon she was mimicking his actions, stripping the shirt from his torso, baring his broad, bronzed chest to her perusal. Beneath her exploring hands, his skin was warm and smooth, yet the muscle beneath as hard as granite. As her fingers combed through the manly sprinkling of down they brushed against the twin nodules of flesh, which hardened against her palms as she watched.

And there with his heart thundering against her cupped hand, she looked up at him propped upon his strong arms to accommodate her need to explore and discover, and she savored the passion that turned his blue eyes languid and gentle as he observed her in turn.

"Don't stop on my account," he encouraged in a husky voice when her hands drew back.

With a sweeping motion, she caressed him again, her thumbs feathering against his nipples once more. He arched toward her, his weight heavy against her wrists bent backward, his chest so close . . . so close. . . .

Lifting her head, she kissed each one in turn.

Ty gasped in delighted surprise. Collapsing against her, he rolled, dragging her with him. "Two can play that game."

Serra found herself on top, straddling his still-clothed hips between her bare ones. Reaching up, he

302

untied the ribbons of her chemise, which dropped about her waist, exposing her breasts. His hands splayed against them, the very core of his palms circling the nubs, and just as his flesh had responded to her caress, hers sprang to life beneath his.

Hard and aching, her nipples pressed against his hands. Raking his fingertips over them and down her arms, he cuffed her wrists. Then spreading her arms wide, he urged her to bend from the waist, moving slowly downwards, nearer and nearer, until her bosom swayed a mere whisper away from his lips.

Closing her eyes, she shivered with expectation, remembering how delicious his mouth felt caressing her breasts. She filled her lungs and waited. And waited, feeling as if she might explode if he didn't touch her soon.

Pursing his lips, he blew gently, his warm exhalation fanning over one aching breast and then the other, and yet he never made physical contact. The anticipation and the want grew so intense that she wiggled in her loving bonds, arching her back and begging him to do what she knew he planned on doing.

His tongue snaked out, tipped one nodule, then drew back. She voiced her delight at the moment of pleasure and then cried out her frustration when it ceased, trying hard to press against his mouth. But he held her firmly away, refusing to give in to her demands. When at last her floundering subsided and she grew limp, he caressed her once more, just as fleetingly. The fact that he taunted her on purpose drove her wild, and she renewed her struggle.

Soon it was a mindless game, a searing sweet torture. When she grew still, he loved her, but the moment she tried to direct his actions, he pulled back, waiting for her outbursts to subside.

Finally drained of fight, air rasping in and out of her lungs, she hung suspended over him, little moans of defeat trickling from her parted lips.

"Look at me, Serra."

Her lashes fluttered open, and as she watched he lowered her body so her breast filled his mouth. Drawing it deep, he laved it, loved it, worshiped it, did all of the things she'd imagined and more. And because he had made her wait the sparks of pleasure were more intense than ever before as the dammed floodwaters of desire washed over her like the rising morning tide.

Then he freed her wrists, his hands circling her back to draw her down as he buried his face against her heart. Entwining her fingers in his dark hair, she clutched him to her fiercely. It was good, so good.

But soon that wasn't enough. She wanted more.

As if he read her body's language, his hand moved down between them to feather across that most sensitive of womanly places. Remembering how he had teased her only moments before, she grew perfectly still, preparing herself for the torturous pleasure sure to come. Her breath coming hard and heavy, her legs straddling his hips trembling with desire, she threw her head back in wanton display. Yet she dared not move.

His palm slid downwards, warm against her belly, which shivered with her need. But still she remained statue-still. Then his fingers found their mark, gently strumming until the music filled her to capacity, heart and soul, so loud within her she could feel the vibrations in every part of her, in all of those places he had caressed—her fingertips, her arms, her breasts. No longer able to help herself, she lifted her body and pressed against him to take all that he offered her.

His hand slowed, suspending her there at the pinnacle like a soprano sings a long note just before the finale. She feared to inhale, to move, to cry out her need for completion. Yet when he sat up, laying her back against the mattress, the intensity of her pleasure never wavered as he continued to play her like a finely tuned instrument, one specially made for him.

He covered her, his body uniting with hers with a swiftness that wrung vocal approval from the very depths of her soul, so strong and sure were his actions. Yet he continued to direct her soaring sensations, centering them deeper within her body, his instrument no longer his hand but that part of him filling her completely.

What finally sent her plummeting over the edge was his emotion-laced avowal whispered against the hollow of her throat.

"I love you, Serra," he exclaimed as he buried himself deep within her, and her own cries mingled with his as they consummated their marital union.

Afterwards, she curled in the crook of his arm, her face pillowed upon his shoulder, their bodies still joined in love, their heartbeats synchronized. His fingers located and outlined each knob of her spine, moving downward in a caress tempered by the afterglow of their lovemaking.

Shutting her eyes, Serra savored his touch, listening to the strains of the fiddler's music wafting through the open window from the floor below them as the celebration continued through the night. But she didn't care that the world went on without her, as the only existence she wanted or needed was here and now, in the arms of Tyler Ramsey.

Then her heart came to a thundering halt, remembering all too well the last time he had made love to her. That next morning she had woken to find him missing, gone from her life, thinking that he would never return. But tonight she wouldn't sleep, as she couldn't bear the thought of waking to find he had slipped away like before. First, she tried to deny her foolish doubts and then rationalize them, for indeed they were childish and unfounded. They were married now, and nothing would ever separate them again. And yet each time she closed her eyes, the uncertainties seeped back into her mind like unsettling ghosts, refusing to be dissipated by logic. The best way she could think of to assure herself that he would stay and to keep the fears at bay was to . . . to . . .

Shifting, she slowly examined him, all of him—his well-muscled chest with its matting of fine, dark hair, his flat, hard belly, the fascinating part of him that made him all man. Quickly, she diverted her gaze and returned it just as fast. He was her husband now, and what she was thinking wasn't wrong or lurid.

Flipping over in his arms, she draped herself across his warm, familiar body, her hand running down his naked flesh until she reached her objective. Ty seemed so vulnerable lying there, his arms flung wide, his chest rising slow and even, his body muscle-hard yet relaxed and, oh, so beautiful.

Forming a circle with her fingers, she eased her hand down around him ever so gently, unsure whether her actions would please him or not. Did a man like to be touched so by a woman, or would he find her boldness distasteful? All she had to judge by was her own reaction. She adored it when he caressed her with his hands. But Ty never moved, and she couldn't be sure if he had even felt her clumsy attempt to arouse him.

Did she dare be so brazen again? She slid her hand down him, so slowly and tightly he had to feel it.

Then his finger curled about hers, tightening her grip and moving her hand in a strong, decisive stroke.

"It appears I have one of those rare women who can't seem to get enough," he said in a voice pebbled with sleep.

Serra caught her breath, unsure if he praised or admonished her, yet she noticed he never allowed her fondling to stop.

"Would that be so awful?" she asked, taking up his rhythm and mastering it until he gave her free rein to do as she pleased.

"Awful?" He laughed. "Most men would give an eyetooth to be so blessed." His final word came out as a groan. Capturing her wrist, he brought her caress to a halt. "But even so, I can take only so much blessin'."

Scooping her beneath him, he rolled to position himself between her thighs. The feel of his manliness, so ready, so eager, left no doubt in her mind that he had liked very much what she had done to him. "Then share a little of that blessing with me, if you will," she instructed, draping her arms about his broad shoulders and planting a kiss upon his parted lips.

Which he willingly did long into the night. Even

307

the music from the merriment below grew thin and finally faded. The crunch of carriage wheels on the street below, rolling away, drifted through the open window beside the bed. And still he loved her, teaching her the ways not only of her body but also of his own.

The last sound Serra recalled was the twittering of a nest of hungry sparrow fledglings demanding to be fed even though the sun had yet to crest the eastern horizon. Lying in Tylers arms, her body sated, her mind so exhausted she could think of nothing but sleep, she drifted off, confident that her husband, her lover, her best friend, would still be there when the new day dawned.

Chapter Eighteen

The clatter of pots and pans being banged together right outside their bedroom door woke Serra with a start. Mindless of her state of undress, she sat up, her long hair hanging in tangles in her face and across Ty's chest, where she had fallen asleep what seemed like only a few moments before. But the sun was high in the sky now, spilling through the open window to create a windowpane pattern across Ty's naked torso.

"What is all that racket?" she asked, blinking in confusion, her heart clattering against her rib cage almost as noisily as the disruption.

Ty opened one eye, lifted his head slightly, and listened. "Shivaree," he mumbled sleepily, dropping back down against the pillow and attempting to reclaim a comfortable position.

"What?" She tossed the coppery mass out of her eyes and, suddenly self-conscious, stretched for the sheet crumpled at the foot of the bed to conceal her nudity.

Ty reached up and stopped her, using his hands to cover her bosom. There was nothing modest about his gesture as he gently kneaded her flesh, drawing the nipples between his fingertips, rolling them until they responded to his satisfaction. His gaze focused on his actions, and she realized that not only was he going to ignore the worrisome noise that grew louder by the minute, but he had no intention of offering any further explanation as to the reason people stood outside their door banging kitchen utensils.

"Ty!" She caught up his hand, demanding his attention.

"Hmm?" he answered, circling her rib cage and drawing her closer to better enjoy her lush nakedness.

"This shivaree . . ." Frowning, she placed her hands upon his shoulders and squirmed to escape. "What does it mean?" she demanded.

"Mean?" He frowned slightly at her lack of concentration on what he found important. "It doesn't really mean anything. It's just the townspeople havin' a little fun." Then he shrugged his wide shoulders when the concern wrinkling her brows failed to dissipate. "It's meant to disturb the newlyweds and keep them from each other, but they can bang away all mornin'. It won't stop me." He planted a kiss upon her breast, then enveloped its fullness with his mouth.

The rabble-rousers grew bolder, taking up their pans and smacking them against the door.

"Hey, you in there," called a masculine voice, followed by spurts of laughter, "it's time to get outta bed."

Ty growled at the disruption, but he showed his defiance by turning over and tucking Serra beneath him.

"Hey, Ramsey. Give that little bride of yours a well deserved rest. She's gonna be weak at the knees three weeks past Sunday if you keep it up any longer."

Again the crowd outside laughed at the ribald insinuation, whipping up the racket against the door once more.

Serra stiffened in his arms. "Ty, maybe we should do as they request."

Ty sighed, his gaze darting down to take in her naked beauty beneath him. "I suppose," he said, rolling off her and onto his back. "Knowin' that bunch of rowdies, if we don't do what they want, they'll bust down the door and join us."

"Ty, they wouldn't?" Serra scrambled from the bed and began frantically searching for bits and pieces of her clothing. Then when she thought about what he had just said, she spun around, dressed in her shift, to confront him, finding Ty already in his pants strapping on his gun belt. "You know who those people are out there?"

At this point something massive slammed against the door, and swearing that the wood buckled under the weight, she emitted a little shriek.

"I know them, darlin'," he assured her, placing his arm about her waist. "They don't mean any harm. Just get dressed, and I'll take care of 'em."

The door bucked again, and Serra wasn't so sure "taking care of them" would be that easy.

"Back off, you buffoons," Ty shouted. "We're comin'. We're comin'."

But getting dressed, at least for Serra, wasn't that simple. Even with Ty's help, it took so much time that the impatient crowd took up making their awful racket once more.

When at last they emerged from their marital chambers, Serra felt quite foolish dressed in her medieval costume. She blushed as the crowd, all men, eyed her, aware that they knew exactly what she and Ty had been doing the whole night long. But the group said nothing further that might embarrass her and good-heartedly voiced their approval of Serra.

"We woulda been here sooner, boss," one man, tall and thin, announced with a gape-toothed grin and a hardy slap on Ty's bare back, "but we just found out this mornin' that you'd gone and done gotten yourself hitched."

"I'm sure you would have, Lacy, but for your sake, be glad you didn't," Ty replied in a good-natured growl.

There was camaraderie in their roughly spoken banter, and Serra glanced around at all the faces—hard faces, worn ones, ones that seen many struggles and defeats—and she could tell they were Ty's friends, and he cared for them as much as they seemed to like him.

Then she studied them intently. There was something vaguely familiar about the short, thickset fellow to her left. And the man twirling his dirty felt hat in his hands and staring at her sheepishly, she could have sworn she'd seen him somewhere before. But where? These were definitely not the people of Joplin she knew and associated with. And yet . . .

Frowning, she conjured up an image of Ty dressed in his dark clothing, his long drover's coat flapping about his long legs. The man in black who had frightened her half to death that day not so long ago. Could they possibly be the same group of men who had ridden with Ty when he had kidnapped her from the train? Rowdies, he had labeled them. Boss, they had called him. Just who were these men, and how did they figure into her husband's—and her—

life? She looked up at Ty askance.

Putting his arm about her, he smiled down at her uncertainty. "Not to worry, li'l Serra. These men work for me."

"In what capacity?" she asked stiffly, still concerned.

"In the mines, of course," he replied, lifting a quizzical brow. "What else did you think?"

What else, indeed? She saw them masked, following the orders of that ominous man in black who had held up a train and abducted one of the passengers as if it were something they did everyday. But if they had worked for Ty in the mines, then that meant they were employed by her father's company, which in a sense indicated they worked for her — sort of. It was all so confusing, and Serra wasn't sure how she should react as the bunch stared at her in bovine curiosity. Should she scream for help or bestow upon them a benevolent smile?

Before she could make up her mind, the group remembered their reason for being there and they separated the couple, holding Serra back with a show of respect as they hoisted Ty upon the shoulders of two of the stronger men.

"We'll bring 'm back after a bit, Miz Ramsey," her restrainer informed her, doffing his shabby hat. And then they were off, carrying Ty down the stairs into the lobby, leaving Serra to digest the fact that someone had called her Mrs. Ramsey for the very first time in her life.

Feeling lost, abandoned, though she realized it wasn't Ty's fault, she debated whether she should follow the boisterous men or wait for them to return her husband as they had promised. Or maybe she should just go home and change her clothing. Standing there debating her choices, she glanced down the corridor to see Amanda rushing toward her.

Her friend smiled, radiating excitement, and they met halfway in the hall, falling into each other's arms.

"How was it?" the blonde asked, her eyes full of stars, her voice conveying wonderment.

Serra couldn't help but giggle. "To tell you the truth, Amanda, I'm exhausted and sore . . . but so happy I could burst."

They hugged once more. Then Amanda took charge. "Why are you still standing here? There's only a few hours until the parade."

"The parade?" Serra asked somewhat stupidly.

"Don't you remember? Ah, well, I guess you wouldn't. You were much too busy last night when all of the plans were being made. The town has organized a parade in your honor—yours and Ty's, that is. You don't dare miss it."

"But Ty . . ." Serra tried to explain.

"I know. I saw them." Amanda wrinkled her nose with distaste. "Those men. So unsophisticated. But I imagine Tyler Ramsey can take care of himself. Now, you come with me. We have to get you ready."

"Get ready?"

"Of course, silly. You're the star attraction in this fanfare."

"But, Amanda, I don't want to be promenaded about the town like some prize mare."

But her friend wasn't listening. Taking Serra by the arm, Amanda led her, still protesting, from the hotel to the waiting Stokes carriage. There was no sign of Ty or the men who had taken him away, and her heart lurched with apprehension, those foolish fears that had bombarded her through the night returning threefold. What if he didn't come back?

However, once they reached the Langston house, Serra was so caught up in the whirlwind of preparation that there was little time to think, much less worry. An argument ensued between Tess and Amanda as to what she should wear, yet neither bothered to ask Serra her opinion. Finally, as they debated between a sea-foam green silk and an embroidered surah ball gown, Serra quietly made her own selection — a pale blue gown of French faille, much softer and less flashy than the other choices.

Then it was time to go, and again Amanda dragged her down to the carriage, which had been miraculously decorated with ribbons and flowers, from the spokes of the wheels to the harnesses and headstalls of the matched team.

As they headed toward the East Joplin Hill, where the spur of the moment participants gathered to form the parade, Serra watched the sides of the streets, looking for Ty. But he was nowhere to be found.

Four abreast, the marching drill team crested the hill and worked its way down Broadway, banners waving. Standing in front of Dutch Lem's, one of the numerous dance halls that lined the street, surrounded by his cronies, Ty watched them pass. Next came the silver cornet band, playing somewhat rustily due to such short notice, but making enough noise for everyone in town to realize a parade was in progress. People poured out of the saloons to watch, quickly getting caught up in the festivities.

Then he glimpsed what he was looking for. Serra. Sitting in the Stokes carriage being led by the driver on foot, she waved one gloved hand, her cheeks rosy with excitement.

Ty knew at that moment he hadn't made a mistake coming back for her. Regardless of the sacrifice and the problems that arose, he was truly happy that he and Serra were married at last.

Then he glanced about at the men surrounding him. Loyal friends all, some of them not much older than himself, having met them soon after he'd first arrived in Joplin, a wild, idealistic boy with big plans. Then they had worked with him at Langston Mining, helping to make it a success, and had followed his lead with blind trust, even going with him to Webbeville to assist him with his smelting operation. They believed in him, and he wouldn't let them down. And he didn't begrudge them their bit of fun. Now that they had had it and bought him a round or two to celebrate his marital status, they would gladly return him to his bride of less than a day. Oh, how glorious those few hours had been, and he grew impatient thinking about the ones yet to come.

Making love to Serra was any man's wildest fantasy come true.

Catching her eye, he smiled and signaled to her. Watching the relief flood through her, he thought he understood how she felt. She had been willing to give up so much by deciding to marry him—everything that she had worked for over the years—but he would see to it she lost none of her well deserved dreams. John Langston could be bullheaded at times, but he would come around and accept their marriage. And Ty was determined to see to it that she had everything her heart desired. He wouldn't fail her.

316

As the carriage moved abreast, he stepped into the street, setting his pace to keep stride with the horses.

"Ty," she cried out over the boom of the marching band and the noise of the spectators, scooting over in the seat to make room for him.

Swinging up onto the bench, he settled beside her and joined in the merriment, waving and doffing his black felt hat. But once the procession reached Main Street and slowly wound its way through the better parts of town, he solidified his plans.

Bending low, he whispered in the pearllike shell of her ear, "You wanna elope, darlin'?"

She gazed up at him somewhat seditiously. "I beg your pardon, sir, but I believe you're already a married man."

"And proud of it, Mrs. Ramsey. I'm just tired of not havin' all the time alone I want with my wife." Devouring her with his penetrating blue gaze, he remembered all over again just how beautiful she was, how willing and exciting.

She placed one gloved hand in the crook of his arm so trustingly . . . so Serra. "I know what you mean. I've missed you, too," she sighed.

"Then if you're in agreement, I know a very private place we can escape to."

"And just where might that be, Tyler Ramsey?" She lifted one brow in skepticism.

"A romantic little cabin not too far from here," he cooed in her ear. "In fact, I like to abduct innocent young women and take them there just to have my way with them," he added in a theatrical voice.

"Ty," she exclaimed, slapping his wrist and pulling back. "You're impossible."

"To the contrary, ma'am. I'm quite easy," he drawled.

317

Smothering her amusement behind one gloved hand, she looked up at him with adoring amber eyes. "How can we possibly get away?" She dipped her head at the crowd lining the streets on both sides and then at Amanda sitting in the opposing seat.

"Trust me. Just follow my lead."

The parade reached a corner and slowed as the marching groups navigated the turn. The carriage halted, and at that precise moment Ty jumped from the vehicle and reached up for Serra. Swinging her down, he gathered up her hand in his and began running. Amanda's shrill protest followed them, and Serra spun about in the street and waved back at the other woman, laughing. "Thank you, Amanda. I really appreciate all that you have done."

"But where are you going?" Amanda called back.

Thinking Serra was about to launch into a long winded speech and tell the world their secret destination, Ty jerked her around before she could answer and ducked through the crowd, pulling her behind him.

"Ty, slow down," she cried, stumbling over the long trailing hem of her gown.

But he was on a roll and not about to be stopped. Instead, he wheeled about and scooped her up in his arms, carrying her the rest of the way to the livery stable. Once they reached the quiet interior of the barn, he lowered her to her feet, taking one long, assessing look at her.

"Not dressed for speed, are you?"

Serra glanced down at her clothing and then back up at him, reddening. "I guess not."

"Not to worry, love. I've got it all worked out," he assured her. Grinning, he stepped into the first

318

stall—an empty one—pulled out a traveling case, and handed it to her. "Tess packed it. I'm sure everything you need is there."

Setting the suitcase on a bench, she opened it and rummaged through the contents. Seemingly satisfied, she snapped it shut again.

"Aren't you gonna change?"

She glanced about. "Change? Here? Now?"

"Why not?" He opened the door to the empty horse stall and swept his arm wide in a gentlemanly gesture. "There's nobody watchin'."

Hesitating only a moment, she slipped into the makeshift dressing room. While she changed, he set about saddling his horse.

Once she emerged, dressed in a simple divided skirt and blouse, Ty found her more beautiful and intoxicating than ever. A bandit's woman, ready to ride to the ends of the earth to snatch a moment alone with her outlaw lover.

Why did that fantasy pursue him so? He jerked the cinch so tight that the big black gelding turned his head and snorted a protest.

"Sorry, boy," he mumbled, loosening the leather strap just a tad. Perhaps his flights of fancy represented freedom to him in its most glorious, abandoned form. Pivoting, he lowered the stirrup on the saddle and laced his hands, offering her a boost up into the seat.

"Cochise!" Ignoring Ty's intertwined fingers, she moved to the front of the horse and rubbed his velvety nose.

Ty lifted one brow, surprised by her outburst, amazed she'd even remembered his horse. "Of course. Did you expect another?"

She hugged the beast as if he were a long lost

companion. Turning her head, which pressed against the animal's muzzle, she gave Ty a wary look. "I was told that you had sold him."

"Cochise? Never." He eyed the two, his wife and his horse, and couldn't believe the old four flusher allowed her such liberties. He normally didn't tolerate such overexuberance. "Only a fool parts with a good horse or a good woman. I'm a lucky man to be able to claim both." He swept her up, depositing her in the saddle, then he swung up behind her, pulling her back against his chest as he gathered the reins in his hands. Then they were off, navigating through the town by way of back streets. In no time at all, they were speeding down the road leading north out of town.

He held her close, inhaling deeply of the sweet smell of lavender in her burnished hair just below his nose. *Ah, Serra, it will be good between us. I promise you, you'll want for nothin', or by damn, I'll die tryin'.*

The ride took several hours, but Serra had no complaint. Lying in his arms, safe, secure, as far as she was concerned, they could have gone on that way for eternity. But once they ascended the familiar rise just before reaching the cabin, he dismounted and swung her down beside him to walk the rest of the way. The dirt path wound through a field of wild chicory and blue sage that was as high as her waist, waving gently in the breeze as if it were blue liquid.

Just ahead she saw the rock fence. Only it wasn't as she remembered it. The once-lopsided gate had been rehung on its post, the tall grass carefully trimmed from beneath so it could swing freely.

But that wasn't all. The cabin had been renovated, too. The porch no longer sagged, the broken railings had been fixed, and it had all received a recent coat of whitewashing. Even the old rocking chairs had been painted, and the stones of the building looked as if they'd been scrubbed clean. And from what she could tell, there were curtains on the front windows. Curtains! White and lacy.

"Ty," she said fervently, spinning about. "When did you do all of this?"

"I've been livin' here for a while." Reaching the gate, he swung it open in invitation, leading both her and Cochise inside.

In the distance she saw a black and white cow grazing, and a flock of chickens pecked in the dirt around the shed. It was all so different, so domestic. It might not be fancy, but it was perfect in her eyes. Tears of joy welled and brimmed over. She couldn't help herself.

"Oh, Ty!" she cried. Pivoting, she threw her arms about his neck, pressing herself against his long, lean frame.

"What's this for?" he demanded, as if her enthusiasm overwhelmed and surprised him.

But his voice, roughened by the emotions he tried to hold in check, gave him away. Lifting on her tiptoes, she planted a sweet kiss on his lips. He quickly took charge, dropping Cochise's reins and circling her waist with his arms, turning the gentleness to passion, hot and demanding.

Still breathing hard, he released her and stepped away. "Don't you move." Hurrying to where the horse cropped at the tender shoots of grass, Ty unsaddled him and dropped the tack over one the new porch railings. Then he was back to her, sweeping her up into his powerful arms as he carried her into the cabin.

Serra couldn't believe the transformation inside. Everything sparkled. The table and chairs had been repaired and waxed. Even the old iron bedstead gleamed with a coat of paint. And in the corner was a small dresser, the top covered with a colorful scarf in an attempt to give the room a more feminine appeal.

Touched in the deepest recesses of her heart, she was aware that he had made these improvements with her in mind. Whirling about, she expressed her delight. "Oh, Ty. It's beautiful."

"Welcome home, Serra," he said quietly.

And home was just what it represented to her.

To say they made love then would be an understatement. They made magic, christening their essence with eternal commitment, their hearts with undying devotion. And afterward as they lay in each other's arms, listening to the melodic sounds of the night settling about them—the lowing of the cow, the distant howl of a lonely coyote, the orchestra of the crickets that seemed to whir in rhythm to the flash of the fireflies framed in the door which had been thrown wide to allow a breeze to cool their love heated bodies—they found that all of their needs had been sated. Plagued with neither hunger nor thirst, fears nor ambitions, there existed just that moment and each other. They drifted off to sleep that way, with no worry of discovery, as their isolation was total and complete.

However, they awoke the next morning ravenous, in need of bodily sustenance. Dressed in a plain skirt and blouse, Serra looked the part of the country wife as she slipped an apron about her waist. Taking up the ends, she headed outside to collect eggs, finding several in a little hollow in the far corner of the shed. Returning to the house, her folded over apron laden, she saw Ty coming in from the pasture toting a pail of fresh milk.

A shyness invaded her. Shading her eyes with her free hand, she called to him exuberantly. "I found more than enough eggs for breakfast."

They met in the pathway leading back to the cabin, almost hesitantly, which seemed rather strange after the recent hours of passion they had spent in each other's arms. Then Ty circled her waist, and she dropped her head upon his shoulder . . . trustingly. Together they entered their honeymoon haven full of hopes and dreams.

It was naive of her to take such joy from the simple little tasks of everyday living, she supposed, but for Serra they were the purest of experiences. And though she knew it couldn't go on indefinitely, she could pretend for a little while, couldn't she? They were pioneers surviving off the virgin land, tilling the soil, watching the crops grow to maturity, and harvesting. Ah, the fulfillment of the harvest. She looked up into her husband's face and experienced the blissful thrill go through her. As if the realization of her dreams hovered just beyond her fingertips. All she had to do was reach out and grasp them. Taking up Ty's empty hand in her own, she squeezed it, willing the moment to last forever. If only it could last forever.

"Wake up, Serra. I'm goin'."

Serra's eyes snapped open and focused on Ty's beloved face. "Going? Where?" A tinge of uncertainty colored her question, and she frowned.

"To town. Webbeville is only a few miles to the east, and a man has things to do, you know."

Her expression deepened. "When are you coming back?"

"Not to worry, darlin'." He brushed a finger on the lines between her eyes and kissed her on the lips. "I'll be home for supper."

She watched him ride away on Cochise, his broad shoulders straight, his pistol that he'd not worn since their arrival the week before strapped to his thigh.

Though she tried to ignore it, the haunting fears she'd thought bested crept up her spine. What if he had tired of her? What if he should decide not to come back? Lifting her work-roughened hand, she waved him off, her heart lurching as he crested the hill and disappeared. Only then did she allow the brilliant, confident smile to fade from her lips. It wouldn't do for him to have seen her crying.

Fighting down the flaring uncertainties, she turned to her daily domestic chores — washing the dishes and making the bed. As she dusted the furniture, she couldn't help but notice the differences. By the door, the saddle stand and the peg he hung his holster on stared back at her — empty. It was as if his presence had vacated the tiny cabin. . . .

She couldn't stop herself. Running to the dresser, she jerked open one of the drawers he used for his clothing, fearing to discover it barren as well.

"Thank God," she said aloud, finding it brimming over with his clean shirts and stockings, items she had lovingly washed with her own two hands. Turning around, she shoved the drawer closed with her backside and stood that way for a moment, trying to collect her shattered nerves, chiding herself all the while. "You're being foolish, Serra. Ty will be back.

You do him a terrible injustice to think any less."

But an injustice or not, the hollow fear refused to leave her alone, and she went crazy trying to devise ways to keep herself occupied through the long day.

First she took down all of the curtains and scrubbed them—not that they needed cleaning. Then she stripped the bed she'd just made and washed the linens. Hours later the clothesline sagged, filled end to end, her morning work flapping in the breeze like signal flags.

But she still had a long time to go until she could begin to expect to see Ty coming down the road. Regardless, she paused just as she had every hour or so to gaze up toward the ridge.

By late afternoon she'd convinced herself that all was well, and he had merely gone to town like he'd said—not run off and deserted her. Still she found no solace. Why had he gone? They had plenty of supplies, so it couldn't be that. Her imagination took charge, inventing all sorts of rationale for his need to leave. None of her thoughts brought comfort.

Standing in the yard, scattering corn chops to the chickens, she suddenly realized she knew nothing about Ty's life—what he did, where he went, who his friends were.

By the time the sun rode low in the sky, the curtains were rehung, the bed freshly made up, and a simple meal simmered on the stove. Serra stepped out on the porch and dropped down onto one of the rockers, exhausted from her chores. However, she wanted to look pretty for Ty when he returned. Dressed in an attractive calico gown, she spread her skirts and waited. He would be coming over the rise any minute now.

She would not jump up like some ninny and let

325

him see how anxious she had been all day. No, that just wouldn't do. Instead, she would remain in her chair and calmly wait for him to enter the yard before she rose to greet him.

Had he had a good day? she would ask, accepting the lighter pieces of his gear as he unsaddled the horse and turned him out to pasture. And he would tell her what news he had from his visit to Webbeville, little pleasantries and gossip, nothing more. Then he would take a deep sniff and ask what she had cooking for dinner.

Chicken and dumplings, she would inform him, and he would roll his eyes in husbandly appreciation.

The sun dipped lower, the last fingers of light piercing the sky like golden swords. The hill before the cabin remained unchanged, barren of activity. Rising, she stepped inside to light the lanterns and stir the contents of the iron kettle one last time.

She wasn't worried. Ty had assured her he'd be home by suppertime.

Pausing on the threshold, she surveyed the landscape. It was much too dark now to see, and she might as well move inside to wait.

Gathering up the utensils, she went about setting the table for dinner. She softly whistled a carefree tune as she placed the forks and knives on blue checkered napkins.

Then she walked back to the doorway and listened, straining in the darkness to hear the sound of Cochise's iron-shod hooves on the pathway. Crickets whirred and the cow mooed, demanding to be milked.

Bella, the black-and-white holstein. Serra frowned. Ty always saw to the cow's needs. She'd never milked her—at least not by herself. Ty had taught her how, of course, in case, he said, she ever needed to perform the task, but . . .

The poor old thing bellowed again, this time louder and longer.

It was apparent she was going to have to see to the chore herself.

Resentment speared through her. Ty had promised he would return by now. Maybe she should just ignore Bella and let him see to her whenever he got back. But she didn't have the heart to stand there and listen to the animal's obvious discomfort.

Washing her hands and donning an apron, she took up the pail and the lantern and hurried across the yard to the shed. The cow followed her, stopping in front of the feeding trough, looking at her expectantly with those big bovine eyes.

"He should be here, shouldn't he?" Serra declared. Tossing some grain into the feeder, she carefully anchored the lantern on a bale of straw, stationed the stool, and set the bucket beneath Bella's hindquarters. Resting her head upon the warm belly of the beast, she groped underneath. It took her a moment to place her hands properly, and even then the first few squirts missed the pail, hitting the ground or the shed wall.

She paused and brushed a wayward strand of hair from her face, using her elbow. Hunching down again, she repositioned her hands, finally getting her aim right and managing to squeeze more milk in the bucket than on her own shoes. She pumped and strained for at least a half hour before she finally gave up. There was only a cup or two in the pail, the floor was soaked along with the hem of her dress, and the cow was nowhere near milked out.

But her palms were cramped, and Bella grew impatient with her clumsiness and began to kick. It would just have to do until Ty came home.

Taking up the pail, which was coated with dirt and hairs, she snorted in self disgust and sloshed the contents out the door onto the ground. There would be no chilled milk in the spring house in the morning. Well, that's what Ty got for being so late.

By the time Serra marched into the house, she was so angry she dared Ty to show his face. She changed her dress and turned to the stove. Lifting the lid on the supper, she wanted to cry out loud. Gone beyond a little extra simmering, the dumplings were heavy and chewy, the chicken dry and overcooked.

Ruined. It was all ruined. And Tyler Ramsey was responsible.

Slamming the lid back on the pot, she banked the fire in the stove, not caring that the meal would grow cold. Then she sat down at the table, pushed aside the plates and tinware, and dropped her head on the wooden slab in utter defeat.

What a fool she'd been all day long, thinking he would return.

Ty had deserted her out here in the middle of nowhere and probably had no intention of ever coming back.

The tears streamed down her face in rivulets, washing away the dreams like sand between her fingers. Gone. Gone. What was she going to do now?

Chapter Nineteen

That's how Ty found her. Lying facedown on the table, her head cradled in the crook of her arm. He didn't miss the telltale tear tracks on her exposed cheek, the wetness on her lashes spiking them together.

"Serra?" He shook her gently, combing his fingers through her coppery curls that caped her shoulders like filigree.

Her lids fluttered, and her amber gaze touched him. "Ty!" she cried, still half asleep, pushing up from her chair and throwing her arms about his neck. Then she reared back just as quickly and shoved him away. "You're late," she informed him, spinning away and presenting her back.

His gaze skimmed over her rigid shoulders, her stiffened spine, and he understood what other men meant when they talked about the chains of marriage. His wife was chastising him as if he were a wayward child. "I'm sorry, Serra, but it couldn't be helped."

She didn't seem to care for his thin explanation or his apology. "Dinner is ruined. And I had to handle milking Bella all by myself."

He could swear he could hear her foot tapping. Lifting one brow in speculative curiosity, he wondered what would turn his loving wife of only a few days into a shrew. "I'll eat it cold." He reached out and clamped down on her shoulder. "And Bella was grazin' contentedly when I came in. Did you have much trouble?"

"Enough." She whirled about to confront him, brushing away his hand. "You had no right, Tyler Ramsey."

"No right?" He felt the resentment rise, age-old probably from the time of Adam and Eve, but he held his tongue. He tried once more to take her in his arms.

But she would have no part of him. "Where were you?"

"Serra, I told you," he replied, keeping his voice low and even. "I went to town."

"What for?"

He could hear the cry of desperation in her voice. What was wrong with her? It was as if she didn't trust him. "Like I said before, a man has things to do."

"Damn you, Ty," she cried, her hand rearing back and flying in his direction.

Trapping her wrist inches from his face, he accepted then and there that he would have to meet her head-on. "What the hell's the matter with you, woman? I told you I'd be back this evenin', and I am." He reeled her in, holding her tightly to his body even though she squirmed and fought. "Halfway here Cochise threw a shoe, and I had no choice except to walk him home. Hell, Serra, I wasn't late on purpose."

She continued to balk and to struggle. Then at

last his words seemed to sink in, and she collapsed against him. Her tears—the last thing he'd expected—came in a flash flood, soaking the front of his shirt.

"What is it, Serra?" Holding her at arm's length, he forced her to confront him.

"Oh, Ty, I thought—I thought—" She choked on a sob that kept her from finishing.

But he had a good idea what she'd been thinking. He pulled her close once more and just held her, rocking her, understanding her fear of being deserted probably better than she did herself. Abandonment had been a part of her life for so long, and he couldn't deny he had contributed to the problem as well by promising to come back for her when they were youngsters and then letting her down. "Serra, shh, shh. I'm here. And I swear to God it's gonna take a lot more than that to keep me away from you."

As her crying slowly subsided, Ty glanced around at the cabin that had been such a safe haven for them and realized its time had passed. He had no choice but to go to Webbeville each day. The smelting project was beginning to get off the ground, and he had to be there to see to the running of the operation. It was wrong to leave Serra out here to cope with each day by herself.

"Listen, Serra, tomorrow you come with me."

She sniffed and raised her head, giving him a doe eyed look. "Tomorrow? You're going back to town again so soon?"

"I have to, darlin'. My work is there."

"Your work?" The tears welled, and he was afraid she would start crying all over again. "I don't even know what you do." Desperation laced her words.

"Then I guess it's time I told you." Guiding her to the table, he sat her down and joined her, facing her, entwining his fingers with hers.

And he told her everything—all about his trip to Chicago and his purchase of the patent, all about his plans. Well, almost everything. He left out the information he had gleaned regarding Lionel Chelsey. Information that could very well change their lives if he allowed it to. But he wouldn't let that happen. Not to Serra.

Reaching up, he brushed the hair from her eyes and smiled. "How would you like to find a place in town, Mrs. Ramsey? Close to my work. Maybe you could come in and even help me some in the office."

Ty saw the spark ignite in the amber depths of her eyes, and he knew that he had said the right thing— at least for her.

"Do you mean it, Ty?"

He hesitated only a moment, wondering if it would be better for them both to just tell her the truth. "Of course, darlin'. If that will make you happy."

Perhaps it was the events of the long day, or just the workings of a tired mind, but Serra experienced a dream so real, so frightening, that she woke up in the darkness shaking.

Her initial instincts were to reach out for Ty. Thank God he was there beside her, warm and reassuring, even though he slept soundly, unaware.

At first she tried to push the nightmare visions away, so awful were they, but then she found herself lying in the darkness, straining to recall every aspect of her dream and make sense of it.

332

She was young, no more than a baby really. She remembered distinctly the terrible fear coursing through her. And the pain. Instinctively, she folded her arms about herself in protection. Oh God, she had hurt all over, yet the agony had seemed such a natural part of her.

There was a boy, so young, too, and yet so wise. And she knew it was Ty from the color of his hair and eyes, from the way he called her li'l Serra, but she had no recollection of him at that age.

Nestled together on the cold, littered floor beneath a stairwell, huddled in a worn blanket, the Ty in her vision had soothed away her tears and pain. Just as he'd earlier done that night, assuring her he'd take care of her always. Then in the dream, he had made her promises of good things to come for both of them. She had accepted his words just as readily as she'd believed him when they'd sat across the old table from each other hours before, talking about moving to Webbeville.

Serra frowned. Did she really want to leave behind the wonderful times they'd had in this cabin? Did she want to share her life, her man, with the rest of the world?

Pressing her body to mold about the contours of his much larger one, Serra wasn't sure she was ready to face the outside. And yet the thought of each day spent waiting, wondering, worrying about Ty was just as intolerable.

When he turned to her sleepily and wrapped himself against her, the meaning of her dream became suddenly quite clear. Their love, their marriage was still so innocently new; that's why they had both appeared in her illusion as such small children. The pain represented the growth, the maturity of their

333

love. And the fear was the unknown, her own uncertainty about moving to town. Yes, it all made perfect sense to her now.

She must learn to let go and trust him, completely, irrevocably, without a single hesitation. Ty would never do anything to hurt her and would see to it nothing else did, either.

Smiling, she drifted back to sleep, unafraid of the future or of her dreams.

Webbeville was nothing like Joplin. It bustled with its self-importance like any other small mining town and yet it lacked the refinement, the solidness. The streets were dusty. None of the technical advancements that made Joplin so unique appeared to have taken root there. In other words, Webbeville was just run-of-the-mill.

Clinging to Ty's back as they rode through the town, Serra took it all in and was somewhat disappointed. But she said nothing as he reined the horse into the livery stable and dismounted.

"Mornin', Mr. Ramsey," the liveryman said, taking Cochise in hand, tying him to a post, and patting his silky neck in appreciation. "Will you be wantin' him ready this evenin' again?"

Ty whipped off his Stetson and dusted it across his pant leg. "Not today, Samuel. We're gonna stay in town tonight. But I would appreciate you keepin' your eyes open for me. My wife needs a mount."

"Does she ride good?" the farrier asked, looking Serra up and down but saying nothing directly to her.

She shook her head, but it went unnoticed.

"Tolerably," Ty answered the question put to him

334

about her.

The man grinned. "I know just the little mare for her. Gentle enough a baby could ride 'er."

"And I expect cheap enough a workin' man can afford her," Ty replied in the same easygoing horse trader voice.

"I'll see what I can do, Mr. Ramsey. Come back this afternoon, and you can decide for yourself."

The two men shook hands, and Serra suspected Ty had just managed to purchase her a horse.

From the stables, he led her down the main street several blocks to a ramshackle building tucked back in an alley near the railroad tracks. Once they entered the big warehouselike structure, Serra was amazed at what she saw. The inner workings belied the quiet exterior. A big machine rumbled, setting off mechanisms that made the floor beneath her feet tremble. Men were everywhere, many she recognized from the morning after their wedding, shoving jack into a metallic cavern that seemed insatiable.

"I had no idea," she murmured.

"What?" Ty asked, apparently unable to hear her over the engine's roar.

"I said I hadn't imagined your operation to be so large." She glanced about, wide-eyed.

Ty laughed and circled her shoulders with an arm, pulling her close. "Believe me, it's not nearly as impressive as it seems at first glance, but we'll make do." He frowned, and Serra couldn't begin to conceive what would be worrying him. His business looked so important . . . so successful.

But before she could ask him about it, he steered her to a small office in the rear of the building.

Stationed in a corner, she observed him, transfixed, as he became the businessman, receiving several men, some of whom she recognized, answering their questions, sometimes following them back into the main part of the building, but always resolving their dilemmas and sending them on their way.

Then another man appeared in the doorway, better dressed than the others and out of place in the factory. The minute Ty spied him, he shot her a wary look and frowned. Hustling her out of the building, he explained away his haste. "I figured you would prefer to freshen up at the hotel before lunch."

He deposited her in a room and left before she could bombard him with questions regarding his strange and sudden behavior.

Well, let him go for now. Dropping her fists on her hips, she watched him stride out the door and down the hallway. He would be back in a few hours for the noonday meal, and she would pin him down then, demanding answers.

Ty appeared in the dining room on schedule. Sitting at a table waiting for him to join her, Serra had a moment to observe him undetected. There was a grimness about his mouth she'd never noticed before, but the instant he spotted her, he smoothed the look away, replacing it with a smile that was all Tyler Ramsey—self-assured, almost arrogant, laughing—revealing nothing of his inner turmoil.

In the space of time it took him to reach the table, Serra realized he was hiding something from her. Did it have anything to do with that man who had come to his office this morning? More now than ever, questions burned her tongue, demanding answers.

"I have good news for you," he announced the moment he sat down across from her, dropping his black felt hat on the table.

Serra's heart lurched. He was going to tell her what was going on without her having to ask. She leaned forward in anticipation.

"There's a small house on the south side of town that's for rent. I figured we could go by there after lunch and take a look at it, if you would like."

"A house?" That was not at all what she'd expected him to tell her. "I—I suppose," she replied, hiding her disappointment.

"What's wrong, Serra? I thought we agreed movin' into town would be best. I thought that would make you happy."

"It does, Ty." She reached out and took up his hand, trying to reassure him and herself. "Truly, it does."

They ate their meal in strained silence. Once the dishes were removed, Serra straightened in her chair, her determination pushing her to confront him. "Ty?"

His gaze fastened on her, unwavering.

"Who was that man in your office this morning?" There, she'd asked him.

He continued to stare at her, then his blue eyes darted to the left and returned. "It's just business, Serra. Nothin' for you to be concerned about."

Should she press him? God, she wanted to, and yet . . .

Her mouth lifted in a slight smile "I wasn't concerned, Ty. Just curious. It was as if you didn't want him in the same room with me."

"Serra, that's nonsense." He stood, adjusted his hat on his head, and reached for her chair to assist her up, dismissing her observation and the subject all in the same stroke. Taking her elbow, he commandeered her out of the hotel.

But she was not about to be daunted so easily by his show of disapproval. "Then if it's nonsense, Ty, just tell me what he wanted."

There in the middle of the street, he twisted about, clutching both of her upper arms, and for a moment she thought he was going to yell at her. Instead, he sighed. "You won't let it rest until I tell you, will ya?"

She shook her head, her chin notched in righteousness.

He began walking again, and she could practically see the wheels in his mind spinning, formulating his answer as carefully as a mountain climber selects his footing.

"Franklin Gaskell works for me in many capacities." He paused to judge her reaction.

Her return look demanded he elaborate.

"One of his jobs is to scout for cheap sources of jack. His latest acquisition was from Langston Minin'."

"Isn't that good, Ty?" She clutched his arm, her feet flying in order to keep up with his longer strides. "You and my father working together again? Why would you not want me to know?"

He shrugged, maintaining his silence and his speed. Several blocks later, he finally subsided on both accounts. "I just didn't want to upset you, Serra."

They continued walking. She supposed his explanation seemed logical enough, but she still sensed there was more to it than what he had told her. The one thing she did believe was his statement that he didn't want to upset her.

Fifteen minutes and many steps later, they reached their destination. The house was small, just as he

338

had said, and set back from the street among several tall oaks. It was a pleasant enough place.

The inside was furnished, nothing like she'd grown accustomed to in Joplin, but it made their cabin look poverty-stricken, which in truth it was if she stopped to think about it.

"Do you like it, Serra?" He turned, waiting for her reaction.

She wondered at the way he acted, always seeing to it she was satisfied, letting her make the decisions. This was not the Ty she knew, yet she could find nothing to balk at in his acquiescent attitude. It was as if he felt he had something to make up to her.

"It'll do fine," she answered.

Then and there he made the arrangements to rent the house as it stood, including linen and dishes.

A strangeness settled upon her shoulders when Ty left her alone to acquaint herself with their new home as he trudged back to the hotel to settle their account and gather up their meager possessions. She brushed aside the nagging feeling, assuring herself Ty was behaving like any other new husband, concerned with her well-being and happiness. She should be pleased, not suspicious. In fact, she should be delirious, she thought as she wandered back up the stairs to the bedroom to sit on the edge of the hand-crocheted coverlet.

This was their very first real home—if one didn't count the tiny cabin where they had spent their honeymoon. She threaded her finger through the ornate needlework. Looking back on the situation, the bungalow hardly qualified as much more than a temporary haven.

In the distance she heard the rumble of a spring

thundershower, and she rose, moving to the window. Folding back the lace curtain, she watched the rain begin, several pedestrians scrambling for shelter as the squall whipped its fury on everything in its path.

Ty would wait for the weather to clear, she told herself, taking the initiative to light a lamp and settle in the rocking chair in the corner to wait out the storm, confident it would only last a short while.

But as the afternoon waned and the rain continued at a steady rate, she began to wonder if it would ever end. Having had plenty of time to think, she'd spent the hours wisely. She wanted to assure Ty that she was indeed a blissful bride and that she would do everything in her power to make him happy as well. But as far as his business was concerned, she would never interfere in it again. Reconfirming her trust in him, which she needed more than anything, Serra wanted to make love to Ty to prove she meant what she said.

The idea of taking the initiative intrigued her, blossoming into a full-blown fantasy that turned her melancholy into high spirits. Yes, she would meet him at the door garbed only in her underclothing and would make wild, passionate love to him right there in the front parlor. She giggled at the prospect of such an unusual christening of their new home and blushed. That would show him how pleased she was with all that he did for her.

It took her only a few moments to strip down to her chemise, and as a last show of uninhibitedness, she tossed that aside, leaving her dressed in only her corset cover and drawers. Then she stationed herself at the front window to watch for his return, hoping he would show soon before she lost her nerve.

When at last the rain slackened off, she saw him

riding toward the house astride Cochise at as fast a clip as he dared on the mud-slick road. Behind him he towed another horse, most likely the mare he'd bought for her.

Serra smothered her glee, realizing he was as eager to be with her as she was with him. Confident she would take him by complete surprise with her unorthodox greeting, she could well imagine the appreciation in his eyes when he entered the front door.

The moment his boot heels connected with the porch flooring, she flew to the couch in the parlor and arranged herself in what she hoped was a most seductive pose.

She waited in the growing darkness for him to enter. The door swung open, and she heard him remove his coat and hat and hang them on the hall stand in the breezeway.

"Serra?" he called out. "I'm home."

His actions, his words, were like a dream come true for her. Her heart hammered so hard in her chest that she thought for a moment she'd gone mute. "In here, Ty," she answered in as husky a voice as she could muster.

"Why are you sittin' in the dark? . . ." His gaze found her and steadied, taking in her seductive pose. "Jesus!"

She rose and sidled across the room to where he stood soldered in the doorway between the foyer and the parlor. Winding her arms about his neck, she rose on her tiptoes.

"I was waiting for you to join me," she purred, placing a hungry kiss on his parted lips.

Which he tolerated, but gave nothing in return.

Opening her eyes, she lifted her mouth, and in

341

that moment she realized something was wrong. Terribly wrong.

"What is it, Ty?" she asked in a small voice racked with concern.

"I'm sorry, Serra." He glanced down the full length of her, his hands, one of which held a telegram, running appreciatively down her supple waist and over the flare of her generous hips. "God knows, I want this as much as you . . . but it's your . . . it's John Langston."

"Father?" She released him and automatically reached for the wired message in his hand. "He's here?" All she could envision was the angry, vengeful man who had tracked them down once, then taken his wrath out on Ty. But they had made their peace, she and her father; he had accepted their marriage even if he hadn't approved.

"No, love. It's not that." Ty paused and dragged her to his chest.

To her surprise, she heard the sob erupt from deep inside of him. "It's been comin', I suppose. I just didn't think it would happen so soon."

"What, Ty? What's happened?" she demanded, a terrible dread coursing through her.

"He had this growth in his belly. Six months ago the doctors in St. Louis took it out as best they could. They all agreed there was a good chance it wouldn't bother him again. Only time would tell."

Serra heard what he was saying and recognized the distress, the disbelief in his voice, even though his words said otherwise. "A growth? You mean like a . . . cancer?"

He nodded, his chin rubbing against the top of her head, a gesture she would have savored under different circumstances.

A terrible guilt assaulted her. Her father was ill and no one had bothered to tell her. In her ignorance, she had gone against his paternal wishes and now . . . "Oh, God, Ty, is he dead?" she sobbed.

"No. No." She felt the wetness of his tears against her scalp. "But apparently the growth has returned and is spreadin' rapidly. The message was from Dr. Jacobs, askin' that we return."

"Then we must hurry." Tearing away from his embrace, she headed upstairs where she had left her clothing.

Minutes later, she was dressed and ready to depart.

They left Webbeville, riding into the orange glow of the dying sun. It would be dark by the time they reached Joplin. She prayed it wouldn't be too late.

Chapter Twenty

Serra sat beside the great canopied bed, holding her father's hand tightly in her own. She looked up at Ty standing at the footboard, where he'd stationed himself the moment they had entered the Langston house, refusing to give up his protective position.

Oh, God, how she loved her husband and understood him now more than ever. So many of his actions made perfect sense, like his refusal to strike back when her father had beaten him that day at the cabin; he had feared to injure the older man if he had fought to even protect himself. What courage his submission had taken, what strength . . . what love.

And now he stood there, stone-faced, as her father berated him for taking away his only daughter, for being a worthless rogue he should have left to the law all those years before.

"Please, Father," Serra interjected, not truly understanding what he was raving about, but trying to soothe away his anger by osmosis through the back of his hand, which she squeezed and caressed.

His hand, so frail and thin now. Oh, God, she should have recognized the signs long before, but she had been much too busy worrying about her own selfish needs. "You must rest. The doctor says you have to conserve your energy."

She caught Ty's eyes and tried to smile, to assure him that her father didn't mean the terrible things he said. It was just the illness, the pain he suffered. Ty stared back, his blue gaze cold, devoid of any expression. It was obvious to her that he was reliving some event from his youth, one she knew nothing about, something he and her father had shared.

Langston's tirade halted abruptly, and he focused on her. "It's all yours, Serenity. I should've never said otherwise. Do you hear me?" He lifted himself up as if he intended to rise, and Serra feared for his failing health.

"Of course, Father." But she had only a vague idea of what he meant.

When finally Langston drifted off into an unsettled sleep, Serra released his hand, somewhat reluctantly, and placed it beside his body grown noticeably thin in the short time they had been gone. Rising, she touched Ty on the shoulder as she passed him, indicating her need for him to come with her. For a moment she thought he would ignore her request, stubbornly refusing to leave his onetime guardian's bedside.

"Ty, please," she pressed her appeal. Their gazes met and held. He followed.

Once they reached the sanctuary of her room — their room now — she spun about to face him. "You should have told me, Ty." This was the first opportunity they had had to speak since arriving, and there had been no time during the long nocturnal ride there. Both of them had centered their attention on pushing the horses as fast as they could.

345

"He didn't want anyone to know," he justified, understanding her questions without having to think about it.

"But I'm his daughter. I have a right to be informed."

The silence was thick and heavy, unbearable. "I didn't see what good it would do."

"I could have helped him." She groped to express herself. "Somehow compensated . . ." Her statement trailed off, unfinished both outwardly and in her mind.

"Compensated? How, Serra? By not marryin' me?"

Serra trapped her bottom lip between her teeth, completely taken off guard by his candor, unsure of how she felt deep down inside. Pressing the heels of her hands against the ache in her temples that always seemed to plague her whenever she was torn, she squeezed her eyes closed.

"No, Ty," she finally answered, fearing she had paused too long and he might think her insincere. She glanced up at his lack of response.

But he was already gone.

He hurt. Shoulders hunched, braced to meet head-on the mental foe, Ty moved like a silent shadow through the streets of Joplin, no particular destination in mind. Oh, God, how the betrayal cut him deep. Not only John Langston's, but Serra's as well.

Serra. Shoving his hands into his pockets, he flattened his mouth in angry denial. He had thought her loyalty ran as deep as the love he harbored for her in his pathetic heart. He should have known she would choose her childhood desires over anything he could ever offer her.

Not sure how long or how far he had wandered, he stopped to get his bearings. Music, loud and bawdy, beat a rhythm in his brain. How had he reached Broadway, that no-man's-land of vice connecting the town on the two sides of the river?

Ah, well, it was appropriate. Just as John Langston had said he was a no-account rogue who should have been left to the mercy of the law long ago. Just like Jesse James and Billy the Kid.

Stationed in the swinging half doors of Dutch Lem's, he fought the urge to enter and couldn't quite pinpoint why. Then the past tumbled in around him, recalling that first day of his arrival. He had been such a scrawny little bastard when he had stumbled into Joplin, but at least he had possessed the beliefs that all things were possible. That and his ability to pick any man's pocket. He wondered, just wondered, if he still had it in him.

Flexing the fingers of his right hand, a ritual of so long ago, he stepped inside the bustling saloon. At the bar he ordered himself a shot of rye, his cool blue gaze flicking over the other occupants of the room, mostly miners and laborers, a paltry lot to select from.

Then he honed in on his most likely victim—a wiry little man well into his cups, his wallet peeking from the breast pocket of his flapping jacket, just begging to be lifted.

A flutter of conscience rippled through Ty as he sized up his mark. He blinked and shook his head, wondering if the liquor clouded his brain so easily. Funny, he'd never experienced those feelings of hesitation before. Turning away, he hunkered down over his drink to contemplate this newfound facet in his personality. Throwing the burning rye down his throat, he suddenly realized it wasn't morals that plagued him, it was fear. Hell, he was scared to death someone might catch him in the act of pilfering another man's pocket.

Just when and were had he gone soft? Not only in the heart, but in the guts?

Slamming down his glass, he ordered another.

"Why, Tyler Ramsey. We haven't seen you down here in a coon's age."

Ty turned his head, his gaze fastening on the mileage-worn redhead as she moved in, so close he could smell her cheap perfume, see the rice powder clogging her pitted face.

"Not since you celebrated your gittin' married," she elaborated and chuckled, the sound coarse and grating as sandpaper. "What's the matter, honey? The missus givin' you hell?"

He smiled. "Hell ain't the half of it." He lifted his glass in a salute.

The woman took the drink from his hand and tossed it down her own throat in one gulp. "Looks to me like you need more than a stiff drink." Slapping the empty glass back on the bar, she ran her hand suggestively down the front of his shirt to rest on the buckle of his belt.

He signaled the bartender to fill the shot glass again. "You could be right." He downed the whiskey in one swallow. "But then you could be wrong."

The picture that held his imagination was Serra's glorious coppery hair falling about her soft, white shoulders . . . the way she had greeted him at the door of their new home in Webbeville, willing and, oh, so loving. But, hell, paradise hadn't lasted long.

He draped his arm about the dance hall girl and

348

allowed her to lead him toward the stairs.

"Tyler Ramsey, you no-good slug."

Jesus Christ! Had all the females he knew ganged up on him? He stumbled forward in the darkened hallway of the Langston house, pushing past Tess, trying to ignore the girl's tirade. Her fist caught him between the shoulder blades. Not that the well-aimed punch particularly hurt, but it was enough. He spun about to face her on unsteady feet. "Damn it, woman, leave me alone."

"You smell like a brothel," she railed back, her face inches from his. "Don't you dare go in there with Miss Serenity until you bathe the stench off your body." Her gaze flicked down over him, knowingly.

"Hell, Tess, when did you become Miss-High-and-Mighty's personal watchdog?" He made a move as if he was going to shove her aside.

The serving girl stood there undaunted, a barrier between him and his destination, and he realized she had no intention of budging, no matter how he insulted — or threatened — her. He sobered a bit and straightened.

"I didn't do anything, damn it," he growled "God knows I tried, but . . . I didn't."

Somewhat mollified, the servant hustled him toward the bedroom he had used during his days of residence in the house. "I'm glad to hear that, Ty, but Miss Serenity might not look upon you with such kind eyes. She's got a lot on her mind, and she doesn't need a drunken lout of a husband to contend with."

Tess's words brought back the pressures, the reason he was in this sorry state to begin with, trying to forget. The tragedy tumbled in around him as concern unclouded his liquor-fuzzed brain. He frowned. "John? How is he?"

"Sleepin' at the moment. Much easier now that his daughter is back. You did the right thing, you know, bringin' her home the way you did."

"The right thing?" He grimaced. "For who? John Langston?" He shook his head and made a sound of derision. "It sure the hell wasn't best for me."

"You don't know that for sure." Tess clutched his arm, forcing him to look at her. "I thought Miss Serenity's arrival was the worst thing in the world that could happen to me. I saw the way you looked at her, craved her . . . ignored me. Don't you think that hurt, Ty?"

He blinked several times in rapid succession. He'd never really considered how his feeling for Serra might affect others. He and Tess had shared their moments, but she had seemed so willing to let it go. "I'm sorry, Tess. I guess I just didn't think."

"I'm not lookin' for an apology. Good things have come of it, of you marryin' her. Good things for me." She pushed him into the bedroom and tried to slam the door behind his back.

He spun about and stopped her, his curiosity piqued. "What things?" he asked.

Tess smiled secretively. "I got me the best damn beau any woman could ask for."

"Monte?"

Serra stared at the man standing at the front entrance and wished now she'd not taken the initiative to answer the door. But the butler was upstairs seeing to some of her father's private needs, and she had been right there in the foyer when the knocker had sounded.

"Serra? When did you get back?" Monte Stokes stared at her dumbfounded, as if he were as embarrassed by the unexpected encounter as she was.

"Last night. I learned about Father just yesterday."

"I see. How is he doing today?"

"Better, I suppose." The conversation lagged at that point, and Serra wondered just why the man was here on her doorstep if he hadn't realized she was home. "I'm sorry, Monte," she stumbled over her forgotten manners and backed out of the doorway. "Would you like to come inside?"

He readily agreed, removing his hat as he entered.

Serra glanced nervously up the wide staircase. Tess had informed her that Ty had returned early that morning, somewhat worse for wear and in a surly mood. After the terrible words they had had last night, what would her husband say if he should come down and find her entertaining an ex-suitor?

She automatically ushered her guest into the front parlor, indicating he should take a seat. Perched on the edge of a wing back chair, she smiled, not really wanting to be there but in all politeness feeling she must. "So . . . how is Amanda?"

Monte smiled, apparently feeling comfortable with the subject of his sister. "She and Amos Ledbetter are inseparable." He shrugged. "At least at the moment."

Serra leaned forward, a feeling of joy for her friend shooting through her. "She sounds serious about this one."

"Could be. But I doubt it. Amos is not really sophisticated enough for my sister's needs."

Silence trapped them in its heavy hand the air thick with their discomfort. Then overhead she heard the thunder of fists pounding on a door.

"Serra?" Ty called her name . . . well, if she had to be honest, he bellowed it like a wounded, irate bull.

Serra tried to pretend she hadn't heard the summons, and Monte's gaze lifted momentarily to the ceiling, then fastened on a point over her head.

Oh, dear. Ty was up and apparently Tess had spoken the truth. He was in one of his surly moods all right. Her heart hammered, and, oh, how she wanted to jump up, race out of the room, and tackle head-on her mannerless husband, but protocol wouldn't allow it. Instead, she must pretend his outburst never occurred. She smiled at Monte.

He reciprocated. "If you need to see to . . . something, Serra . . . go ahead."

"Oh, I—it wouldn't be polite to leave you here alone."

"It's all right, really. If you would just let Tess know I'm here."

"Tess?" Somewhat confused, she lifted her brows, her lashes fluttering. "You mean the Tess that works here?"

"Yes. Tess."

Serra popped up like a wounded spring cut loose from its bindings. "Of course. I'd be happy to." In the doorway she spun back around, wondering if perhaps she'd not heard him correctly. "Tess?" she asked once more.

"Tess," he confirmed. "We made plans to go on a picnic today."

"A picnic? Of course." She reddened and raced

352

from the room, realizing Monte's intentions. And she had had the nerve to question him like some interfering old biddy. Once in the privacy of the foyer, she paused to collect her wits about her, to gather her aplomb. Tess and Monte?

What an oddly matched couple.

The shatter of glass issued from upstairs, and she hurried forward as her name echoed through the house. "Serra, I want to talk to you. Now," came Ty's insistent demand.

She tried to pin her thoughts on something other than the upcoming confrontation. Tess and Monte. Maybe it wasn't such a mismatch. Actually, once she thought about it, they were well suited.

"Tess and Monte," she mumbled as she lifted her skirts and tackled the stairs.

"Ma'am?"

She paused midway up. "Tess."

The servant was dressed in one of the simple gowns that she had passed on to her. It was much too youthful for Serra now that she was a married woman, but it looked wonderful on Tess.

"You have a caller downstairs."

Tess blushed. "Oh, Miss Serenity. I didn't mean for you to—"

Serra smiled. "It's all right." She truly meant what she said, even if her voice did sound a little shaky.

The servant stared up at her askance.

"Really. I don't mind. In fact, I can't see that I would have much say about whom you see."

In that brief moment they shared a sisterhood, and Serra reached out and hugged the girl. "I'm happy for you, Tess."

"And I'm happy for you, too, Miss Serenity."

The explosive demands from upstairs were repeated, and Serra looked up to see Ty striding toward her. "Yes . . . well," she replied with firm resolve, "I hope there's reason for you to be."

With that, she gathered up her skirts in determined fists and marched forward to meet her husband halfway.

Ty saw her frown as she glided toward him, a beautiful woman in every way. But he'd learned a long time ago that beautiful women meant trouble. Somehow along the way, he'd forgotten that lesson—or ignored it—temporarily. He waited until she reached him, then took possession of her arm and led her back up the way he'd come.

"Tyler," she hissed between her teeth, yet she made no attempt to pull away from him. "You are making such an unnecessary ruckus. We have guests in the house. Besides, what if my father should hear you carrying on this way?"

"To hell with all of them, Serra." There in the hallway he grabbed up her other arm and had to keep himself from shaking her. "I need to talk to you, damn it."

His gaze skimmed over her—the slender column of her neck, her breasts rising and falling with each purposeful breath she took. He wanted to have more than a conversation with her, but words would have to suffice for now. The door to her room stood open, the way he'd left it when he'd barged in there, thinking she was inside and ignoring him. Whipping her through the opening, he slammed the barrier shut behind his back, then forced her to sit down on the freshly made bed.

He stared down at her, watching the way she studied him, her amber eyes widening with that look she always gave him when she had every intention of getting her way. Now that he had her undivided attention, his decision to just tell her like it was, to demand an answer to a straightforward question, didn't seem so . . . necessary. No, damn it. He had to know. He soldered his lips together in determination. He had to know now.

"After all the things Langston said about me, are you sorry you married me, Serra?" He had asked her that same question last night. If she hesitated to answer him again . . .

He watched her features contort, her throat convulse. Hell, he didn't know what he would do if she admitted to reservations.

Her face lifted just high enough, and her bottom lip began to tremble.

Ah, Serra.

How he wanted to crush her to his heart. Instead, he waited for her answer.

"No, Ty. I'm not sorry." Her amber eyes cast down, then swept back up. "After all of the things Father said about me, do you regret our union?"

Did she mock him? He studied her for a moment, the way her lashes brimmed with emotions, and decided her question was sincere. How could Serra doubt him after all he had done? If she did, then it meant he had failed miserably in his quest to protect her, to give her the one thing she needed most — security. Dragging her forward against his chest, he feared to let her go. "No, Serra, no. What he says to me doesn't matter. None of it means anything as long as I have you."

"Then you must understand why I humor him, why I never chastise him when he starts in on you."

She bowed her head against his chest, the weight like heat to melt the calluses surrounding his heart. "Oh, God, what if he should die now that I have finally found him? I couldn't bear to lose him again," she sobbed. "Not so soon."

Ty took a deep breath and held it so long he thought his heart would surely burst with the need to protect her, to see to it Serra got whatever she desired. Let her have her precious dreams; to hell with the truth. He was the only one who seemed to give a damn about it, anyway, the only one who had anything to forfeit with its concealment.

"You won't lose him, darlin'. He's a strong old cuss with more vinegar and starch in his veins than blood. Don't you worry." Reaching up, he stroked her soft, silky hair. Her pride and glory. Dear God, he couldn't begin to imagine life without her. "I promise, Serra. I'll see to it nobody takes that away from you."

As much as she would have liked to stay there, wrapped in the protective, blanketing arms of her husband, Serra finally unfolded herself and stepped away. There were too many chores that needed tending. Too many responsibilities demanding her attention. For now, she would have to be satisfied with the knowledge that they loved each other. And Ty. Dear, sweet Ty. As if he sensed his presence in the house served only to upset her father more, he quietly slipped out, telling her he would be back—later.

When she had followed him with concerned eyes, he had turned to assure her, "I promise not to be gone long. Just want to check on things at the minin' company, make sure it hasn't gone to ruin during my absence. It's destined to be yours one day, you know."

Dipping her head in acceptance, she thought nothing more about it. Time didn't allow her to. Duty called. There was so much to do to see to her father's comfort.

Pausing in the hallway, she checked the watch pinned over her heart. The doctor who attended him would be there in less than two hours. Oh, dear, she wanted to see that he was bathed, his bedclothes changed, his hair neatly brushed—all things to make him look and feel better. And it did seem to her he was improving daily. As if her arrival had spurred him back on the road of recovery.

An hour later she sat beside him, as was her custom when all the chores were completed, and they shared a few private moments together. Taking up his hand, she contemplated his thin face, weatherworn and tough as old shoe leather, and yet there was a fragility just beneath the protective surface.

"Shall I read to you, Father?"

Langston's eyes, brown and warm when they lit on her even though they sunk deep into their sockets, spoke for him.

"What would you like?" She reached for the stack of books she'd collected from the downstairs library and began shuffling through them, reciting the titles. Try as she might, she couldn't help but notice how heavy each volume seemed. She was tired, oh, so tired, but she refused to let her father see it.

Then Langston's hand settled on her, stilling her nervous movement. "This one?" she asked, looking up to find him studying her intently.

The book drifted back into her lap.

"Does he make you happy, girl?"

357

Serra knew of whom he spoke. Ty. She hesitated to answer, fearing to upset him, and yet to try and avoid the question might only serve to suggest that she wasn't happy. Wouldn't that upset him even more? Pushing the books aside, she took up his hand once more.

"Yes, Father," she confessed. "I love Ty very much. I believe I always have and always will."

In the next few seconds she witnessed the change as it occurred, knowing that her father had at last come to accept the inevitable. Love for this craggy, sometimes gruff old man came full circle. "You know, Father, my feelings for Ty doesn't diminish my love for you."

He sighed. "I know that, girl. I was just worried that he might take undue advantage of your generous heart. I guess I was wrong."

"Then you'll be gentler with him, won't you? For me?"

He smiled thinly. "Hell, girl, next you'll want me to apologize to him."

"If it's not too much of a strain on your vocal cords." She laughed and he followed suit, their moment of gaiety mingling in the sun-filled room.

"Excuse me, Miss Serenity."

Serra glanced up at the butler's intrusion.

"The doctor is here and wishes to see you downstairs."

"The doctor?" Dousing her laughter, she took up the pin watch attached to her bodice and frowned. "He's early. Well, it doesn't matter," she said carelessly as she released her father's hand and stood. "I'll just see what he has to say, and we'll be back up to check on you."

Leaving the butler to attend the patient, she hur-

358

ried down the stairs, her heart thundering. What did Dr. Jacobs have to say to her that he couldn't talk about in front of her father? *Oh, please, please, don't let it be bad news.*

She raced into the front parlor, prepared for her father's physician. Instead, she came face to face with the mesmerizing intensity of Lionel Chelsey's dark gaze.

"Doc," she cried, surprised yet immensely relieved as she fell into the circle of his familiar arms.

"Ah, dumpling," he cooed his condolences. "I came as soon as I heard, and to offer you my services and support in your time of need."

She leaned back and smiled up into his kindness. "To be honest, I can use all the help I can get. How long can you stay?"

"As long as you need me."

"Oh, Doc, I can't tell you how good it will be to have a medical mind in the house all of the time, especially when it's yours." Pressing the side of her face against the lapel of his dark coat, she closed her eyes in genuine pleasure.

"Not to worry, Serra. We'll get through this together, you and me. Just like we always do." He patted her head with affection.

"And Ty," she added, backing up a bit so she could look at him, joy tipping her words with excitement. "You can't imagine how wonderful he has been."

"You mean that boy, Tyler Ramsey?" Knitting his brows, Chelsey held her at arm's length.

"Oh, Doc, I know you had your reasons for not liking him—he did treat me rather shabbily in the beginning when he thought my claim invalid—but that's all different now. We're married and very much in love." It was so important to her that the men in her life all got along. She'd resolved the problems between her father and Ty; why not with Doc as well?

"You're what?" His grip on her arms stiffened, painfully so.

"Why, Doc!" Somewhat irritated that he was being so stubborn, she tried to brush his hands away. "I thought you would be happy for me."

"When did this happen?" He shook her so hard that her teeth snapped together.

She knew he didn't like Ty, but she couldn't fathom the intensity of his anger. "Just a few weeks ago," she replied, "but —"

"Ah, Serra, don't you realize what you have done?" Dragging her toward the sofa, he forced her to sit down. "You've gone and given that cadger the footing he needs."

"Whatever do you mean?" She brushed back a strand of wayward hair, pushing down the confusion within her.

"Don't you see, Serenity?" He settled beside her, sighing with self-appointed wisdom. "Tyler Ramsey wants control of your inheritance now that you have usurped his place in your father's will. What better way to accomplish his goal than by marrying you?"

Serra swallowed her disbelief. No. Doc had to be mistaken. Ty loved her. Besides, he had his own business, his own wealth; why would he want Langston Mining? Then she remembered that he had gone down to the office just this afternoon to check and make sure all was well. But that didn't necessarily indicate that he contrived to take possession of the business.

"No, Doc, you're wrong," she countered with firm

conviction. "You've misjudged Ty completely."

"Have I? Then why don't you ask him what happens when a married woman inherits? You'll have no control of your money, Serra. You won't have any say at all in its distribution. There'll be no sharing with those who have helped you, supported you, given you the education and the opportunity to take your rightful place."

Slowly it dawned on her that Chelsey spoke about himself, and it took her by surprise that he would be so bold in his assumptions. Perhaps he did have a right to expect compensation in return for all that he had done for her, but he talked of her inheritance as if it were his, of her father's death as if the loss held no consequences. How calloused and crass; how unacceptable. "Doc, please, I don't want to discuss this now." Her hands moved to her temples in a show of reluctance.

"Then when will you want to talk about it?" Chelsey pushed. "When it's too late? When Tyler Ramsey has his greedy hands on all of it, and he casts us both to the side?"

"No, Doc, you mustn't say things like that," she chided. "Ty has no intentions of betraying me in such a fashion." The throbbing in her temples intensified, and she automatically began to massage them, trying desperately to eradicate the debilitating pain, the doubt oozing into her mind, the thunder of the physician's strumming fingers.

That sound. It was so familiar, its rhythm forcing her will at bay, as if a plate of glass slid between her and reality. She could see it, but she just couldn't grasp it any longer. The only thread left her was a voice—his voice making demands.

"Serra, you will confront Tyler Ramsey and insist

on an answer."

"An answer about what?"

Serra's head flew up to find Ty standing in the parlor doorway, so real, so tall, so self-assured, his black Stetson clutched in his gloved hand, giving Chelsey a look that offered no welcome. Then he turned to her, his cold blue eyes demanding an explanation for the physician's presence.

Ask him, Serra. Do it now, an inner voice commanded, but she fought down the urge. Ty would never use her for his own personal gain. Rising to her feet, she joined her husband, determined to keep tempers aligned and under control. "Tyler, Dr. Chelsey has graciously offered his medical knowledge to help Father," she informed him, thinking that would defuse the situation.

Ty's gaze flicked down, assessing the other man. "We don't want your kind of help, Chelsey."

Serra gasped at his brusqueness, and she found herself standing between the two men, a hand planted on each of their chests, keeping them apart. "Ty, Doc, please," she pleaded.

"Ask him, Serra. Ask him what he intends to do with the Langston fortune once he gets control of it," Chelsey ordered, his lungs wheezing with angry resolve.

Try as she might, she couldn't help herself. Turning to Ty, she spoke the words, hoping—no, praying—he would deny the accusation. "Is it true, Ty? If Father should die, would you have the right to take control?"

Serra knew him well enough to recognize the guarded stubbornness as it slowly masked his face. His jaw worked as he formulated his answer. "Yes, Serra," he admitted at last in a strong, unemotional voice. "As your husband, I would have every right." He leveled a steady gaze upon his opponent. "To protect both you and the assets from wheedling scum," he continued his explanation to her even though he no longer looked at her, "I would do it without hesitation."

"There, see. I told you," Chelsey declared with a confident smirk.

She turned to Ty, seeking a retraction, something, anything to counter the terrible truth of his confession. "You would do this to me, Ty?"

His hard, proud gaze never flinched, never expressed even an inkling of regret that he had deceived her so. "Darlin', I would be doin' you a favor, not an injustice."

His betrayal rose like bile in her throat. This wasn't the first time he'd forsaken her, and she accepted with resignation that it probably wouldn't be the last . . . the cold, calculated way he grasped her heart and squeezed until she could feel it shattering into a thousand irreparable pieces. And he never even blinked an eye as he watched her slowly disintegrate. Where once love had filled every nuance of her soul, a new feeling sprouted in its place, growing, expanding until it became fullblown. The hate clotted in her blood, giving her a courage and strength she'd never thought, never wanted to possess.

"Get out," she ordered, taking a threatening step toward him, an inner part of her finding it hard to believe that she spoke to him with such venom.

Ty held his ground, as if he had every valid reason.

She raised her clenched fists to emphasize her sincerity. "Did you hear me, Tyler Ramsey? Get out!"

she shouted.

Once the tidal wave of her outburst had settled into silence, Ty took up his hat, placing it on his head at a cocky angle. "If that's what you want. But you know, Serra, my leavin' doesn't change a damn thing. I'm still your husband."

"Don't worry, dumpling. I have friends in high places. I'll see to it you get an annulment," Chelsey interjected, almost gleefully.

Ty's attention riveted on the doctor, hard and hawkish. "Not likely, Chelsey," he challenged. "You have no grounds. Serenity Langston, Serra Paletot." He shrugged his wide shoulders. "No matter what name you call her by, she's still my wife in every way."

Like the cock that crowed announcing the disciple Simon's denial of his God, she heard his third betrayal. Her last vestige of hope withered and died upon the echo of his words. He still didn't believe her claim to the Langston name; apparently, he never had. He'd lied to her, deceived her, and now he mocked her. Her heart couldn't take any more.

Her fists smashed down against the broad expanse of his chest, lifted, and descended again. "You are a blight upon my life, Tyler Ramsey," she sobbed. "Get out!"

He touched his black gloved fingers to the brim of his hat. "All right, darlin', I'm gittin' out." He took a step backward. "But I'll be there, always there, Serra. Our lives run too deep and too long. I hope you don't come to see that when it's too late."

Then he was gone, and Serra knew, this time, there would be no miracle . . . no reprieve.

The dream in all its vividness came crashing down on her hard and heavy. Serra struggled to swim free of it, tried and failed, unable to stop the horror from sweeping her up into its midst. The nightmare was the same as before. She a little girl, a toddler really, and Ty a small child himself, there in some dark corner huddling together, shivering with cold and fear.

"Papa hurt," she blubbered in a baby voice.

Ty lifted the corner of the filthy sackcloth and dried the streaking tears from her dirt-crusted face. "Someday, Serra, it'll all be different for both of us. Someday," he promised, and oh, God, how she wanted to believe him.

She awoke with a start, automatically turning in the big canopied bed and seeking his warmth. And then she remembered the devastating events of the day.

Ty was gone. She had sent him away.

Lying there in the darkness, alone, she sorted through the still crystal-clear vestiges of her dream, trying to remember details, something, anything that would confirm or deny that there was any reality in the vision. Chewing on her bottom lip, she sat up in bed. Dear God, what if there was something to her dreams? What if Ty was a part of her past she couldn't recall in her conscious state? What if he were right? What if she wasn't Serenity Langston?

Her mind threw up barriers, rejecting the preposterous idea. Her memory of this house, of her parents, was much too vivid. But there were the other images of a father, and they weren't of John Langston.

Then and there Serra accepted that she couldn't go on any longer without knowing the truth—all of it—whether it pleased her or not. She must get to the bottom of the situation, and the only way she could see to accomplish that was to return to the origins of her conflict: her youth.

New York City. Yet the thought of such a monumental undertaking unnerved her.

Then she thought of her father, lying in a bed just down the hall, possibly dying, believing she was his long lost daughter, trusting her to have told him the truth. Was it fair to him if he was being deceived?

Regardless of the dangers, she knew then that she couldn't live with a lie, couldn't continue in darkness, never sure of who she really was—Serra Paletot or Serenity Langston.

She glanced at the mantel clock ticking away in solemn innocence. Two-thirty. Rising from her bed, she began to pace, making her plans. She considered her choices: to go it alone or to take someone with her. But whom? Tess? She shook her head. The servant had her own life now. Besides, the girl was needed to see to the smooth running of the house during her own absence.

What about Dr. Chelsey? She mulled over the idea for a few minutes. Then something primeval squelched that thought before she could explore it further. There was this feeling—nothing she could confirm, really—that left her wondering if the physician somehow was behind the deception.

Then Ty, she finally settled on. She would ask her husband to accompany her. No. If he already knew something and hadn't told her, why would he be willing to help her in her quest? Besides, she thought, lifting her chin, this was something she had to do on her own, prove to herself.

Hefting down her valises, she set about packing

essentials and nothing more.

As she closed the lid on the last suitcase her heart flipflopped in her chest. New York. Dear God. That part of her life was so far away, so long ago . . . so frightening. She only hoped she had the courage and stamina to carry through with her convictions.

Chapter Twenty-one

The ferry chugged away from the Jersey shore, churning the already muddy waters of the Hudson, striving to gain position among the many boats clogging the busy river. Serra settled her baggage about her legs and took a seat near the front of the craft, knowing the trip wouldn't take all that long and yet wishing it would stretch on forever.

Her destiny awaited on the far shore, answers to questions that had plagued her day and night on the long train ride across the country. The reoccurring nightmares seemed to grow larger in scope the nearer she drew to the end of the line. Where once she was merely confused, she now was certain there was substance to the bad dreams. Confident that she would find the explanations she sought, she wasn't so sure she was ready to face what she discovered.

When finally the ferryboat maneuvered so that its bow aimed toward Manhattan, Serra had a full view of the harbor, awe inspiring in its majestic clutter. Off to her right, she could see the back view of a statue. Even from that distance, she could tell the feminine figure was colossal in size as it canopied over Bedloe's Island. Glancing about at her fellow passengers, she searched for someone to question. She settled on a small woman huddled on a bench across from her.

"Excuse me, please," she queried, leaning forward.

The woman, rather worn and yet Serra couldn't be sure of her age, looked up but said nothing.

"The statue? What is it?"

"Where've ya been of late, girlie?" the woman chirped in a thick Irish brogue like a downtrodden sparrow pecking at a crust of bread. " 'Tis Liberty Enlightenin' the World, ya be lookin' at."

"Liberty, of course." Serra dropped back against her seat. "I remember hearing about such a project just before I left New York. I had no idea it had been completed," she murmured, mostly to herself.

"Aye, ya've been gone a long time, haven't ya, lass?"

Serra smiled. "A very long time."

"Have ya kin waitin' for ya on the other side?"

"No." Serra shook her head, wondering if perhaps she did have relatives somewhere in Manhattan, wondering if she might possibly run across them in her search.

"If it's work ya be seekin'," the woman continued, her mousy gaze drifting over the quality of Serra's clothing, her baggage, "I wouldna be too hopeful if I was ya."

"No, no. I don't need a job," Serra assured her with a smile.

The woman leaned forward and glanced about. "Then I suggest ya not tell that to everyone ya meet, or you'll find yourself the victim of pickpockets and petty thieves." Sitting back, she cradled the old straw bag she held to her chest. "And hold that purse of yours closer to ya. Its string could be cut before a

369

leprechaun could stash his pot o' gold."

Serra gathered her belongings to her, a terrible sinking feeling settling in the pit of her stomach. What if she couldn't find her way around the huge city? It had been a long time, and her memory was choppy at best. Besides, look at all the changes that had taken place over the years. What if things weren't the way she remembered?

But that was ridiculous. She would find a good hotel on the Upper East Side and from there take a cab wherever she needed to go. The driver would know the way. There was absolutely nothing for her to worry about.

Regardless, she clutched her purse to her bosom, wondering, dreading just what awaited her on the other side of the river.

Yet when the ferry docked at the depot, everything went amazingly smooth. In no time she located a small boy—actually, he hustled her business—to help her with her luggage and hail a cab. She glanced around, seeking the Irishwoman who had been so helpful on the trip over, deciding to offer her a ride to her destination, but the old woman was nowhere to be seen. It was almost as if the bustling city had swallowed her up.

With a sigh, Serra turned to step into the waiting cab. Reaching out the window, she tipped the baggage boy generously for his time and efforts.

His eyes lit up, and he grinned at her as if she were some angel of mercy. "Thank ye kindly, ma'am. And may God bless ya," the boy shouted as the vehicle rolled away from the busy station.

May God bless her indeed, she prayed, pressing her shoulders against the leather seat. Once enmeshed with the traffic, the carriage lumbered through the teeming, crowded streets. Within minutes Serra was lost, realizing she was no match for the city on her own.

"What the hell do you mean, Tess, you don't know where she's gone?"

Ty dominated the entrance to the Langston house, his broad shoulders filling up the doorway as he pushed his way past the servant, beginning a methodical forage of the downstairs as if he expected to find Serra hiding from him behind a piece of furniture.

"Just as I said, Tyler Ramsey," Tess insisted, following in his wake, her fists plopped on her hips with indignation. "The mornin' after your departure, she simply left without an explanation. She didn't even inform the staff. Even Dr. Chelsey couldn't seem to get anywhere with her."

"That son of a bitch." Ty paused in his futile search and towered over the girl. "Is *he* still here?"

"No. Chelsey hightailed it the day after Miss Serenity left."

"Did you contact the sheriff? Did you report her missin'?"

"There be no need, Ty." Tess tried to catch his arm, but he pulled away. "It was obvious she left because she wanted to. She packed several bags."

Halfway up the main staircase, Ty spun around on the steps and asked, concern knitting his dark brows, "John? How is he takin' all of this?"

From below, Tess shrugged. "He's not sayin' a word except to ask each mornin' if she's returned yet, as if he expects her to at any time. I think he knows somethin', but he's refusin' to say anything."

Well, he would see about that. Angling back around, Ty continued his ascent, taking his benefactor's room by storm. He was surprised to see Langston sitting up, a healthy color to his cheeks and a large breakfast on the tray across his lap.

"John," he said, trying his damnedest to sound deferential to the older man.

Langston looked up from his morning newspaper, his disciplined brown eyes peering over the top rim of his reading glasses. "Tyler," he greeted, as if he wasn't at all surprised by his ward's sudden appearance at the foot of his bed. "I thought you would come." He folded the paper several times and laid it beside him on the coverlet. "You sure took your sweet time about it, boy."

"Where is she, John?"

"You walked out on her. I'm not so sure you have a right to know that information."

"She sent me away."

"Ah, yes." Langston shook his head. "Well, she told me about that." Stripping off his spectacles, he folded them, sitting them on top of his discarded newspaper. "You know, if I'd listened to my Laura Lee every time she got emotional and ordered me out the front door, I would have worn a dog path between here and the old Bateman House." Langston chuckled. "Boy, you got to learn to read your woman better'n that."

"My woman?"

"Hell, you married her, didn't you?"

Ty nodded with suspicion. "Yes, sir, I did."

"You're damn right you did. You took my little girl and made her your woman."

Ty stiffened and squared his shoulders, preparing for the tirade to begin—again. Only this time he

372

wasn't so sure he would just stand there and take it, without Serra to temper his own anger.

"She's gone back east, son," Langston finally said in quiet compassion, the first time in a long while that he'd spoken to Ty so kindly.

A rush of unbidden emotion raced through Ty, softening the tension in his body, the resentment in his heart.

"God knows I tried to talk her out of it." Langston's voice broke on a sob, so unlike the man of self-control Ty had come to know, had learned to respect. "Had I been half the man I used to be, I would have made her forget all this nonsense about gittin' to the truth. Hell, the only truth that matters is that she's found her way home."

Ty heard the cry for forgiveness in the other man's uncharacteristic outburst, and if the truth be known, he felt for John, truly understood and forgave him for his weaknesses. But a vision of Serra alone, trudging through the streets of New York, filled his mind, and Ty's heart quickened with fear. A disdainful frown creased his face. Then an even more terrible possibility struck him.

"Damn it, John, do you know where Chelsey's gone?"

"That old quacksalver?" Langston snorted, but his derision turned into a choking sound, which took him several minutes to recover from. "I suspect he tucked tail and headed home when he didn't have any more bones to pick over. I wouldn't tell him where she went."

Remembering the physician's file on Serra that he had read, which made him suspect Chelsey had powers to make people do and say things against their better judgment, Ty pressed. "Are you sure,

John? Are you sure you didn't tell him anything?"

"Hell, boy, I may be sick in the body," he growled, "but I ain't touched in the head. I'd remember if I told him."

Ty relaxed somewhat. Surely Langston was right. A person would have to remember something as important as that.

Serra stepped from the Fifth Avenue Hotel, a prestigious building of white marble a full city block in size, as Jimson, the doorman, held open the door for her. He tipped his hat and smiled as he signaled for a waiting cab to approach the curb.

As she settled herself inside the vehicle, the driver asked, "Where to today, Mrs. Ramsey? Going slumming again this afternoon?"

Serra didn't particularly care for the term *slumming,* but apparently that was a common pastime of the idle rich in the city, a status she had been elevated to by the hotel staff. The mysterious woman from Missouri who spent her days touring the Lower East Side, with no apparent destination in mind. Cabbies vied for her fare, a most profitable one. Laughingly, Jimson had told her she was known on the streets as "our lady of the cab." Everyone was curious about her intentions.

Serra wasn't all that certain of them herself. She had taken to exploring every street, every alleyway, hoping to come upon something that would fit the image in her mind, a vision that had recreated itself night after night in her dreams, more vivid in each recounting. A rambling, decayed frame building, several stories high, surrounded by streets so narrow a carriage couldn't turn around in them even in desperation, shouldn't be that difficult to locate. But so far she'd not had any luck.

Today she'd finally dredged up the courage to pay a visit to the Children's Aid Society. Perhaps they would shed some light and hopefully some information on her past. She wondered if they would even remember who she was.

"Amity and Broadway, Jimson."

The doorman relayed her orders to the driver. As the carriage took off down the street, Serra leaned back against the aging leather seat and closed her eyes. She hoped today wasn't as fruitless as its predecessors.

The hired vehicle threaded its way out into the slow-moving traffic on Broadway, heading south along the crowded thoroughfare. Serra watched the scenery inch by inch, just as she did at every outing. The neat city blocks were dotted with trees and gas lights, lined with competitive hotels to rival the one she stayed in and other multistoried buildings. So tall she couldn't see their tops from where she sat, the structures housed the fashionable businesses of the city—Tiffany and Company; Arnold Constable and Company; Lord and Taylor with their magnificent show windows, just to name a few The prestigious upper section of Manhattan.

The carriage came to a stop, and Serra peered out the window to see if they had reached their destination so quickly, only to find the way so jammed with other carriages, wagons, carts, and omnibuses that it seemed impossible to her to untangle them. The drivers, including her own, vent their frustration by shouting curses and insults at each other. And then uniformed policemen arrived, barking orders, snagging teams by their harnesses, and within minutes they were on their way once more.

Not too much farther the vehicle lurched to another stop at the corner she'd requested. Serra had the sudden urge to demand that the driver take her back to the safety of the hotel. Viewing the streets from the security of her cab was one thing; now she was expected to venture forth into the teeming hostility on her own.

When at last the driver unlatched the door and swept it open, he cocked his head at her show of reluctance.

"This is the corner you asked for, ma'am, Amity and Broadway."

And, yes, indeed it was. There across the street she ferreted out the address she sought, crammed between two other buildings, all of brown stone and iron. The home of the New York Children's Aid Society.

Clutching her reticule, Serra ventured forward, blinking. There was nothing familiar about the building itself. Not that she'd expected it to be, as the orphans were lodged elsewhere; this was simply a reception office where interested parties could inquire and hopefully make donations to the cause, and where records were kept.

Instructing the driver to wait, she stepped into the street, judging the slow-moving traffic as she navigated her way through the conglomeration of people, animals, and vehicles. Once inside the building, Serra jutted out her bottom lip, huffing in relief. Nothing had prepared her for the harrowing experience of crossing Broadway. Noting on the register that the Children's Aid Society was on the second floor, she took the stairs, determined now to complete her task.

A young gentleman, not much older than herself really, rose from a small desk near the door to greet her when she entered the office. She didn't recognize him, but apparently he sized her up for quality and came forward most eagerly to welcome her.

"I would like to see Mr. Charles Bracing," she announced, recalling the name of the man who had been in charge of the program six years before, the person responsible for the founding of the Society several decades before that, a face she remembered coming to the home from time to time.

The gentleman leveled his gray eyes on her, giving her a strange but kindly look, and replied in easy grace, "I'm sorry, madam, but Mr. Bracing is in Switzerland. Geoff Tanner," he introduced himself. "Can I assist you in some way?"

Serra hesitated. She had wanted to speak with someone familiar, someone who might recall her situation. Someone who would be interested in helping her glean the truth. Contemplating this Mr. Tanner, she surmised he probably couldn't have worked there long enough to meet any of her criteria.

"Perhaps if we shared a cup of tea . . ." he urged, politely waiting for her to supply her name as he settled her in a chair near the one window in the office.

And what name should she offer him? Langston, Paletot—Ramsey? Worrying her bottom lip, she began pulling her gloves from her fingers. "Mrs. Tyler Ramsey."

In the process of making a pot of tea on an old stove in the corner, Tanner spun about, an opened blue and white caddy with a spoon poised over it still in his hands. "I once had a friend by the name of Tyler Ramsey."

Serra's heart quickened, and she leaned forward. "So tell me, sir, what became of this friend of yours?"

Setting aside the brew, he took a step toward her, his brows knitted in consternation. "The records are incomplete. In the spring of eighty-one, he was sent west to be placed out, but when the agents returned, they had no knowledge of his whereabouts. They claimed the adoption papers had apparently been misplaced and lost."

"Ah, yes, the Reverend Millboone and his abominable wife," Serra stated emphatically, shaking her head as a memory of the two filled her mind.

"You know them?"

"Only too well, Mr. Tanner, and I can assure you that they lied."

"I've always suspected that," Tanner said, edging closer. "But how did you know that?"

"Because, sir, I was on that very same orphan train. Once we reached Missouri, Ty managed to run away. He found his own benefactor without the aid of the Society."

Slapping his knee, Geoff laughed out loud. "That's the Tyler Ramsey I know. He always was one to do things his own way." He moved to a file cabinet on the other side of the room and pulled open the top drawer. Rummaging through the records, he came upon the one he sought. Spreading the portfolio open, he draped it in her lap.

The picture was faded, somewhat out of focus, but there they were, all thirty of them, lost waifs, eyes round with fright — all except Ty, taller than the rest, a look of belligerence on his youthful face, so dear, so handsome.

"Which one are you?" Tanner prompted.

Serra startled and glanced up at the man's interested face. She smiled and pointed to the child whose hair frizzed about wan, uncertain features. "Here. Serra Paletot." She tapped the photograph. "Do you remember me?" she asked hopefully.

After a moment of contemplation, he shook his head. "I'm sorry, Mrs. Ramsey, I honestly can't say that I do. But, then, I didn't actually join the Society until after Ty's departure.

"He was good to all of us, you know," he continued, "encouraging us to make something of ourselves, to take advantage of every situation." He smiled in remembrance. "Nobody could pick a pocket like Tyler Ramsey. Even when he was in the orphanage he would sneak out at night, and he'd check on all of us at the Five Points, make his rounds to the hot spots of the rich off Broadway, and then distribute his spoils with those of us who refused to see the benefits the home had to offer. There's many a night when I would have gone hungry or maybe even frozen to death if it hadn't been for the generosity of Tyler Ramsey." Again his gaze swept over the quality of her clothing, her shoes, her fine kid gloves, her expensive feathered hat. "He's done well for himself, then?"

"Well enough," Serra answered, realizing just how lucky she and Ty were, and feeling somewhat guilty about her lack of gratitude. "But I'm not here for my husband's sake, Mr. Tanner. I've come to find out more about my own circumstances. I thought perhaps you could help me."

"You mean the Society."

She nodded.

Tanner frowned. "Have you a brother or sister you're trying to locate?"

379

She shook her head, sensing that Tanner had been through this before. "I just need to know where I came from, something about my parents . . ." She trailed off when she saw his frown deepen.

"I'm sorry. It's policy, you know, to keep the records private. I—I just don't know," he stammered.

"Please, Mr. Tanner."

For a moment they stared at each other, Serra hopeful, Tanner uncertain.

"Very well," he finally agreed. "For Tyler. I suppose I owe him that much."

Together they spent the afternoon becoming friends, combing through the records, which were painfully sketchy, containing nothing more than she already knew. She'd appeared on the doorstep of the Baxter Street facility wearing a woman's expensive paletot, the note proclaiming "Please take care of Serra" pinned to the collar. Nothing more. Except that in the registry beside her name was written: "From the Five Points, Miss Hannah Evans."

"Geoff, who is this Miss Evans?" Serra asked, her finger running over the scrawled name as if it were written in gold ink.

Tanner's gaze flicked up and over her, assessing. "Miss Hannah recruited for the Baxter Street Home. Years ago, she spent hours scouring the Five Points, talking with the children, encouraging them to come forth, to turn themselves over to the care of the Society. She was the salvation of many a wayward soul—including my own."

Serra's brows knitted. "Why don't I remember her?"

"Unless she commandeered you from the streets, you wouldn't. She rarely came into the orphanage itself except to check the files and add whatever she

380

could to the records. Like what she did for you. I have to admit, though, she usually wasn't so brief in her notations."

"And where is Miss Hannah now?" she asked quietly, noting his reference to the woman in the past tense.

Geoff sighed and sat back in his chair. "She goes into the orphanage in the afternoons to spend time with the children. But, Serra, you must understand," he cautioned her, his hand covering hers in gentle restraint, "she's so old now. Her energy, her memory, just aren't what they were at one time."

But hope glimmered in spite of his warning. At least the woman was still alive. "It's worth a try, isn't it?"

Tanner smiled. "I suppose."

Serra rose. "I have a cab waiting below. We can go right now."

Without further protest, Tanner escorted her across the street and gave the driver directions to the Baxter Street Home. But when she urged him to join her in the hired carriage, he shook his head and fastened the door. "I can't close the office, Serra. I have a duty to stay here. You understand, don't you? Just in case one of the children or a benefactor should decide to come in."

And she did understand, admiring his dedication to helping others, the unrepressed glimmer of hope he harbored in his heart. A hope he had passed on to her. Miss Hannah Evans. Impulsively, she reached into her reticule and took out all the money she had placed in there that morning. Stuffing the wad into the hands of an unsuspecting Geoff Tanner, she curled his fingers about it. "Thank you, Geoff. Use this in a way that will benefit the children best."

His gray eyes widened, and he took a darting glance about. "Mrs. Ramsey," he said reverting back to a more formal address, "this is a lot of money. Are you sure?"

"I'm sure. In fact, you can expect a sum each month." She patted his hand, which was fisted about the donation. "It's the very least *I* can do."

"All right. If you're sure you can afford it. You just tell Tyler Geoff Tanner remembers. Tell him he was right."

With a nod, Serra smiled sadly as she called to the driver to proceed. She doubted she would ever see Ty again, but she didn't say that to Tanner.

Then they were off, crawling through the district south of Houston Street, where beyond the grandeur of Broadway the side streets teemed with bourgeois businesses—butchers, bakers, small clothing shops unwilling to compete with the better stores. And behind the facade of these shops hid the multitudes of factories and warehouses, the sweatshops disguised with ornate Corinthian columns, Palladian windows, and French dormers.

Finally, they reached the steamy interior of the Lower East Side. Though Broadway itself presented a respectable face, just beyond, the sidewalks showed the wear of the many immigrant feet that traversed them. Turning down one, the carriage's way was no longer impeded by other traffic but by the street vendors—the hurdy-gurdy man, the hot corn seller, the soft drink peddler, the bootblack, each one shouting about his or her wares in an effort to outdo the competition—and the hordes of children who claimed the filth-lined streets as their playground, a place of refuge from the crowded tenements that offered only squalor and darkness.

She shivered, reliving what it had been like, recalling and trying desperately to forget. But the images, the smells, were too sharp, too real to be ignored.

When they reached the orphanage on Baxter Street, Serra couldn't believe the filth and stench surrounding the old building, an oasis of hope in the bowels of hell. She remembered it well.

The cabbie handed her down, but when she asked him to wait for her, he shook his head in refusal. "I'm sorry, ma'am. The dips would steal me blind if I did. I'll come back around for you in an hour, though."

Serra agreed, knowing the man would return if not out of loyalty, then out of a need to collect his hefty fare for the day. She nodded. "An hour."

As she watched the carriage roll away, her insides roiled with apprehension. She was alone now, on her own to face whatever the Fates decided to unveil. Turning, she confronted the soot-streaked building, disembodied images flashing through her mind, none of which made much sense—a small child crying, another comforting.

She pressed the heels of her hands to her temples. If only these nagging pictures would present themselves with continuity. If only she could make herself remember. And then a terrible thought struck her. What if Miss Hannah Evans failed to recall just as she had all of these years? Notching her chin, she refused to accept that she'd come all this way to leave empty-handed.

The moment she entered the orphanage, familiar sights and smells confronted her. As she spoke to the director, introducing herself and explaining her reason for being there, she became aware that she was being watched through slit doors and the grills above them.

The children. She smiled to herself, remembering how it was whenever anyone had come to actually visit the home. Always there was the hope one of them would be adopted, each praying he or she would be the lucky one. She heard their muffled whispers, the shuffle of their small feet, as they vied for space, but she pretended not to notice.

At her insistence to see Miss Hannah, the director sent her to a small room in the rear of the building. The sight that greeted her squeezed her heart until it bled.

The old lady sat hunched among a group of youngsters, her back to the door, sprigs of white hair peeping from an out-of-style bonnet, her voice as brittle as aged parchment as she spoke to them softly, offering encouragement. The children were cleanly dressed, their faces washed, their hair brushed back, and yet there was something about them to suggest disorientation, a newness to such care and consideration. And there remained the tell-tale signs of abuse — an eye swollen and red, bruises on exposed limbs, the haunted, distrusting look that took time to dissipate.

As she stood there unnoticed in the doorway, simply observing the woman as she worked, a strangeness mantled her shoulders, almost as if cold fingers wove their way about her throat and began to squeeze. The pain these children suffered seeped into her body, twisting, wrenching a response from her she didn't wish to give.

Familiarity. Her hand crept to her throat where the blood pounded out the sickening sensation of knowing just what they experienced. She had felt

384

their pain, lived with it just as they did, and oh, God, somehow she had managed to escape the horror of it all by shoving the memories into the deepest recesses of her mind.

And then one of the children, a little girl who couldn't have been more than two or three, held out the mangled fingers of her left hand to the old woman. "Tiss, Mith Nanna," she cried in a soft baby lisp, pressing her flesh against Hannah Evan's wrinkled mouth. "Papa hurt. Papa hurt."

Serra clutched her own fingers to her heart, and the tattered remnants of truth she had squirreled away with such efficiency came tumbling down around her. "Papa hurt," she murmured, remembering a hulking figure towering over her as she cowered on the floor, the feel of a belt buckle digging into the tender skin of her own arms and legs, her exposed buttocks and spine. A great sob leaked from her sealed lips, and she covered her mouth to squelch the sound.

It was at that moment that Miss Hannah heard her cry and glanced over one sloping shoulder. Though her wrinkled face wasn't really familiar, the compassion in her sparkling blue eyes that spoke of life and vitality was. Eyes like those had soothed away her pain, her fears long ago. The eyes of Tyler Ramsey.

Serra stumbled backward, as if someone had slapped her in the face.

And in truth, reality had done just that. The truth was, John Langston couldn't be her father. The truth was, she was a nameless child of the slums of New York, Serra Paletot. No amount of wishing and dreaming could ever change that fact.

"Is there something I can do for you, dearie?"

385

Hannah Evan's reed-thin voice beckoned to her.

Serra knew at that moment she didn't want to unravel the truth any further. It would crush her as surely as if she were to dart in front of a speeding train. Pressing the knuckles of her hand against her open mouth, she shook her head and edged out of the room.

Down the hallway she ran, the clatter of her own feet loud in her ears. At the end of the corridor, she flung open the door. More memories bombarded her as she stared into the dormitory that had housed her for all of those years. There. There. In the far corner. The very bed she had slept upon.

Spinning, she raced out of the room, forgetting to shut the door behind her. Instinct guided her flying feet. She had trod these floorboards for so long, how could she ever forget her way?

As she passed through the sewing room, several older girls glanced up from their work. She had learned her stitchery right here, sitting in that very chair, needle in, needle out, perfecting her skills for hours, a craft meant to provide a living someday in the sweatshops.

But she had escaped it. Somehow she had been fortunate enough never to have to ply her wearisome trade. And she wasn't so sure she deserved such deferential treatment.

Dear God, she should have never come here. If only she had stayed home and been satisfied with what she'd had.

Serra came to a shaking halt at the kitchen exit leading into an alleyway. Home? She laughed inwardly without mirth. What right had she to call any place home? As she fled through the unlocked door, she crashed into a line of wooden crates used to store garbage. The hem of her dress caught on a piece of ragged wire and tore as she spun to free herself. She stumbled on, the heels of her shoes sinking into the muddy ruts.

Once she reached Baxter Street, she paused long enough to catch her breath and get her bearings. Spying the front of the orphanage building now several blocks to her left, she searched up and down the street for a sign of her cab.

An hour he had said. How long had it been? She glanced down at the pin watch on her lapel. Twenty minutes at the most. She should go back inside to wait. But, oh, if she did that, she would surely lose her mind.

She began walking in the opposite direction. Crossing a side street, she caught the name: Franklin. She paused at the corner and stretched to peer down the filth-lined lane, left and then right. One of these streets eventually ran into Broadway. If she could only locate the main thoroughfare, she would be safe and could find her way back to the hotel, perhaps even locate another cab.

At the next intersection, a hurdy-gurdy man cranked his organ to the delight of a crowd of dirty-faced urchins. She reached into her purse for a coin to drop into his tin cup, determined to ask directions. To her horror she came up empty-handed, remembering that she had given all of her cash to Geoff Tanner. What a fool she'd been, an optimistic dunderhead. Now she was at the mercy of a cruel, unfriendly city with no money, no cab, no sense of direction.

She glanced about, seeking some avenue other than returning to the one place she had no desire to ever see again, the Baxter Street Home.

"You lost, miss?"

Serra whirled about to confront an angelic-looking boy of no more than six or seven.

"Which way to Broadway?" she asked, wishing she had a coin or two to offer in exchange for the information.

The boy looked her up and down, took in her fine clothing, and grinned. Ty must have looked a bit like him at that age. "I'll be glad to show you."

Serra hesitated. Should she trust him? Had he been older, she would have refused his offer to help. But he was so young, so pitiful-looking with his watery eyes. Besides, she had been one of them—once.

She nodded and began to follow his lead, telling him a little about herself and how she'd once lived in the orphanage. The boy listened as they walked, and he seemed genuinely interested as he wove a path through the throngs. Recognizing a store as they passed it, Serra felt certain he led her in the right direction. Several blocks later when they crossed in front of a run-down tenement building from which a cluster of dirty-faced children poured, following them, she was no longer so confident.

"Are you sure this is the way? I don't remember the cab passing such a building."

"A shortcut, miss," the boy assured her, fingering his filthy cap with an equally dirty hand. "You know the cabbies; they always take the longest route. That way they can up their fare."

That hadn't necessarily been the case. The drivers she had hired had been more than honest with her.

Serra came to a halt, her gaze darting from the angel-faced lad to the group, a gang composed of both boys and girls somewhat older than her guide. She sensed it was no accident that she was here and

388

they were there.

"Please," she appealed to the small boy, hoping to share an affinity with him since they came from similar backgrounds, "take me back to the home."

But it was too late. The group surrounded her. Ignoring her protests, they stripped her of her reticule, tearing her lapel as they snatched the pin watch from her bodice. One brave girl, her tangled hair as fiery as Serra's, even grabbed her hat and tugged, pulling it from her head. Her hands empty, her clothing further ruined, her hair tumbling about her shoulders in disarray, Serra cried out in protest. As quickly as they had accosted her, her attackers scattered to the four winds.

Then she saw a pair of the urchins disappear into the run-down building from which they'd come. Something within Serra, something basic and primeval, snapped, a sense of righteousness that these, her peers, would dare to treat her so shabbily, and she followed them. Finding herself at the mouth of the tenement building, she stepped inside the dark tomb, uncertainty snapping at her heels.

An acrid stench rose up to greet her, burning her nostrils, and she faltered, clasping her hand over her nose and mouth as she stared at the far wall, which was stained and in many places stripped to the bare boards. Her heart flailed against its prison, thundering until it filled her ears, drumming a loud warning.

Get out, that inner voice demanded, yet her feet inched forward, one step at a time, her hand reaching to grasp the broken banister of the winding old staircase.

Glancing up the rickety stairwell, she saw nothing in the bleak space above her. Then her gaze darted downward and caught sight of an old burlap bag stuffed beneath the ground floor steps.

Papa hurt!

Serra pivoted about, searching for the speaker. There was no one there. "Show yourselves, damn it," she snapped, spinning like a runaway top.

Come on, li'l Serra, I'll protect ya.

"Ty? Answer me. Where are you?"

Silence mocked her plea, except for the scuffle of tiny rodentlike sounds issuing from beneath the staircase.

Stooping, she peered underneath the landing, fully expecting to find someone there. The space was empty, the burlap bag a prelude to the pile of old rags that truly looked more like a rat's nest than a bed. But as filthy and as pitiful was the sight, she recognized it for what it was—a child's bed.

"Ty!" Her voice rang out with distress. She and Ty had once shared such a hovel and had felt themselves privileged. The scenario was all too familiar—this building, the terrible stench, the children.

"Miss, ya best get outta here."

She gasped and whirled about to find the boy who had led her there in the first place peeking out from a doorway, nothing but his dirty face revealed, his eyes so wizened in their sockets that she couldn't help the cry that tumbled from her lips. Her hand to her throat, she backed away, tripped over a loose floorboard, and turned, fleeing into the trash-filled street.

And she ran from all of it, but mostly from the terrible truth that had its talons sunk into her and refused to let go. She had no idea which way she went, and at the moment she didn't much care. She just had to get away from that building, this neighborhood, the nightmare that was all too real now.

Sucking air into her burning lungs, she clung to a street sign, hanging there as if she were a bit of flotsam at the mercy of the tides. Lashes fluttering, her amber eyes climbed slowly upwards. She couldn't believe what she read.

Broadway. The letters spelled her salvation, and yet her fears still beat against her insides like trapped butterflies. Which way? Which way?

She saw the carriage coming toward her, recognizing it as a cab, as safety on wheels. Unable to believe her luck, she straightened, lifting her arms to flay the air, and began shouting, "Here. Stop. Please."

"Whoa." The clip-clop pace of the horse slowed as the driver pulled back on the reins. She was rescued. Dear God, the nightmare was nearly over. A giddiness settled about her. Once she got back to the hotel, she assured herself, she would deal in a clear-minded way with the information thrust upon her in the last few hours. And she would find a rational solution.

The carriage halted in front of her, and cupping her hands about her mouth, she started to shout her destination up to the driver over the din of the street noise. But then the door of the cab opened voluntarily.

"Serra."

The sound of her name spoken by a familiar voice caused her to spin about.

She glanced into the black depths of the vehicle. Dark, penetrating eyes stared back at her.

"Doc?"

It was as if an angel had swooped down and plucked her from harm's way.

"Get in, dumpling."

"Oh, Doc," she cried, practically throwing herself up the single step and through the open door. "I don't know how you found me," she prattled, "but you can't imagine how glad I am to see you."

Smiling, Chelsey latched the carriage door and rapped his knuckles on the ceiling. The vehicle lurched forward and Serra dropped back against the seat, exhausted, rung dry of all emotions, her eyes drifting closed now that she had been miraculously delivered from certain disaster.

Then the wheels in her mind began to churn, taking up the tempo of the undercarriage. It had been Doc who had convinced her she was Serenity Langston, Doc who had helped her dredge up false memories and hopes . . . Doc who had deceived her.

Her eyes flew open to find him contemplating her as if she were an insect pinned to a felt board, a specimen for him to observe, nothing more. Straightening beneath his scrutiny, her need for answers bolstered her courage.

"You've known the truth all along, haven't you?" she demanded in a voice roughened with disbelief.

In silence, they rode for what seemed an eternity, their gazes locked. Then finally the sides of Chelsey's mouth curled upwards, and he crossed his arms over his chest in complete understanding.

"And, so, what do we do now," she asked, her heart crying out for him to deny her accusation, "— now that I know the truth?"

"We could go on with our little charade, Serra. John Langston is more than happy to accept you as his daughter."

Was there no one in this world she could rely upon?

"And then when he dies, we can divide up the booty. Right?" she snapped.

"And why not?" Chelsey confirmed. "It won't do him any good where he's going."

As she listened to the wheels revolving beneath her seat, Serra knew she could never agree to such a dastardly plan, not even to save her own sanity. She shook her head, first slowly, then flipping it from side to side with calculated intent.

"No, Doc, I refuse," she whispered, her head picking up speed to whip back and forth so fast that the world took on a cockeyed angle.

"I was afraid you might say that, you foolish chit."

Like bat wings, his caped arms rose, up and over her, blotting out the ray of sunlight streaming through the window beside her. A smell, so sweet and suffocating, filled her nostrils. She struggled against the rag pressed to her nose and mouth, denying this final betrayal.

"No, Doc," she implored, but her words were muffled as she managed only to suck the dampened cloth deep into her mouth.

Then the world went spinning, black, black, down, down.

"Ty," she cried out, but only silence and defeat answered her.

Chapter Twenty-two

By no mere accident, Ty discovered Serra's where-abouts. After several long, unproductive days of scouring the city, checking with every possible hostelry, making demands, offering bribes—and threats, when necessary—he finally located her at the grand Fifth Avenue Hotel. Worn from his long trip, his clothes dusty and not at all appropriate for a sophisticated city like New York, he stormed into the hotel and met with another round of resistance.

"I'm sorry, sir," the long-nosed desk clerk stated. "But the lady's room number is not available." He stared down at the proffered money in Ty's hand, as if to touch it would mean instant contamination. "Not at any price."

Begrudging admiration and gratitude shot through Ty. At least he could be sure Serra would be safe in such an establishment. Stuffing the bribe back into his pocket, he leveled a hard look upon the other man. "Then be so kind as to send a messenger to her room to inform her that her husband waits for her downstairs."

The desk clerk gave him look for look, and Ty could easily read the other man's thoughts. Somewhat skeptical that this uncouth, travel-stained . . . gentleman could possibly be married to someone as wonderful as their dear Mrs. Ramsey, at first he hesitated. But then a private discussion between the clerk and the doorman brought forth an admission. "I can't do that, sir. Mrs. Ramsey has yet to come back from her outing of yesterday. Quite frankly, we're all a bit worried, as she always returns by the end of the day."

"Just where did she go?" Ty demanded of the doorman.

Jimson shrugged. "Took a cab and went slumming as usual, sir."

Again Ty opened his wallet and checked his impatience, this time tempered with genuine fear, in order to track down the particular cabbie who had taken Serra into the Lower East Side district.

The driver whined about how she had stiffed him, and only when Ty encouraged him with Missouri-style perseverance did he finally confess to dropping her on a corner of Baxter Street, near some of the worst slum areas of the city.

"How could you do something so damn cold-hearted?" Ty reviled, releasing the little New Yorker with such roughness that the man fell back against his carriage, startling his horse and making it rear in fright. "Damn it, man. She's a lady all alone in the streets of New York."

"I told her I'd be back in an hour, but she never returned to our agreed location."

"Why didn't you check on her?"

"And leave my cab unattended in the Five Points?" The man barked a derisive laugh. "Hell, if I'd done that, the dips would've stolen it as sure as I'm standing here now."

Ty couldn't deny the truth in the other man's words. It might have been nearly seven years ago since he had lorded over the back streets of the Lower East Side, but he doubted things had changed all that much. The slums had simply moved farther uptown, claiming more territory.

"Then the least you can do is take me to where you dropped her off."

The man eyed his rustic attire — his tight-fitting denims, open collared shirt, cowboy boots, drover's coat — and shook his head. "I'm not too sure I should do that. The streets of New York are no place for . . . someone like you."

Ty snagged him by his coat collar once more and gave him such a vicious jerk that the cabbie's eyes bugged in fear. "Don't try me further, mister. I've had one hell of a week, and it doesn't look like things are gittin' any better."

They came to a hasty agreement. Ty promised not to turn the man inside out if he retraced the route he'd taken with Serra just the day before.

Jumping into the carriage interior, Ty found it impossible to relax. Damn it. He had to find her. They'd come too far together for him to lose her now. Why had he been such a fool? He should have made her see how much he needed her, not tried to cram down her throat how much she needed him. He had promised to take care of her, and if he failed in that one aspect of his life, then there was nothing worth living for, anyway.

As the carriage worked its way through the dusty city streets, Ty made a promise to himself. Nothing and no one would stop him now. Serra was all he had that mattered.

396

Serra awoke in the darkness to a squeamish stomach and a foul, almost metallic taste in her mouth. Moistening her lips, she inhaled deeply, then wished that she hadn't. The feeling of nausea intensified, and she had to squeeze her eyes shut in order to fight the sensation down.

She tried to lift her hand to cover her mouth and found the task impossible. Flexing her knees was just as difficult. Alarm cascaded through her. It seemed her hands and feet were restrained.

Fear balled in the pit of her stomach, and the queasiness rolled over her again as she began to struggle against her bonds. But soon her fight subsided. It was either give that up or something much more indelicate.

Dear God, where was she? Lying in the blackness, she calmed herself, her fingers crabbing about the limited circle of her reach.

She lay upon a bed, a rough muslin sheet of indeterminable cleanliness beneath her. There was not much else she could tell from her exploration.

Her final memories came back in flashing bits and pieces. The discovery of her true identity, the attack by the street children, the nightmare flight through the city streets. She must look a fright, her clothing torn and wrinkled, her hair in tangled disarray. A madwoman to anyone who didn't know her. Then she remembered Dr. Chelsey picking her up.

"Doc?" she called, surprised by the hoarseness of her own voice.

A match flared, its blue flame hissing as it was touched to the wick of an oil lamp. Then his face bent over her, the shadowy play on the hollows and hills of his familiar features taking on a demonic demeanor.

"How do you feel?" His hand, so cool to the touch, clean to the smell, pressed upon her brow, pushing back the tangled red skein. His question, a clinical one, Serra surmised, didn't imply he inquired about the state of her soul.

"As if I might be sick," she replied as discriminatingly as she could, praying to God she could control the queasiness.

He chuckled and patted her cheek. "It will pass before long, dumpling, and then we will talk."

Serra lowered her lashes and waited, her mind as well as her stomach churning like butter paddles agitating milk. Where was she? What did Doc plan to do with her? Beads of perspiration popped out along her hairline when her questions went unanswered.

She could hear him shuffling about the room, but she dared not look, not until this horrible feeling in her stomach passed.

And eventually it did. As if he knew just how long to wait, he hovered over her, running his hand lightly along her face once more. "Better?"

She nodded, sensing it would be foolish to deny the truth. "Please, Doc, let me go," she pleaded softly, trying not to sound too desperate. While she'd been lying there, she'd worked it all out in her mind—just what she would do. She could sew tolerably. Seeing the girls in the orphanage ply their needles reminded her of that forgotten talent. Finding a job wouldn't be all that hard. The sweatshops were always looking for willing, competent hands.

"I'll say nothing. I'll go my own way," she promised, choking on a sob, realizing there was no reason to expect anyone to care if she did just disappear.

She heard him click his tongue and knew he

shook his head. "I'm sorry, Serra. It's not that easy. I can't take that chance."

"Then we can go back." she declared, changing her line of tactics. "I'll tell John Langston I made a terrible mistake. He'll accept that explanation from me."

"You don't begin to understand, do you? I don't care what John Langston thinks of me. The old besotted fool thought I couldn't make him tell me what I wanted to know. But he was wrong. He couldn't fight my powers, either. Just like you, Serra." His face became rigid with determination. "Too much is at stake now to risk taking such chances."

She heard his fingers begin to drum upon the unpadded arm of the chair in which he sat.

"No, stop that," she cried out, closing her eyes and fighting bravely to block out the overwhelming sound. A sound that did things to her — terrible things.

"Serra, you will do as I say."

"No. I won't. Not ever again. I won't listen to you." She struggled against her bonds, trying hard to concentrate on anything but the beckoning beat of his strumming.

To her relief, the noise ceased. The only sound left was the racket created by her heart pounding in her ears.

Then he was standing over her, his watch suspended from his long, spidery fingers.

Serra averted her eyes, refusing to look as the pendulum swung in front of her.

"You must pay attention, Serra, if you want me to help you. I can help you, child. I can take the pain away."

She shook her head and clenched her eyes tight.

399

Then his fingers dug into the tender flesh of her cheeks, forcing her face around.

"Doc, why are you doing this to me?"

"Because, my dear, it is what's best. I have failed twice. I can't do so again." He took a deep breath and let it out slowly. His jaw worked, the watch growing still in his fingers. "It all began so long ago. No harm had been intended. Just take the child, demand the ransom, and return her. It was supposed to go so smoothly."

Staring off into space, Chelsey frowned. "But it got complicated, and when the little brat became ill, I thought I could handle the situation. I'm a doctor, am I not? No hospitals. I could restore her health.

"But she died, and we had nothing," he continued. "Nothing, do you hear me? We disposed of the body, fearing every day our part in the crime would be discovered." His face contorted, his dark eyes taking on a wildness she'd never seen before.

Serra knew fear . . . abject terror, her pulse racing like a runaway train.

"Then when Mrs. Babison appeared not long after that, it was like we'd been given a second chance."

Babison? Babison? Serra racked her brain to remember the name. The woman who had been at the Chelsey house when she and Amanda Stokes had paid their surprise visit.

"She knew all kinds of details about the Langston household, little things only a family member or a nanny would know. She wanted revenge for the shabby way the Langstons dismissed her after the child's disappearance . . . wanted her share of the take. All we needed was someone to play the part of Serenity."

That's why Mrs. Babison had seemed familiar to

400

her. The nursemaid . . . in the picture of the Langstons. She was the same woman.

"When we found you, Serra, we couldn't believe our luck. You were perfect—your hair, your age, even your name lent itself to the transformation. I have never met a more willing subject. It was so easy." His face contorted. "Until that damned Tyler Ramsey butted in. And now I have no choice except to put things back the way they should be."

The watch began to swing, back and forth, back and forth. "You are sleepy, Serra. You cannot resist the need to close your eyes." His commanding call offered an escape from the crushing affirmation. If she wasn't Serenity Langston, then what did it matter who she was? John Langston would brush her aside, and so would Ty once he realized he didn't need her to stake his claim to the Langston fortune. She had no purpose, no future, no ambitions to keep her going, to keep up her fighting spirit.

Let go. The voice seemed to come from within her, ordering her to give in to the mesmerizing lure. Her lids grew heavy and began to sink.

Then she heard another voice calling to her, deep and resonant. *Serra, li'l Serra. I'll come back for ya. I promise.* Ty? It could only be her deepest desires surfacing, but still she listened.

"No-o-o-o-o." She snapped her eyes open and shook her head, dissipating the fog.

Before her cry could fade, an astringent odor enveloped her, filling her mouth, her nose, her eyes each time she tried to take a breath, and she struggled to avoid it. Then a flood of confusion rushed over her, hot and searing. She heard herself sobbing, the sound abandoned, unrestrained, and oh, God, it felt good to let go so completely, to express her un-

401

happiness, her defeat, the loss of her dreams.

"Not to worry, Serra," Chelsey told her, his voice so soothing. "I'll take you where you'll find peace and happiness."

Peace and happiness? Yes, that was what she wanted. To be shielded from the bombardment of things she didn't want to face.

Odd. Serenity might not be her name anymore, but serene was how she felt as she sank deep, deep into the secure recesses of oblivion.

"Yes, she was here." The orphanage director, new since his days there, gave Ty an unsettling look. "She asked to see Miss Hannah, but once your wife met with her she seemed upset and then she simply disappeared, we think heading out of the kitchen exit."

"Miss Hannah Evans?" He remembered the kind old lady. Miss Hannah had been the one to aid him in his rescue of Serra, had known Serra had a father still living, but had held her tongue, giving a little girl the one opportunity to escape the terror of her childhood. A father would have meant a complication, as he might not have been willing to sign the surrender form, even though he cared nothing for his daughter. It had been Miss Hannah who had written the note, "Please take care of Serra," wrapping the child in one of her own cloaks to keep her warm.

Miss Hannah. He smiled and then the expression metamorphosed into a frown.

Had she told Serra the truth?

Ty gritted his teeth. Damn it. He should have been the one to tell her.

"Did my wife say anything that might give a clue

to her whereabouts?"

"Only that Geoff Tanner at the main office had sent her here."

"Geoff Tanner?" The image of a scrawny kid of the streets with a big chip on his shoulder filled his mind. "He finally saw the light, did he?" Geoff was the one person who would still have contacts among the streets. The one person who might be able to help him locate Serra.

Like a lost shadow, Serra followed quietly as Doc led her along the docks, whorls of early morning fog making her feel as if she were in a dream. Her mind blurred, her tongue thick and unresponsive, she didn't resist when he pushed her head down so her chin scraped her breastbone, instructing her to say nothing and keep her face hidden. Laying claim to her arm, he steered her forward, watching her with his dark, commanding eyes as he approached a small guardhouse nestled among the piers.

"Blackwell's Island," he announced, slipping the permit from the Department of Charities and Corrections through the iron bars to the man on the other side of the window.

"Which institution?" The man looked up, glancing over Serra's shawl-covered head with minimal interest, then as quickly dismissing her.

"The Lunatic Asylum," Doc answered.

"She's a quiet one."

"At the moment," Chelsey replied, his fingers drumming impatiently on the barred sill.

The asylum? Fear-nurtured confusion welled within Serra. She stiffened. The home of the damned and the forgotten. But she wasn't crazy, was

403

she?

The shriek erupted from deep inside of her, earthy, unfettered, and she was powerless to stop it. But that was how it came, unexpected and total whenever she wanted to protest. The guttural cry seemed to be the only verbal expression she was empowered to make, other than to babble nonsense just as she was doing now. Trembling, her knees gone rubbery, she swooned.

Arms, strong ones, caught her, and she leaned into them, allowing them to support her. She consented to follow as they led her forward through the ever-thickening fog.

Then she was sitting, the ground beneath her rocking. She glanced about, saw the lapping waves of the river, and wondered almost hysterically in her delirium if she had finally mastered the art of walking upon water.

And it appeared that way as she shot forward without effort, the piers behind her swallowed up in the thinning mist that danced about like ethereal spirits, the opposite shore with its granite seawall touched by an unexpected streak of morning light growing steadily closer as she watched it.

Peace and happiness, Doc had promised her, and she leaned forward, willing herself to move faster. With the way the sunbeam played upon the island, it did seem to offer a pot of gold at the end of the rainbow.

But once they reached their destination, the heavenly illumination was snuffed out like a giant stage light. In the distance, a chain gang of gray-striped prisoners toiled to repair the seawall where it had crumbled. Bodily lifted from what she now realized was a boat, Serra saw clearly these shores held no promises, only destitution.

Turning, she tried to scramble back into the boat. Instead, she stumbled and went down on her hands and knees, a cry of agony tumbling from her lips. Again she was lifted, her arms and legs flailing the air.

"Let me go. I'm not crazy," she managed to shriek in a lucid moment, her fists balled and swinging.

She heard them laugh, these men who handled her as if she were a sack of old laundry, as if she were immune to pain.

"They all say that," one of them declared, tossing her down onto a cot and strapping her to it.

Then she was lifted into the back of a wagon, bed and all.

"Doc?" she mewled, her head lolling back and forth as she sought to find the one person who could stop this nightmare, could make these men understand she shouldn't be treated in this fashion.

Her answer came from the iron wagon wheels as they rolled and squeaked down the dirt lane, and in Chelsey's silent face as the corners of his mouth curled upward in victory.

Peace and happiness, he had promised. She knew instead she had just entered the gates of hell's damnation. And once they closed behind her, there would be no escape.

Sitting across the table from Geoff Tanner, Ty lowered his glass of untouched beer. "It's as if the city has swallowed her up."

"I shouldn't've let her go by herself," Tanner blurted out in self-condemnation, wiping foam from his lips as he sat back and shut his eyes.

"That's not the point. If we're here to put blame

405

where it belongs, I should never have allowed her to get far enough away from me to get into trouble. I should have told her the truth myself and not let her find out from others. Others who might not be so carin' or understandin'." Ty's mouth angled downward, feeling as if the weight of the world rested on him.

Geoff's hand settled on his hunched shoulder. "Not to worry, Ty. If she's out there, then we'll find her. I have my connections on the street, you know, people who still remember Ty Ramsey." He smiled reassuringly. "The Robin Hood of the street arabs—bootblacks, newsboys, and pickpockets—is not so easily forgotten. Even the younger ones have heard about you, my friend, how you went west. They talk about you, sure that you moved on to fame and glory."

Ty smiled. Why did the children of the streets all have the same dreams and ambitions, their lawlessness to know no boundaries? He had been no different. "Like Jesse James and Billy the Kid," he declared, expressing his inner most feelings.

"Yeah, just like them." Geoff cast a sweeping scrutiny over Ty's rustic attire—Stetson, boots, drover's coat, his beard and mustache. "I must say you do look as if you stepped out of a penny dreadful."

Ty glanced up to see the teasing, yet speculative smile play across the other man's face. Understanding flashed between them. Give these kids the champion they yearned for. . . .

"It just might work, you know."

"The little scamps will flock to you," Geoff agreed. "I daresay they'll be a fountain of information."

"Do the secret passages still riddle the Five Points the way they used to, serving as lines of communication?"

Geoff grinned. "Does a lady sport underwear?"

They rose in unison, dropping coins upon the table to pay for their unfinished mugs of beer. Together they strolled out into the streets of the Lower East Side.

White. All around her the pastiness of solitude – the walls, the ceiling, the uniforms of her wardens.

Serra screamed and bucked a protest as a woman twice her size began stripping her of her clothing. On a table in the corner she spied the white gown intended for her, meant to steal her identity.

Firm hands held her down — not that they were hurting or cruel, but they brooked no defiance — squeezing her about the throat until she couldn't breathe.

Gasping for air, for life itself, Serra succumbed to the demands upon her. Lie still, accept the degradation.

And it was the worst kind of humiliation to have them look upon her uncovered body, as if she had no rights, no modesty. But then they thought her crazy, no longer capable of human responses. A mindless animal.

They were wrong.

The moment the strangling pressure relented so the clothing could be pulled over her head, Serra bounded forth, brushing the detested gown aside. Reaching a doorway, she glanced down the hallway. All the same — white, white, white. She ran, unsure if she raced toward freedom or deeper into the bowels of misery. But she would continue until either something or someone stopped her or she managed to escape.

The tackle came from behind. Falling forward, the side of her face and her palms slapped upon the waxed alabaster floor, she felt stinging agony radiate through every nerve in her body. Her arms twisted behind her back, her hands secured at the wrists, she was hauled up without an expression of concern.

"Please," she cried, her voice so strained with emotion and pain that it cracked. "You have made a terrible mistake. My name is Serenity Langston." No, no, that wasn't true anymore. "I mean Serra Paletot — no, Ramsey," she corrected, knowing in her heart that she did indeed sound crazy, unable to even tell them her name. "You have to believe me. I don't belong here."

No one bothered to answer her, to even acknowledge that she had spoken. Stuffed into the gown, she was then strapped once more to the bed, one leather band secured across her forehead.

"Please, please, you must listen to me," she pleaded, but her will to fight began to fade.

A hand pinched her nose, forcing her to tilt her chin. When she gulped for air, there was nothing she could do to stop the bitter-tasting liquid from filling her mouth. Choking, she tried to spit the foul medicine out, to hold her breath, but her warden's patience outlasted her empty lungs. She swallowed, felt the burning bitterness slide down her throat. Then it was as if parts of her evaporated, first her hands and feet, then her arms and legs.

Down, down she plunged, where her name and the colors around her no longer made a difference.

The smells were worse than he remembered, the filth and litter so deep Ty wondered how he had managed to remain healthy long enough to escape the squalor years ago, how the dirty, wary faces surrounding him were able to survive it.

Where did they all come from, these street urchins ranging in age from mere babies to gangling youths, and why did God in all His mercifulness allow such a nightmare to continue? He glanced at Geoff Tanner and saw his own misgivings mirrored in the other man's face.

"A lady," he told his attentive audience, fingering his Stetson and hunkering down as if they sat about a campfire swapping stories instead of in a tenement courtyard about a burning barrel of trash to chase away the late night chill. "Very pretty, her hair the color of pennies." Reaching into the inside pocket of his drover's coat, he took out the sack and began distributing the bits of copper to emphasize his point.

Eager hands reached for their share, fair or not. A penny meant a loaf of bread or an ear of hot corn to eat. Five cents, a real bed indoors even if it was lice-ridden, or a bottle of rotgut gin to fend off the cold, whichever the recipient might find the most enticing.

He remembered well — oh, God, how hard that particular decision had been to make each night. The easy way would have been to accept the oblivion the liquor offered. But there had been Serra, and he had chosen to share with her the pittance he had scraped up during the day to keep them fed and dry.

Getting himself and Serra out of such surroundings was all that had been important at the time, as if by their escape, the horror, the filth would magically no longer exist. Staring all about him at the hardened, yet youthful faces, some bleary-eyed with drink, he realized just how wrong he had been. There had been no miracle; he had merely turned his back on others not so fortunate or of such stalwart constitution.

And now it seemed Serra had become once more the victim of life's wretched reality. Standing, he glanced again at a silent Geoff Tanner and frowned, the horror of it all invading his very soul. Dear God, let one of these pitiful, streetwise souls have seen her.

A little girl, maybe eight or nine, sashayed forward, planting indignant fists upon her rag-covered hips, a feather-crested hat much too large for her head covering her tangled mop of red hair, so much like Serra's had been at that age. She eyed Ty up and down, taking in his demeanor, his western attire.

"Are ya really Tyler Ramsey?" she demanded.

Ty contemplated the hat nestled in the fiery curls. It was something like Serra might wear. He nodded, solemn-faced, his heart racing, hoping.

"They say you was the best there is," she continued her questioning. Beside her stood an angel-faced boy, much younger. Her brother, if looks could be counted upon.

Ty allowed one side of his mouth to lift. "I still am," he declared, snagging the little fellow's hand before it could further explore the interior of his coat. Turning it palm up, he pressed several more coins into the grubby center, fisting it about the money.

The boy snatched the gift, squirreling it next to his heart. Then his rheumy gaze darted to his sister and back to Ty. "We seen her, mister."

Containing his excitement, Ty squatted down eye

410

level with the boy. "Where?"

"Wanderin' the streets."

"Shut up, Ralphy," the girl said, pinching her brother on one dirty ear and tugging.

The lad brushed his sister's hand away.

Ty felt the instant tension in the youthful crowd and recognized it for what it was. Distrust. Desperation. Fear. He glanced about, touching on each face, so innocent to what life had to offer and yet so battle-scarred, with an openness he prayed conveyed his understanding.

"Can you show me where you last saw her?"

The little boy snaked another look at his sibling. She glared. He turned to the group about him, seeking their permission.

"Ah, go ahead, Ralphy. Show 'm," consented a lad of about sixteen, who seemed in charge of the motley group. Meeting Ty's appreciation over the heads of the younger children with a rare smile, the older boy continued. "You may not remember me, Mr. Ramsey, but once you shared a loaf of bread with me when that was all you had."

Ty smiled. "Can't say that I do, son, but it's enough that you recall."

They moved as a single unit, through one of the basement passages that led under the street and came up in another building several blocks away. Holding a torch high above his head, Ty must have looked much like the Pied Piper leading the scurvy rats of Hamelin back into the streets.

"Here," little Ralphy stated, pointing down a garbage-lined alleyway. "We cut her purse strings and took off," he explained sheepishly.

Oh, God, he could see her now, frightened, alone, harboring the knowledge that she had emerged from

411

this environment, no longer sheltered by her dreams that she was more than just another homeless street waif.

"And you didn't see her again after that?"

"Actually, I did," Ralphy confessed. Imitating a turtle, he tucked his head between his shoulders as if he knew his admission would be frowned upon by his peers. "She weren't like all the others," he said in his own defense, "so I followed her. Then when she found her way back to Broadway and got into a carriage, I left her be."

"A carriage?" Ty wanted to shake the boy, to make the information he possessed tumble out at a faster pace. "You mean a cabbie picked her up?" If that were true, why hadn't she returned to the hotel?

"Well, sort of, but there was a man inside."

"A man?" A terrible fear shot through him. Strange men didn't pick women up in the streets of the Lower East Side, not unless . . .

"Did you get a good look at him?"

Ralphy stood there, staring up in silence, his watery eyes anything but encouraging. "No, not a good one."

Frustration welled up within Ty, blending with the fear already there. Damn it. There were thousands of men who might have picked Serra up, a woman alone, confused in the streets, and none of them would have had noble reasons.

"Serra," he cried out, his desperation echoing through the night. So close, and then it was as if the trail came to a sudden end, and he was powerless to stop it.

He couldn't believe it was over. He couldn't accept that he had lost her. But in his heart he knew his chances of finding her now were slim at best.

"Mister," Ralphy said, tugging at Ty's drover's coat with timid fingers. "I might not of seen 'm good, but I think the lady called him by a name."

A resurgence of hope coursed through Ty, and he swept the little urchin up into his arms. "A name? What name?" he demanded.

Ralphy squinted, his small face contorting with concentration. "I can't swear to it, but I heard her call him . . . Doc."

Ty grew perfectly still. "Doc?" The fear of the unknown increased twofold upon discovering the name of his adversary. He looked to Tanner and saw that the title meant nothing to the other man, but to Ty it meant worse than if the boy had said Satan himself.

"What is it, Ty?" Geoff asked.

"Lionel Chelsey," he replied. That half-crazed quack was capable of worse than anything Serra might experience in the hands of a street hustler. "If the boy's right, then her very life is at stake, and every minute we lose could very well be her last one."

Chapter Twenty-three

Chelsey. Even though he didn't comprehend, Ty acknowledged the awesome powers that man held over Serra. He could control her mind, her desires and dreams. Just how far the son of a bitch would go, he couldn't be certain.

But first he had to find her. Where could Chelsey have taken her that wouldn't have aroused suspicions? Ty's mind churned, grinding out possibilities. There were so many locations and so little time. He'd need a small army to check them all out.

Pausing, he glanced about him at the youthful faces turned to him in expectation. He had such an army. One that could get results where others might fail. But would they be willing to help him? And if they were, could he trust them?

Did he have much choice?

"I need your help," he announced.

At first no one moved, and then he saw the looks pass among the older ones. For a moment he thought they might turn their backs on him.

"What's in it for us?" asked the group's leader, the same boy who had earlier admitted that Ty had once helped him.

The demand for compensation didn't offend him; to the contrary, relief flooded through Ty. He could handle that stipulation, knowing firsthand how it was on the streets. The older boys were in charge, and it was up to them to see to the younger ones, who would do as they were told, all for the benefit of the whole.

"A ticket outta here for those willin' to participate," he pledged.

"What do we have to do?" the lad continued the negotiations.

"Locate Doctor Lionel Chelsey, the man who abducted my wife off the streets."

"And once we find him?" There was not even a hint of doubt that they would succeed in his young voice.

Ty's eyes narrowed. "You report back to me. He's mine."

Within an hour the networking was set up. Children poured in from every corner of the Five Points, more than Ty ever imagined might volunteer, two dozen, maybe more, so many he wondered how he would manage to keep his promise to them all. His mouth flattened. Somehow he *would* see to it that each and every one of them was given the chance he promised them.

Like soldiers they reported for duty, taking their assignment to be checked out from Geoff Tanner—one of the many seedy hotels of assignation, a dance hall, a boarding house, or maybe one of the innumerable tenement buildings—and then they scampered off as quickly as they appeared.

Less than twelve hours later, Ty had what he sought. A man fitting Chelsey's description had taken a flat near the East River Bridge, accompanied by his daughter who he claimed to be of poor constitution. And in truth no one had seen her except for when he had carried her limp form in the day before and then out just this morning, so bundled up nobody had any idea what she looked like. Chelsey had just returned to his rooms alone as the young investigator had left to report his findings.

Serra. Ty swallowed down his fear, replacing it with an anger of such intensity it nearly blinded him. What had Chelsey done with her? Had he simply murdered her and carried her lifeless body to the wharves and dumped it? No, he assured himself. Chelsey needed her alive if he wished to get his clutches on the Langston fortune—alive, but out of the way. The urge to confront the man, to squeeze not only his intentions but the very life out of his worthless body, left Ty shaking. But he had a better punishment in mind for the good doctor. He smiled, the expression anything but pleasant. Taking several of the older boys aside, he put his plan into motion.

"There are only a few places he could have stashed her," Geoff offered his analysis. "A hospital, perhaps, or some kind of institution."

"You mean like an insane asylum?" Ty narrowed his eyes. Chelsey had the power to make Serra speak a lie. Could he also control her mind so she acted deranged? He found it hard to believe that she would succumb voluntarily to something as detrimental to her own well-being, and yet . . .

"You know him best," Geoff stated.

Yes, a madhouse would serve the doctor's purposes precisely. Serra would be kept constrained and isolated. And even if she did protest, who would listen to someone thought to be crazy?

"I think that's where we'll find her. How do we get there?" Ty rose, ready to depart, confident that Chelsey would be going nowhere until he returned.

"Ty, it's not that simple. First of all, there are several lunatic asylums that serve New York. However, the most likely one is isolated out on Blackwell's Island in the middle of the East River."

Isolated. Instinct told him they were on the right track. "Then that's where we will go." He stood.

Geoff mimicked his actions. "Wait a minute, Ty. The state penitentiary is on that island as well. It's a virtual fortress. No one sets foot on its shores without a government permit, and that could take a while to obtain."

"I don't have a while." Pushing away his coat, he drew forth the concealed pistol. Spinning the cylinder, he checked each bullet chamber to make sure it was loaded. Then he slid the gun back into its holster, his fingers resting lightly on the handle. "This is the only permit I need." He headed toward the street.

"Ty, please." Tanner followed in his wake. "You've got to understand. This is not the wild West, where you go in guns blazing. You try a stunt like that here in the city, they'll escort us on the island with pleasure, but in prison gray and white stripes." To make his point, he grasped Ty's upper arm and turned him about. "If you're determined to attempt this, then let me try to talk our way onto the island first."

Hesitating only a moment, Ty nodded. He would give his friend the chance he requested, but if Geoff's way proved ineffectual, he would do it his

417

own way. Nothing would stop him from finding Serra. He hailed a cab, calling his destination to the driver as he whipped open the door.

"And, Ty," Tanner continued, jumping into the interior right behind him, eyeing the Stetson he wore. "Get rid of that damn thing, will you? The more normal we look, the better our chances are to succeed."

Pulling off the hat, Ty draped himself out of the carriage window and dropped the black felt Stetson with the silver conchae onto little Ralphy's head. "Watch this for me, will ya, boy? I'll be back for it," he assured him with a smile, his cobalt-blue gaze roving over the cluster of youths who had followed him out into the street. "I'll be back for all of you."

At Geoff's recommendation, Ty waited in the carriage as the younger man approached the barred guardhouse on the docks to try and convince the official to let them pass. Studying his surroundings as if it were a Missouri landscape, he noted how a stack of crates lined the way almost to where his friend stood. He switched his attention to Geoff, watched him gesturing, pointing toward the vehicle in which he sat. Ty could catch snatches of the conversation.

"His wife is there by mistake . . . her life could well be in danger."

But the guard shook his head, refusing to bend the rules even in an emergency.

Geoff reached into his breast pocket. Ty smiled as he saw his friend offer the guard the hefty bribe they'd both decided might sway reluctant authorities.

418

It seemed for a moment that the man would accept it as he allowed Geoff to press the money into his hand. He even counted it and looked up, smiling.

Then everything went awry. From nowhere, more guards appeared, surrounding the hapless Tanner, taking him into custody.

"Damn," Ty swore, his hand moving down to his gun when the watchmen, once they'd subdued a protesting Geoff, turned toward the carriage. He debated his choices, refusing to just sit there and wait to be taken. Behind bars he would be of no help to anyone, especially Serra. There was only one way to handle this situation—his way.

Slipping out of the vehicle through the open window on the far side, he caught the eye of the driver and lifted his weapon, aiming it at the unsuspecting man. "Start moving slowly, straight ahead, toward those crates," he ordered, waving the pistol in the direction of the loading dock less than a hundred yards away.

More afraid of his fare than of the approaching authorities, the man complied, whistling softly to his team.

They began to roll forward.

"Hey, you," one of the guards shouted at the driver. "Stop."

"Keep goin'," Ty insisted, keeping pace with the slow-moving vehicle, hoping he had enough time to reach the concealment of the cargo before the sentinels reached him.

Just in the nick of time, he ducked down behind several staved barrels. His gun cocked and ready, he watched the police surround the carriage. The moment they discovered the inside empty, they began a search, fanning out across the docks.

Inch by inch he wormed a path through the crates until he came within a few yards of where Geoff was being detained.

His friend hadn't given up, as he continued his dialogue with his captor. "This can all be explained. You've got to understand. Mr. Ramsey fears for his wife's life."

Easing his way around until he crouched just behind the guard, Ty raised his gun and planted the barrel in the middle of the man's back. "Turn him loose," he said with quiet authority.

The guard stiffened. In the distance the search party continued to move in the opposite direction, heading away from the docks, assuming that their suspect would seek to escape the area.

"Easy," Ty ordered, pressing a little harder against the man's rigid spine.

Once Geoff's hands were released from the cuffs, Ty rose and pulled the hapless lone guard back against his chest, repositioning the pistol against his temple.

"Now," he said, "I want you to pass us."

"I can't do that," the guard croaked. "You don't have any papers."

Ty looked up at Geoff's distressed face and grinned. "The man wants paper. Go in the guardhouse and find this gentleman what he needs."

Geoff scampered away and returned a few seconds later with a sheet of blank paper just the right size.

"I want you to put your stamp on it and make it look authentic," Ty ordered, pulling back the hammer of the gun with a loud, insistent click.

"You're crazy," the guard declared, but with amazing speed he complied, stamping the outside of the folded sheet with an official-looking seal. Just as quickly, they cuffed him to a pipe on the floor of the small building, gagging him for good measure with the bandanna from Ty's neck. Hopefully, that would give them enough time to reach Blackwell's Island.

Racing down the pier, they selected a boat. Ty jumped aboard, and from his rocking position below, he stared up at Geoff. "You don't have to come if you don't want to. I'll understand."

"I suppose," Geoff replied with a crooked smile slashed across his face. "But once we find Serra, our actions sure will be a lot easier to explain. I really have no desire to spend time in jail waiting for you to turn up."

Together they nosed the confiscated craft toward the opposite shore. Ty knew it wouldn't be easy to pull off their ploy; in fact, now he realized how unlikely it would be that he would even locate Serra. But he had to try. Something deep inside of him — call it gut instinct — assured him she was somewhere on that island, and if he didn't find her, she would never leave it.

Once they reached the far docks of Blackwell's Island, they were met by the prison sentinels. His heart thundering in his throat, Ty flashed the fake papers when the guard asked to see them. Fortunately, the formalities were lax on that side of the channel, as visitors never got that far without the proper documents. But it was only a matter of time before an alarm would go out once they were discovered missing on the city side.

Ty glanced around at the many buildings — alms-houses, hospitals, workhouses, the large, ominous penitentiary, and more. He had no idea which one held the insane. Hell, it could take all day just to figure that out.

"This way," Geoff instructed, heading toward a building on the north side. "I've been out here a couple of times as a representative of the Society."

Ty was only too glad to have Tanner with him, and he willingly followed his friend's confident lead.

At first she thought the thundering noise was made by running feet. Her eyes closed, Serra strained, listening, hoping that perhaps there was someone out there, someone who cared. But no, the sound never grew louder or softer, just remained steady.

Thump, thump. Thump, thump. Her hopes plummeted, realizing that she heard the beating of her own heart, a prisoner as surely as she was.

Slitting her lashes, she glanced about her surroundings. Nothing had changed; it was still all white, as if the purity of the color could somehow wipe out the horror. From a small window high above her head a ray of sunlight, striped with the shadow of bars, splashed across her chest. Her movements were restricted by the straps upon her arms and legs; she was thirsty and hungry and her head ached abominably, but at least she was aware of it all. At least she was alive.

She held herself perfectly still, willing her heartbeat to slow down. The loud sound subsided, leaving a void, one eventually filled with other noises. The screams and wild cries of a woman farther down the hall. A door slammed, another one squealed open. A crash so near, Serra turned her head toward the entrance of her cubicle.

Nothing.

The waiting, the not knowing; it was too much. A panic, one that claimed her time and again since Doc had brought her here, washed over her like a rising tide. Dear God, even if she wasn't insane at the moment, if she stayed here, underwent the rigors of the abuse called treatment much longer, she would eventually lose what little sanity she still possessed.

Then they entered her room. Their white coats flapping, the three women and one man hurried in, surrounding her bed. Hands were upon her, but she was used to that by now. Holding herself in check, she willed herself to remain calm. She would give them no reason to think her crazy.

With steady eyes she watched them unstrap one arm, roll up her sleeve, and check her pulse.

"Good morning," she offered, hoping she sounded cheerful, alert . . . sane.

Surprised faces angled toward her. "Good morning, miss. Are we having a lucid day today?" the man whom she assumed must be a doctor asked. Looking up from his chart, he signaled to one of the nurses.

"The sun is shining," she announced brightly. What an inane statement to make, but with the rays of light beating down on her, it was the first thing to pop into her mind. At last someone was talking to her, listening to what she had to say. She glanced up at the tiny barred window overhead. "I miss the sun. You can't imagine how glorious it can be high in a clear Missouri sky." Speaking from the heart, she looked to each face for their reaction. What she caught was a glimpse of the brown medicine bottle concealed behind the nurse's back.

"Please," she whispered. Her amber eyes darted from face to face, settling on the doctor's. "Can't you see that I don't need that?"

It was as if she'd never spoken, her head forced down so it could be secured in place. They didn't care if she belonged there or not. All that mattered was the treatment their chart indicated.

"No, no," she cried out, struggling to escape the confinement, the injustice of it all.

"Serra?"

She heard the frantic call of her name thunder in a familiar voice through the hallway and accepted that her mind must have finally snapped.

"Ty," she screamed in desperation, knowing it impossible for him to be there, but nonetheless fighting against the hands restraining her, covering her mouth and nose, pinching off her air until the blinding panic began to constrict about her. And still she refused to give up, clinging to consciousness as if it were life itself.

"You can't come barging in here like this." The doctor's voice conveyed surprise and indignation.

"Watch me." It was as if an avenging angel spoke.

Her captors pulled back, and Serra took a deep, gasping breath, filling her lungs with oxygen and hope. Someone held her, crushing her, but she didn't fight it, sensing these arms held no malice, only love. Looking up she found him, praying only that it was no delusion she saw but truly her ominous man in black there to rescue her.

"Ty?" she whispered hoarsely, clutching his solid

424

manly frame. He had come for her, had come to take her home, to safety. "It was Chelsey who brought me here. Chelsey who kidnapped the real Serenity Langston," she confessed, unable to squelch the words tumbling from her lips, "then convinced me that I was her. I believed him, Ty, truly I did," she sobbed. "I never meant to perpetuate a lie."

"Shh. Shh. I know, Serra, I know," he soothed as he released her from her bindings and gathered her up against his heart, pressing gentle, reassuring kisses on the top of her coppery head.

Closing her eyes, she gave herself up to him, to his strength. It no longer mattered who she was, just as long as they were together.

Then she spied the weapon he cradled in his hand. Fear and confusion rocketed through her. "Ty?" she asked, touching his fist circling the gun.

He didn't respond, helping her from the bed to stand on unsteady legs. "Where are your clothes?" he demanded.

She shook her head in uncertainty. "I don't know. They took them," she replied, indicating the medical staff.

"Look here. You have no authorization to remove a patient from my care," the doctor began, stepping forward.

Ty leveled his pistol at the man's heart, his deadly intent only too obvious. "I have every authorization. Now get my *wife* her clothing."

For a moment it seemed as if the physician would refuse to cooperate, but then he signaled to one of the nurses, who took out a bundle from a cabinet behind her.

With trembling fingers, Serra donned her wrinkled gown. *It's over,* she kept telling herself, glancing up at Ty's hawklike face and the physician's resigned one, sure that once they left the building everything would be all right.

Then to her complete surprise, Geoff Tanner barreled into the room. "Ty, they're coming," he warned, his anxiety whooshing in and out of his open mouth, nothing like the calm, sophisticated gentleman who had helped her only a few days ago at the Children's Aid Society. "We better hurry."

Before she could question either of them on their strange behavior, Ty shoved her behind his back, urging her toward the exit. Once in the hallway, he pulled the door closed, securing it from the outside, locking in the asylum staff. An immediate barrage of indignant fists pounded upon the barrier.

When she hesitated, Ty pulled her forward. A thousand questions burned for answers, but she held her tongue, sensing that danger still lay ahead.

"Ty, what have you done?" she at last demanded when they reached the front door and she spotted the armed guards in the distance, hurrying toward the building en masse.

"Only what I had to do," he replied, dragging her down beside him. Calmly, he situated himself near a window, using the wall as protection so he could examine his gun, spinning the cylinder to check the bullet chambers in an automatic gesture.

"He's taken on city authorities," Geoff informed her in a matter-of-fact whisper that belied the worry shining in his gray eyes. He squatted down beside them and glanced out of the window at the horde of policeman converging on them. "And I think maybe . . . he's taken on more than he can handle."

426

"I can handle it," Ty announced calmly, leveling his pistol at the approaching men.

Serra met Tanner's concerned look with one of her own. She didn't doubt that her husband could take them all on. Just like Billy the Kid and Jesse James, she thought, her gaze flicking over Ty once more. Out to challenge the world and best it. Reaching up, she grasped his arm, so muscled and taut, a man in every way. And yet needs drove him that no mortal should have to contend with.

"Don't do this, Ty," she pleaded, squeezing his arm, trying to convey the love she harbored in every cell, in every drop of blood in her body, through her fingertips. "There's nothing you have to prove."

"You're wrong, Serra." His cobalt-blue eyes swept over her, lingering on her open lips with a longing she felt as if it were her own. "I've had to justify my existence since the day I was born." He focused on her restraining hand for just a moment, then he returned to his business of making preparations for the inevitable fight. "Besides, what choice do I have? What choice do any of us have when it comes right down to it?"

"We all choose," she insisted, urging him to listen by capturing his face between her hands, forcing him to look at her. "We decide whether to spend our time fighting—or growing. I know. I fought who I was, where I came from for so long, wanting to be more, wanting to be someone special. But I'm not some pampered lost child, just a product of the times—a street urchin, nothing more. I'm learning how to make the most of my origins . . . trying to accept that they are good enough.

"Ty," she continued. "You're many things—arro-

427

gant, bullheaded—but you're not a killer. You are not Jesse James or Billy the Kid. You're Tyler Ramsey, and I love you for who you are."

His attention riveted on her with an intensity that stilled her heart, his free hand drifting up to collect a fistful of her radiant coppery hair. "You are special, Serra, very special to me." Then his gaze softened with remembrance and he chuckled, squeezing the fiery curls and letting them sift through his fingers. "I told you your hair would be your pride and glory some day, didn't I?"

She smiled. "Yes, you did." She covered his hand with hers. "You also told me you'd take care of me."

"I am, Serra, I am." Emotion choked him and he pulled her near, his hand cradling her head against his thundering heart. "The only way I know how."

An unbidden tear leaked from her amber eyes, to be absorbed by his dark shirt. *Please, please, let him listen to me.* "Then if it's me you want, our love that matters, give up this crazy need to prove yourself."

"I can't allow them to take you back in there, Serra," he replied in his own defense.

Pressed against his chest, she heard the sob he fought to restrain gathering there. "Surely the police will listen."

"I think she's right."

Having forgotten the other man was there, they both glanced at Geoff in surprise.

"So far this has only been a minor scrape," Tanner continued. "Chances are they'll haul us in, but we can take them to Chelsey and prove our cause was just—even if our methods were a little irregular."

"Serra, is this the way you want it?" Ty asked, his face revealing nothing of what he felt.

428

She nodded. "No heroics, Ty."

The approaching guards neared the building. Ty stood, slipping his gun back into its holster beneath his drover's coat. Serra and Geoff joined him on the front steps, and together they waited as the men surrounded them.

Quickly, they separated Ty, stripping him of his weapon and forcing him to his knees with a roughness that sent Serra flying to protect him.

"Please, can't you see he's not resisting you?" She suffered his pain, his humiliation, as they cuffed his hands behind his back; but she was proud of him, the way he towered over them all when they let him regain his feet.

The blue-clad officer examined her from head to toe. "Who are you?"

Serra's heart thundered. What if they didn't believe them and forced her to reenter that awful place? Lifting her chin, she clung to her faith that good eventually triumphed over evil. "I'm his wife, Serra Paletot Ramsey," she answered with pride.

Ty glanced at her, his gaze softening, then he looked away, his face once more hard and unreadable.

Relieved that Serra was safely off Blackwell's Island, Ty allowed the officer to lead him up the steps into the police station. Cuffed just as he was, Geoff Tanner maintained his silence, but Ty could read the misgiving in the other man's eyes. He knew that fear all too well; every boy from the streets of New York did. Once you entered the doors of authority, there was a good chance you'd never come out again. Mi-

nor scrape or not, the possibility couldn't be ignored. But this was how Serra wanted it — no heroics.

He watched her standing proudly a few feet away
as she began to speak, attempting to explain the situation to the officers. How Chelsey had turned her
over to the asylum and his dastardly reasons for doing so. Why her husband had come to her rescue.
They listened, making a few notes, then turned to
Ty.

"Is this true, son? Is she your wife?"

He nodded.

"Can you prove it?"

"The inside pocket of my coat, there's a marriage
certificate." He stood patiently as the officer rummaged around in his coat.

"What about this man, this Dr. Chelsey? Do you
know where to find him?" The officer studied the
document for a moment, seemed satisfied, and deposited it on the nearby counter.

Ty gave him the address of the flat where the children had spotted him, confident that if plans went
as they were supposed to, his young assistants still
held Chelsey at bay.

"Bring this Dr. Chelsey in for questioning."

An hour later, the officers returned with Chelsey
in tow. Cool as they come, he spied Serra standing
off on her own. Without losing a beat, he rushed to
her, gushing with false concern over her safety.

A tug-of-war of emotions shot through her as Doc
pulled her close, expressing his relief. As cruel as he
had been to her the last few days, there still re-

mained the memory of his kindness, his guidance through a difficult time in her life.

"Ah, dumpling, I was worried," he said in his most caring voice. "You should have stayed put, not run away from the hospital." Then he turned to the officers. "My Serra isn't well, you know. One moment she is lucid and the next—" He waved his hand in the air to emphasize his meaning.

"Damn you, Chelsey, you lie."

As fast as a striking rattler, Doc spun about to face his accuser. The sight of Ty standing there caught him off guard. Serra placed a restraining hand on Chelsey's jacket front. Without warning, he grabbed a revolver from the holster of an unsuspecting officer, pulling her back against his chest.

"Get that whoreson away from me, or I swear I'll shoot her."

Cold metal rested against Serra's temple. Her knees began to quake, her heart running wildly in its prison. Never had she been so scared. She compressed her lips, fearing that should she move even the slightest, Chelsey might actually carry through with his threat. He was quite capable of doing so, she realized.

Ty pushed forward, his wrists still cuffed behind his back, brushing away the hands that attempted to hold him in check. "Let her go, Chelsey. She's not the one who foiled your plans. I am. I've known all along what you were up to. I'm the one you want." He took a bold step toward his adversary in challenge when the physician refused the bait.

She gasped at his foolish bravery, knowing Doc would have no compunction about killing him. But the pistol pressed harder against her skull, and she stilled.

"Did you enjoy the reception committee I sent around to your flat to keep you entertained in my absence?" Ty continued his brazen taunts.

"So those little demons were your doing, besieging me, driving me half crazy with their antics and threats." The leveled gun at last swiveled about, pointing at Ty's unshielded heart.

"No, Ty," Serra cried out, struggling to escape Doc's clutches.

It was enough of a distraction. Ty came flying forward, crashing against Chelsey's much smaller frame. Serra found herself thrown to the floor, out of harm's way, but she was immediately upon her feet again.

The shot roared, echoing through the police headquarters like a deadly beast seeking its target.

Looking down at Ty slumped over Chelsey, Serra's mouth went dry, her heart coming to a skidding halt so painful that she clutched at it. She feared the worst.

"Ty," she cried, shoving toward him, but the officers were there first, keeping her at a distance, screening her from the ugliness and danger.

Someone lifted Ty up. Others fell upon Chelsey, wrenching the gun from his fist as he raved and slobbered like a mad dog, and pinning him to the ground.

She saw the crimson ooze on Doc's hands, his shirtsleeve. Ty's blood.

She screamed, certain of what she would find once she reached her husband. "Let me through," she demanded, and the crowd of blue-clad officers parted.

Then she saw him. Slouched forward, his face

hidden, Ty didn't seem to move, to breathe. The red stain on his shirtfront spread like hot, angry lava, his life forces spilling forth, and she feared there was nothing she could do to staunch the flow. If only she'd not insisted that he give himself up. Bound and helpless, he had still found it necessary to prove himself. To protect her. She had told him that was what she expected of him, but she hadn't meant for him to sacrifice himself for her sake.

Throwing herself at his feet, she cradled his head to her heart. "Oh, Ty. I was wrong. I was so wrong," she sobbed, so sure he wouldn't answer her, couldn't hear her.

Then his arm was about her, free from its bonds, holding her against his uninjured shoulder. "I know you said no heroics, darlin', but I just couldn't help myself," he defended in a weak murmur.

The sob tumbled forward, a combination of the release from the long terror and the joy of finding him alive, yet fearing he still might be in danger of not surviving. Then she found herself laughing amidst the weeping, not sure really why, except that it relieved the pent-up tension of the last few days. "You big lug, I love you," she declared through the tears.

"Ah, Serra, I love you." He squeezed her lightly. "God knows I always have."

Together they watched as the officers dragged Chelsey away, screaming like the lunatic he'd claimed her to be. Try as she might, Serra couldn't find it in herself to despise him. For years he had treated her well, even if he had used her innocence and dreams for his own advantage. The worst she could dredge up was pity for a man who had allowed his greed to override the little bit of good in him.

"What will happen to him?" she asked the officer who helped her rip away Ty's shirt and attempt to stay the rivulet of blood until medical assistance could reach them.

"There will be a further investigation, and any others involved will be brought to justice," the officer informed her, offering her another wad of cloth to replace the soaked one in her hand.

Doc's wife and Mrs. Babison. She made a mental note to supply their names to the authorities as accomplices to the physician's crimes, once Ty was taken care of.

"Based on my years of experience and on what happened here today," the man added, "I wouldn't be surprised if he ended up in the very same asylum he had you committed to. A just ending, wouldn't you say?"

Just perhaps, but Serra didn't wish such a punishment on anyone, not even Lionel Chelsey. She nodded in silence, hoping that the man who had been her guardian for all of those years would somehow find the peace and security within himself that he had promised her.

But Doc had chosen his path, just as she chose hers now. Ty was all that mattered to her. He couldn't abandon her now. Brushing away a stray lock of dark hair from his forehead, she smiled down on him, willing her own strength to enter his weakened body.

"No more heroics, darlin'," he promised her, his head dropping back into her lap, his eyes drifting closed.

"No more foolish dreams," she vowed to him, gracing his temple with a gentle kiss of commitment, her wet lashes fluttering down over her amber eyes.

Then she watched them ease his large frame onto a litter and place him in the back of an ambulance. Accepting the solidness of Geoff Tanner's shoulder as a brace, she climbed aboard.

"He'll be fine, Serra," Geoff assured her, though his face was masked with concern.

"I know," she adamantly agreed, fighting her own inner doubts, as the wagon lurched forward. "I wouldn't let it be any other way."

Chapter Twenty-four

Joplin, Missouri
July 4, 1887

Serra glanced about at the children. All twenty-seven of them, their youthful faces alight with hope and excitement as the holiday parade moved down Main Street, horns blaring, drums thundering, cymbals crashing.

"Miss Serra, I ain't never seen nuthin' like this before."

The sparkling amber eyes framed by the bright red hair reminded Serra of herself so long ago. Only she had been frightened and alone—and full of delusions. This child's dreams, as well as those of all the others, would be realized without the pain of trial and error. She would see to it.

"It is wonderful, isn't it, Kerry Ann?" Placing her gloved hand on the little girl's head, she draped her other arm through Ty's good one, the one not cradled in a sling. Smiling up at him, she knew what he was thinking as his cobalt-blue eyes danced with merriment. She couldn't help but remember herself.

They had just left the hospital, Ty's recovery

amazingly quick considering that the bullet had struck very close to his lung. Kerry Ann had been waiting for them at the bottom of the building's steps, the hat she had pilfered from Serra perched on her head, as impertinent an imp if ever they'd seen one. Leading her brother Ralphy forward, her other hand stationed in the middle of that feathery confection to keep it from falling off, she had insisted in no uncertain terms that Ty hold up his end of the bargain.

"What bargain?" Serra had demanded from her sheepishly grinning husband.

"In my zeal to find you, darlin'," he'd explained, "I promised probably half the street population of New York a home with us, including this little minx."

To say she'd been surprised would be putting it mildly, but she hadn't been angry. In fact, during the long hours of Ty's recovery, she'd come to grips with her own past and had then racked her brain to think of ways to help the homeless children herself. Her vow to Geoff Tanner to send money wasn't enough, but to take a regiment of unruly children back to Missouri hadn't even crossed her mind. It had just seemed like too large of an undertaking.

And it had been hard work organizing the children, making sure that each of the ones who had helped in locating her was in turn found. Geoff Tanner had been invaluable, tracking them down, encouraging the parents of the few that had them to sign the necessary surrender forms to free the children to a new life that offered the hope of advancement.

But the hardest part had been convincing Geoff to come with them as well. At first he refused to even consider her offer. But then he had spent several hours with Ty, alone in their hotel suite, and he emerged with his mind changed.

Serra looked up at her husband standing on the Joplin sidewalk beside her, then she glanced at Geoff several feet away, the children sandwiched between them, still wondering what had passed between the two men all those weeks before. She supposed it didn't matter, only that Geoff was here now, for without his help this whole project would have been near to impossible.

Once the holiday fanfare passed, Ty covered her kid-gloved hand resting on his forearm with his own, and he moved forward to cross the street, his long, lean body a bit thinner from his days of infirmity. But in Serra's eyes, he was just as devastatingly handsome as ever.

"Are you ready, Serra?" he asked as they reached the other side of the thoroughfare. "John is eager to see us."

John Langston. A pang of guilt speared through Serra, and she tucked her bottom lip between her teeth, worrying it along with her doubts. Accepting Doc's responsibility in the crime, seeing his wife and Mrs. Babison arrested and jailed for their participation hadn't been that easy. But facing the man she had deceived into thinking her his daughter was the final and most difficult hurdle she must confront. She knew she must talk with him, tell him the truth, but she wasn't sure she had the strength to crush him so. Especially with his own failing health. Without glancing at Ty, she nodded.

Ty paused to look down at her. "Are you sure, darlin'?"

"No, I'm not sure, but it's what I must do."

"*We* must do," he corrected. "I should have told

him long before. It would have saved us all a lot of grief."

But the fact that he had held his tongue served only to confirm to Serra how much he truly loved her. And he had never insisted that she make this confession; the choice had been solely her own.

"Yes, together," she agreed with a firm nod.

Turning the care of the children over to Geoff's capable hands, Ty directed the motley-looking group to the Joplin Hotel just a few blocks away, where he had arranged for rooms until a proper facility in town could be located. "Keep them out of trouble the best you can," he ordered the younger man.

Like a flock of gangling goslings, squawking and gawking, Geoff herded them forward, the group capturing the attention of the locals gathered to enjoy the parade. Serra smiled. Joplin was in for a most interesting time dealing with their newest citizens. But in the long run, knowing each of the children as she did, the town would eventually benefit from their unique talents.

Across the street at the livery, Ty arranged for a carriage to take them to the Langston mansion. Once they arrived, the vehicle wheeling into the familiar circular drive, uncertainty gripped her with its cold fingers. If Ty hadn't been there, reaching up to assist her to the ground, chances were she would have changed her mind and bolted. But he was there, and she accepted his offered hand.

The house with all of its elaborate gables and fretwork on the outside seemed more like a tomb when they were ushered in by the silent butler.

"Father?" Serra queried, realizing she had no right to call John Langston by that name, but she couldn't find it in herself to label him otherwise.

439

"Upstairs with the doctors, waiting for you, Miss Serenity." The butler managed a sad smile. "He refused to give up until you got here."

She hurried forward, running up the stairs without much thought to protocol. Even if he wasn't her flesh and blood, if she had no right to claim this house as home, John Langston was more like a father to her than anyone else in her life. She loved him dearly and wished that she could be the one thing he wanted and needed: his daughter.

The thunder of her hard-soled traveling shoes was muffled by the hallway carpeting, but the pounding of her heart remained deafening, at least in her own ears, as she raced toward the entrance to his rooms.

So dark and quiet, a gloominess prevailing where once sunshine had dominated. She knelt beside the bed, found the cool, thin hand buried among the covers, and dropped her cheek against the open palm.

"Serenity," Langston said in a barely audible whisper, stroking her coppery hair with parental concern. "At last you're home."

She nodded against his fleshless hand, once so strong and capable, unable to find her voice to answer, to say what she knew must be said.

Then she felt Ty's presence behind her, and she drew strength from him as he touched her shoulder with concern and love.

"Ty," Langston acknowledged the younger man's arrival, eyeing him with alertness, attempting to pull himself up in the bed.

Serra placed a restraining hand on his wasted shoulder, fearing his reaction would be negative.

"I see you found her, boy."

"Yes, sir," Ty replied in quiet respect.

"Good, good." Langston settled back against the pillow with a tired sigh. "My daughter's in the best of hands now."

Serra caught Ty's blue gaze for a brief moment. She had to tell Langston, end this deceptive farce. She had to do it now before it went any farther. Staring down at her hand clasped in the older man's frail one, she gathered her courage. "Sir," she began, and faltered just as quickly.

"What is it, Serra, girl?" he urged, his dark eyes sunken and thoughtful.

"There's something I must tell you." Again she choked on her convictions, unable to go on.

Langston's hand reached up and cupped her chin, tilting it so they stared at each other. "I feel a confession comin' on." He smiled so reassuringly that she found the courage to continue.

"My trip to New York. Like I told you, I went in search of answers."

"Ah, yes, the truth you young people put so much stock in." He gave Ty a strange look, then returned his attention to her. "I assume you found what you went lookin' for."

She nodded.

"And now you've come to tell me that you aren't my daughter after all."

Serra blinked rapidly, revealing her surprise. Had he known the truth all along? "You must believe me," she cried. "I never meant to deceive you. I honestly thought I was Serenity Langston when I came here. I never intended to cause you or anyone else pain."

"Serra," he said softly. "Serra Paletot—now Ramsey. A name to be proud of, girl.'" He smiled wanly, his thumb brushing against her petal-soft lips that

441

trembled with emotion. "I'm not the old, blind fool you all thought I was." He glanced up at Ty, then back at her. "But I decided a long time ago, the truth didn't matter so much. You were all I wanted in a daughter, all that Serenity would have been if she were still here. Over the last few months, you have been more a child of mine than any other."

Serra didn't try to inhibit the flood of tears.

"All except one, perhaps," Langston continued. "I was lucky enough to have you come into my life when I least expected it, but I was also given by God's own grace a son any man would be proud to claim." He looked up at Ty with eyes of genuine love. "Can you ever forgive me, Ty, for the way I've treated you?"

Beneath his beard, Ty's tan face flushed. Knowing her husband the way she did, Serra sensed he fought an emotional battle of his own.

"There's nothing to forgive, John. You gave me a chance when nobody else would. If it weren't for you," he explained with a wry smile, "chances are I would have ended up . . . well, I don't think my life would have worked out so well."

Like Jesse James and Billy the Kid—a victim of his own misguided fortune, Serra finished his statement in her own mind. Glancing at the two men most important in her life, she read the same conclusion on their faces.

A sudden realization washed over her, so crystal clear she couldn't believe she'd never seen it before. This was what family was truly about. Not necessarily the bond of blood, but the affinity of the minds and the hearts. Family knew what the others were thinking and feeling and aligned themselves to fit into the pattern of human frailty and imperfection

442

found in each of its members. But most important was the love and the ability to forgive. To praise when it was called for, to guide when the need arose, to understand when there was no other recourse.

Here in this room, Serra Paletot, an innocent abandoned so long ago, found what she'd been searching for all of her life. Family. John Langston with his heart of pure gold had made the culmination of her dreams possible. And though she recognized the fact that she would lose him soon, it didn't mean the end of what she'd only just discovered. Family perpetuated. When one generation stepped aside, another took its place.

There were twenty-seven souls just waiting at the Joplin Hotel, more than willing to take up the family crest and proudly carry it forward into the future.

The solution seemed so clear to her. There was plenty of space right here in the Langston mansion to house them if they converted some of the rooms and renovated others. She would see to it that John Langston's final days were rememberable ones. What finer medicine would there be than to suffuse the silent gloominess with the laughter and joy of children filled with the hope of living?

She glanced at her father—yes, that's what he was to her now and always—and found him resting peacefully, the lines of worry about his drawn face smoothed and relaxed for the first time that she could recall. Bending over, she planted a gentle kiss upon his brow and rose, the excitement of her solution burning to be shared.

"What is it, Serra?" Ty asked, following her as she departed the room.

She smiled. Yes, family meant sensing the change in one another. Slipping out into the hallway, she closed the door behind them and pivoted about.

"We'll bring them here," she announced, flying down the corridor to assess the empty bedrooms on that floor alone.

"Who?" he asked, trailing after her as she flung open the door of one of the never-used rooms.

"Why, the children, of course, silly. Who else would I be talking about? We can divide them up by age, putting the younger ones near us. Some of the older ones can take over the empty servant quarters, and Geoff—"

"Whoa, whoa, woman." Ty clamped her shoulders and spun her around to face him. "Are you sure this is what you want to do?"

Straightening, she lifted her chin with conviction. "Can we do less for them than John Langston did for us? Don't you see, Ty, this is a matter of family tradition."

His bemused look softened with understanding. "Ah, li'l Serra, when you told me so long ago all you wanted was family above all else, I had no idea you meant such a big one."

She laughed, almost shyly, unsure that he approved of her plan but confident he would go along with it if she asked him to. Slipping into his arms, her own curled about his neck, and she arched up against him. "The bigger the better."

"We'll need more beds, enough for an army."

"We can order them."

"Cook will probably raise the roof."

"Then we'll raise her salary and get her an assistant."

"And what about John?"

444

"He'll welcome their company and their unrelenting spark of life. Can't you just imagine him with Kerry Ann?"

"You've got an answer for everything, don't ya, darlin'?"

"No, but we'll find them as the need arises," she replied in all seriousness.

"Then I suppose we should share this grand revelation of yours with the others." With a resigned sigh, he released her.

Returning to the Joplin Hotel, they entered the front lobby. Chaos prevailed there. The children being as children will, seemed unable to settle down. Like fleas, they infested every nook and cranny of the three-story structure. And in the midst of it all sat Geoff Tanner in front of a tall potted palm that trembled as if it were alive instead of invaded by curious children, calmly conversing with the last person Serra expected to see.

"Amanda," she called out, releasing Ty's arm and hurrying across the lobby.

The pert blonde whirled about, her pretty face flushed with excitement. "Serra!" she cried in return, rushing forward in greeting. "I have met the most wonderful man," she announced in a hushed whisper. "Can you imagine right here at the Joplin Hotel, and he's come here all the way from New York City. New York, Serra. A gentleman of true sophistication." She batted her lashes in the way only Amanda could do.

Serra swallowed her amusement and glared at Ty over the blonde's shoulder to squelch any biting remark he might have considered saying. No "hello" or "how are you" from her friend, just an instant launching into what was happening in her own life.

445

She smiled with patient understanding of how Amanda's mind worked. "I see you've met our dear friend, Geoff Tanner."

"*You* know Mr. Tanner?" Amanda shot a look at the two men standing together, attempting to rein in the kids.

"Actually, he's an old acquaintance of Ty's."

"Really. I never gave much thought to where your husband came from." Her look of perplexity instantly changed. Like a cat on the hunt, she watched her prey. "Tell me, is Mr. Tanner married?"

"Totally unencumbered," Serra replied. *Unless you count the twenty-seven children in his care,* she didn't say.

Amanda smiled. "Then we'll just have to see about changing all that, won't we?"

Serra laughed aloud. Ah, yes, family was a glorious thing. It was time Amanda Stokes settled down. Who better than Geoff Tanner? "I see no reason why we can't begin right now."

Taking Amanda in tow, she led her forward, putting the confused blonde in charge of six of the rounded-up children.

"Are these yours?" Amanda demanded to know.

"That, and twenty-one more," she informed her friend, hurrying away to snag two of them coming out of the washroom. Reining them in, she turned them over to Amanda and Geoff, who seemed to be working surprisingly well together, then she headed in the other direction to continue her search.

In the hallway of the second floor, she ran into Ty on a similar mission. Laughing, he captured her about the waist with his good arm, wheeling her about to face him.

"There was an old woman who lived in a shoe," he teased in limerick, grinning. "Who had so many children she didn't know what to do."

Lifting her fist, she cuffed his uninjured shoulder, frowning her resentment. "I'm not old, Tyler Ramsey," she declared with mock indignation, then she couldn't help herself. She laughed at the imagery the nursery rhyme evoked. "But I'm not sure I know what to do—not all of the time," she admitted.

"What about now, Serra?" he asked. His face turned serious, intense with need. "Kiss me," he demanded.

Closing her eyes, she willingly complied, the touch of his lips on hers as sweet as any nectar she'd ever tasted. Definitely the right thing to do. Then in the distance, she picked up the sound of running feet, childish cries of glee. She pulled back. "Little Ralphy. I think I hear him."

"He'll wait for just a minute. I doubt he can do that much damage in a few short moments." Bending his head, he captured her mouth once more, branding her with the passion they had held in check for so long.

Passion. It was as much a part of her dreams of family as any other, the part she savored the most, she had to admit, as the familiar feelings and tensions only Ty could arouse in her whirled about her, drawing her down, deep into their wondrous clutches.

To love. To belong. There was nothing more in life she desired. She gave herself up completely to the magic Tyler spun about her. Well, almost completely. Without losing a beat, she reached out and snagged the wayward child by the arm as Ralphy darted by, holding him firmly as she surrendered her heart, her love, to the one man who deserved it.

Tyler Ramsey.

Like Jesse James and Billy the Kid, she mused. A man with a destined course, whose fate was written in the stars, but Ty would be remembered for the good he gave the needy world, a giving that had only just begun.